D1031784

THE
HEART
OF
HELL

ALSO BY WAYNE BARLOWE

God's Demon

THE
HEART
OF
HELL

Wayne Barlowe

TOR

A TOM DOHERTY ASSOCIATES BOOK

NEW YORK

This is a work of fiction. All of the characters, organizations, and events portrayed in this novel are either products of the author's imagination or are used fictitiously.

THE HEART OF HELL

A Tor Book
Published by Tom Doherty Associates
120 Broadway
New York, NY 10271

www.tor-forge.com

Tor® is a registered trademark of Macmillan Publishing Group, LLC.

Library of Congress Cataloging-in-Publication Data

Names: Barlowe, Wayne Douglas, author.
Title: The heart of hell / Wayne Barlowe.
Description: First edition. | New York : Tor, 2019. | "A Tom Doherty Associates Book."
Identifiers: LCCN 2018057443| ISBN 9780765324566 (hardcover) | ISBN 9781429988360 (ebook)
Subjects: | GSAFD: Fantasy fiction.
Classification: LCC PS3602.A775626 H43 2019 | DDC 813/.6—dc23
LC record available at https://lccn.loc.gov/2018057443

Our books may be purchased in bulk for promotional, educational, or business use. Please contact your local bookseller or the Macmillan Corporate and Premium Sales Department at 1-800-221-7945, extension 5442, or by email at MacmillanSpecialMarkets@macmillan.com.

First Edition: July 2019

Printed in the United States of America

0 9 8 7 6 5 4 3 2 1

For Laura, my heart of Heaven.

Were it not for her Light, this book would not exist.

Long is the way and hard, that out of Hell leads up to the Light.

JOHN MILTON
Paradise Lost

THE
HEART
OF
HELL

1

ADAMANTINARX-UPON-THE-CHERON

The blue star comforted her.

She could not explain the emotion, why its cool hue, so different from the surrounding sky of fire, bespoke salvation. She only knew that it did and that she wanted to embrace it.

She was a brick. Roughly three feet long, two feet high, and two feet wide, she was a block, dense, dark, and dry. Only one of her eyes, exposed upon her upper surface, its brilliant blue iris startling against the deep, raw umber of her rugose skin, gave the oblong form any sense of life.

The soul who had been called by her companions Bo-ad had been made into a brick, identical save for the twisting, puckered textures on her sides to the millions upon millions that she had seen and ignored when she had been able to walk the streets of Adamantinarx.

Lying alongside her fellow souls, incorporated into the steps of a great plinth, she dozed in the oppressive heat, her thoughts turning like the slowest of wagon wheels. Her sluggish mind seemed to take hours to complete the simplest thought, to reason through the most obvious conclusions. The best she could do was to try not to think at all, to let the events of the street that stretched before her wash over her and manage as best she could to understand them.

The memory of her transformation was so traumatic that she

tried to evade it, to push it away. But as much as she thought to deny it, it reappeared, blocking any recollection from the past that might offer comfort. And so she was forced to obsess about it, revisiting in painfully slow and excruciating detail the moments before she had become a brick. What else was there to do?

She had stood with the other condemned souls, trembling uncontrollably with the nearness of the demons, aware of what was about to befall them. Her future was to be that which all souls feared the most—a future of eternal inactivity. To become one of the uncountable trillions of bricks that gave structure to the chaos of Hell—this was true damnation. It was the demons' most efficient, most lasting punishment for souls like her who had not been sufficiently broken by their overlords. Somehow, from the moment she had arrived in Hell, she had always known it was to be her fate. Her awareness had been too great, her anger too sharp, and her resentment too obvious.

He had been near enough that, had she been foolish, she could have reached out and touched him. Near enough, too, that she had seen the countless embers burning in his flesh and smelled the acrid brimstone scent of him—a scent so pungent that it took little effort to recall. And every tiny aspect, every minuscule feature of his fierce and bony face, was, even after so much time, vivid enough that it still frightened her. She had never before been so close to a Demon Major and, knowing she was mere moments away from her fate, she had required every bit of her will to remain standing, let alone confront him. She had hated the shaking, the weakness, before a master. In the end she had known, despite her self-perceived independence, she was no different from each of the quivering souls who stood next to her.

It had taken a very long time for her compacted mind and body to adjust to its new state. She had, at first, felt feverish, then suffocated, had wanted to scream, had wanted to cry, and ultimately had wanted to truly die. But all of that was out of her control and eventually she simply lay heavily in place, breathing, screaming, and crying in her mind.

Around her the city had pulsed, growing until the moment that the Lord of Adamantinarx decided it be torn apart. She had known nothing of the reason for this but had heard a great deal of noise, sounds like the demolishing of buildings, and seen clouds of dust rising into the air. Some time after that, things grew still and then the bright cobalt star had appeared in the sky, its sudden appearance a mystery to her. Beneath it, the great statue of Sargatanas reached some five hundred feet into the sky, its arms held wide, its six wings outstretched, its head engulfed in an immense billowing torch of flame. Because of the position of her eye she was forced to stare up at it for the remainder of eternity, a bitter and unending reminder of the demon who had taken her limited freedom from her. Somehow, she did not think her position a coincidence but more the product of vindictiveness for her temerity.

The statue's voice—the incessant roaring of its fiery head—seemed like a challenge to the thunder of Hell itself. Even so, with that furnace voice and the ambient sounds of Hell fading into the background, she would most often close her eye and will herself to sleep. And so she thought to pass eternity.

A scuffing sound, sharp enough even with her muffled hearing to seem very near, roused her and she painfully opened her crusted-shut eye. Immediately hot ash and tiny cinders forced her to blink rapidly, their stinging bringing a precious tear to her lower lid. It oozed out and began to pool in her eye, clouding her sight so that all she could see were the molten colors of Hell. For a short time she saw nothing distinctly, straining through the tear shimmer to focus on the limited field of vision that fanned out above her. When the tears had burned away in the heat and she could finally see clearly her world was largely the same as ever—the black statue rising into the cloud-torn sky, embers floating in chaotic, swirling eddies, the tops of buildings that ringed the Forum of Halphas.

A demon's shape, tall and angular and aglow with burning sigils, could be just seen a yard or so away from her. She strained unsuccessfully to give detail to the vague form, rolling her eye to the side until the compressed muscles behind it seemed as if they would snap. While she was used to the ebb and flow of passing travelers, worker souls and those who stopped to look up at the blazing statue, this was an occurrence the likes of which, after her many months of enervating punishment, she could not remember. No one purposefully came this close—there was no point to attempt to look upon a statue so tall from such a close vantage. A wave of terrible dread spread through her crushed body, a sensation so potent that, for a moment, she almost felt alive. It was a higher demon who approached, she knew not just from her own reaction but from the two adjacent bricks that were to either side of her. Their tiny tremors were unmistakable.

She closed her eye. The pain of trying to see who stood near her was almost unbearable.

Over the roar of the flames she heard the shattered-glass intonation of demonic words exchanged, and knew there to be more than one of them standing in proximity. She could, with difficulty, understand the demons' tongue but could only distinguish a few of the barely heard words. One word—a name spoken with reverence—was repeated. *Sargatanas*—the Lord of Adamantinarx, the Demon Major who had ordered her punishment. How she hated him!

She opened her eye a fraction, trying to draw as little attention to herself as possible.

Both demons were almost atop her. The nearer of the two carried a carved bone staff while she could now make out a winged demon who stood a few paces off. Both appeared to be looking down, searching the plinth for something. She watched them through her slitted eye and with each foot they drew nearer she could see and hear more. The wingless one was darkly robed and had the head of some horrible beast, all moving teeth and hornlets and ridges, while the other, wearing a leather satchel that hung from a buckled baldric, was deep red from head to wings to clawed feet and seemed more well formed.

"I am sure it was the one just in front of you," she heard the farther of the demons say. "Lord Valefar showed me." He paused. "Truly, I should have dealt with this sooner."

"Really, my lord? They all look alike. I cannot recall—it was quite some time ago and did not seem important at the time. It might have been this one," said the other demon. "Or *this* one." And suddenly she felt a sharp stab as the beast-headed demon's staff was jabbed into her exposed upper surface. Her eye flashed open with the pain of it.

"It *is* that one! See, Abbeladdur, it is just as I said. Look at that eye!"

The beast-headed demon leaned forward and peered into her eye.

"Your memory is good, Eligor. Better, it would seem, than mine."

She watched as the red figure approached and knelt, his wings sweeping behind him. The demon called Eligor extended his hand and placed it gently upon her. He began to gingerly brush away the ash that had collected upon her, careful to not let any get into her unblinking eye.

"And," Abbeladdur said with a tinge of disapproval as he, too, stared down at her, "the expression has not changed either. I remember it now. Pure defiance."

The demon Eligor said nothing but leaned in even closer to Bo-ad, pursed his bony lips, and blew the remaining ash from her. And then from under his robes he produced a heavy, curved knife and slid it from its sheath. Unreasoning terror gripped her and she closed her eye.

Why have they sought me out among these countless other bricks? Was it because I dared to challenge him—Sargatanas? Will they finally destroy me for it? And why is he not here, himself, to do the deed?

She felt one of Eligor's hands upon her and the blade of the knife prying her away from her companions on the plinth. With a dull scraping sound she was freed from the step and then lifted easily and placed upended upon the flagstones. She could now see the two demons without straining. For the first time in many transits of the red star Algol she could see the city around her and she was amazed.

What has happened here? Where are the old buildings?

The great infernal metropolis that had been Adamantinarx was no more; in its stead were vast tracts of land adjacent to the Acheron that either were devoid of any structure, had the traceries of foundations upon them, or had new, low buildings rising modestly from the ground.

She was surprised by the more intimate scale of the new city. Gone were most of the more grandiose structures. Here and there a few recognizable survivors stood—tall, solitary buildings that had been, for the most part, constructed of native stone. And in the distance, high atop the Central Mount, stood the palace, changed in small details but essentially the same. These few buildings were the exceptions. The city, as she knew it, was gone.

There was more to puzzle her. She saw innumerable workers laden with bricks or stones, but nowhere to be seen were any of the familiar bone scaffolds that had been such a ubiquitous feature of construction. In fact, she noted, none of the bricks were made of souls either. And, most astonishing of all, the workers themselves were a mixture of souls and demons!

Bo-ad's thoughts were interrupted by the abrupt sound of the winged demon sheathing his knife.

"It is time to make amends, Chief Engineer. Long overdue, really," she heard Eligor say.

The demon named Abbeladdur said nothing but came very near and, raising a clawed hand, began to trace intricate patterns in the air around and above her. The thinnest of fiery lines outlined a human form that lingered briefly and then vanished. And then, with a word, he backed away.

She felt a rushing wave of sensation as of countless motes of energy gathering and washing through her. Every cell in her crushed and convoluted body was reawakening, feeling pain and pleasure in equal measure. It was an ecstasy.

It was her resurrection.

In a flicker of memory Bo-ad recalled a moment long ago when she had been working and a cinder storm had descended with little warning, roaring in like a beast and terrifying the souls around her. Unlike her fellow workers she had not sought shelter but had instead remained out in the open, challenging the storm to take her and destroy her. She had been enveloped in a pelting whirlwind of tiny, blazing embers that had burned her skin with a ferocity that made her cry out, a whimper that turned to a shout of defiance. The storm had etched its name upon her, faintly pitting her skin with slow-healing wounds. But it had also made her feel alive.

Her body unfolded in painful twitches and jerks as it warmed and filled and she could feel her desiccated limbs grow supple, the black fluid that served as blood in Hell stirring and reaching into her shriveled fingers and toes. And then she was herself again, lying upon the flagstones at the base of the plinth, a brick no more.

She lay still, eyes closed, barely breathing, hoping that her newfound freedom was not some sad manifestation of her dreaming, imprisoned mind. If it was, she did not want to let go of the wonderful feelings that were spreading through her, the movement of hot air upon her body, the barely perceptible, soft fall of ash upon her sensitive skin. She could hear the two demons moving and speaking in whispers and then she became aware that one of them had knelt over her. She opened her eyes and saw that Eligor was peering into her face intently.

Slowly she raised a hand and ran it over her thigh, her hip, and then over her ribs. She felt different, smoother, and, more than that, she could not feel the orb that had been so much a part of her. *Ah, proof . . . this is, indeed, a dream.*

Dream or not, she wanted only to lie there upon the flagstones; she knew anything more would move her forward toward the unknown.

"Soul," a hoarse voice whispered.

She did not respond. But the voice gently repeated the word.

With great reluctance, Bo-ad opened her eyes. Redolent of brimstone and vast in his steaming blood-hued robes, the demon Eligor loomed above her, hand extended. She did not take it, but instead, propping herself up first with her elbow and then, less steadily, with her hands she managed to sit upright. She ached, her muscles trembled uncontrollably, and her breathing was labored. And with each painful inhalation she began to doubt that she was dreaming.

Eligor rose and straightened his robes.

"Can you speak?"

She looked up at him and swallowed, working her parched throat, testing it, fearing the pain that might come if she tried to talk after having been silent for so long. She made a short, dry sound and found the pain of the effort nearly unbearable.

"I can, demon."

If Eligor was startled by her obvious lack of respect he did not show it. Nor did she show her surprise at his use of the souls' language. He reached beneath his robes and withdrew a small flask, unstopped it, and proffered it to the soul. Reluctantly, she reached up and took it, pausing for a moment to look at it suspiciously. She could just see a small glyph floating within the translucency of its carved, stubby form.

"My name is Eligor. And it will help," he said quietly, his accent minimal.

She sipped it and felt stronger as the warmth of the thick liquid spread through her, reviving the fibers of her body. She put the flask to her cracked lips again and drained it completely. The liquid found its way to her trembling limbs and they grew stronger, more supple, and almost immediately she felt steady enough to attempt to stand. She rose slowly and when Eligor reached out to help her she again avoided him and he withdrew his hand. The trembling continued, but she was, she thought, stronger than before she had been pressed into a brick.

Bo-ad stood, chin down, the hot wind swirling around her, bits of ash and detritus pelting her.

"Why?" she said in a voice firm enough to carry over the sound of the wind and fire. She was careful to keep any bitterness from her tone. Or fear.

"It was Lord Sargatanas' wish. The lord that you spoke to so . . .

directly before you were reduced. I found his written thoughts about you among his scrolls. And I also found his instructions. They were quite specific."

"Why isn't he here himself?"

"He is gone. Or more properly, he has gone back." A flicker of a smile passed over the demon's bony face. He swept his hand out toward the city. "There was a great war. And everything changed."

"Why would *I* care?"

Eligor stiffened slightly. "Because in some ways he fought that war for you. Because you opened a door into his soul that might otherwise have remained sealed. And because now you are free."

Bo-ad said nothing. She turned away and looked at the rubble and the scaffolds and the space where she had lain and the distant fire in the sky. When she turned back her expression had darkened.

"This is why you have brought me back? To tell me I am *free*? In *this* place?"

"Yes. That was his wish. It is why this structure was not torn down. Until now. He wanted this to happen when things were again calm."

"In this place, demon, freedom can exist only for you and your kind. It has no meaning for a soul."

Bo-ad heard the slow, irritated intake of breath as Abbeladdur took a threatening step toward her. It was unclear if he understood the souls' tongue—he had contributed nothing to the exchange—but it was obvious that he was able to sense her hostility from the tone. She hoped that her unblinking stare masked the fear that suddenly stabbed at her. As if in answer, the fires that laced Abbeladdur's form flared ominously and her trembling grew perceptibly. With a deep breath and an upraised hand, Eligor motioned him to stop. An unmistakable expression of disdain creased the beast-headed demon's muzzle, but rather than confront his companion he growled something and walked a short distance off pretending to examine the statue's colossal foot.

"It has meaning now," Eligor said, turning back to Bo-ad, "if you choose to let it. You are not the first soul to be told this. In fact, you are among the last. We wanted to make sure there would not be another war . . . a war of eradication . . . before *you* were freed. We needed to know that the souls would not attempt a rebellion of their own."

Are we always just that close to extinction here? Unconsciously, Bo-ad reached for the small pendant—her statue of the White Mistress—a talisman she had always used to comfort herself. It was gone! And then, through the miasma of recalled pain, she remembered *him* probing her wounded flesh just after she had been crushed, searching for and finding something. It had been the statue! Why had he wanted it? She knew she could not keep the disappointment from her face and knew, too, that Eligor had seen it.

Without hesitation he reached into his satchel and produced a necklace—the missing necklace—letting it dangle from two curved claws for her to take. She looked with incredulity at it as it moved erratically in the wind.

"In time, he truly regretted taking this from you."

She took it and slowly tied the fine new braided cord around her neck. Her mind was racing with the shock of rebirth and the newness of what she was learning of the changes to the world around her. There was too much for her to understand and too much that she knew she would never understand about these creatures and, in particular, Sargatanas. Someday she might ask this demon, but now was not the time. Not in her present state of confusion.

A brief wave of regret passed through her. Whether it was his own idea or not, Eligor was trying to do his best to compensate her for her treatment. But centuries of punishment and oppression would not so easily erase the fear and hatred she felt for her former tormentors. As conciliatory as he was, she would make no effort to befriend him.

"You said your lord's instructions were quite specific regarding me. What were they?"

"To see you walk again, to return your treasured necklace, and to give you anything that you wanted within reason."

She was stunned; it was an act of generosity, more than that, an act of *kindness* unheard of in Hell. An act unlike any she ever heard of by a demon. And yet, from what she was beginning to understand, Sargatanas had not been like any other demon.

What do *I want?* For the first time in Hell, she found her normal decisiveness challenged. As she stood regarding Eligor and his companion she only knew that she wanted to be away, to be anywhere but where she was. So often when she had been toiling in the streets of Adamantinarx, she had burned to know what lay beyond the walls of the city, beyond the Acheron, far out into the Wastes. She had seen many travelers arrive through the great gates and had envied each and every one their ability to move freely about. She had stolen every opportunity to study them, their foreign garb, their strange Waste-born mannerisms, the goods they had brought with them, and she had formed a thousand questions about them. Now, with this offer from a demon she had never known, she felt it was all within her grasp.

Eligor looked at her expectantly. The wind had died down somewhat and she could hear the shouts of workers and the sounds of their chisels upon rock some ways off.

"Do you know who I am . . . *was?*"

"Yes," the demon said. "Lord Sargatanas knew even while he spoke with you. It was his Art, his special skill, to know. When he gave me my instructions he told me that I could, at my discretion, give you your self back. He gave me a glyph for this purpose, *Boudica*."

As she heard that name, she saw the demon raise his hand and from it a simple three-character glyph flared from his palm. This he gently pushed forward and, moments after it vanished against her skin, she felt as if a slight breeze brushed through her chest.

The soul stood transfixed, unable to speak as, for a fleeting moment, she smelled something forgotten, something so sweet and aromatic that it overpowered the acrid pungency of brimstone and set every fiber of her soul alight. It was the unmistakable earthy scent of the forest, and with it, like countless leaves falling in seamless layers, her memories came back to her. She closed her eyes and for a time the faintest smile played upon her mouth and then, quite suddenly, her face grew grim.

When she opened her eyes, she saw that Eligor was watching her very attentively and that even Abbeladdur was peering at her from some distance.

"I want to know about my daughters." The words came out so plainly that they seemed flat, unemotional.

"This is not something I can tell you about," Eligor said.

"Can't or won't?"

"When Lord Sargatanas concluded that he wanted you brought back it was already too late to discover the truth about their whereabouts," Eligor said patiently. "While he could understand your life, it would not have been in his power to shed light upon the lives of your kin. The Books of Gamigin—the Books of the Souls—were no longer in Adamantinarx."

"This means nothing to me," the soul once known as Bo-ad said.

"These are the soul books that speak of every soul who was ever consigned to this place. If your daughters were here those Books would speak of them. When the city was threatened by the tyrant Beelzebub's legions, Lord Sargatanas had them as well as what was left of the Library spirited away for safekeeping, fearing that the Fly would, in his rage against the rebellious souls, either have the Books destroyed or, worse, use them in some way unforeseen."

The soul took a deep breath and slowly turned away from the demon. She could almost taste the newly born frustration in her dry mouth. Though she had only just recovered her lost life, she could feel the upwelling of her maternal imperative to know her daughters' fate, the urgency to help them in any way she could. Trying to keep her voice steady, she said, "I see the broken bones of a city, demon. When *will* these Books be returned?"

"The city is being mended," Eligor said stiffly. The flames of his head grew briefly in intensity and the soul was quick to perceive a more formal edge to his voice. "Three centuries of Zoray's Archers under the command of my lieutenant, Metaphrax Argastos, are to set forth shortly for the Wastes to recover them. They will be guarding the retrieval caravan. You may join them, if you choose. And, after the Library is brought back and installed and you have learned what you will, you may go where you please."

Boudica saw the winged demon turn and nod to his companion in the direction of the palace—a sure sign the conversation was at an end—and realized she had pushed him perhaps harder than was prudent, that a potential ally was on the verge of casting her aside. He began to move away.

"Eligor . . . I *will* do as you suggest," she said, allowing a tone of contrition to shade her words. "I'll accompany them out to the

Wastes because I have always wanted to venture out and see them for myself. And when I return I hope you will help me to find out what I seek."

The demon stopped in mid-stride and turned to her.

"I know it is hard for you, Boudica, without having been in the Rebellion yourself, to understand that not all of us are your enemy, but it is true. Many of us no more want to be here than you. But, with his departure, my lord, the Ascended Sargatanas, showed us that we have choices in Hell . . . free will, if you like. It was his gift to us. Let him look upon you from Above, as surely he will, and see that you used it well."

"I will try, Eligor."

But even as she acknowledged Eligor's words and understood the sense of them she could not help but be surprised with the fervor he showed regarding his departed lord. It bordered on a reverence that went well past the lord and subject relationships of Hell. She would have to remember this and be more careful. If for no other reason than to simply survive.

Eligor hesitated, stroking the beard-like bones of his chin, looking at the soul as if reconsidering her, and said abruptly, "Come, we will go to a place where you can stay until the expedition leaves."

The blood that flowed anew in Boudica rose and, while her daughters' plight never left her mind, she felt a sense of exhilaration. It was a new world and she was free.

2

THE FROZEN WASTES

Hail pelted him like the drumming of a thousand clawed fingers as the ice squall roared across the ash-black ice with little to check its furious progress. Only the polished, fang-like karsts that reached into the deep slate-blue sky, stubborn in their resistance to erode away, stood as obvious impediments, and these clearly bore the smoothed scars and hollow pits of the wind's primacy.

He remembered it all—the endless ice, the unpredictable winds, the sudden storms, the mind-numbing emptiness. Most of all the chill air, cold and free of ash, reminded him of the azure firmament of the Above, insulting him with its similarity.

He hated it all.

The renegade Chancellor to the deposed Prince Regent of Hell, former Grand Master of the Priory of the Fly, Adramalik had been past the Margins, and now the Frozen Wastes, but once before to pay respects to Abaddon. He had never set eyes on the fearsome Lord of the Underworld and that was fine with him, but the fact that he had undertaken the journey spoke for itself. And he had never mentioned his motives for contemplating approaching Abaddon to the ofttimes paranoid Beelzebub. His pilgrimage had been at a time before he had sworn allegiance to the throne in Dis, a time when he thought he might have served either master. In the balance, even with the Prince's defeat, he felt he had made the right choice. In all the millennia of his life in the First City and its embattled environs he had, through ingratiating obeisance and blind obedience, insulated himself against the need to venture back to the icy Wastes. To anyone who had asked, he had vowed never to return. And yet here he was, the thoughts of his life of excess and comfort a bitter and distant memory.

Swathed in tattered skins and crouched against the furious wind, he watched as the black beads of hail and small bones, made round and unrecognizable by the wind, clattered and slid across the dark, shiny surface of the ice. Who knew where the bits of bone had come from, or from what, or, for that matter, how old they were? He imagined that someday they would simply vanish after breaking apart into finer and finer pieces.

Adramalik's gaze penetrated deep into the ice below his feet. Dimly seen, beneath the shadowed, translucent veil of ice, was another world, a world that glowed from the channels of brilliant blue fire that lit it from below. It was a realm of mystery that made the demon shudder from more than its terrible radiance. Those low fires, warm enough only to melt the ice a hundred feet above them, created a vast network of channels and caverns throughout the ice sheet, a frigid parallel landscape that lay many hundreds of feet below the surface world. No demon had ever been there or, if they had, had ever returned to tell of it. With all the fiery horrors of Hell around them, it was this cold unseen world that spawned the most horrific tales that fleshed out the nightmares of the Fallen.

Adramalik shifted so that he could part the folds of his cloak just enough to peer out into the windstorm. The ice pellets obscured his vision somewhat, but he could distinguish the half-dozen huddled shapes of his fellow refugees, their scarlet skins molded by the wind and ice around their bodies. Both Brigadiers Melphagor and Salabrus, his trusted lieutenants, had succumbed to their wounds along with five lesser Knights. Their fiery swords would be missed. The six surviving Order Knights were all that remained of his life in the former capital of Hell, all that had survived the great, final battle in the dome and the equally great privations and threats of their journey. No longer a functionary of the Prince, Adramalik was now their leader simply by rank—known to them as Grand Master—and he was all they had to cling to. Now, without question, they had followed him into the most remote and unknown reaches of the world. If ever he had doubted the courage of any of them, after what they had endured to this point, he could no longer.

He could have flown to Pygon Az as he had done in the distant past, but to do that would have meant leaving his Knights behind to follow on foot, their battle-damaged wings having rendered them incapable of flight. They would never have made it this far without him.

Even as he reflected on his companions, he saw a large shadow occlude the fires below and then skim away, lost to the gradual opacity of the ice. He shook his head ruefully. This was no place for a demon. He pitied those who had had the misfortune to Fall here. And doubted they had survived for long.

With a final, spiteful gust of wind the ice storm abated and Adramalik rose, shaking away the loose pellets and newly melted water from the creases in his skins. The heat from his smoldering body had created a foot-deep concavity in the black ice and his clawed feet, ankle high in steaming meltwater, had to grip the ice firmly to keep from slipping. The Knights were rising around him, gathering their few precious possessions—relics of their lost existence—and patting away the small, obsidian-like beads of ice.

Adramalik searched the horizon. He knew the boundary marker was somewhere nearby. His bearings were not what they could have been. The streams of magnetism that wound invisibly through-out Hell were tamed and bent near the cities but were notoriously unreliable in the adjacent Wastes and nearly unfathomable in the far-flung Frozen Wastes. With no significant landmarks the traces of those streams, the strange new, fixed blue star and Algol's vaguely seen eye, were all with which the refugees had to nav-igate.

As he was the only demon among them who had actually walked the streets of Pygon Az, the Knights looked upon him in a very real way as their compass. He would take them to their salvation, so far from the wrath of Sargatanas' demons that they could finally stop looking over their shoulders. But their ties to Adramalik went deeper than that of a guide. He alone had been responsible for their induction into their Order as well as their be-havior as Knights. And he alone was responsible for the final de-cision to vacate Dis. The Knights' hasty departure had been born of a mixture of self-preservation, obedience, and loyalty to him. With little left to him besides their companionship, Adramalik was acutely aware of the codependence that had grown so strong among them. Even so he had to maintain his leadership role and bolster his image in their eyes. As with any group of powerful and potentially threatening demons, he was aware of their conceiv-able opportunism and did not want to provide them any small sign of weakness. Weakness on his part would lead to disloyalty and disloyalty would inevitably lead to his destruction.

"We are not far now," Adramalik said over the dying wind with little conviction.

One by one they joined him: Chammon, Rahab, Vulryx, Demospurcus, Beleneth, and Lucifex. Each of them bore the clear signs of recent combat. All had been wounded in the Rotunda battle and bore ugly, untended, and unhealed scars that were visible beneath their frayed cloaks and sheared armor. Serious as they were, none had cut deep enough to destroy them. Most apparent were Beleneth's hacked-off forearm, Rahab's cleft forehead, and Lucifex's broken lance head, a prize from some vanquished Flying Guards demon that protruded from his upper chest. With his characteristic mixture of bravado and studied indifference Lucifex—spawn of a succubus courtesan and a Knight—refused to have it pulled free, a decision the other Knights secretly mocked. Layered upon these obvious wounds were the unmistakable traces of their subsequent escape through the Wastes, the Margins, and now the Frozen Wastes. Adramalik, too, bore obvious battle wounds. He had been pierced in three places—one an ugly puncture in his cheek—but he had hardly noticed the superficial wounds in his haste to retreat. Only now, in the cold, did their tightened and crusted suppurations annoy him. In hindsight, he knew he had been fortunate, that with these wounds he and his fellow demons had gotten off lightly. Had any of that lord's captains captured him after the battle his and his Knights' fate would have been certain.

As Adramalik looked at each of them the Knights made weary eye contact with him, wordlessly nodding their readiness. They were stretched to their limit but not to their breaking point. A fire to survive still burned deep within them, pushing them toward their goal. Adramalik was proud of them, proud of their fortitude, proud that they had endured so much. But as much as he admired their strength, his anger and disappointment were equally profound. When they had fled Dis their number had been double what it was now and he was uncertain whether he could leverage any amount of power with so small a company wherever he settled. And for potentially losing that advantage he blamed the forsaken Frozen Wastes.

Adjusting their weapons and belongings, the small party set off. Adramalik, as always, led the way, casting a simple glyph of light a few yards ahead more to give them something to follow than for its weak effulgence.

Like a weight sinking upon him, Adramalik felt the dulling burden of monotony return. Of all of the tortured regions of Hell, the Frozen Wastes were, in his mind, the most relentlessly mind numbing in their stark absence of variation. Only the few wind-blasted karsts that pierced the thick ice from deep below afforded any real visual relief. At least, he thought, they were not being pursued, for, clearly, there would have been nowhere to hide.

With steam pouring from their heated bodies, the demons resumed the strange, sliding gait that had taken them slowly across the ebony ice flats. They had quickly learned that the heat of their ember-flecked soles was so intense that it formed a slick beneath their feet that never allowed them the solid purchase they so craved. Standing in place was risky and falls were frequent and when the wind grew in intensity, despite the demons' efforts to dig their claws into the hard ice, their progress degenerated to a deadening trudge.

The ice sheet was like a living thing, cracking and buckling and sending rumbling groans and creaking screams into the frigid air. As they shuffled along, the party no longer took notice of the sounds. At first, when they had entered the Frozen Wastes, they had been startled, looking about anxiously when they heard the sudden cries of the ice, their apprehension at the sounds' origins manifold. But, after so long on the ice, they had grown so accustomed to the sharp sounds that none of them flinched. Adramalik noticed that they had not, however, grown used to the enormous apparitions that floated before them mere yards from the ice's surface, tendrils wavering and forms distorting as if in the throes of a body-stretching torture. Conjured by the moaning wind of the dark ice particles that settled restlessly upon the sheet's surface, they seemed to follow the party, to shadow their steps. It was impossible not to notice the faint traceries of glyphs that twined within them and Adramalik worried that, perhaps, the ice-cloud apparitions were less a natural product of their surroundings and more some kind of thaumaturgic sentinels sent by some unknown demon lord. But, he reflected time and again, there was little he could do to influence them and so he and the other demons tried to ignore them.

Even as the blue star stayed fixed, strangely never rising or setting, Algol dipped slightly in its shallow traverse of the darkening blue-gray sky as the Knights moved slowly toward their promised goal. Adramalik had told them many times about Pygon Az, the Black Ice City. Their enthusiasm for the stories had, like a carcass being bled, drained away long ago when the realization of its distance and the hazards reaching it had set in. It was a place in which the Grand Master had spent considerable time and that he had regarded more as a punishment than an abode, and this sentiment had unintentionally seeped into his description of the city. But the logic of the far-flung capital's choice as a favored destination was irrefutable. With its former ruler, Lucifuge Rofocale, long gone, it seemed to Adramalik perfect as a safe haven and, more important, ripe for a political takeover.

The party crested a low rise and watched a flight of Ice-shears slowly flap off, their sharp, distinctive honking filling the cold air, their glowing spots all that remained visible as their forms faded into the sky. As the demons' eyes followed the Abyssal flyers, in the distance they saw the marker that Adramalik had found so long ago. He hoped that none of the Knights could sense the almost palpable relief he felt upon seeing it once again.

Split in two huge pieces, the floating wedge-shaped stela was crusted upon its windward side in a thick layer of gale-burnished black ice. Below was another stone wedge, inverted, with its pointed edge thrust deep into the ice. Joined only by the brilliant blue connective sigils of Rofocale, it, and the dozen others like it, served as a boundary marker delineating, in this case, the southernmost edge of his bleak territory. As with all such markers, it served also as a catalog of sorts, a listing of the founding demon's exploits in war and peace. While its form was simple in contrast to the markers Adramalik had so frequently seen outside Dis, it was impressive nonetheless for its remote location.

The party drew nearer the twin stones and Adramalik, whose eyes were especially keen, began to read aloud some of the inscriptions. They were ancient, compelling words and he wanted the Knights to hear them and to know whom their former lord, Beelzebub, had so easily dispatched.

"'I, Lucifuge Rofocale, Demon Major Lord of Pygon Az, Bearer of the Order of the Fly, Grand Marshal of the Severing Blade, upon having descended in my Fiery Glory from the forsaken Above and established these borders of my Realm, have captured and imprisoned those miserable native creatures that call themselves Salamandrines numbering in the tens of thousands, and thus have I made safe the lands surrounding my great City.'"

Adramalik paused. The Knights were staring out into the ice beyond the rise.

"Something is out there, Grand Master," Demospurcus said evenly. Adramalik heard nothing in his voice to belie fear. They had all seen enough of what the Frozen Wastes could offer to be neither surprised nor concerned.

"Something is always out there," Adramalik said. "I think this one has been following us." He turned back to the floating boundary marker. Lucifex had separated himself from the party and was slowly making his way to the buried portion, the radiance of its glyphs edging him in brilliant blue.

"Ever the one to lead the way, eh, Demospurcus?" Adramalik said, nodding toward Lucifex.

The Knight grunted. As the most recently inducted Knight, Lucifex was both the least experienced and the least cautious of the remaining Order Knights. Adramalik had marveled that he had survived this long. And because of his relative inexperience he had become something of problem to them all. Even now, Adramalik saw how the others looked to him to see if he would call the young demon back, but instead, shaking his head slightly, he resumed reading.

"'I, Lucifuge Rofocale, Demon Major Lord of Pygon Az, upon having Descended in my Fiery Glory from the forsaken Above and having established my capital—'"

A deep groan reverberated beneath their feet, lingering as a vibration that made each of them simultaneously look down into the ice. Adramalik thought he saw a shadow darken and shift, but he could not be certain. He pursed his lips and continued, "'. . . and having established my capital upon the river Lethe, have, by crushing a million Souls, erected a Great Temple unto Lucifer the Lost to honor him and keep his memory vivid. And upon having erected this Great Temple in Lucifer's memory I sacrificed to him those tens of thousands of captured Salamandrines that served me as workers and, as further tribute, I used their blood to paint the Temple black. . . .'"

From the corner of his eye Adramalik noticed that Beleneth and Chammon had drifted a few paces away as if to follow Lucifex's rash example.

They do not share my interest in this place. How could they? They lack the foresight. I saw what Rofocale was trying to do with his canonizing of Lucifer. And I know how it outraged Beelzebub. He forbade me ever mentioning it. But I remembered.

He took a deep breath to call them back when the ground suddenly jolted and he heard a sound like a thousand giants' bones cracking. With an earsplitting roar, a giant form burst upward from beneath the ice sending massive frozen chunks and demons alike into the sky. Before he was able to attempt any protective glyphs Adramalik was knocked roughly to the ground by Rahab, pinned momentarily by his flailing body.

What Thing has the Wastes disgorged?

He heard the other demons' cries as, one by one, they smashed back onto the ice.

Was it drawn to my guiding glyph from below? Did it follow us all this way? Stupid to have used it!

A rain of jagged ice shards tumbled upon him as the enormous, bellowing creature pulled itself free from the tunnel it had opened.

Like some terrible nightmare-statue come to life it was huge, dark, and shiny and along its bony flanks were the strange glowing markings that resembled glyphs but were not the forms of letters. Steam, born of the warmer habitat beneath the ice, poured from its heaving sides as it angrily shook the chunks of ice away from its spined and beaked head. Adramalik saw the massive floating claws it had used to burrow its way to the surface reattach to its paws, the unknown magic of their disarticulated anatomy amazing and intimidating. He had never seen such a large ice dweller; to him no two Abyssals ever seemed quite alike, but this one was exceptional. *What birthing pit of a hellmouth is spewing out these nightmares?*

Adramalik pushed Rahab roughly off him and scrambled to his feet, trying to determine the whereabouts of each of his Knights.

Of those who had been thrown into the air, only Chammon was on his feet and he was barely visible behind the great beast, while the others were just regaining themselves. Suddenly, to Adramalik's amazement, he heard laughter. Turning back toward the marker, he saw Lucifex, sword aflame, madly charging the creature. *Of course! Imbecile!* Instead of sending out a protective glyph for all of the demons, Adramalik was forced to cover the impetuous demon's pell-mell charge with a lesser, individual glyph.

Fool! This creature is too large for any single demon to take down, let alone one with so little experience!

As if it had read the Grand Master's mind, the Abyssal pulled its hind legs free of the tunnel entrance and spun toward Lucifex with a roar and a hooked paw, effortlessly sending him sprawling and sliding on his belly across the ice. The glyph had held. Had Adramalik not acted with haste, the demon would have surely been destroyed. Irritated, he turned his attention to the other Knights. Each was now standing, weapon in hand, and with a quick command glyph he ordered them to form a circle around the creature. The demons responded quickly, sliding into positions roughly equidistant, and he shot out a shielding Glyph of Protection that covered them from above but allowed them to wield their swords. He joined them and, as one, they drew their flaming swords and began to advance confidently, tightening the cordon around the beast.

When the Knights were a few dozen paces from the creature, Adramalik saw it reach for two heavy chunks of ice from the tunnel's edge and purposefully hurl them at Chammon and Vulryx. Both demons twisted away from the missiles as the ice boulders crashed into and were boiled away by the defensive glyph barrier, but the Knights' posture changed somewhat. As they crouched, their movements slowed and the Abyssal took advantage of this to bombard them each with ice boulders. Seeing that it could not penetrate their shield, it began to throw chunks at their feet and each demon found he needed to melt a path with his sword, sending disorienting clouds of vapor into the clear air. It was, Adramalik thought, no stupid creature.

Nonetheless, the cordon tightened. As the demons slowly approached it, the Abyssal drew up and ceased pawing for ice chunks, seeming, for an instant, to be appraising the situation, seeking out potential weaknesses in its adversaries. And it found none. The flaming red swords of the Knights, now being waved almost tauntingly out before them, seemed to confuse it, and instead of charging in any one direction it hunkered down, bristling its many spines in some kind of defensive posture. It let out a very deep rumble.

Upon reflection, Adramalik was never sure what the creature did next to cause so much mayhem. As he and his Knights came within swords' distance of the Abyssal it seemed to puff out a cloud of impenetrable darkness, a billowing shadow so dark one could only just see the glowing markings on its flanks. From within that cloud, accompanied by the creature's echoing snarls, came a whirlwind of blows, a phalanx of disembodied claws that catapulted three of the demons far into the air and out of the fight. From the corner of his eye, Adramalik saw their stunned forms lying on the ice, motionless. *At least their ashes are not upon the wind!*

With his protective glyph ring disrupted Adramalik saw each standing demon hurriedly light his own weaker defenses, intricate, sizzling webs of glyph charms that each had crafted through eons of individual combat. Demospurcus, shrouded in red-violet ribbons of writhing glyphs, raised his sword overhead and, roaring, charged into the unnatural darkness. Adramalik saw the ribbons fade into the shifting shadow cloud and then saw only his flaming sword rising and falling, stabbing and slashing. For a moment he hesitated, debating whether he should follow the Knight into the cloud, but then, as he watched, the sword swung in a long curve, ascending upward in an arc higher and higher and then higher than any wingless demon could jump. And suddenly, without warning, the great head of the Abyssal thrust out of the dark cloud and there, high above and dangling by one leg, was Demospurcus still flailing his sword at the beak that held him aloft.

Adramalik leaped forward, taking wing, and with sword extended hurled himself at the massive head. He had hoped to distract the monster into dropping Demospurcus, but instead the razor-sharp beak snapped fiercely shut, clipping the demon's leg off at mid-calf and sending the shrieking demon plummeting to the ground, a trail of ash emanating from the wound. The Grand Master knew he would only be able to deal with the urgency of a wound as grievous as that if he could quickly dispatch the Abyssal. He aimed for the creature's eye socket and plunged his sword deep into its pallid eye and into the orbit behind. Clinging to the bony head, he gritted his teeth as the animal roared in pain and tried to dislodge him, shaking its head until the demon found himself briefly hanging by his sword hilt. Adramalik flared his wings and, pulling backward, yanked the sword free, leaving a smoking, bubbling wound that sprayed him with bitter fluid. Without hesitating he raked another eye with the fiery blade and then, with the fight gone out of it, the animal reared back into the dissipating cloud of darkness. Through the veil of shadow, Adramalik saw it frantically search for the hole it had sprung from and then, finding it, claw its way back down under the ice. Its whimpering cries faded quickly as it retreated into the caverns below.

Descending hurriedly, Adramalik fell to one knee before Demospurcus and quickly laid his hand on the demon's leg. Though the wound was not fatal, it was serious. Its gathering ash had eaten its way nearly up to the Knight's knee and the Grand Master found that he needed no fewer than three battlefield glyphs to stop its advance. He crouched there for some time, waiting for the other stunned Knights to regain themselves. At first, only Lucifex and Vulryx joined him, the former looking serious and contrite. Adramalik did not acknowledge him.

Slowly, on unsteady legs, Rahab and Beleneth joined their brethren gathered around their fallen comrade, a mixture of relief, exhilaration, and anger written upon their tired faces. It was clear that Demospurcus would not perish, but it was also clear that he would be a burden until they could reach Pygon Az. When Adramalik rose, each knew that they would not halt during their journey until they were within the walls of the Black Ice City.

Adramalik looked at Lucifex pointedly. "He is *your* responsibility, Knight. See that he makes it to Pygon Az alive. Let him perish and I will prove to you that I do not care if I lose *two* demons."

The Knight nodded gravely and carefully gathered up the barely conscious Demospurcus, pulling him with some difficulty onto his back.

The demons set off, moving more slowly across the ice because of the demon-encumbered Lucifex. Countless times Adramalik saw him nearly fall only to quickly catch himself with a well-placed foot or an outstretched arm. Gradually he found himself letting go of his anger toward the Knight and his impulsiveness, realizing pragmatically that he had so few fellow demons from Beelzebub's former court that it would be foolishness to ostracize or humiliate any one of them.

The party crested a ridge and saw the bend of the river Lethe, silvery against the dark ice. Beyond, the jagged spires of Pygon Az appeared, the city's black towers seeming to grow from the very ice of the Wastes, its fires tiny pinholes of glittering light that outlined its walls. The umbral clouds of an ice storm hung in the skies overhead and, as the demons felt the first pricks of shard-fall, it descended upon the city, obscuring it until only the fires winked through the shimmering curtain of ice.

Slowly, ice shards plinking noisily on their armor, they made their way to the city's giant gates. They were almost as large as the gates of Dis, itself, and were coated in frozen stalactites of black ice. The demons stood before them, gazing up and panting. Over the shard-fall, the billowing sound of the giant blue-flamed braziers atop the walls greeted their ears. From beyond, there were no sounds.

"These gates and walls are huge, Grand Master," Chammon said. "Who could they possibly be defense against out here?"

"Abyssals?" Adramalik ventured. They had not been erected when he had last visited the city. To his knowledge, Abyssals did not attack settlements. "Walls are never a bad thing . . . except when one is trying to breach them. I am sure we will soon find out why they are here."

With that, he pounded with the pommel of his sword upon the slick surface of the gate, and moments later, without inquiry from within, the massive doors parted and the demons entered Pygon Az.

3

THE WASTES—EMBER FIELDS

With every hissing footfall, Lilith and Ardat Lili dislodged a hundred flakes of glowing ash, tiny embers that rose weightlessly in a glittering wake behind them. And yet with every step that took them away from Adamantinarx, Lilith wondered why her sorrow did not diminish. She had known, in her heart, that Sargatanas was going to succeed, had known he would be torn from her forever. Part of her was angry with him even as she had told him she would not be. She cursed herself for not having learned from her experience with Lucifer just what parting from Sargatanas would feel like.

It was a hollowness beyond her imagining.

Lilith stepped easily through the ash. Her bird feet gave her a distinct advantage over her companion as they crossed the stinging Ember Fields. The ground layers of thin tissue, burned, flakey, and easily disturbed, were hard on Ardat's feet, but, deep in her own thoughts, she said nothing. Punished by the Fly for doing Lilith's bidding, Ardat had escaped an eternity worse than most in Hell. When she had spoken of it, and that had only been once after awakening from a dream of blind terror, she had told Lilith what it had felt like to be suspended high above the Prince's Rotunda, a peeled skin devoid of rational thought. Her mind had been eaten away, emptied, and the very few thoughts she had had were flighty and chaotic, echoing the flies that had surrounded and penetrated her.

Lilith kicked her feet through the smoldering embers, certain she would never be able to repay her handmaiden for the evils she had endured. She only hoped that she could always be there for her when the nightmares came.

The faint roar of a firestorm could be heard and Lilith knew that shelter must be found. The Ember Fields would become alive with whirling pillars of incandescence within which they would never survive. The pair pressed on toward a distant rocky outcrop, a dark oasis in a sea of radiance. They would rest there until the storm passed, huddled beneath their makeshift Abyssal-skin shelter.

Just as Lilith's feet gained purchase on the volcanic rock the first winds began to press her garments against her. She turned to help Ardat up onto the rocky shelf and saw the concern in her face. Having traveled from city to city solely with the heavily protected caravans, Ardat was less than experienced in the wilds of Hell, whereas Lilith's time spent in the Wastes before the Fall had taught her much about survival that even the demons themselves did not know.

They found a small, sheltering hollow carved by the wind in the outcropping and set their packs down within it. Lilith pulled the overly long scabbard of her sword over her head and then the strap of her small bag and heard the faintest of clinkings from within. She had been careful to pack the dozens of small, obsidian phials in finely shredded vellum made from the wind-strewn remnants of Dis' extinct bureaucracy that she had found and gathered up on her last visit to the ruined capital. The phials were empty, but, she reflected, even in their emptiness they represented the true reason for her journey. This venture into the depths of

Hell's Wastes was about regaining a soul. It was about filling those phials with a cure. It was about Hannibal.

The war with Beelzebub was long over. Hell's new capital, Adamantinarx-upon-the-Acheron, was rising once again, well on the way to being rebuilt not with soul-slave labor but with a willing alliance of souls and demons. This was truly Sargatanas' legacy, a legacy of hope in a place where no one but he could have envisioned it.

But Lilith kept her ears open to events elsewhere in Hell. Adamantinarx was not Hell, it was but a benign part of a greater, less forgiving whole, and Lilith knew well enough not to judge the world by what she saw in its once greatest, most progressive city. Disturbing tales from far-flung cities began to filter back to her of conflicts arising directly from the outcome of the war and from the new status imparted to souls. But the most troubling of all the stories was the one Eligor brought back from the wards of Dis. What he reported to Put Satanachia after his visit with the Soul General had been troubling enough that Lilith herself had undertaken the long trek to the ruined capital.

Escorted by a full, elite cohort of Furcas Legion *malpirgim,* Lilith wandered the flat acres that were the once-crowded streets of Dis. Above it all hung a vast sigil—Satanachia's symbol of dominance and possession. And below it the twisted alleys, the grandiose boulevards, the sagging and ulcerous domiciles, the pompous and overblown buildings of state, existed only in memory, leveled by Mulciber in his efforts to protect the Fly. Gone, too, was the Wall that he had built from those bricks. So much was gone. Everywhere, etched upon the glass-smooth surface of the ground, were the geometric marks where the foundations of the tens of thousands of buildings had stood. The Keep, that demon-made mountain of flesh and bone and blood, was all but gone, its single, stark surviving portion—Moloch's Tower and the area immediately around it—all that remained. Gone, too, was the famed Wargate. She was not at all dismayed that the dark, seeping tumor that had been Hell's first and largest city was gone, that its sullen and corrupt bureaucrats, its persecuted throngs, its horrific legions, and most of all its hierarchy of prideful and paranoid demigods, Demons Minor and Major, were destroyed. But most satisfying was the knowledge that the unclean creature that had tortured her in mind and body for eons, the Prince Regent of Hell, the Fly, was no more.

Conversely, Lilith did frequently wonder why her protégé, Hannibal, had so definitively taken up residence in the former abode of his enemy, Moloch. She tried hard to deny the obvious answers, but the longer he remained in seclusion, the more the rumors and her suspicions disquieted her. And so, with Eligor's tale echoing in her mind, she packed her kit and made the journey to Dis.

Now, standing before the shattered and deconstructed remains of Beelzebub's fortress, she wondered whether she had been overly concerned and whether Eligor might have misread the signs. Either way, she wanted to see Hannibal for herself.

The cohort brought her across the rubble-strewn lava moat that had once been Lucifer's Belt, the naturally enhanced defense Beelzebub had built around his Keep. Very little remained exposed, with only small expanding patches of lava visible between the massive chunks of melted mortar that had been Mulciber's Wall. Those souls who had comprised it, the majority of Dis' damned, had been lost forever, congealed, one indistinguishable from the other, by the lava's fierce heat into solid, inseparable blocks. It was this rubble that was, respectfully, being cleared. Eventually, the lava would reclaim the place. Lilith clambered over the sharp chunks until she reached the base of the structure, where they began to set up camp.

Looking up, she saw the pointed, broken base of Moloch's Tower floating high overhead. Architect General Halphas had provided invocations to keep it floating. The ground beneath it was a network of concentric circles filled in with lava—evidence of where the Keep's vast underground chambers had been and where Semjaza had been held captive. The tower itself was intentionally impossible to reach save by Flying Guard demons who had to gain special permission to access it. The souls and demons working on demolishing the remnants of the Keep at its base were prohibited from gaining access to the tower itself. This was by Satanachia's design. While the tower—Hannibal's residence now—was not to be touched, everything else was to be demolished. No part of the Keep was to remain intact.

Lilith saw workers, souls and demons alike, moving about, claw-tools in hand, surefooted through the crumbling debris. She watched them for some time and, even from a distance, she noted how different their interactions were. The ancient relationship of overseer and slave was no longer in evidence. Demon and soul seemed intent on coexisting, performing their tasks side by side with seeming harmony. It was a reality of which Lilith had, in the past, only dreamt, a reality brought about by the reforms that followed Sargatanas' rebellion.

The tower loomed above and Lilith asked the Demon Minor she had traveled to the capital with, a commander named Dramyax, how she might gain access. Sent to Dis to organize workgangs, Dramyax seemed distracted and reluctant to help. He was, Lilith knew, a demon of little imagination.

"Perhaps you can send a glyph skyward to seek a flyer?"

"Perhaps." Dramyax's eyes were elsewhere.

"Perhaps Lord Satanachia can be apprised of your unenthusiastic service to me?"

Immediately a glyph soared, and in a few moments a Flying Guard demon appeared. Dramyax bowed cursorily.

With no more words exchanged she was carried aloft the hundreds of feet to the tower's broken, floating base. He brought her to the foot of a long staircase and without a word opened his wings and was off. Lilith shook her head and, wasting no time, began to ascend, her clawed feet easily grasping the narrow struts of the bone steps. A damp, fetid odor filled her nostrils, the scent of ancient, severed conduits and eviscerated substructures. Climbing through what little was left of the Keep was a harrowing experience for her. She recognized some of the shattered halls and organic passages; the chambers and their destroyed furnishings and all of it made her uneasy. The passage of time had not dimmed her horrific recollections of the Fly and his insatiable appetites, of that untrustworthy monster, Chancellor Adramalik, and his brutish Knights, of the twisted, pathetic Prime Minister Agares without whose help she could never have survived, of the thing that had once been Faraii, of her trysts with the noble, Ascended Valefar, and finally of her first hopeful thoughts of Sargatanas.

Halfway up the ragged pile, she paused and peered down through a gaping hole at Dramyax's demons hard at work setting up camp. They were well-disciplined troops. Dramyax was a good commander, tough but fair despite his shallowness, and during their march to Dis she had watched his troops repulse small bands of freed souls who had taken to the regions between the great cities. While the souls had proved to be tenacious fighters, they had never posed much of a threat. But during these minor engagements, Lilith had, for the first time in Hell, experienced a firm dislike for humans. This had not been her vision for them.

Pulling her skins in closely around her, she resumed her climb passing curious workers who stopped to look at and bow their heads at the White Mistress as she passed them. Her popularity among the souls as Sargatanas' consort had risen even beyond what it had been when her name had been whispered among the damned before the Rebellion. Now it bordered on open reverence.

Roughly a thousand feet up, Lilith marked a change in the degree of demolition around her. Large gangs of demons and souls were toiling with fervor and, at this height, the tower's base began to look less like the remnants of a building and more like a giant, talon-shredded cadaver. The winds picked up, bearing upon them the overpowering scent of decay, flapping the raked flesh and shaking the loose bones that dangled from the tissue. Lilith's toes clutched the smooth bone steps a little more firmly in the face of that noxious wind. Great buckets on long sinew ropes carried torn flesh and foul detritus past her, on their way down to be emptied into the surrounding lava fields. To be cleansed, she felt.

Nimble as she was, the ascent took hours. Some of the blasted pieces of the Keep were accessible only by climbing narrow staircases that were exposed to the open air. These she negotiated with great trepidation. Eventually, she stepped up and onto the uppermost platform of the Keep and felt the tingling tug of vertigo in her thighs as she gazed, once more, down at the seemingly tiny demons below. The exposed heights were all the more powerful due to the relatively narrow platform, and she backed away from its edge. Lilith pursed her lips, the only gesture she would allow herself that might have been interpreted as evidence of nerves. Rising high into the dirty clouds loomed the exposed and shattered shaft of Moloch's Tower, a rough-sided soul-brick cylinder—

the only such building still extant in Dis—that terminated in a jagged and aggressive crown surrounded by giant floating claws. With the thick mantle of flesh that had covered the Keep now gone, much more of the spire was revealed. It was stained and ugly, even by Hell's standards, and, by its survival, albeit broken, somehow defiant. And at its apex, she knew, was the abode of Hannibal. How he reached it she could not guess. As she pondered this question, a winged demon separated himself from the other demon workers just below and rose to the platform where she stood. He landed lightly, and she saw that he left his wings half-open, angling them against the wind. He was a burly, barrel-chested demon, probably a former flying infantry soldier, scarred by battle and work. As he approached, Lilith was relieved to note that the inextinguishable fires upon him burned away the scent of decay.

"My name, my lady," he said, his voice gravelly, "is Sheggaroth. We received word of your imminent arrival and I volunteered to escort you to the tower's top." The demon knelt clumsily. "Are you ready?" he said.

Lilith nodded.

"My lady, I have been up there," he said, indicating the tower top with a flick of his spine-crested head, "more than once. It is a . . . an unpleasant place."

Something seemed to be troubling him, but Lilith was reluctant to press him.

"I have some familiarity with 'unpleasant places,' Sheggaroth."

The demon nodded, stood, and extended his arms and Lilith, enfolded in his embrace, allowed herself to be lifted into the air. It was a short flight, with the ash-flecked winds buffeting them, but Sheggaroth was a strong flyer and he landed surely upon the sill of the narrow panoramic window that encircled the tower's chambers.

"Please wait here if you would, Sheggaroth," Lilith said.

"Of course, my lady."

She dropped carefully and quietly down from the windowsill into the ancient stone-flagged chamber that had apparently been Moloch's living quarters. No lamps were lit and only the vague silhouettes of the room's sole architectural feature—a raised platform where beddings were present—could be seen in the gloom. An indefinable, heavy scent permeated the place despite the wind that ebbed and flowed, a disturbing muskiness that Lilith had not encountered before.

She slowly made her way farther into the large, high-ceilinged room, her red eyes adjusting rapidly to the darkness. Moving slowly through the wedge-shaped chamber and avoiding the many heavy columns and the waist-high sharp-cornered ledges, she passed through a threshold and came finally to a wide, round anteroom marked by a shallow circular depression. There she saw the twin stone troughs that she knew had housed Moloch's fearsome Hooks and saw the runnels that had filled them with the crimson blood of the souls he had dined upon. As she approached the oblong receptacles she let out a gasp—one of the troughs was filled nearly to the lip with blood, thick and red and smooth. Everywhere, large bloody footprints covered the floor.

And then she saw him, seated on the only piece of furniture that she had so far seen in the chambers, a magnificent throne carved of jet, rescued, she was sure, from the Keep.

"I knew you would come. Eventually." His voice was low and rough. "Welcome."

"Hannibal," Lilith said softly in the souls' tongue. Her ability to speak to souls had improved since the Rebellion. "Thank you. I'm sorry I came unannounced."

"It's good to see you again, unexpected or otherwise, Lilith. I don't have visitors . . . the last was Eligor . . . and so I require little in the way of furnishings. If you like, there are some skins in the other room that you can drag—"

"I am fine standing." She could just see the trough out of the corner of her eye. And was that a cage at the opposite side of the room?

"So, tell me, how is our world since our great lord has Ascended?"

"It is a changed place. Improved in many ways, still dangerous in many others."

"From what I've seen, in my few journeys, Hell has now become a place of imagined freedoms. The Salamandrines have a saying: 'You can channel lava in any direction you like, but it still burns.' This prison of our sins is no less hot for our achievements."

Lilith heard something in his grating voice, something distant and pained.

"You haven't found your wife, Imilce?"

"No. I have searched far and wide. She is gone. Lost to me."

"I will see if—"

"Lilith," he said angrily. "I'm over it. Do nothing. If she is here in Hell I will never know. And that is probably just as well."

The shadowed form of Hannibal seemed to twist on his throne. Lilith could not see his eyes. She moved forward, hand outstretched as if to comfort him.

"Is there any way I can help you? What is it that you need?"

Hannibal gave a short laugh, guttural and dangerous. "What I *need* is to finally be one with my god, Lilith. Now that you have set me on that course, now that he is so much a part of me. Isn't that what every living soul craves? Even when love or fear of one's god requires of them acts so questionable, so irrational, so unspeakable, that living becomes unbearable? I've listened to too many souls here in Hell who have tried to explain why they are being punished—that this god or that one made them do something otherwise repugnant. I listened and I understood why they had done what they did. In my case, my god was a monster. He asked me to burn my baby alive. And now I am becoming one with him. How can I argue with such bliss?"

Hannibal rose from the throne and approached Lilith so swiftly and aggressively that she could not step away.

"Was this what you had in mind for me, Lilith? *Look* at what my salvation has wrought!"

Lilith saw a figure that was caught somewhere between tortured humanity and degraded godhood. He stood much taller than she remembered, his arms huge, asymmetric, and muscular, his legs strangely jointed and inhumanly powerful. A low blue flame coursed over him and when she looked at his face, through that shimmering fire, she saw many cold blue eyes now open and glaring down at her.

A copious amount of drying blood still dribbled from his mouth, down onto his chest.

"Hannibal, I'm sorry."

"No sorrier than I. I betrayed myself, my fellow souls, and now, by becoming *this,* my dead daughter. All for Sargatanas. His price to Ascend was steep indeed." He moved away, his gliding stride long and supple.

"I think you should go now, Lilith. I crave solitude. That is all there is for me now."

Lilith's chin dropped and then she turned, heading back toward the window and Sheggaroth.

"And Lilith," Hannibal whispered hoarsely, "do not send Mago here to try to comfort me. I have found that I cannot be trusted with souls, no matter who they are."

For a moment her eyes lit, once more, upon the trough and the footprints and then she realized that along with Hannibal's some of them were smaller—the bloody footprints of a soul. Without asking Hannibal about them, she moved away from him, her strides lengthening as her relief to be leaving grew.

The protective Abyssal skin across the small cave entrance was still shaking, but the storm was passing, burning itself out as it rose into the sky once more. Lilith's hand was clenched around Ardat's, too tightly perhaps, but the feel of another so close was comforting to her. The wind-driven fire spouts that had been mountain high were playing themselves out, tracing swirling corkscrews of burning embers across the ash. When the winds had died down completely, she cautiously parted the skins and saw the entire world ablaze in a coruscating cloud of settling embers. She stepped out and raised her face into the floating cinders, feeling the tiniest of stings as they landed upon her. It was quite beautiful but, she knew, also quite transitory. To find any beauty in Hell was always a small miracle.

Ardat began to break down the shelter and with Lilith's help they were soon back en route to the distant Wastes. It was her mission to seek a cure for Hannibal and there was only one demon who she felt could help her find it—Buer. The demon was nearly a legend and his whereabouts were unknown, but she would find him and then she would return and save Hannibal. Again.

4

ADAMANTINARX-UPON-THE-ACHERON

Preparations for the expedition to retrieve the Books were nearing an end and, after much impatient walking of the half-rebuilt streets of Adamantinarx, Boudica was more than ready to leave. The Wastes caravan, which consisted of many dozens of harnessed Abyssals, awaited only the arrival of the three centuries of demon legionaries that would protect it.

Boudica, her packs and bags at her feet, leaned against a new stone pillar, watching as the heavy silver-red creatures were laden with supplies. Since the Rebellion, she had learned, the demons had been actively rounding up and breeding Abyssals, using them in all the many ways that they had once used souls. The demon cavalry had needed to completely retrain with fast-running Skin-skippers, a difficult and dangerous animal, yet an animal otherwise ideally suited to their needs. The draft creatures Boudica now stood before, *bul-ata,* as the Salamandrines called them, were now fairly ubiquitous, as they had proved to be hardy and strong, perfect for the lengthy journeys outside the city. Each animal was nearly twenty feet high, with thick-carapaced, blunt-spined bodies and numerous jointed legs covered in horny plates. As with most Abyssals, the creatures bore an erectile spine, in this case dorsally located and surmounted by an elaborate natural light-producing lantern. She could see that the *bul-ata* were capable of carrying massive amounts of cargo hanging from their rows of spines and she knew that they would need to. Apart from the Library, once it was recovered, they would be carrying provisions for the long march, as little forage for demons and beasts alike was readily accessible on the march. The demon drovers, their club-like guiding sticks in hand, were holding the shifting animals' thick bridles, keeping them in line as they were packed. The clatter and jostle of provisions being loaded, the noisy, shrill calls of the animals, the muffled words of the demons chatting among themselves, all filled her ears, just as the pungent sweet-smoke aroma of the *bul-ata* filled her nose. There was a simple pleasure in watching all of the frenetic final preparations, especially since she had to do nothing. Her only concern was her complete unfamiliarity with the animals and her lack of experience riding them. But that, she knew, would take care of itself with time.

She saw Eligor before he saw her. Taller than most of the worker demons, she spotted him quickly, recognized his color, the way he carried his wings, the purposeful stride, and finally his glyph. He paused to give some instructions to one of the drovers and then, spotting her, he made his way past the baggage to her side. She saw that he carried a few bundles and somehow knew they were meant for her.

"Greetings, Boudica. And are you ready to leave our great capital?"

She looked up at him, straight into his burning face, and said plainly, "I can't leave here quickly enough."

"Only so that you can then return just as quickly?"

"*Only* so that I might find my daughters, Eligor."

The demon nodded. "I know." A thin smile played upon his bony lips. "Lord Satanachia gave me a few things to give you for your journey. To aid you in finding them." And with that Eligor untied the skin from the long bundle he had been carrying. The skin fell away and the hilt of a sword was revealed, a sword scaled to the hand of a female soul.

"I asked Lord Satanachia to have this forged for you. He obliged by having his own sword maker produce it. It was crafted after the kind of weapon you were familiar with in your Life. But it is made of metals and techniques not known in your world."

She took the weapon, regarding its finely made handle and blade, and resisted the overwhelming urge to heft it in her hand, to hold it overhead, and to swing it with all the pent-up fury she had contained for eons. Instead, she smiled coolly at Eligor. She bore him no grievance and was, she knew, in fact, in his debt. He had done everything possible to free her of her past existence in Hell and she would not forget that.

Before she could thank him, a piercing cry interrupted them and Boudica saw a half-dozen especially large, recalcitrant *bul-ata,* being brought up to the others and tied to the laden creatures' harnesses. Each bore intricately worked trappings that looked decidedly non-demon. She turned back to Eligor with a quizzical look upon her face.

"Those beasts are for barter. They are bred for their size and strength. Safe passage through the Wastes is not always assured and the Salamandrines are notoriously difficult."

Eligor opened another satchel and withdrew a small, round item fashioned of bone and some golden metal. It looked very old and heavily used, its surface details darkened and rubbed smooth from handling. Small glyphs, inlaid in metals, decorated its sides. He handed it to her. It was large for her hands and she found it lighter than she had expected.

"That is an ancient Finder set to guide you to this city from anywhere in Hell. Press all of the glyphs at once and you will see."

She did as he instructed and a fiery and pointed glyph sprang up and hovered a foot above the device.

"It follows the magnetic fields, growing in size until you are here. It was created long ago when we first founded this city. Lord Sargatanas had a number of them made for those flying demons who were ordered to explore the far-flung Wastes and they served their purpose well. But now, with the city's geomantic place in our world and minds firmly established, we demons have little use for them. That said, it is a rare piece." Eligor paused and turned his head. "Ah, Metaphrax approaches."

She heard nothing. And then, after a few moments, just above the sounds of the animals and drovers, Boudica could make out the low tramp of countless feet accompanied by the slow, rhythmic striking of weapons upon armor of the approaching centuries of the newly renamed Argastos' Archers. Metaphrax Argastos was nearly Eligor's height, winged like him, battle scarred, and crusted in the circular phalera-disks Boudica knew to be trophies. He had a hardened, efficient look about him that she remembered from her own warriors. There were some who took to the art of war as if it were that for which they had been created, and this demon had that look. He turned his fierce gaze upon her and, despite herself, she was impressed by his obvious intensity. A glowing serpent of interconnected glyphs wended its way around him, moving ceaselessly and illuminating his body and face with a random fiery light. It was a mesmerizing effect and Boudica found it hard not to stare.

"So, this is the female soul who is to accompany us, yes? Armed and ready for the Wastes, I can see." Boudica heard the slight tone of something bordering on mockery.

"More than ready. She spent quite a long time waiting for just such a chance to get away, Metaphrax. And she has good reason to journey out."

"The caravan seems ready, as well," Metaphrax said, looking away and peering up and down the jostling line of pack animals. The archers were already taking up positions on either side along the flanks of the creatures. Boudica saw that each carried an odd bow that appeared as if it could also be broken apart and used as a pair of curved swords if need be. She suspected they were formidable weapons.

Metaphrax extended his hand to Eligor and the two demons clasped each other's forearms.

"I will bring the Books back to Adamantinarx or be destroyed trying."

Eligor nodded and said, "May Sargatanas' spirit be with you."

"And may he guide and guard you."

Boudica heard the exchange and was surprised by the two demons' apparent reverence; Sargatanas had, indeed, changed things in Hell.

Eligor clapped his junior officer on the arm and then turned away. She watched him depart, an odd mixture of emotions playing upon her mind. He had given her the freedom she had craved, had shown her more kindness than any other demon. And, yet, he was still one of them.

"Come, Boudica. You will ride at the front with me and my lieutenant, Styjimar," Metaphrax said. He was walking slowly in an effort, she guessed, to allow her to keep up, and she picked up her belongings and followed him. When she reached the head of the column she saw a handler offer him the reins of his mount. She carefully watched him insert his foot into a toehold carved into one of creature's armored plates and climb upon the lead *bul-ata*'s back. A second creature, only slightly smaller, stood adjacent and he indicated with a flick of his head that it was her mount. She eyed it suspiciously, walked to its side, and raised her hand overhead to grab the soul-scaled stirrup. Without asking, the demon leaned down from his creature, firmly grasped her hand, and lightly tossed her onto her saddle. She settled easily into the smaller, padded saddle the demons had crafted for her and unsheathed and grasped the short, spiked guiding stick as she had been shown.

Almost immediately Metaphrax gave the signal and the column began to move forward. The shuffling of the many Abyssals' countless legs created a susurration that, while loud, Boudica found surprisingly relaxing. Any of the fears she might have had regarding riding them soon vanished altogether. Slowly, they trudged past the many grand buildings with their freshly gilt domes, the myriad new dwellings built now of stone, over the newly cobbled avenues, and down toward the massive rebuilt pylon once known as the Gate of a Million Hearts that led to the bridge across the milky River of Tears. Now its newly carved talatat depicted the Ascended Sargatanas, a familiar motif on walls and buildings.

The mist-laden air became clammy and not a little oppressive and she and the others grew silent, the well-known dispiriting effect of the waters settling upon them. Neither demon nor soul was spared and each grew quiet and descended into a somber reverie.

As the caravan made its way across the statue-lined bridge, Boudica peered down into the river she had reflected upon from a distance of time and status for so many centuries. Its thickly rippling surface seemed only barely translucent, almost viscous, and she had the impression of tiny creatures schooling about in infinite numbers in the slow whirlpools, purposeless and desperate. Some of the souls believed that they were the tears of the despairing, rendered somehow to life, each one a pained or sorrowful thought.

The great river's breadth surprised Boudica. Perhaps it was the malaise the Acheron engendered, but it seemed to take longer to traverse than she would have imagined. Once they had crossed the bridge the air remained thick and it was some time before the river's effect wore off. The road, vestige of a wide and spear-straight avenue emanating from the city's heart, began to fade away into the creased and pocked ground-skin until finally, even with Adamantinarx's distant palace still visible in the miasma, it vanished altogether.

The *bul-ata* were in their element and Boudica now saw the obvious advantage to the creatures' many legs. The wrinkled ground, for all of its low unevenness, was no challenge whatsoever to them and she relaxed with the gently swaying motion of her mount. With a new sword upon her back and the city that had kept her prisoner for so long fading into the ashy sky, Boudica, for once in her existence in Hell, felt contentment.

With the caravan's steady progress into the region between the cities, Algol's position in the sky became Boudica's sole measure of time. When she had been a worker in the time before the Rebellion, the labor-gangs had been worked in regularly timed shifts and these had, to all the souls, been a means whereby time had been calculated. According to Metaphrax, Algol was an excellent if difficult navigational aid, and he took pains to show her how, with the use of a simple cord with odd knots and little carved weights, the star's seemingly erratic risings and fallings were made predictable. *So great,* Boudica thought, *is the need for rational creatures to measure time that even in the timeless realm of Hell, a realm of perpetual gloom, a method had been created.* It took her some time to be able to manipulate the device, fashioned as it was for demons' larger hands and seated, as she was, upon a moving beast's back. But eventually she could follow the star's subtle movements just enough to calculate the passage of time.

The terrain between Adamantinarx and the smaller cities of its outlying wards varied little. Boudica saw low, sharp-ridged hillocks as far as the horizon, thin rivers of lava zigzagging through them, and the occasional stands of arterial trees swaying where there was no wind. As she peered down at the ground she saw it move of its own accord, slight ripples, barely perceptible tremors, a twitch and a wince as they passed over it. She found it ironic that in a place of such sublime suffering, a place regarded as that of the dead, this land was so alive. But she knew that it was alive in a way that was terrible, alive but less than alive.

"It is something between Life and Death," Metaphrax explained when Boudica inquired about the nature of the land. "We had nothing like this in the Above. Our world was beautiful and the Life that permeated it emanated, by its grace, from the Throne. This 'life' comes from something, something . . . foul. Beelzebub mandated it. It was his idea, born of nothing but perversity. The Fly and his court wanted to put their corrupt mark upon this world when they arrived. This is their doing. All of this was born of a single dark invocation. Once started, it spread like a plague very quickly. And changed the world we found when we Fell."

"And the Salamandrines? What of them?"

"The Fly wanted them exterminated. Only they are not easy to exterminate. We found that out the hard way . . . over millennia. They became, in our minds, the Men of Wrath. The hated Others. At least that was what the Fly wanted us to think."

She thought about that as they progressed toward the true

Wastes, spoken, as it was, by a demon. She thought about what she guessed he had lost or given up and then what she had, as well. They shared lost worlds and lost dreams and that made her feel a strange kinship with this taciturn Demon Minor. But he was a demon, nonetheless, and she found it hard to remain anything but wary of his motives and his intentions.

The infernal landscape provided Boudica with one disturbing revelation after another. Fascinated and repulsed, she watched as seemingly flat ground would suddenly sprout foot-high writhing carpets of fingers disquietingly human in appearance, or massive pale, dead eyes that would roll toward the caravan beneath blinking, sticky lids. Or slices of skin-like terrain that would peel off and float bizarrely before them only to corkscrew back into the ground. Or smooth-sided hills that were quiescent until they passed, only to split at any random point and grin at her with their shredded clay-hued mouths, spewing sounds and odors from deep within that made her shudder. Metaphrax barely took notice of them, save to spit upon the more egregious of them as he rode past. Boudica saw him do it, and saw, too, how his hot sputum caused reactions. The dark smile that crossed his bony face almost amused her.

Behind her the lengthy caravan traveled in relative silence. While a constant array of squeaky sounds emanated from the tireless *bul-ata* and their bulky harnessed goods, the drovers and the centuries of archers remained quiet; the steady tramp of their feet was accompanied only by the jangling of equipment and weapons.

As the travelers left far behind the environs of their city, Boudica watched Algol carefully, frequently using the corded calculator and trying, with some difficulty, to measure what would seem to her to be a day. The abstraction of it made her grow weary and she soon found herself staring into the low, dark clouds that moved raggedly over the landscape. As a worker, she had, during the infrequent rest periods, stared into the sky as respite from the realities of the city around her. She was quite familiar with the variety of ember-flecked clouds that passed over the city, with their dense appearance and the strangely formed symbols that swirled within them. Here, out of the confines of the city, she saw them for what they were—huge rafts of darkness, split by flickering red lightning and amorphous flocks of fiery embers that raked through the sky. And when the clouds seemed to touch the ground she thought she saw huge, lumbering forms moving within the shifting veil as if they were taking advantage of the concealing curtains of gloom to move about. She did not ask Metaphrax about them, each time suspecting that it was simply a fabrication of her tired mind. But every time she peered into the distant clouds something seemed to be stirring and it made her uneasy.

Metaphrax sent aloft a glyph that halted the column and ordered a general dismount. As she swung her leg over the broad back of the *bul-ata,* Boudica found that she was, in fact, more tired than she had realized. Her tingling toes found the foothold with some difficulty and she landed harder on the ground than she had intended. She saw Metaphrax turn his head at the sound and then turn away and she felt a slight surge of embarrassment. Brushing the ash from herself, she looked about, feeling rather diminutive amidst the much larger demons and beasts. Presently, the three centuries of archers broke out broad, square flensing axes and began to carve out a campsite perimeter from the fleshy ground as the beasts behind them were formed up into a rough square. The heavier packs were removed.

Boudica stood by her mount, resting her tired legs by holding on to the harness, and took in all of the activity, perplexed by what seemed to be serious precautions.

"When the Rebellion ended," Metaphrax said, "souls were free to go out and leave the cities. They did this in great numbers, but once they found themselves away from our protection they banded together in large communities. Sometimes this helped fend off Abyssals and the Salamandrines. Sometimes it did not. The Wastes are littered with the sundered still-living remnants of those failures. Since then, small, heavily armed hordes of souls have begun to roam the Wastes near the cities, preying upon wayward caravans and solitary travelers."

"And yet you do nothing about them?"

"Nothing. Other than fend them off when it is necessary. That was the outcome of the Rebellion. They—you—are now a People of Hell."

Boudica watched as great rectangular chunks of ground-flesh were stacked and put heavily in place to form walls half again the height of the demons. The work went rapidly. The demons were powerful and well trained. Once the wall was completed, she saw most of the archers stow their axes and take up a relaxed watch, sitting at the edge of the ditch they had created. Metaphrax, for his part, looked satisfied with his well-disciplined demons, and Boudica watched him set off to walk the perimeter, more out of duty than any real necessity.

With her kit and her corded device in her hand, Boudica curled up amidst a pile of unloaded freight. While true, reviving sleep was not something she would ever experience in Hell, she knew if she closed her eyes her mind would slow enough that she might drift off a bit. As had been the case since Eligor had reawakened her memories, disjointed images of her Life flashed in her mind, so fleeting that any resonance was lost before it took hold. Instead, she had confused and blurred visions of lush green foliage and rocky outcrops and animals. She saw a large red spotted deer, antlers and pelt stained with blood, fending off a pack of wolves. And then he was gone and Boudica sank into the fitful, infernal realm of near sleep.

When she awakened, it was with a start and she knew almost immediately that something had happened. The archers were standing and kneeling in battle lines three deep, their strange bows at the ready and conjured, fiery-shafted arrows in their hands. Two of the nearby *bul-ata,* clearly distressed, were making keening sounds and had heavy iron darts protruding from their armored carapaces. Many more were sticking out of the ground and along the upper edge of the improvised wall.

The demons seemed poised to react but apparently were waiting for a command from Metaphrax and, when Boudica scrambled atop a pile of packs to better see whatever might be over the wall, she saw the Demon Minor, bow in hand, standing with a small contingent of archers and one of the huge *bul-ata.* Behind it she saw a party of skin-shrouded individuals whom she, at first, took to be souls. But when she saw that they were much taller than souls but not quite as tall as the demons she realized that they were Salamandrines. They wore heavy, strangely cut skin garments that hid their true silhouettes, and their odd movements, slightly jerky and crisp, almost implied that they were jointed differently than both souls and demons. From her vantage point it was hard for her to make out any real details of their accoutrements, but one item that was prominent on the half-dozen Men of Wrath was the long, slender sword that each wore slung over his shoulder. And these blades were echoed in the long line of Salamandrines who sat upon dangerous-looking Skin-skippers behind the six figures speaking with Metaphrax. One Salamandrine, apparently a chieftain, stood conversing with the demon, while just behind him a standard-bearer carried a banner composed of the anthropomorphic skins of souls that flapped in the light wind.

The demon was speaking and gesturing, his demeanor one of composed command, and then, with little ceremony, he handed the *bul-ata* over to the Salamandrines he had been addressing and then turned his back and walked steadily back toward the enclosure.

Boudica watched as one by one the line of Salamandrines turned their steeds away from the demons' encampment. The Skinskippers' patterns of glow-lights almost looked like the demons' own glyphs, and as she watched the riders depart into the low, dark ash she was left with the impression of twinkling lights melting away into the darkness. As she climbed down from the piled baggage, assisted by Styjimar, she was not wholly certain as to why she felt an odd admiration for the Salamandrines. She had barely been able to see them. But the feeling was there.

"And that is how we ensure safe passage from here to the Far Wastes," Metaphrax said somewhat smugly to Boudica as he re-entered the encampment and walked past her to Styjimar. But, as camp was broken down and the *bul-ata* were made ready, inchoate fears suddenly struck her and she wondered whether it was really that easy to buy the Salamandrines' indifference.

With her mounted and once again heading steadily toward the distant Wastes, Boudica's uneasiness did not dissipate. The shadowed land seemed perfectly suited to canny warriors who could vanish into the low hills like ash on the wind. And now, as she gazed into the low-hanging, smoky clouds, she not only thought she saw the huge, vague forms that had seemed so elusive earlier, but she also now thought she saw parties of mounted Salamandrines, fading from hillock to hillock, just out of plain sight.

Eventually, she gave up speculating and simply assumed that the caravan was being followed and watched from afar. On occasion she would catch Metaphrax, too, looking into the distance through hooded eyes, his expression unreadable.

The caravan proceeded into a landscape that grew more strange to Boudica's eyes with each hill that fell behind them. Great, fleshy formations rose from the ground, many of them looking to her like the enormous bodies of giants cast upon the gray landscape and rotting back into it. She wondered if it was possible that that was exactly what they were.

Wending its way through valleys created by these imagined or real giants' splayed limbs, Boudica glimpsed strange, furtive animals flitting from one distant shadow to the next, and she heard them, too, hooting or screeching their warnings to one another. Flocks of sharp-winged predators streamed in and out of the smooth flesh-walled chasms of the promontories while brief flashes of fiery lights bespoke other packs of creatures living amidst the cliffs' charnel-strewn bases. In fact, Boudica realized, the infernal world outside of the cities was anything but empty of life.

"These reaches are rarely hunted," Metaphrax commented. "The creatures here are living as did their ancestors who once lived outside Adamantinarx. Before the great hunts and the exterminations. They are thriving and abundant, but with the new order of things and the spreading outward of souls and demons these beasts will undoubtedly vanish."

"I can't tell with most of them if they are dangerous," Boudica said.

"All of the beasts in Hell are dangerous," Metaphrax said. "And now, with the Rebellion over, we have added a new and hungry and numerous one to this world." He looked at her, his meaning clear, his smile ironic.

5

PYGON AZ

"The city is empty," Chammon said.

"So it would seem." Adramalik tried not to let his own surprise and dismay creep into his voice.

"But the gate opened."

"Perhaps it was never locked and the wind moved it." Even as Rahab said it, Adramalik knew it not to be the case. The gate was far too massive to be affected by even the strongest gale. And when he had rapped upon it with his sword it had not budged. Clearly, it had been opened from within—probably by some simple glyph sent from somewhere in the distant palace. Which meant they were being watched, and that made him uncomfortable. But the uneasiness he felt was born more of the stark contrast between the windswept, open streets before them and the ancient memory he had of Rofocale's bustling infernal city.

The demons found the streets barely easier to negotiate than the endless dark ice tracts of the Frozen Wastes. Originally flagged in the roughened souls typical of most infernal metropolises, the streets were now sheathed in a thick, even layer of smoky ice that seemed as if it had been polished perfectly flat by a million feet. This Adramalik found odd, as he clearly remembered the streets to have been carefully maintained and easily trod upon.

The party made its way past the low, dark outer buildings, each one's roof surmounted by low, shimmering blue flames. Though it was called the Black Ice City by all in Hell but its own inhabitants, its name, Adramalik knew, was something of a misnomer—legend said that the city was built of ice. While the ice surrounding the city was indeed black from the ash content, the dark buildings themselves were constructed in the same manner and with the same raw material—souls—as were all the other infernal cities. And, much as it was to be expected, progress regarding the liberation of the souls had not quite caught up with this far-flung realm. The buildings were positioned much as the Grand Master remembered. But something suddenly struck him as he peered up into the dark sky at the roof line. The once-intricate cornices decorated in Rofocale's typically extravagant style had been crudely chopped away, resurfaced into a simpler, more stark form of ornamentation. Angular, repetitive forms had replaced the curving, flamboyant, zoomorphic shapes that had given the entire city a strange, hallucinatory feel. In all, it had been a very atypical city in Hell, a city very much reflective of the Prince-in-exile who had once ruled within it. Now, with the changes obvious only to him, he felt it resembled Dis more than any other city for its severity. But just as the Fly's penchant for overblown grandiosity had been a clue to his ego, Adramalik could not help wonder if this stark new aesthetic was indicative of Pygon Az's new ruler's temperament.

Demospurcus' groan cut the air and Adramalik saw Lucifex carefully set him down and prop him against the icy side of a building. The thick ice surrounding the wounded demon began to melt almost immediately and the dark surface of the bricks emerged. The other demons watched as the heat from their comrade quickly melted the ice upward exposing the wall. Suddenly a long, broad row of bulges that ran the length of the wall was revealed and within the cascade of sheeting water a series of blinking, twitching heads appeared. Water poured from their noses and mouths and the sound of coughing and retching filled the demons' ears.

Adramalik looked at the surrounding buildings and saw that each bore the same wide swathe of small bulges and knew that countless heads were embedded in their mortar. As a design motif, it was unlike anything he had seen in an infernal city and yet, from an aesthetic standpoint, it appealed to him. And, it was practical, as well. If, as he suspected, the souls' eyes were still functional, it would mean that each building could, in effect, be an agent of the city's court, a means whereby the court could keep track of souls and demons alike. It would take some powerful invocations to create and control the massed visions of countless souls, but a high-level Conjurer—most certainly a Demon Major like Agaliarept—could achieve it. And undoubtedly had. There seemed no other explanation for the arrangement. But who was this reclusive demon, settled into this inhospitable kingdom?

Adramalik pulled back and saw the other demons also staring at the wall. Chammon had his dagger out and was taunting some of the heads for sport, dragging its tip back and forth across their wincing faces and watching their reactions, while Vulryx was voiding himself against the wall, a fiery stream of urine melting the ice into clouds of steam. The Grand Master grinned. His Knights were ever the disrespectful pranksters.

A faint scuff from behind and down the avenue made them turn simultaneously. Seven fiery swords were drawn and fired as one and Adramalik saw a strange figure followed by a small retinue advancing toward them. His tall and gaunt silhouette, from a distance, was an intricate assemblage of shapes, some dangling like the skinny arms of Abyssals while others protruded in curving arcs. As he approached, the Grand Master saw the forms more clearly; most were finely carved obsidian or bone ornaments that had been thrust into the bone and flesh of this Demon Minor. He wore the skin of a large soul stretched over his body, the soul's hands hanging limply from his own wrists. There was a distinctly barbaric, almost primitive look to his adornments, something very unlike the customary manner in which demons decorated themselves. His head, in particular, seemed the focus of extraordinary attention with several large, crescent-ended blades thrust deeply into his skull, cutting all the way down to split his lips.

Adramalik was nearly as intrigued by this ornately decorated demon as he was by the small group of souls who hung in the shadows behind him. Garbed in long flesh robes, none had heads, their necks cleft cleanly across. And yet they seemed as aware of their environment as any demon or soul he had encountered.

The gaunt figure stopped before them, his ornaments rattling as he pulled his robe around himself.

"Why are you here?" Adramalik heard the effort in the demon's voice to control his destroyed lips. His words were overarticulated and cared for, but the random sibilance was never far away.

"We seek audience in the court of Prince-in-Exile Lucifuge Rofocale, the Lord of Pygon Az. We are fugitives from Dis and thought to seek asylum in your city."

The Demon Minor turned his head to look at each Knight in turn. "Fugitives from Dis?" He paused, the doubt evident in his narrowed eyes. "We offer *no* sanctuary here. The former Lord of Pygon Az is no longer regent."

Adramalik feigned surprise. "Is this so? We heard nothing to suggest he was deposed." His Knights betrayed nothing.

"Not only *did* you know of his demise, but you were, in all probability, present when it happened. I know who you are, *former* Chancellor Adramalik." He turned and regarded the other demons.

"And this sorry band is all that is left of what used to be a very formidable brotherhood. There was much speculation in my Lord Ai Apaec's court about where you might turn up . . . some, including myself, even believed it would be here. My lord argued that you would never be so bold. Or stupid. Now that you are here, you may, at my lord's pleasure, take up residence. But we *will* turn you over to Sargatanas' demons should they come seeking you."

Adramalik nodded.

"Then, as you already know," Adramalik said, "the Heretic Sargatanas is no more. But his zealots still believe in his cause. Even more so than before. Your . . . prudence regarding them is duly noted."

Even with this reception, he and his Knights had no desire to leave. Quite the contrary. And the likelihood of demons from Adamantinarx venturing this far into the Frozen Wastes to find a handful of renegade demons was fairly slim. Bold or stupid, as this gaudy figure had said. And the misbegotten spirit of post-war reconciliation was far too strong in Sargatanas' demons. As for this upstart lord who had assumed Rofocale's throne, he mattered not at all. From what he could sense, this lord was no Demon Major—with Lucifuge gone he knew of none in this frozen realm—and therefore would pose no difficulty to him or his Knights.

"I thank your lord for his hospitality and understand his decision should the issue of our safety arise." He paused and then added, "However, we can take care of ourselves."

The Demon Minor shrugged almost imperceptibly. He turned and with a slight flick of his head beckoned the Knights to follow.

Adramalik glanced at his Knights and they fell in behind him, Lucifex swearing as he gathered Demospurcus up. A few paces behind them shuffled the headless throng. They seemed to be the lackeys of the ornate demon, tied to him, perhaps, by their inability to see. He would study them and their relationship to this demon.

Without turning, the demon said, "You are wondering about my name and my role here."

Adramalik betrayed none of the annoyance he felt at having his thoughts so easily perceived. Was it an Art or was it simply that obvious?

"Once, I was called Xipetotec. But here I am called the Bearer of the Knife."

"I see no knife."

"I bear it nonetheless."

Adramalik made no further comment. He hoped his irritation had been concealed. Mostly.

They advanced through the city, taking one of its six gradually ascending main avenues in toward its heart. Laid out in a precise hexagram, Pygon Az's center had been dominated by a six-spired palace that had, in Adramalik's opinion, looked like solidified black flame. Lucifuge's wildest imaginings had come to fruition in his palace, a place where his baroque tastes could be indulged without the judgment of his peers. All that was gone now.

Algol set and the sky darkened. The air was unusually clear and cold and visibility across the black city was perfect. With blue-flamed torches and braziers lit, every icy detail stood out against the dark sky.

The palace, altered by its new lord, rose in a six-sided pyramid, steeply and aggressively. Its dark sides were tiered and braziers outlined the squared-off parapets. Partial, round-tipped crescent-vanes surmounted each tower so that the overall effect was of a full crescent composed of six giant sections. Little was left of the original buildings and Adramalik even wondered if they had been built over or razed to construct this stern edifice. Perhaps he would see evidence of them when they were closer.

Vulryx picked up his pace and moved closer to him. Careful to not the let the Bearer hear him, he whispered, "Grand Master, the streets are empty. Where is everyone?"

"No idea, Vulryx, none."

Vulryx dropped back, staring briefly at him and then glancing warily about.

Adramalik remembered Pygon Az as a flourishing city despite its frigid location and distance from the other major cities in Hell, remembered, too, the cohorts of the Ice Legions as the ubiquitous backbone of the place. He shook his head slightly. Nothing about this city was as he had represented it to his Knights. What were they making of it? Would they lose their respect for him? Would they mutiny and cast him out onto the ice? He would have to watch them carefully, gauge them for any signs of discontent. Just as he had done back in Dis.

As they drew nearer to the city center, the Bearer discharged six glyphs that raced ahead, disappearing into the low buildings around the palace.

The demons and souls continued on toward the palace and began to climb the low, wide steps that accommodated the gradually rising ground of the palace's foundation. Had there not been steps, the purchase on the icy, angled street would have been nearly impossible for any demon's clawed foot.

The nearer they drew to the palace the more ornate the buildings became. Giant statuary, sheathed in black ice, motionlessly mimed the great and obscure events of Pygon Az's distant past: noble generals triumphing over long-dead Salamandrines, subjugated Salamandrines in every imaginable pose of supplication bested by great demon warriors. Adramalik remembered them as they had been, clean and free of ice, maintained by a lord who had been proud to rule here. Disconcertingly, none of the statues had heads.

Huge black gates guarded each of the six entrances to the palace, their sloping walls and towers dully gleaming from the ice that encased them.

"You will be housed within the palace precinct," the Bearer said, without sounding especially interested. "Each of you will be in a separate domicile."

"That is not acceptable," Adramalik said with as much imperious authority as he had ever used in Dis.

"It is that or nothing. You can all find yourselves back out on the ice with only the Pit to comfort you."

That caught Adramalik up short. He had tried to sublimate his awareness of that place's proximity, to keep his memories in check, to not even mention it to his Knights. The Pit had been a nightmare within a nightmare, a place he had visited so long ago but never forgotten, a place of such overburdening darkness that the very fires of Hell were a comfort by contrast. He hoped that the Bearer's words had not been overheard by the demons, but when he turned to gauge their reactions he was dismayed to see the grim expressions on their tired and wounded faces. They had heard.

Eventually, the party reached a series of ice-slickened streets arranged neatly at the base of the hexagonal array of towers. As they were set into the sloping hill at the palace's base, the streets were canted, something that would have been no problem had the flagstones not been sheathed in ice. A short distance from the main avenue they traversed, Adramalik saw a blue glyph hovering over a one-story domicile and the Bearer nodded toward the first demon in line. Vulryx nodded back, not a little resentfully, and, accompanied by one of the Bearer's headless functionaries, made his difficult way to the domicile's entrance, within which both vanished.

This process was repeated until each of the Knights was dispatched to his own domicile. It was all very efficient, and yet something about it troubled him. When the Bearer finally nodded to him, indicating the low, dark, elaborately ornamented building, Adramalik gave the demon a long look. The Bearer turned to confront him, his ornaments swinging and clattering.

"You will be summoned when my lord wishes it. Do not attempt to enter the palace before then."

Adramalik did nothing to acknowledge that he heard the warning. Instead, he turned and followed his guide, who, despite his obvious deficit, found his way to the domicile's entrance with complete ease. There was no door. Adramalik could not reason through why one wasn't needed.

As he crossed the darkened threshold, a dozen strong hands grasped him roughly and pulled him within.

6

THE VALE OF THE FREED

The scent of countless souls hung heavily in the air as the two travelers gazed out over a vast, bowl-like depression in the dark and folded landscape.

They had followed a steadily rising trail that eventually cut its way through some low karsts until finally, just as they both wondered if they could negotiate any steeper a grade, the trail opened on to a flat mesa with the panorama of the Vale spread before them.

After Sargatanas had Ascended and the souls had found themselves emancipated there had been a general and predictable exodus from the cities. Lilith had seen the steady flow of souls, liberated from their terrible existences, twisted and bent but quietly jubilant that they were no longer forced to be in proximity to their fearsome jailors. Standing on what remained of the palace parapets, she had wished she could talk with each and every one of them, hear their stories, understand their relief. She had felt, in some ways, responsible for their release. Had she not, even before Sargatanas' encouragement, seeded the souls with her many statues, hoping against hope that one would rise and challenge the demons? And had not Hannibal been that one, her greatest soul champion? She sighed with the thought of him, even now as she gazed into the smoky distance.

"Are those soul roads, my lady? There . . . and there?" Ardat was pointing at parallel scratches that crisscrossed the plain.

"Yes, Ardat, the lighter ones. The others are trackways made by Abyssals." Lilith turned to look at her handmaiden. "How long have we been away from Dis?"

Ardat looked inward, trying to calculate the time. "At least . . ."

"At least long enough for you to call me Lilith, yes?"

"Yes." Ardat smiled. It was a small concession to one who had given so much.

"We will have to be careful, down there among the souls, Ardat. While some have tried to lead them, none, from what I have heard, has been able to govern them. Each town is a separate entity and rivalries have been growing." She paused to peer into the distance. A thin bolt of red sigil-lightning flashed for an instant. "I truly do not know what we will find down there."

With a deep breath, Lilith headed toward a rough cut in the mesa's side and swung herself down, beginning the descent to the valley floor. Ardat gathered her robes and followed, tentatively at first and then more confidently.

Lilith moved easily down the cliffside, her strong hands and bird feet grasping the crusty wrinkles, folds, and bloated organs that covered its surface. More than once she put her hand on a ridge only to have it split apart to reveal yellowed and slimy teeth. And each time she pointed silently to Ardat, who carefully sidestepped the fetid maw.

Sword practice, Lilith reflected, had honed both of them physically, sharpening their reflexes and toughening them. It was, in Lilith's mind, inevitable that in the course of their long journey they would be set upon, if not by renegade souls or demons then certainly by some Abyssal.

Lilith kept a watchful eye on Ardat, who had more difficulty negotiating the irregularities, but despite the occasional brief misstep, there was never any need for her to assist her handmaiden.

Nearing the mesa's base, she saw the wall beneath her feet end, leaving a farther than comfortable drop for the pair.

Ardat climbed down beside her and the two dangled their feet for a few moments before letting go. Lilith landed easily, but Ardat fell and rolled amidst a clattering slide of scree. When they stood, Lilith saw, to her relief, that Ardat had only a few scrapes to show for the descent and fall. She turned to look at the cliff's base and saw a vast network of large, gnawed hollows reaching far into the darkness of the mesa's belly—clear evidence of Abyssals. From within she smelled a rank odor and shuddered, glad down to her soul that she didn't have to enter the caves.

She stood for a moment, unsure of why the dark, descending recesses stirred something deep and unpleasant within her. And then a sound from Ardat swept away her gathering thoughts and made her turn and she slowly walked from the troubling caves.

Stretching before them, enclosed by the low mountains, was a largely featureless, undulating plain dotted with the occasional steaming fumarole and low hillocks. There were no lava flows to ford or fissures to leap across, no sharp-rocked pumice fields or yielding pock-pans that might indicate sub-infernal Abyssal colonies. It was, in all of Hell, a valley most conducive to the habitation of souls. And, Lilith knew, it explained why they had flocked here by the countless thousands.

"That way?" Ardat said, pointing into the distance to a low rise surmounted with what seemed to be a walled enclosure. Small curls of dark smoke coiled up from it.

Lilith nodded and the two set off.

The image of the caves' mouths did not leave her and, together with the arid landscape, vague and ancient recollections long suppressed began to coalesce. Memories of a time and place so remote that she shook her head, astonished she could call them up with such clarity.

Anger was her constant companion in those distant days. Anger and wrathfulness. She had been betrayed, cast away, and transformed and, for all that, she had vowed she would become something the human race would whisper fearfully in the dark about for millennia. She owed them nothing but terror.

"What is it, Lilith?"

Lilith set her jaw. "Memories. Very old memories. From a time before I first met you."

She could feel Ardat's eyes upon her.

"This landscape, this heat . . . it seems cooler here. It reminds me of the Land Between the Two Rivers. You remember. When I arrived there it was little more than a swamp, a place of fishermen and reed weavers. Who could have foreseen what was to rise there? That souls . . . humans . . . would have begun their journey toward civilization in such a place?"

"At the time, I could not have cared less. I hated them all with all that I had become. And that was a far cry from what I had been. When life was breathed into me I was beautiful, joyful, a creature of the sunlight, a being who reveled in her independence and freedom but who could have been happy with someone to love. But I wanted to look my love in the eyes as an equal, not as chattel, and that was to be denied me. Wrathfully. After my fall, I was changed. I was made to be inferior, and then to feel inferior." She nodded toward her feet. I was made to be ashamed of who I had been. And made to be ashamed, too, of what I had become. I feared being seen and, so, I walked in the cool shadows of the night."

Lilith did not glance up to meet Ardat's eyes but instead focused on her scaled feet and their every deliberate step. She had walked through so many generations of humans that she had stopped counting them. And only when she had arrived in Hell had she stopped hating them.

"I had kept to myself for millennia, wandering through the desert of my soul. I was so lonely and disappointed. And that turned to bitterness, then hatred.

"The first village was the hardest and the one I can still remember the most vividly. It was a peaceful place, a swamp-side collection of a dozen reed huts. The villagers were harmless fishermen who laughed with their children and wove mats during the sweltering days, fished in the violet evenings, and made babies in the night. I watched them from the reeds for quite a long time, still and unblinking as one of the tall, predatory birds that waited at the water's edge. And I knew what I would do to them.

"I waited until a terrific storm descended upon the swamps and then, at night, I made my way to the first hut, a simple dwelling that I knew contained a man, a woman, and their baby. They lay naked only feet apart and I went to him and, with a hand across his mouth, I slowly roused him. I remember his eyes, wide in the darkness as I climbed atop him, the sweat on his skin, his hands on my thighs and buttocks, his manhood deep within me. I was something he would never forget. We moved together in the darkness for hours. His woman stirred but did not awaken and the baby woke, saw me, and stared. The look that man gave me was a mixture of sudden fear and primal lust. When he came deep within me, that look almost instantly turned to remorse, pain. And my heart leaped. I savored the conflict within him and the conflict to come with his woman. I left him with scratches he could never explain away.

"That night I visited two more men. And while they planted their seed inside my body, I planted mine within their souls. Both gave rise to their own demons. I was a sower of discord, of a yearning that could never be fulfilled. But that was not enough. I was not finished with that once-happy village.

"I waited until the winds and the rains stopped and then until the storm of angers and accusations that rent the villagers asunder abated. I waited and watched and counted their babies. There were ten. I took them, one by one, making it look like the women's jealousies were the reason. And the swamp embraced every one of those babies, taking them each to its watery bosom."

Lilith looked up from her feet. Avoiding Ardat's gaze and noting her silence, she stared straight ahead at the village. Something seemed odd about the walls surrounding it. Was the heat making them look as if they were moving?

"I left them with the sounds of their keening and screaming ringing in my ears, left them to wallow in their anger and grief, left them to finally realize that it was not their doing but mine. This I did, happily, to countless villages along the two rivers. And it was not long before I came to relish what I had become. A creature of the stormy nights. A predator. A feared legend.

"That is how I began to punish them, not for what *they* did but for what the Throne did to me. I could not think of a better way to strike out at the Throne than to prey upon its favorite children. And that is why I am here. My terrorizing them was one thing and that alone would have been enough to put me here. But my anger toward the Throne . . . that was something else. Lucifer understood that, Sargatanas less so.

"You know the rest. When you and I found each other in Kish, I had already made my way into the king, Etana's, royal bed. He was so filled with pride, so angry that he had no offspring. You and I kept him childless for what must have felt to him like centuries—"

Ardat stopped her with a hand on her arm and pointed at the
wall. And Lilith's breath caught in her throat. Countless arms
were reaching out to them and, as one, the souls tightly lashed
to the fleshy walls cried out for release.

Lilith, one hand hovering over the handle of her sword, gently
pushed Ardat behind her and moved ahead. The path leading to
the enclosure—she could now see it was a small soul village—
would take them through a narrow gateway and she was concerned
that the souls, arms outstretched, hands grasping, might make
ingress difficult. As they got closer, the souls began to cry out and
claw at the air, grabbing the passing traveling skins of the two
wanderers. With grim faces and some effort they managed to
wrench themselves free of the dozens of hands. They tried not to
inflict wounds on the souls, but it was nearly impossible to not
bend or twist the strong fingers, causing shrieks from the souls.

The village was a shambles. Like most soul settlements, the low
buildings were made of the very ground itself. The massive, fleshy
bricks were nothing like the soul bricks of the cities. These were
mindless lumps, featureless and without spirit but organic nonetheless. They lay one atop another, oozing their dark ichors in long
rivulets that pooled at the walls' footing. They had been flensed
in great quantities from the ground, leaving only the black substrate to walk upon.

Large carpets of thinner tissues surmounted the buildings, veins
dangling in clumps and streamers from their cut sides, and these
twitched with the oncoming of Lilith and Ardat.

It was readily apparent that there had been a fierce struggle
within the walls of the settlement. Before them, strewn atop the
black matrix, lay a confusing, writhing assemblage of torn and
mangled limbs, torsos, and heads that were striving to reconnect
themselves. Even had the pieces managed to claw their way next

to one another it would have been to no avail. As far as Lilith was aware, once dismembered a soul could not be made whole again without an Art.

Had the Salamandrines done this? She had heard about the negative effect the soul exodus had had upon the Men of Wrath. How their territories had been compromised and, too, how the nomads had moved farther and farther away from settlements, embittered. But had they come back to vengefully reclaim their lands? She knew what they were capable of doing to souls and demons alike. Had their rage finally grown too much to bear now that the souls had been released? She could not see any obvious telltale signs.

Without a word, Ardat and she separated and ducked into the dozen squalid buildings that had served as newfound homes to the souls. The small rooms contained only Abyssal-bone furnishing, broken and in disarray—neither found anyone intact within. The interiors were dark, foul smelling, and humid and they were both relieved to exit them and walk back toward the gate with the hope of talking with some of the bound souls.

Tied to the flesh wall with nets of their own newly dried tendons, the mangled souls were able only to move their arms. When they were not reaching out toward the two travelers, they were ineffectually clawing at their bonds. Most were gagged by the tightened netting and it was only after moving down the line some hundred paces that Lilith found a soul—a male—able to speak coherently. And when the souls were questioned as to who was responsible for this atrocity, a single word was uttered from a dozen mouths.

"Souls."

7

THE PYROCLASTIC FALLS

She felt the dull rumbling through her saddle long before she heard
it. Gradually, the intermittent vibrations had gathered in strength
and intensity until they had blended into a low and continuous
shivering. Slight tremors had been passing beneath the *bul-ata*'s
pointed feet for some time as the caravan had made their way
toward the great volcanic dome that so massively deformed the
horizon.

The plains that lay just before the massive distant volcano were
unusual in their conformation. In a world filled with the most ap-
palling geographies, Boudica had never seen a skin field dotted,
as this one was, with what looked to her eyes like low, familiar
tumuli. Chieftains had been buried in her land under such mounds
but never in such numbers or so close to one another. The demons passed them with uneasy glances, shaking their heads as if
even they were confounded by Hell's endless, dark revelations. Apparently, these hummocks were new to them, as well. Boudica
stared at the nearest mound, as she passed it, and she saw it trembling. But as common as movement upon the fleshy surface of the
ground was, she felt there was something more to this shivering,
almost as if something from within was trying to come free. As if
to punctuate that thought, a sudden thin spout of liquid burst from
the mound into the air, covering its rounded upper surface in slick

fluids. Metaphrax, she could see, paid it no heed, and this she found reassuring enough to shift her gaze to the looming mountain.

It was named in the demons' tongue Yalpur Nazh—the Pillar of Flame—and it was clear how the by-product of this massive mountain had gained that name. Towering into the liverish sky was an unsettling plume of smoke and fire that emanated from this, Hell's largest, ceaselessly erupting volcano. Crisscrossed by flickering red lightning, the glowing plume was, she had been told, held perpetually in place by the constant superheated infernal updrafts—an unnatural wonder unlike any other in Hell. No demon dared fly too near the roiling clouds for fear of getting caught up in those updrafts.

A wide field of hardened lava pierced the ground-flesh, gradually growing indistinct in the ashy gloom, between the caravan and Yalpur Nazh. The folds of the intervening hills looked sharp and difficult to traverse and the demons eyed them with an apparent degree of reticence. Sooner than she would have liked, the caravan reached the mountain's foothills and Boudica watched Styjimar, on the lead *bul-ata,* slowly make his way atop the first of the narrow hillcrests. Soon his form was only visible by the stalk-light of his mount. This region would be a challenge to both demon and beast and she was, once again, grateful for the plodding surefootedness of her steed. Despite that she was breathing heavily.

Metaphrax turned to look at her and then dropped back to her side. Above the roaring of the volcano he shouted, "Do not despair. We will stay a safe distance and ride upon the flank of Yalpur Nazh. It will be three days' hard march, but on its other side we will find much calmer land!"

She nodded and the demon urged his *bul-ata* forward. Boudica could hear the scrabbling sound of his mount's many feet as they tried to gain purchase on the smooth, hardened lava. And then it was her turn and, knowing her creature would be reluctant, she coaxed her *bul-ata* forward with a tap of her riding stick to its cranium. With a small trill the creature took its first steps on the inclined lava and, like the beast ahead of her, it took a few moments for it to get used to the relative lack of traction. More than once her creature slid backward and she found herself nearly toppling from its back. To ensure that this never happened, she cinched herself to the ornate saddle with some dangling straps—a makeshift measure but one for which she was grateful.

Once atop the network of ridges the caravan moved slowly, scrabbling along in single file with two dozen archers filling the gaps between the lumbering beasts. She could not hear them for the rising din of the volcano, but she could see them shouting to one another, even occasionally laughing. Some things, she thought, like the ageless rough banter of soldiers were universal. She remembered her own tribesmen—her Iceni—fierce and empowered by hatred and by her, laughing while they marched on the foreign enemy's capital. And laughing, too, as they burned it to the ground. She could not help but smile faintly at the recollection.

The caravan moved steadily upward upon the angry flank of Yalpur Nazh and, as they edged closer to the incandescent pillar of smoke, the roaring winds gained in ferocity, threatening the demons' already-precarious footing. Scalding ash descended upon them and soon she saw that none of them were conversing. Infrequent command glyphs from Metaphrax were sent backward to indicate changes in course or warn of obstructions. Little else was possible.

Eventually, even in this difficult terrain, Boudica found the volcano's mind-dulling din and the monotonous pace and the swaying of the *bula-ata* beneath her soporific. She gazed with heavy-lidded eyes out across the Wastes, out and back toward Ada-mantinarx, and sighed. So much time spent there and so little to show for it.

Her gaze lowered to the strange field of mounds and then she started. *What was that? Movement? Or a trick of the heat and wind and falling ash?* As she peered into the veiled distance, it appeared that the mounds were disappearing. And, in their place, dark objects were appearing, moving slowly en masse toward them.

What are *they . . . some kind of predator that hides underground waiting to pounce on hapless prey?*

She tried to shout, to get Metaphrax's attention, but he was intent upon the path ahead. She wanted to urge her beast forward, to pull up alongside him, but it was impossible—the footing was too tenuous and the path too narrow. Instead, apprehensively, she looked back toward the shapes and her breath caught. They had picked up considerable speed and her eyes widened as she could now see that they were some kind of large creature bearing other, smaller ones upon their flat backs. As they drew closer, just as they began to angle up the lava foothills, she could not see any legs and realized that they were floating, gliding rather than running, over the terrain. And she also understood, in an instant, that the Abyssal riders were Salamandrine men. They had lain in wait, buried within the fleshy mounds!

The first wave of Salamandrines crashed into the rear of the caravan before the rearguard demons could react. Boudica craned in her saddle and saw the archers flaming up their *ialpirg* projectiles for their bows, but the narrow procession made it difficult for them to see around the lumbering and panicking *bul-ata*. The Salamandrines carried long swords and thick-hafted lances, which they wielded with both hands, guiding their hissing mounts solely with their legs. Boudica could see the expertise with which they rode, the deftness and precision with which they slaughtered the demons, and a sense of nervous admiration gripped her. With each gliding pass, the attackers sent one or two of the heavy, screaming *bul-ata* toppling, their riders thrown into the deep troughs of the lava hills. Some of the Salamandrines with lethal thoroughness plunged after them, only to arise moments later with bloodied and ash-covered lances.

Later, upon reflection, it had seemed to Boudica that it took quite some time before the archers had reacted and the first *ialpirg* had risen into the air. In reality, the archers were an elite unit and highly trained and she was sure it could not have been more than a few short moments. Hundreds of the fiery conjured arrows rose in an incandescent wave, but few were seen to reach their targets. The driving ash pellets, the immense updrafts, and the equally strong blasts from the Salamandrines' mounts' exhalation-siphons caused the missiles to fly erratically away like embers on the winds.

One by one, Boudica saw the *bul-ata* behind her topple, and each one that fell underscored the diminishing likelihood of bringing home the lost Library. The success of her personal quest was slipping away as well. The possibility of her discovering the whereabouts of her daughters was diminishing before her eyes. Dread rose up in her throat like bile. With each cohort of archers slain, it became apparent to her that it was only a matter of time before she was set upon. She was doomed to fall, along with her beast, into the deep ravine, to fall victim to a lance thrust followed by probable dismemberment. And there she would lie, for all eternity, a quivering, disassembled pile of body parts unable to move and lost to all. The thought terrified her. Twisting in her saddle to face the back of the caravan, she unsheathed her sword, determined to strike at least one blow before succumbing.

A brilliant flash of red light from behind her, from the head of the procession, made Boudica spin around. Metaphrax Argastos had arisen. Ascending from his saddle on fiery wings, he held above his head a terrible lance, its head coruscating with writhing and hungry symbols. His conjured ribbons of luminous glyphs had grown in size and agitation and now moved sinuously, protectively, around his already-armored form as he rushed toward the attackers.

His audacity, undoubtedly as he had hoped, drew them away from the caravan. The threat he represented was clear, potent, and undeniable and the gathering Salamandrines wheeled their floating mounts, charging the flying demon with a startlingly shrill war cry.

Squinting through the maelstrom of ash and embers, Boudica lost count of the Salamandrines somewhere after thirty—the swarming melee and Metaphrax's intermittent pulses of dazzling light made a more accurate count impossible. She was amazed at the demon's fearlessness and courage and his ability to fend off so many attackers drew her profound admiration.

At first, the Salamandrines appeared hesitant—some broke off to attack the wingless Styjimar—but most steeled themselves to address the Demon Minor. The fury of Metaphrax's attacks seemed unstoppable and Boudica saw five of the warriors toppled from their mounts cleft by the burning lance. But it was not long before the warriors understood his rhythm, the timing of his swings, and the reach of his lance. Deftly, they darted in, jabbing up at him with their own lances, missing more often than not, but connecting with enough frequency to slow him down.

One blow caught Metaphrax just between his glyph ribbons and his actual armor, causing one of his phalerae to glow. It looked like nothing to Boudica, but when the Salamandrine pulled his lance away she saw the demon pause, drop his arm for an instant. It was enough.

Upon the signal of a horn, four masked warriors converged beneath him, chattering loudly to one another. As they skimmed past her, Boudica could see them seating their lances and pulling heavy, weighted nets from behind their saddles. They were, it seemed, laughing. This was sport to them, not the deadly struggle that she would have thought of it.

For Metaphrax, bellowing with each sliding thrust of his lance, it was no sport. The demon still moved lightly, his wings constantly changing up their beats to dodge and parry the many lances that tried to find their way through his guard. Time and numbers were not on his side and Boudica saw more Salamandrine lance heads thrusting upward, jabbing closer and closer to his body. Even a warrior demon had his limits and, while many attackers were sent to their death, the number grew fewer and fewer as the fight wore on.

Finally, through the aerial melee, the four net bearers drew close enough to let fly their spinning nets and each, expertly launched, tangled around the shoulders and wings of Metaphrax. The weights bore him downward until he set down on the smooth hillside, for a moment a vision of grace and sadness. And then the Salamandrines set upon him and that vision turned to one of ugliness.

Pummeling the demon into submission with the hafts of their lances, the warriors managed eventually to tie the demon into the nets so that any movement, any chance of escape, was impossible. Despite this, the fire in his eyes never dimmed and he silently glared at them, until their laughter faded away.

Boudica's face was grim. Metaphrax had treated her well, with dignity and respect. And whether it was because Eligor had ordered it or it was his own intention, she had grown to respect his stoic warrior's way back. This was not how she would have hoped the demon would have met his end.

As she watched his plight, the Salamandrine in command rode up alongside her *bul-ata*. His unmasked face, beaked and scarred and pallid, seemed filled with hatred and there was a coldness in his four white eyes that nearly made her shudder. *Men of Wrath*. She understood that more now than ever.

A terrible shout brought Boudica's attention back to Styjimar. He had been unseated from his saddle and, now with Metaphrax no longer a threat, more of the wild Salamandrines fell upon him with their lances and swords. Two particularly bold warriors dismounted to better their blows and this proved to be their undoing. For one brief moment she saw the demon disembowel one and split the skull of the other with his sword only for his sword arm to be chopped off at nearly the same instant. It took little time for the killing blow to fall—a simple but effective decapitation—and she saw a dark cloud of ash suddenly blossom where he had lain.

Around her, the remaining archers, thrown into disarray by the falling beasts and the lack of leadership, were being ruthlessly and systematically destroyed, the balance of the engagement having gone the Salamandrines' way with the fall of Metaphrax. The warriors' high spirits had returned now that the demon commander had been subdued and their high-pitched laughter punctuated many of the archers' demises. In all, it was the most grotesque display of battlefield behavior that Boudica had ever encountered, and she had returned from many a blood-soaked field.

The Salamandrine riding alongside her—his many necklaces and ornaments and demons' phalerae clearly bespoke an elevated rank—seemed to be enjoying the brutal spectacle, shaking his raised lance and screeching with every archer destroyed. Before she could react, he turned to her, croaked a command to his mount, and leaped lithely from his gliding steed onto the broad back of the *bul-ata* just behind Boudica. He snatched her sword from her hand and, with a short clacking laugh, slid it into his own belt. She glared at her huge captor, a quiet defiance that garnered her a sharp backhanded slap across her face. She turned away, stunned and trembling with anger.

It was not long before the Men of Wrath had their victory on the flanks of Yalpur Nazh. The Salamandrines, their lances a bristling wall impenetrable to any who might think to escape, encircled the few remaining archers who had not been immediately destroyed. These dropped their weapons and stood defiantly, grim faced. And they did not have long to wait. The Salamandrines set upon them with knives and cleavers and Boudica watched, her face grim, as the riders, brutally careful not to inflict any fatal wounds that might deprive them of their prizes, proceeded to carve away the bony armor and skins of their screaming victims. Once freed of their hides, the writhing and screaming demons were spitted on lances so as not to be turned to ash and cast bodily into the lava of an adjacent pit.

With two Salamandrine hands holding his head still, Metaphrax was made to watch as well. His fate, Boudica knew, would be no less harsh and, she could see from his set expression, he clearly knew this as well.

Once the last of his soldiers was dispatched, the Demon Minor was brought to his feet. He stood a head taller than his captors and he seemed to make a point of this by standing as straight as possible, defiant and proud. Metaphrax Argastos would leave this terrible world in a way befitting his lineage and rank.

The Salamandrine leader strode purposefully up to the demon and unceremoniously spat in his face.

It was the beginning of Metaphrax's end. Boudica had seen many a chieftain and many a haughty Roman meet their end in similar ways. Her own warriors, men and women alike, had killed their prisoners in ways that still troubled her and she, too, had executed the more important enemies without so much as a second thought. When the Salamandrines began their slow execution of the demon she could not help but shudder.

Knowing full well that any deep cut or limb removal might result in the sudden and total destruction of the demon, they began to carve away at him in a way that she saw would last for hours. They began by taking squared-tipped blades and prying away his most valuable possessions—the hard-won phalerae that were lying in thin sheets across his breast and each of which bore silent testimony to his many one-on-one victories with higher demons. They did not come free of Metaphrax's chest easily and, with each one painfully removed, Boudica could hear a shrill hiss and see the Demon Minor's body stiffen. These now-glowing disks they held aloft, cawing shrilly, for all to see and the Salamandrines rejoiced, shrieking as if each one was a victory of their own. A dozen times the knives found a disk and twisted it loose and a dozen times she saw the demon weaken by degrees. But he never faltered and she could not help but feel pity and admiration for him.

The leader of the Salamandrines looked toward Boudica and gestured to her. Sullenly, she dropped to the ground, still a bit dazed. A few warriors surrounded her and dragged her before the demon. Boudica looked up at him and saw nothing in his expression.

The Salamandrine pulled Boudica's new sword from his belt and handed it hilt-first to her. And she suddenly understood what they expected of her. For an eternity the Demons had been enemies to both souls and Salamandrines alike and in that moment she knew they would do her no harm. But, too, she realized there was no avoiding what must come next. This was to be the price of her freedom.

Boudica looked down at the straight, narrow sword in her hand. Once, so long ago that it now felt like a dream, she had had little else in her hand but a sword. Now it seemed so odd that here in Hell she should be reunited with the very instrument that had put her in this place. She hefted it and its weight seemed right, familiar. Its blade reflected the towering fire above her and for a moment it, too, seemed to be made of fire. Was it an omen of things to come?

Metaphrax was roughly pushed to his knees.

Boudica drew back a step, her breath short and shallow. She did not want this. Despite all of the indignities suffered at the hands of the demons, she did not feel that this demon deserved her retribution. She looked into his vacant, silvered eyes and saw only herself.

The Salamandrines, growing restless, turned first to her and then back to their leader. With an impatient hand gesture he spoke and jerked his head toward the demon. His message was obvious.

She looked at Metaphrax and the sword in her hand. The roaring fire, the burning embers, the intensity of the Salamandrines' gaze all seemed to fade away. She stepped forward, and before she could stop him Metaphrax grasped the point of her sword and raised it to the deep and vulnerable cavity in his chest where his angelic heart had once been. Time itself seemed to stop.

"You must do this, Boudica. Not for me," Metaphrax said, the light back in his eyes. "But for your daughters."

She hesitated, but suddenly she could feel him pulling the blade, inch by inch, into his chest. Knowing that the Salamandrines would not be satisfied with anything but the most purposeful gesture, she silently uttered the words "I am sorry," and thrust the full yard of metal into him.

Metaphrax erupted into a black cloud and then he was gone, only his dark disk remaining in the ash.

Boudica, covered from head to toe in dark ash, turned slowly back to her captors and offered the sword, hilt-first, to them. Instead of accepting it, one of the Salamandrines knelt and scooped up a handful of Metaphrax's ash and, unfastening a skin bladder, poured a small amount of dark liquid into the ash. With one finger he mixed it, and then dipped his sharp-nailed finger into the black paste.

He reached out and gently grasped Boudica's arm and wiped it clean. Then, without any warning, he began to incise a pattern into her skin, his nail digging into her flesh. The ash mixture, she knew, would leave a raised scar. Had she been truly alive, a creature of her old world, she would undoubtedly have cried out, but her existence in Hell had inured her to pain. When he was finished he spat on her arm, wiped away the blood and ash, and stood up.

She looked at her arm and was surprised by the flowing delicacy of the volute form. The stinging would fade, but this symbol of her first demon destroyed would be there forever.

8

PYGON AZ

Somehow, Adramalik knew this trip to the palace—by his count the fifteenth—would prove fruitful. Every journey he had taken to be introduced to the new Lord of Pygon Az had ended with him being left unfulfilled and frustrated. He never made entry into the Audience Chamber, never set eyes upon the throne or its occupant. Each invitation, brought by a scuffling emissary of the Bearer of the Knife, was sealed with a glyph and the demon had ceased opening them after the tenth. Instead, he handed the folded skins to the two dozen headless souls who shared his miserable domicile and watched them fight over the skins as if they could actually read them. At first he laughed when he saw them clawing and tussling, but with the third offering he merely turned away and relished his momentary privacy.

This trip to the palace proper was identical to all the preceding. Exiting the domicile, the emissary and he briskly walked the three hundred paces to the imposing palace gate, passing the forty-seven statues of Lucifuge's ministers, the ice-encrusted heads of which lay at their pedestals' bases. The gate, a portal three times the height of the average demon, was draped in sword-sharp icicles nearly half that length. Once the pair passed through the gate, Adramalik focused, as he always did, upon the main residence and palace. It was nothing like his memories of the place. The extravagances of Lucifuge's fantasies lay in broken heaps under ice many feet thick. And rising above was an austerely simplified edifice that rankled Adramalik with its defacement. *Who could have so callously scraped this palace clean of its ornaments, leaving them in miserable piles where they fell?*

Not usually one to care about palace adornments, Adramalik could not help but resent everything he was learning about Pygon Az's new ruler.

The approach to the palace had once been a maze of magma-warmed black-watered pools—one of Lucifuge's more inspired visions—each in the shape of power-inducing sigils, each successive one more potent and elaborate than the last. Now the fantastic pattern of pools bubbled red, filled to the top with souls' blood. The fountains were still, but the effect of the red against the black of the ice-coated stonework was wildly different than he recalled.

The emissary never paused, never broke step, despite his lack of a head. Adramalik had, long before, grown accustomed to the silent strangeness of the inhabitants of Pygon Az, to staring at the smooth and frozen stumps of their dismembered necks. This character was no different. His step was firm and sure, his manner abrupt, the language of his body distant. The many unseen magnetic fields of Hell were, once, the sole means whereby demons had managed to navigate the dark and ever-changing realm. Perhaps these headless individuals used the same invisible maps, albeit on a much smaller scale, to negotiate their frozen world. Adramalik's curiosity was only fleeting.

The route took them past a short pylon with four heavy, carved Abyssals holding up the archway and then into the palace grounds proper. Here it became clear that the building's façade had been crudely chipped apart and roughly cleaned away. The remaining shards littered the ground forming weirdly shaped low tumuli, held fast to the stone paving by ice.

The wind was picking up and Adramalik could smell a sharp tang riding it. Blood. Not the sickly sweet, turned scent of former angels' blood. Souls' blood, pungent and metallic. The source was not the pools he had passed. They lay upwind. He narrowed his eyes. The heavy scent was being sucked out from the palace entrance just ahead.

Just inside, Adramalik saw the Bearer of the Knife, head bowed, waiting in the shadows.

"Chancellor," he said, his lips working past the jewelry, "presently I will be taking you into my Lord Ai Apaec's Audience Chamber. You will follow his court protocol . . . you will not look him directly in the eye, you will remain on one knee, palms upon the floor, and you will not speak until spoken to. And when you do, you will refer to his lordship as 'my god.'"

Adramalik was careful to make his feelings about these rules clear without uttering a word. He had never been subjected to this kind of indignity in the Court of the Prince Regent of Hell and was not encouraged by what it said about Pygon Az's master.

"These are simple rules. Rules by which you will abide." The Bearer's voice was firm. He was staring at Adramalik. "Rules which will allow you to keep your head."

Adramalik opened his arms and bowed his head. If he needed to show such obeisance to merely survive then he would. But he would not forget.

The final threshold beckoned—the last archway between him and this new lord—and the two figures crossed into the Audience Chamber. And even Adramalik, hardened as he was to the sights of Hell and his lost lord's Rotunda, was stunned at the transformation of the space.

It was a huge room—nothing on the scale of the Rotunda but appropriately sized for a lord of Lucifuge's rank and stature. What had once been a heavily carved ceiling had fallen into disrepair with large areas having cracked off leaving deep, scarred pocks. No furnishings remained and the windows that Adramalik re-called pouring a rich, cold light upon the assemblies had been covered over, traded, for the most part, for a few inefficient braziers at the room's periphery. Their path to the throne, which the Chancellor could just discern in the distance, was flanked by shadowed hillocks of heads. Adramalik needed to no longer won-der about the citizens of Pygon Az. Their bodies might still walk the streets of the Black Ice City, but their minds lay elsewhere.

The Bearer's silhouetted form strode on, his goal obvious now—a well-lit dais that Adramalik knew from the past. His nar-rowed eyes strayed to the piles that rose irregularly around him. Most were in shadow, but he could make out the features of the heads writhing as he passed, disdain evident upon their cracked lips. Their eyes, filled with anger and pain, followed his steps. Some of the heads began to shake, causing minor avalanches. In moments, Adramalik found himself stepping around clusters of heads that had rolled from the piles onto the unswept floor. He swore under his breath with each sidestep until, losing his temper, he merely kicked those wayward heads out of his path as he moved forward.

Suddenly a deep moaning arose from a large pile just before him and he searched the mound for the cause until his eyes alit upon a small pack of fist-sized Abyssals that were tugging at the flesh of the heads beneath them. Scavengers in the throne room! Each bore an interesting blend of horn-sheathed nippers, serrated-toothed hooks, and distended jaws, all emanating from fat maroon bodies that glowed with faint patterns. They were indelicate and undis-criminating feeders, plucking loose fleshy bits from wherever their limbs fell, restlessly sidling from one head to the next. Their constant, clumsy motion upset the heads, setting off the small cascades that Adramalik had at first thought were a result of the heads themselves.

Adramalik saw a dozen or more headless warriors carrying long-handled clubs arrayed before a low platform. Atop the dais stood two impassive throne guards, each bearing large, staffed-mounted *tumi* blades. Rising behind them was a pile of flesh and bones that occupied the same spot where once had stood Lucifuge Rofocale's elaborate throne. But before the Chancellor could focus on the seat and discern whether any remnant of the once-resplendent throne still existed beneath the layers of offal, his attention was drawn to a huge warrior—a champion, who shuffled and pushed his ponderous, bone-decorated body through the assemblage and squatted down before the Bearer, a club-like arm held before him threateningly. He was nearly twice the height of a soul and thick around like one of the pale, bloated worms that Adramalik had frequently seen sliding through the shadowed alleys of Dis.

The Bearer indicated a spot for Adramalik to position himself directly before the huge soul. The Chancellor glared briefly at him and then, with a show of unhurried dignity, Adramalik gathered his skin robes and dropped to his knee. The Bearer remained standing, the occasional clinking of his adornments the only indicator of his proximity.

Now that he was closer, the Chancellor saw a huge seated figure, headless like all the other throne-room occupants, its texture and hue almost indiscernibly different from the necrotic flesh that surrounded the huge seat. It was, he guessed, some long-dead god's body, even larger than that of the squatting champion. Apart from the steady rise and fall of its massive chest, it remained motionless, waiting, it seemed. A thrill of fear coursed through

Adramalik. *What is this creature capable of? Why the headless theme throughout this kingdom?*

Even as he pondered these questions—questions he had asked himself long before he had been brought within the palace confines—he heard a loud shrieking rise from the Abyssals and, along with that shrill sound, a clattering as of innumerable hard-shelled bodies blundering into one another. The sound faded, replaced by another—a hollow breathing that grew louder, closer.

Suddenly he felt something brush past him. And then he saw it—a large, dark form that scuttled upon eight attenuated legs toward the throne, leaping from one small pile of bone to another until it reached the seated giant. Pivoting, it arranged itself delicately, obscenely, upon the shoulders and then, thrusting short spines through the throat beneath it, pulled itself down upon the neck of the figure. It inhaled deeply and, as it did, the massive figure came to life, spreading its arms in a slow, pantomime of welcome. Simultaneously, Adramalik heard a dull, whispering chant begin from the countless heads. He nearly turned, startled by the deep sounds that so many throatless heads produced.

"You seek refuge. For now, you have found it." The voice was deep and Adramalik imagined that it found its resonance in the thick throat of the massive body it squatted atop.

"Tell me, former Chancellor Adramalik, briefly, of the demise of your lord, the Prince Regent."

Adramalik cleared his dry throat.

"There was a rebellion . . . my god. One that was not easy to ignore and less easy to put down. At first, my former lord, Beelzebub, was convinced that the Heretic Sargatanas was merely attempting to expand his wards. He realized, too late, that this was not the case. When the Heretic Demon rallied the souls to fight for him the weight of numbers made it impossible for the Prince to prevail. His champion, General Moloch, was destroyed, as were the remaining armies of Dis and the Prince himself."

There was a moment during which Adramalik heard only the deep inhalations of Ai Apaec.

"And this Heretic Demon. Does he still walk the burning fields of Hell?"

Adramalik hesitated. "No, my god. He has left our realm."

"'Left our realm'?"

"Some say he is back in the Above. Ascended."

"And what do *you* say?"

"I do not know. And do not care. He is gone. But his influence is felt in the five points of Hell. Souls now have putative equality and are left to fend for themselves—"

"All this I know. What I want to know is why *you* still exist. Why you did not loyally go the way of your Prince. I want to know what kind of creature I am harboring in my nest."

Adramalik nearly forgot himself and rose. "I *am*," he said, his voice barely under control, "the former Grand Master of the Priory and Chancellor General of the Order of the Fly, His Most Exalted Prince Regent Beelzebub. There was no one more trusted by the Prince than me. My god."

"And his trust was obviously well placed. Or so I have been told."

Adramalik sucked in a deep breath, taking a long moment to carefully craft his response.

"I supported my Prince until the end . . . my god."

Ai Apaec studied him. His eyes glittered from within the deep shadows cast by his beetled brows. He was running his broad hand over some rounded object at the throne's side.

"And your very hasty exit from the Prince's Rotunda?"

"There was nothing anyone could have done in the face of Sargatanas' fury. Nothing. Not by me. Not by my Knights. We withdrew rather than be destroyed, my god."

"Very loyal, indeed."

Adramalik ignored the slight.

"My god, how is it that you know so much about those last moments of the Prince?"

"I had, at hand, a witness to those events," Ai Apaec said. He reached down and picked up the object he had been caressing and placed it squarely on the arm of the throne. It was the head of Demospurcus.

Adramalik slowly closed his eyes, hoping that his bowed head concealed his expression. Demospurcus' suffering was at an end. He had been a good, if not impulsive, Knight. There were so few of them left and now there was one less. He was surprised to feel the loss so strongly.

"I see, my god."

"You feel his loss? More than you are willing to admit, yes?"

"Yes. My god." Adramalik found that unnerving.

"I know because I am no stranger to loss. I know what it tastes like." He paused and Adramalik heard the dry, heavy sounds of the huge figure shifting his weight upon the throne. Long, jointed legs stretched out on either side of the scabby legs of the body the god was mounted upon. The great curved talons at their ends scratched across the floor like knives dragged across bare-laid bone.

"Because of your former station in Hell I will tell you how I feel. There are so few demons of high rank that pass through here." The god paused. It almost seemed as if he was talking to himself, musing. "I came to this *place* a god newly fallen. In my day, I had worshippers so plentiful and so eager to please me, to curry my favor for their meager crops, that they willingly, *joyously*, brought me the heads of their loved ones. I was called the Decapitator and

I saw my image everywhere. I was feared and beloved. I was hated and adored. I was the ravenous center of those miserable creatures' lives. But they did not satisfy me; they never could have. They were weaklings, unworthy of having created me. And for that, I let them die, enjoying their famines, their wars, their disease. Their inevitable extinction. I was so sure that I was omnipotent, so sure that my immortality was not linked to their pitiable existences, that I let them go and, in so doing, destroyed myself. Now I sit in a frozen wasteland with nothing. I cannot be what I once was and I do not care to be more than I am. The ice has numbed me."

Adramalik took this all in. His mind, still off-balance from the head that continued to stare at him from beneath the Decapitator's hand, raced with the many reactions he could frame. He could think of nothing to further his and his demons' cause in Pygon Az. They were all at this god's mercy and he could easily decide to destroy them with the wave of a disinterested hand. And then the god, himself, provided the answer.

"If you and your Knights are to stay here," Ai Apaec said, "you must become useful in some way. I have grown tired of the pickings in the palace and hungry for Abyssal flesh."

Adramalik, too, had become hungry for Abyssals. The dull, insistent burning between his legs was a constant reminder of his nearly unbearable lack of sexual gratification. Oh, how he would become a zealous hunter of young Abyssals! This *god* would get them when he was finished with them.

"My Knights and I hunted the plains of Dis often, my god. For sport. We can bring you what you desire."

"Let us see how you do, then, Adramalik. I will expect results within the first setting of Algol. Only the largest Abyssals will do. And variety, Adramalik, variety. For each rise and fall of the

Watchdog that you do not provide me with a fresh kill, I will have one of your Knights brought to me."

The Decapitator patted Demospurcus' head for emphasis and the demon closed his miserable eyes. Adramalik thought he could hear a short, light laugh and the tinkle of metal from behind him. The Bearer of the Knife was enjoying the exchange.

Adramalik nodded his assent. "Yes . . . my god."

The Abyssals that could be found around Dis, Adramalik remembered, had been stocked there for sport. Their ancestors had long ago been exterminated. Somewhat accustomed to the presence of demons as they had become, they were difficult enough to kill with twenty mounted demons at one's side, thought Adramalik. These wild Abyssals, used to the frozen climes, would provide him and his Knights with potentially more trouble than they could handle—all to satisfy the bored whim of a minor fallen god. And large Abyssals—how could he enjoy those? The Chancellor's spirits sank. He looked sidelong at Ai Apaec's crouching champion and thought were things to take a turn for the worse, he was not at all certain he and his Knights could make their way out of Pygon Az.

9

THE VALE OF THE FREED

The hot winds blew through the seventh town with such an unabated fury that Ardat suggested, hand over mouth, perhaps it existed only to cleanse the filth and stench from the buildings. Lilith made no response. Her scarlet eyes were focused on a large, irregular building composed of massive Abyssal horns, bones, and skin that towered a hundred feet above the surrounding squalid huts. At one point, the distant roughly designed pile must have been well maintained, even imposing. It had the self-important, almost ludicrous look of a makeshift palace. But now it had fallen into disrepair, its outer walls, doors, and many ladders hanging askew and flapping noisily in the fierce wind.

Traveling skins whipping about her, Lilith began to move slowly toward the edifice with Ardat a few paces behind. Both could hear eerie, indistinct sounds above the wind. And both were ready to turn and run should they encounter any scavenging Abyssals. The fifth and sixth villages had been host to dozens of Skin-pickers—quick, many-pincered Abyssals that had, over the millennia, developed a taste for easy-to-catch runaway souls. With the onset of soul-upon-soul warfare, the numbers of opportunistic creatures boldly seeking an easy feast were growing.

A long row of curved Abyssal tusks lined the causeway to the palace and Ardat followed her former lady beneath them. Lilith clenched and unclenched her hands as she strode forward, the sights to either side of her tightening her throat, forcing the air out in shallow, staccato bursts. The souls whom they could see were mostly impaled on short, serrated spikes, pierced and tied where they lay and utterly unable to escape their torment. In most cases, as the pair passed them a frenzy of limb-fluttering entreaties followed, creating a sound that Lilith knew she would not soon forget.

The palace entrance yawned before them, a darkened rectangle against an expanse of reinforced tattered skins. The bone framework behind them was exposed in many places, and as they drew nearer to the wide doorway they could see vague silhouetted shapes moving within. Lilith hesitated at the threshold, her fingers running for the briefest moment over the crude carvings that ran up the frame, her nostrils flaring at the dank, heavy air from within.

Lilith knew they were not alone. Before her foot crossed the threshold, scuffling sounds betrayed the souls who tried to move unseen amidst the huge mounds of items that were gathered randomly upon the floor. Shafts of reddish light penetrated the gloom from above, stabbing downward from evenly spaced slits in the lofty ceiling, light beams that were intermittently broken by the shadowed forms that seemed to be gathering before the pair. The gloom did nothing to hide them from her. She was a creature of the night and the palace's interior was, to her adjusted eyes, as light as the world outside. Ardat, however, had no such heightened ability and, careful as the former handmaiden was, Lilith heard her stumble as they entered.

Lilith saw the mounds and knew them for what they were—the pitiable possessions taken from souls in the wake of the marauding mobs that now roamed the Vale. It was a terrible, silent statement of the terror that had befallen those souls who had merely tried to build some kind of life in the infernal realm. There would be no peace for them.

Without warning a great din arose from the collected souls. Screams and barks and the clattering of weapons upon shields broke the stillness and continued unabated as Lilith moved farther into the building. It was an attempt to unnerve her and Ardat, undoubtedly the same tactic that these raiders had used to instill fear into the unnumbered souls they had conquered. Lilith remained unshaken by the sound and, as she finally cleared the mounds, saw them arrayed in two ragged lines leading to an elevated throne.

For souls with little ability to manufacture true and uniform armor, they had exercised an incredible amount of ingenuity in their fearsome panoplies. All wore some striking element of Abyssal remains such as claws or bones or armor or teeth. Many of these were deliberately broken to create jagged and sharpened edges that were thrust deep into their already-malformed bodies, while others were tied on in lapping layers to create grotesque, intimidating silhouettes. From her own Waste journeys, Lilith recognized the nasal spines of Skin-skippers, the elbow-claws of Lesser Gougers, the keeled, luminous plates of Peelers, the heavy eye sheaths of Lava-swimmers, the splayed dorsals of flying Cinderchasers. Nearly ever creature that walked, crawled, or flew was represented in the makeshift armor that covered the raiders and Lilith had to admit to herself that they did, indeed, present a spectacle of raw ferocity. But the attempt at intimidation was lost upon her.

Undeterred, she and Ardat walked the shifting corridor between the armored souls. Each soul they passed tried all the harder to goad them into action with frenzied cry or leveled spear, but neither she nor Ardat raised her weapon. As they drew closer to the foot of the throne, the pair could plainly see the massive dark figure that sat upon the skin-covered seat. It was, as they had come to be known among the souls, a Manifold—a conglomerate of more than one soul created by demons for specialized tasks. While most were comprised of eight or ten souls and used in the legions, some whom she had seen had been composed of dozens of hapless humans, strung together for the most arduous of building tasks. This one, Lilith thought, had probably been some demonic mason's helper—his melded limbs were thick and powerful. The liberation of the souls had not enabled the countless Manifolds to separate themselves—that would have required a demonic Art and vast amounts of time. This one clearly had been impatient to venture into the Wastes and wreak havoc. She could hear his wheezing breath and smell his unclean body. He raised a heavy fifteen-fingered hand and the crowd quieted.

"We are Koh-Gul-Yut the First, King Undisputed of the Vale."

The King sat back, self-satisfied, in a posture of confident power.

"I am—" Lilith began.

"We know who you are. Your reputation is great. Why have you come all this way to my peaceful kingdom, White Mistress?" The voice was strangely high pitched and strained.

"My companion and I cross the Wastes on a mission. Yours is but one of many kingdoms we would pass through on our way." Lilith kept her voice steady, controlled. None could miss the firmness in it.

"And pass through it you shall. I have no interest in detaining you. However, I'm sure you can see that our kingdom suffers from many privations . . . privations that came as a result of your prolonged civil war. I see that you both carry packs—"

"Do not go any further. We will not be paying any tribute to you or paying you *any* obeisance."

The room filled with sibilant murmurings.

Again, the King raised his hand and the marauders fell silent.

"You would insult us before our own people?"

"I would tell you that I am revolted by you, your actions, and your so-called kingdom built on misery and blood. I would tell you, too, that my design for you, for *all* souls, was for your liberation and peaceful coexistence in our shared exiles. Not for the mindless atrocities I have seen throughout this vale. I have let loose a scourge."

"What business is it of yours how we choose to exist? We have our free will back, White Mistress. Just as you hoped for," Koh-Gul-Yut hissed. "Was that *not* part of your design when you spread *these* about Hell?"

The Manifold clutched a pendant around his thick neck, yanked it free, and threw it at her feet. Lilith eyed with disgust the small self-portrait she had carved. With eyes fixed upon Koh-Gul-Yut, she slowly placed her clawed foot upon it and crushed it.

"No. Never."

In one fluid, practiced motion Lilith pulled free the sword Lukiftias-pe-Ripesol, and, for a moment, all was still. She grasped its hilt with both hands and leveled the long blade steadily at the King seated above her. She heard Ardat unsheathing her own blade.

The Manifold clenched his fist. And Lilith wheeled and sliced the two closest souls in half. Springing up the few steps to the throne where the huge King was getting to his feet, she chopped his leg out from under him, her blade cleanly severing the thick calf from its knee. With a shriek, he toppled forward and would have fallen onto her had she not deftly sidestepped the flailing Manifold. Even before he landed, her blade bit into his necks, separating heads from multiple spines.

A few steps below, Ardat was fending off the sudden surge of attacking marauders, swinging her two angled blades in long, almost rhythmic arcs. With each slice a limb fell, but the number of assailants seemed to grow rather than diminish. Lilith looked toward the doorway and could just see shadows flickering across it. The clamor was drawing all of the marauders from outside within the palace confines.

With a roar, Lilith leaped into the fray, sword slashing downward cleaving a soul from neck to groin, clawed feet bringing down another where she landed. Ardat ducked low as Lilith's monstrous, demon-killing sword swung in dangerous circles overhead, easily chopping three of the souls' armored heads from their shoulders.

Ardat slowly backed up the stairs, eyes wide and mouth agape at the whirlwind of destruction that was her mistress. Lilith was a being transformed. All of the pent-up rage at what they had been witness to as they made their way from village to village—all of the horrors of the souls' failed self-rule—was coming out with each swing of the terrible sword.

Lilith, a calm settling over her, reached inward and found that place in her heart that she had visited many times before. It was the empty place she had discovered so long ago when she had stalked the swamps, the place to which she had retreated when the Fly's torments had proved too much for her. There she had watched herself, marveling bleakly at her ability to simply shut everything out and survive. Then it had been a place of salvation. Now it was a place of cold retribution, disconnected and hollow of feeling. These souls were lawless, ungovernable, and as devoid of conscience as the worst of the demons. And they were all the more disappointing to her for it.

She had been instrumental in seeing them freed, had nurtured what she thought would be what little was good in them. Now, without a shred of remorse, she would undo some of what she had accomplished.

Wave after wave of marauder came for her, weapons brandished, shrieks upon their lips. They all fell.

She took no pleasure from her skill with the sword, from the seemingly limitless stamina she showed, from the perfect executions of the souls. No blow was half-delivered, no soul left wounded only. The dismembered bodies at her feet rolled down the growing mound by the dozens, spattering her white robes until she was reddened and dripping.

When the souls began to thin out, Lilith found herself the predator of humans, once again. She pursued those who remained throughout the darkened interior, stalking them through the debris, pushing some into tumbling mounds of looted possessions only to chop them apart, knocking others down to rend them apart with her feet. The last of the marauders fled out into the relative brilliance of the open, infernal air with Lilith close behind. One by one, snarling, she overtook them, her sword held out before her red with the sticky blood of their brethren. And one by one they were struck down until only streaks of crimson gave evidence of their frantic flight, the bloody signatures of their demise.

Ardat emerged, tentatively at first. When she saw her mistress hunched over upon a rock near the village gate, surrounded by the impaled souls, she ran to her, fearful that Lilith was vulnerable to more assaults.

"Lilith! Are you hurt?"

The White Mistress was completely stained a grisly red and it was impossible for the handmaiden to discern whether the blood was that of the souls or mixed with that of some grievous wounds they had inflicted.

Lilith lifted her chin and Ardat could plainly see the tears that ran from her scarlet eyes.

"It is over, Ardat. My love of them. It was never realistic," she whispered hoarsely. "I was a fool."

Ardat put her hand on Lilith's trembling shoulder.

"I thought I could make a difference here. I thought that they could be lifted up from the blood and the shit and the ashes. But it turns out that is where they belong."

Ardat watched her mistress grimly. She had been there through all of the eons during which Lilith had secretly championed the souls, working to covertly elevate them, hoping for them. Ardat remembered well how she had been the instrument of the almost legendary White Mistress, disseminating the small statues throughout Dis and Adamantinarx. Bringing hope to the hopeless. It was all over now.

Lilith rose unsteadily, propping herself up with the great sword. Her exhaustion was clearly more than physical. Avoiding Ardat's gaze, she walked silently to the gate.

Ardat followed and when they both reached the many impaled souls the handmaiden dropped to one knee and began to cut loose the nearest soul. Lilith could plainly hear the gurgling words of gratitude and saw, too, the hope in his eyes.

"Leave him. Leave them all to rot. They are in Hell for a reason. There are no innocents here."

Ardat hesitated and then, sheathing her blade, rose to follow her dark mistress beyond the gate and out into the Wastes.

10

THE WASTES

The small encampment to which the Salamandrines took her was, in many ways, reminiscent of movable encampments to which Boudica had been accustomed all her Life. Light frameworks arranged in rough defensive circles with beasts of burden and war tethered nearby, weaker family members in the center. But those were the only real, superficial similarities. Everything else about the nomads' camp was like something conjured in that fearful state between wakefulness and sleep that passed for rest in Hell.

Boudica waited as the Salamandrine chieftain who had marked her with the design dismounted. He had shown great skill in the way he had piloted the hovering creature using verbal commands or taps on its carapace. Only after he reached up and took her hand did she jump down. The hover creature barely moved as it floated in place, its siphons hissing as it distended three legs. The Salamandrine nodded to follow, and without hesitating she obliged.

The first thing that struck her was how, save for a bone-framed lookout post, the entire circular camp was sunken, nearly to the height of a Salamandrine male, almost twice her own height. It had been hewn into the ground, the backfill being placed in a circular wall around the camp's periphery. Raised a foot above the ground line, but covering most of the opening, were vane-like tent works of stretched Abyssal skin mounted on pivoting bone bases. She realized this eye-level slit allowed them the protection of the ground but also enabled them to see anything or anyone approaching. She imagined that the flexibility of these structures deflected some of the infernal winds as they whipped across the featureless expanses and also served to shed away the embers and ash that would inevitably fill such a pit.

As she descended the chopped-out steps into the camp, she could easily see how the fibrous layers of ground-skin gave way to the base matrix. The resilient black substrate that underlay most of Hell was the texture of almost-hardened pitch, and when she ran a finger against it she felt a strange tingling, a sensation that did not go away when her unshod feet touched the camp's floor. After a few moments she grew used to it and to the odd sense of well-being it brought her.

Boudica was led toward the camp's center by the chieftain. Flanked by four additional Salamandrine warriors, she saw every head in the camp turn as she passed. The looks she got were impossible to interpret. The Salamandrines' beaked faces gave up no clue to her untrained eyes. But the silence that descended upon the camp was unequivocal. She was a stranger here. And that was something to engender suspicion among an already-wary people.

They passed partitions of hanging skins, and as she glanced inside she saw meager possessions arrayed around sleeping skins. The Salamandrines traveled lightly—their possessions seemed to number fewer than ten per partition. At the camp's center were cooking pits and, around them, the elders sat while the young played and mounted mock battles. A zoomorphic idol, half her size, carved from a jet boulder stood at the exact center of camp and seated next to it was an old, nearly blind Salamandrine, robed and adorned with a profusion of jet ornaments. When he looked up, one of his four yellowed eyes fixing her, the stone jewelry rattled against his chest like small bones.

Her captor spoke to the elder chief and then, without warning, grabbed Boudica's arm and twisted it around to display his handiwork. The elder nodded, clacking his beak-like jaws together quietly. He spoke, then, at some length to the chieftain who stood attentively, silently. When the elder finished, the chieftain knelt and the old Salamandrine gently grasped his head with both ancient hands and pecked the crown of the warrior's head once. The chieftain stood and turned Boudica away by the elbow.

While the camp was small, it was subdivided by hanging skins into many small chambers and Boudica found herself completely disoriented by the time her guide left her at her own tiny, empty stall. She curled up on the floor and, as barren of possessions as she was, she felt contentment in her surroundings. It was a strange thing, her sudden identification with the Salamandrines. It was not hard to transpose her own past with their present and see what their grievances were. She would do what she could to understand these people, to fit into their society. What else could she do? She needed them and, perhaps, she could convince them that they needed her.

Algol rose and sank—a span of what she thought would have been three or four moons in her Life—before Boudica felt in relative command of the Salamandrines' difficult tongue. She was a quick learner and devoted herself fully to the task. The beak clicking had been physically impossible to emulate and so she had resorted to snapping her fingers at just the right moment to make them understand her. Not an easy thing when one was engaged in physical activity. She was sure some of them found this comical or even insulting, but no one said a word to her. She imagined it all came across like a human with a lisp or a stutter or both and tried as hard as she could to compensate by being agreeable. The Sala-mandrines, as a whole, seemed to appreciate her efforts, carefully pointing out her small errors but not chiding her. For such a grim race, their deference seemed puzzling. Puzzling until she was told that she had a good enough mastery of the language to understand why she was being treated so deferentially. She was essentially a curio.

K'ah-aka-tuk, her captor and now, unpredictably, her sponsor, made all of the introductions to his clan. There was, first and fore-most, M'ak-aka-tua, the clan chieftain and K'ah's uncle, who had approved Boudica's adoption into the clan.

"He was a once-feared warrior," K'ah told her as they walked past the elder's larger stalls, "a master tactician who had harried the demons for over a thousand full cycles of Algol, bringing much glory to our people and garnering much hatred from the demons. Once," he told her, "our camp-frames had been decorated with over five hundred heads we skillfully liberated from slain demon captains. An uncommonly ferocious firestorm had destroyed these proud and hard-won trophies, but we still remember. Now Elder M'ak holds the most honored position on the plains surrounding K'oba K'ul, the Rising Falls. He has earned it."

"The demons call it Yalpur Nazh. Why is this region so impor-tant, K'ah?"

The Salamandrine flicked his head in one of the many subtle head gestures that Boudica was struggling not only to learn but also to interpret. The pair sat upon a pile of Abyssal skins near the edge of camp. The pyroclastic pillar rose in the distance, its slow turbulence angry and glowing.

"K'oba K'ul rises and falls in an unending cycle, its fiery be-ginning linked to its fiery end. We see that as a symbol of the

Eternal State, of Life and its endless pattern of birth, death, and renewal. We invoke that idea when we engage in *t'lakka,* the ritual eating of our enemies."

Until that moment, Boudica had no idea that the Salamandrines were in any way cannibalistic. She had seen a steady flow of killed Abyssals being brought in by the hunters and assumed that that was the clans' only food source. In her Life, she had heard of tribes that had indulged in similar activities but had not seen it performed. She knew, in a flash of intuition, what she would have to do to fit into this society and knew, too, that she would put a good face on it. It was good to be warned, but the anticipation could work against her, make her seem weak. Weakness was clearly not a state she wanted to convey to these hardened people.

"M'ak must be held in great respect to be the chief of this region, yes?" she said, moving past the unpleasantness she had just discovered.

"Indeed. Other chieftains come from far away to consult him on matters ranging from tribal problems to the more important raids on demon outposts. All of this he wears with dignity and wisdom."

"Clearly, K'ah. I am honored that he allowed me to stay here."

"It is not simple hospitality, B'udik'k'ah. We have never encountered one like you. Of course, we knew of your kind's existence . . . we watched from afar as the demons used your kind in numbers beyond count and in terrible ways. And we felt a certain sympathy for your kind. But we never saw one of you out in the Burning Lands accompanied by demons as you were."

"Much has changed since the fall of the Prince."

K'ah nodded crisply. He served the clan not only as a warrior but also as their spirit-artist, and now he was proving, as well, to be an excellent instructor in the ways of his people.

"What is that thing you wear around your neck? It looks like neither a demon nor a soul."

Boudica's hand went to the carved pendant. It was too complicated to explain.

"Just an ornament. Little more."

The Salamandrine tilted his head.

"Are there others like you . . . other souls sent out with demons on missions?"

"Not to my knowledge, K'ah. All souls, as you must know by now, are free, but, apparently, my standing with the demons was something unique. I could not have known this until I was liberated. One demon, a rather extraordinary lord, saw me as . . . how do I put this . . . that which made him act. Like a spark that lights a great blaze. He rebelled against the ruler of Hell and caused the great changes you have seen. He's gone now." She glanced into the sky, toward Zimiah, the blue star, uncertain as to whether she should pass on the pervasive myth that had grown up around its sudden appearance.

K'ah was silent for a moment, staring out into the Wastes.

"We need to understand our old enemy, to see our world through their eyes, and, perhaps, you can help us with that." He paused. "There is something you will need to do, something that will accord you even greater status among us. Then we can listen to you as one of our own."

Boudica looked down at her sword hilt, running her chalky fingers over the hilt's carving.

"I'll do what I can to help, K'ah. Despite their behavior toward me of late, despite the kindness of a few, I am no friend of theirs."

Again, K'ah bowed his head. He turned once more to look out into the Wastes, sniffing.

"A firestorm is approaching . . . I can smell it. It is still a long way off, but it will come within this Algol-rise. The creatures of the Burning Land will be running before it. It will be some time before they are near. It's an opportunity."

"For whom?"

"You."

"Really?"

"You'll be able to practice your skills. In preparation."

"For what?"

K'ah rose and indicated to Boudica that she should follow. They walked the length of the narrow aisle that led to his stall, passing many Salamandrines who bowed their heads to her. A decorated Abyssal skull hung above the doorframe of K'ah's stall and she saw him part the skin curtain, reach in, and bring out his long, black sword, a heavy coil of rope of tightly braided skin, a short dirk, and a sling. All of the warriors carried similar swords and she recognized them as symbols of rank, something one attained only when one was ready to ascend to adulthood.

K'ah handed her the sword.

"This . . . this is what you seek, B'udik'k'ah. One of your own. It will tell the clan that you are one of us."

She weighed it in her hand, and as she did the small teeth, dried eyes, and bones that depended from its hilt by a cord rattled. It was far lighter than she had expected—half the weight but more than three times the length of her own sword.

"Hollow?"

"Yes. Like a bone. But more flexible," K'ah said. "It comes from a creature called a Great Gouger. Mine was at least five spans of my height." He paused, remembering, as if the creature stood before him. "This I took from one of the many spines atop its head."

"And these?" Boudica said, indicating the rope, the sling, and the dirk.

"These are the ones I used. They all have a purpose. The sling is used to stun the Gouger, the rope to climb upon its back, and the dirk to slay it and free the spine. Once you have killed it."

Boudica's eyes were wide, her mouth agape.

"You can't be serious."

"We will practice with the sling until it's time. The Gouger is a dangerous but slow-moving spirit. And you are an adult, not one of our adolescents. They are thrown into the Burning Lands with no training at all. If they prevail they are warriors. If they perish they are food."

K'ah let that sink in.

"You have an advantage over them . . . you are already skilled in weapons." The Salamandrine took up the sling, stretching it taut, testing it. "You know how a *ha'rakha* works?"

"A sling. Yes. But it's been some time." She could not help but marvel at the universality of weapons.

"It will come back to you." K'ah looked at her intently, head tilted. "I know, B'udik'k'ah, this is rushed. But you need to join us in a way that is beyond M'ak's question."

He looked down, beak slightly parted.

"We need your help."

Boudica nodded shakily. "And I need yours."

She instinctively understood their plight. They were a dying race, but, that said, they were never simply going to melt away into the darkness. Not without a fight. And, now, not without her.

Still, her nerves were showing and she hated it. The Salamandrines' adolescents were half again her height and, while lightweight and wiry, quite strong. Untrained or not, she knew they were used to their harsh, nomadic life, to the creatures—or Spirits as they called them—of their world and their behavior. She had seen enough of the formidable Abyssals in her brief travels and none had seemed as if they would be easy to kill. Having fought the least hospitable environment imaginable, they had won, evolving protective carapaces and armored limbs that seemed impregnable. How could a sling and a dirk prevail against any of them?

K'ah stood and, without a word, disappeared into the camp. Boudica watched his retreating back and then stared down at the black floor, sighing. All this, to find her daughters. Who could have guessed the twists her path was taking to achieve that? Had she really believed she could have simply wandered, unchallenged, through Hell to arrive at their doorstep? It would be worth it, she knew, worth it just to simply hold them in her arms again. She just had to get past this trial. She heard a sharp snort from outside the encampment's wall. The Salamandrine had returned mounted on a fleet Skin-skipper, the reins of a second beast in hand. He held them out, shaking them in mock enticement.

Boudica climbed out of the encampment and approached K'ah, who handed over the reins. Her Skin-skipper sniffed the air, shuffling uneasily on its many jointed legs. She ran a hand over the skin between the plates of its carapace, noticing that the glowing spots upon its skin were cool to the touch.

"Give it a name . . . it will be yours. You're its first owner."

She smiled—an expression undoubtedly unfathomable to K'ah. The creature's name came to her easily, the name of the goddess who had forsaken her in the end of her Life, after all the reprisals, after all the slaughter in her name.

"I'll call you Andrasta." She made a wry face and then said,

"May you bring me the victory in my quest that your namesake kept from me in my Life."

She turned to K'ah. "It's done. Its name is Andrasta. And it and I are ready to begin the training."

Boudica saw the first red drops splatter the pommel of her saddle as she and K'ah set off. Blood rain. Or so it had been called by the souls. It was almost impossible to know whether the droplets were actually blood or evaporated water from the rivers colored by the side effects of volcanism. So many of the rocks contained reddish ores, she reasoned, that it could well have some influence on the rain. She did not give it much more thought, as the rain came down harder, finding the small gaps in her oversized traveling skins and gradually soaking her. The moisture did not last long as her body's heat burned it off quickly. K'ah had promised her a new set of skins—better-crafted garments with hidden pockets and ornaments—but those, he said, would take time to make to her unique, non-Salamandrine proportions.

K'ah led them hurriedly away from the camp, following a tear in the landscape that skirted the low foothills of K'oba K'ul. A scout had run up to him, breathlessly describing a Great Gouger that he had spotted in the foothills tearing up the ground-flesh in search of prey. It was an old individual, and K'ah's eyes had twinkled with the prospect of Boudica's kill. He had virtually run to his mount, Boudica barely able to keep up, and then they had leaped over the camp's wall and into a headlong gallop.

Andrasta's gait took some getting used to. Its movements were springy and it crossed the terrain in long bounds that jarred the soul with every landfall until she learned to move her body with the Skin-skipper's. The rain, which barely slickened the hot ground, did not seem to impede the surefooted creature in any way, but Boudica found herself clutching the front of her hood tightly to keep her face dry.

Ahead, the vast mountain vanished into the ruddy sheets of rain, its tower of fire seemingly rising from no visible source. Only the nearest rocky foothills, now steaming and made wet by the pelting rain, had any real definition, glistening from behind by the light of the sky-borne fires. For all her discomfort, Boudica could not help but be impressed by this alien vista. *What a world I am now in!*

As if to punctuate the thought, a startled pack of Abyssals burst from their dry skin-pocket shelter and nearly collided with the pair, their small, strangely disjointed bodies black and barely visible save for the glowing blue markings on their elongated heads. K'ah veered away just in time and Boudica reflexively followed suit, digging in her spike-shod foot just the way he had shown her. He looked back and nodded crisply, approvingly. It was a small thing, his gesture, but she felt good about it and good about him as well.

She saw the trio of Abyssals dash off pell-mell. Without hesitating he veered back and around into their midst, and she saw him lash out with his sword. The move was so deft and swift and his re-scabbarding so precise, she was not entirely sure of what she had seen. Still moving, he leaned down and retrieved the kicking Abyssal, draping its bleeding, trembling body across his saddle.

The remaining pair of Abyssals ran frantically straight into a cavernous mouth that suddenly roared open in the ground. As she passed, the huge toothed flap of skin closed around the creatures, dark blood squirting from the corners of its shredded lips. She shuddered and turned hastily away. *What a world, indeed!*

K'ah pulled his mount off the trackway and began to coax his mount up the side of a hillock. The terrain quickly grew much steeper and it soon became impossible for the Skin-skippers to progress any farther. They dismounted and cut holes in the ground and tied them down, leaving the beasts to stand, grunting disconsolately, in the rain. K'ah pulled the dead Abyssal from his saddle and flung it over one shoulder.

The pair began to head upward, toward dull, intermittent sounds that were clearly not a part of the volcano's deep, rolling thunder.

Boudica wrinkled her nose. "That smell?"

"The Gouger is not a clean beast."

She began to notice bubbling rivulets of blood streaming down from above, and then small fragments of rock and thin chunks of skin tumbling down the hillside. The sounds grew louder as she and the Salamandrine skirted larger outcrops, keeping out of sight. Then, rounding a tall pinnacle of rock, up in the gloom of falling rain and debris, she saw a massive form pawing at the angled ground with huge clawed hands.

Even through the rain, the beast's light spots shone fiercely, blazing rows of angry red against its slick, dark sides highlighting its bulk. Boudica's breath caught in her throat. *How can I possibly kill that? In the rain? On a steep hill? It's madness.*

She felt K'ah put a hand on her shoulder. He put his beak near her ear and whispered hoarsely over the driving rain and thunder.

"We need to lure it down to the flat ground. See its short rear legs? It's perfectly built for the foothills—its natural home . . . but on flat ground it's clumsy, slow."

She nodded sharply, nervously. So that was the plan. Simple but still fraught. Still, it must have worked countless times. And for adolescent Salamandrines, no less.

K'ah half-rose and let out a piercing whistle. Unslinging the dead Abyssal, he began to swing its still-glowing body over his head, the blood from its severed neck spattering the ground and Boudica.

The Gouger turned abruptly, its heavy beaked jaws filled with offal it had pulled from the hillock, saliva cascading. With a single gulp it downed its huge mouthful. And then a deep, low groan issued from it, echoing in the hills, trembling the ground. The huge Abyssal, its four yellow eyes fixed on the Salamandrine, slowly rose, sending a boulder bouncing and tumbling past Boudica and on into the darkness.

With remarkable control, K'ah turned and began to slide down the wet slope dragging the dead Abyssal behind him. Boudica, shaking her head, followed his lead less assuredly, narrowly avoiding a jagged upthrust rock in her otherwise speedy descent.

K'ah landed easily on his feet at the hill's bottom, and Boudica, spurred on by the monstrosity drawing ever closer, scrabbled furiously and fell clumsily to her knees. Regaining herself, she bolted, trying to catch up to the Salamandrine.

"Your *ha'rakha,* B'udik'k'ah!" he shouted. "Now is the time!"

Boudica shot a glance over her shoulder as she ran. A great cloud of rocks and debris was cascading down the slope and within it the huge shape of Abyssal twisting to stay upright.

K'ah stopped and dropped to a knee. His sword was drawn.

She skidded to a stop and frantically reached into her pouch, fishing out a heavy metal-ore bullet for the sling. In a moment she had loaded it and was twirling the sling overhead, its leather cords whistling rhythmically. And then she turned to face the behemoth.

It was even bigger than she had imagined, a mountain of a creature, thick and heavy and four times taller than K'ah. It sniffed at the dead Abyssal, snapping it up and swallowing it whole. And then turned and bellowed as it began to move toward her, lumbering on short hind limbs, its scythe-like floating claws fanning out from its blunt, round wrists to find her.

She could feel the rush of the air being cut as the long blades tried to slice her. *So much angry meat!*

Boudica let fly and the bullet sped straight, hitting the Gouger in its right eyes. It stopped, spray flying from it, drenching her. Boudica stood her ground, loading another bullet while keeping her eyes locked on the Gouger.

She could see that the creature was keeping one eye closed— her shot had hit home—but the three other yellow eyes glowed balefully through the rain at her. A low, deep sound came from its throat, half moan, half angry challenge. Slowly it began to move forward, each lumbering step making the fleshy ground faintly tremble.

Boudica stood firm, whipping another heavy bullet at the creature's face, and it roared in pain and outrage. She saw that both of its eyes on one side of its face were closed and, just as she had been told by K'ah during the long hours of practice, she seized the moment and raced across the slick ground to the Gouger's blind side.

The animal turned but not quickly enough. Its claws again raked empty air as Boudica lassoed a spine and pulled herself up and onto its side. In moments she was atop the roaring creature, grabbing spines for balance, pulling herself along its armored back, and making her way toward its thick neck, her dirk glistening in the rain.

The Gouger stopped so abruptly in its tracks that she had to grab a dorsal spine to keep from flying out over its head. Futilely, it began to violently shake its neck and paw at the air above its head in an effort to dislodge Boudica. She clung tightly to the spine and twice nearly dropped the wet dirk. But ahead she saw the reason she had challenged this creature, the embodiment of her newfound hope with the Salamandrines—the Gouger's precious spike swaying from side to side with each of the beast's jerky movements.

Steeling herself, she carefully, methodically, leaped from armored plate to plate to the juncture of the creature's wildly bobbing head and neck and, summoning every bit of her strength, plunged the dirk deep into the fleshy cleft. The Gouger groaned in pain and Boudica dragged the serrated blade back and forth through the tendons and into the stiff spinal cord between its vertebrae once, twice, a third time. She felt a snap and the huge armored head jerked forward, sagging limply. With only one breath left to it, the creature lurched forward and slowly sank to the ground without another sound.

Boudica yanked her dirk free and, trembling, made her way shakily to the spine. She knelt and began sawing at its root, a dark fluid pooling around her feet. In a moment she had sawn through the horny tegument surrounding it. She stood and began to twist and pull on the sharp blade, but the tendons beneath it were too tough and it remained loosely in place, like a child's tooth that would not come free. Just as she heaved a sigh, strong hands grasped the spine, twisting it sharply, and the prize ripped away. K'ah knelt and, eyes fixed on her, offered up the future weapon.

"Your life in the Burning Lands begins anew."

11

PYGON AZ

The bone-white Abyssal had been just as challenging to bring down as Adramalik had feared. His Knights, stressed and weakened by their miserable food and lodgings, were not what they once had been.

The Chancellor had watched with grave concern as his Knights had been handed old, poorly kept lances by headless servants and filed out of their domiciles and out onto the ice to search for the god of Pygon Az's next feast. They were unsteady, nervous, their spirits as low, their moods as dark, as he had ever seen them. Which, in turn, made him wary. It was exactly these kinds of low periods that he had tried to avoid back in Dis simply out of self-interest. Unhappy Knights were dangerous Knights and he knew their unease could readily be turned in his direction. What could he offer up now to placate them? He had nothing, no succubi, no exotic feasts, no souls for playful torturing. *Somehow, I will have to take control of them without igniting their wrath.*

In the end, it had been difficult. As they had ventured out of the fetid darkness of their cells, their spirits had not lifted as he had hoped. Nonetheless, while they had no real chance of regaining their full strength, they were still a band of the most potent, highly trained, and merciless Demons Minor Hell had to offer. And this sense of elite power—weak as it might be—bound them together yet. Eventually, with his flatteries ringing in their ears, they rose above their hushed anger and found themselves almost enthusiastic about the hunt. But the nagging wariness never left Adramalik.

When a smaller Abyssal crossed their paths, Adramalik generously offered it up as a potential meal. It was a poor, lean creature, but it provided them with enough to raise their spirits. He did not even venture to ask whether he could take it aside before they cooked it and assuage his needs. He thought of their needs first. Or so he lied to himself. Renewed, with small morsels in their bellies and small jokes upon their lips, they set back out for larger game. And Adramalik breathed easier.

When they came upon their quarry, as pallid as the dead eyes of souls and covered in heavy folds of flesh and armor, it moved quickly to defend itself and the Knights, slipping and sliding in their ice melt, only barely stayed clear of its claws. Adramalik had to admit that Demospurcus would truly have been only a burden had he survived and been forced to accompany them.

Eventually each of their ancient lances found a home in the creature's vitals and it slumped to the ground in a bubbling cascade of dark blood.

They had to chop up the enormous carcass and drag the massive, steaming chunks of meat back through a sudden ice storm. And Adramalik thought he almost saw relief on their ice-crusted faces as the dark gates of Pygon Az reared up before them. The only thing that reduced their collective pleasure at their accomplishment was the knowledge that they would have to accomplish it all over again when Ai Apaec's huge belly grew hollow once more.

The Bearer of the Knife was there to bring them directly to the throne room and for the remainder of the journey to the palace the only sounds were those of the demons' labored breathing, heavy footsteps, and the scuffing of their bloody burdens over the icy flagstones.

When the party made their way into the shadowed Audience Chamber of Ai Apaec, Adramalik wondered how they would manage to drag the meat to the throne, given the obstacles the piled heads presented. This was soon answered. The enormous headless champion strode forward and relieved the Knights of their burden, shouldering the massive chunk easily and striding back to the throne.

The demons saw their new god descend upon the flesh, his godbody left to sit motionless on the throne. As he feasted, his many sharp palps carving through the bloody meat feverishly, his body distended until he could expand no more. The champion reached down and picked Ai Apaec up and gently placed his saggy, bloated body upon the lap of the seated soul and then withdrew to his usual position, squatting, club at the ready. The Bearer walked ahead and then took up his place at the right hand of the throne.

Only then did the Bearer diffidently wave to Adramalik to approach. With a jerk of his head the Grand Master indicated that the other Knights remain behind and then began to make his slow way through the piles of souls' heads. Their murmuring began almost with his first step.

"It rises. . . ."

"Something awakens. . . ."

"It hungers. . . ."

Adramalik peered into the shadows.

". . . It . . . urges. . . ."

". . . Something . . . craves. . . ."

". . . It . . . demands. . . ."

He saw eyes and teeth glittering in the darkness.

". . . from . . ."

". . . from . . ."

". . . from . . ."

He stumbled.

". . . the Pit . . ."

". . . the Pit . . ."

". . . the *Pit* . . ."

And that made him slow his pace.

". . . annihilation!"

". . . obliteration!"

". . . apocalypse!"

The words hit him like a javelin.

". . . *IT AWAITS YOU!*"

And, in that moment, the horror of their words echoing in his head, he knew that he would not be able to resist the Pit. Somehow, deep within his breast, he had known it all along. The pull of the place, the hold it had had over him, was undeniable. He would have to push aside his unreasoning terror and make his way there. And it would have to be alone. Had the words been overheard? He looked back at his companions but saw nothing amiss. His Knights could not know about this.

The sibilant chorus of voices had faded completely as he drew closer to the throne. There, glutted and once again atop the enormous soul, Ai Apaec squatted. He was even more grotesque than when Adramalik had first seen him. The god's body was distended, sack-like, and barely fit upon the broad shoulders of his god-body. His short legs needed to constantly readjust for him to stay atop the thick neck and his palps flicked about leaving dark, glistening rivulets of blood to drip down the broad chest below, pooling where he sat.

Adramalik knelt.

"You have done well for your first effort, Adramalik. Better than I had imagined. I was quite sure you would have lost at least one of your Knights. They are more formidable than I had thought. Which is good because on your next adventure out into the ice I would have you bring back *two* Abyssals."

Adramalik glanced at the hard-won remains of the god's meal. There was more than enough left for a hundred such feasts. But even as he watched, he saw servants begin to push the rent chunks of meat into deep channels of blood that edged the throne. There they bobbed briefly before slowly floating out of sight.

The Bearer of the Knife stepped forward.

"My god, Ai Apaeac, demands that two such creatures should be killed and their flesh be brought back for his pleasure on your next journey to the ice. His appetite has merely been whetted by this first serving. In his generosity and as a reward to strengthen your Knights for their next hunt, he has ordered that a measure of the meat that you brought back be divided among you."

The Bearer prodded a small chunk of meat that had fallen from Ai Apaec's mouth with his staff, a leaving not nearly large enough for him and the five remaining Knights to satisfy their needs.

"Retrieve it, split it as you see fit, and go back to your domicile. We will call upon you again, as we see fit."

Adramalik drew in his breath and, head still bowed, rose. He scooped up the meat and headed back to his waiting Knights. As he passed a shadowed mound of heads, he dropped the chunk of meat amidst the heads and they immediately and noisily began scrabbling for it. He would not, could not, insult his companions with such an offering and was doubly grateful for the meager meal they had found out on the ice. It was a lesson he would not forget.

As he approached them, the Knights formed around him protectively. As one, sullenly and disheartened, they withdrew, but as they crossed the Audience Chamber's threshold great peals of deep laughter echoed throughout the cavernous room and continued until the sound was dimmed only by distance.

Adramalik sat in the dark corner of his domicile, scratching heartening symbols—small incantations—on the wall, surrounded by his scuffling, mindless inmates, weighing all of his alternatives. Much time for fearful, restless contemplation passed. Staying in Pygon Az was no longer a real option for him. He and his Knights were all but prisoners. And, truth be told, he was not exactly sure that in their current state they could break away from the place. They were still seemingly loyal, but it was only a matter of time before they grew mutinous. Ironically, it was probably just as well that they were separated—plans could only grow when they were together. All this considered, he had to make his own plans. To remain within the confines of the city was to accept incarceration and subservience for eternity. The only way, he concluded, to free his Knights would be to free himself first. But would they see the reason of that?

Seizing the moment, Adramalik began to push the headless souls out of his way. Any resistance he encountered he met with the snapping of limbs. At least they could not scream. After only a few moments the majority of the souls who could still walk had scrambled to the four corners, pressed up against one another, shaking. With a slight smirk, Adramalik crossed the threshold of his domicile.

In a city with no one upon its streets, it was not difficult to stay in the shadows and make his way to a secluded spot. He did watch as the countless eyes in the bricks followed him, at every moment prepared for an alarm to be raised. But none was heard as he made his way into the gloom of the Black Temple Lucifuge had built so long ago to honor Lucifer the Lost.

His wings, kept folded for so long, ached and twitched when he finally spread them wide, their flight-enhancing glyphs flaring to life. Still making sure he had no witnesses, Adramalik climbed with some difficulty to the top of a temple spire and only then dared to launch himself into the air. It had proved to be a simple, uncontested thing to leave Pygon Az behind, so easy that he felt angry and bitter at the plight of his now flightless and handicapped Knights. He would have to see if some obscure incantation could revive their tattered wings. Otherwise their lethality was severely compromised. But first he would have to manage to free them, a task that would not be easy. A wave of something akin to dread passed through him as he contemplated his next, dangerous moves. For millennia he had avoided even thinking about the place, let alone what lay beneath the ice. But to the Pit he would go.

He had not forgotten the way—how could he have?—despite the passage of time. And the growing stench on the light wind helped him focus, filling his lungs with the fetor of Hell's depths and his mind with the chaos that was the Great Lord Abaddon.

The terrain below grew more mountainous with waves of black, ice-sharpened peaks reaching up to claw him from the sky. The mountains, themselves, took on an unnatural demeanor, carved into aggressive abstract forms and adorned with parallel grooves to enhance their artificiality. Strange totems surmounted the mountaintops, each lit with a striking blue glyph, each unfathomable to his otherwise educated eye. He knew they were signs of Abaddon and knew, too, that he would never understand them. Had the wind been as it usually was in this realm, fierce and wild and erratic, he might well have succumbed to the mountains' jagged edges. But luck or fate or the will of That Which Dwelt in the Pit was with him and he gained the flattened valley ringed in as it was by towering, dark cliffs, where, ahead, the Pit lay open.

Instead of flying over the Pit itself, Adramalik chose to land some hundred paces away. He needed to steel himself for what was to come.

As he moved toward the opening he felt the once-familiar, almost irresistible rush of air that, growing with each step, seemed bent upon sucking him down into the abyss of the Great Lord's sub-infernal kingdom. *What am I doing? What in Hell's name am I thinking?*

His pace became labored as he fought the wind, but, eventually, Adramalik found himself standing close enough to the Pit's edge to feel its undeniable power. Wind whipping at his wings and robes, he found himself trembling slightly, closed his eyes, and breathed deeply. Which he immediately regretted. The stench of the Pit, despite the downward surge, was nearly overwhelming. What was it? Decaying demons' flesh mixed with brimstone and something else that Adramalik dared not guess. He knew the legends.

Shaking on the edge, he kept his eyes shut for some time until his terrible apprehension subsided.

When he opened them again, a thing was squatting nearby, silently observing him. He did his best not to register too much surprise, but he was sure that it was impossible to completely mask. He stared in silence at the creature. It was a thing wholly unlike anything he had encountered in Hell—neither demon nor Abyssal. It was large, gangly, and bony, had four legs, and sat tall on its haunches on the Pit's edge dangling its long, skinny tail into the void. A ring of dark fire like a wavering crown flared and guttered around its head and within it a mesmerizing glowing black glyph hung. The creature tilted its head jerkily as it regarded him and, distorted as it was, the face it bore seemed somehow . . . familiar.

"What brings you all this way . . . Chancellor?"

Adramalik blinked and his brow knit.

"Has Pygon Az's new lord grown tiresome?"

That voice! I know that voice, that accent!

"He has," Adramalik admitted. "Are you from . . . ?" He waved a hand toward the surrounding landscape. "Or from . . . down there?"

The creature shifted on its haunches, its movements abrupt.

"Down there, of course. But once, not so long ago, I was as you are."

Adramalik's mind raced. And then it all snapped into place— the voice, the odd movements.

"Faraii?"

"I was."

"But how? You are so changed. How is it possible?"

The creature that was once Faraii cocked his head, his dark eyes peering down into the gaping hole.

"Because my god wanted it so."

"Your god? Do you mean Abaddon?" Adramalik could not keep the astonishment out of his voice.

Faraii nodded. "He is down there. Waiting."

"Waiting for what?

"For the time when he will rise. For the time when all this"— he looked around him—"will fall. For the Second World to rise. And for you."

"Me?"

"Yes. Ever since the fall of the Prince Regent, my god has awaited your arrival."

"Your god has a name? Abaddon?"

"He has many. The Salamandrines whisper theirs . . . T'Zock. The World Eater. T'Thunj. The Lord of the Second World. To them he is a prophesied savior. A harbinger of the return of their world to them. But yes, you may think of him as Abaddon. But you must never address him directly. That is for me to do, for I am beloved of him."

Adramalik blinked. Apart from the physical changes wrought upon the demon, he hardly recognized the inner soul of Faraii in this supplicating monstrosity that spoke to him in worshipful tones of his master.

He unfolded his wings and Faraii turned and cantered to the Pit's ragged edge. The stench from below was less than inviting and Adramalik hesitated. This *was* why he had come all this way. Something had drawn him to this moment. And, to his profound amazement, he had been awaited.

Adramalik approached the edge and found himself fighting to remain steady against the storm of air rushing downward. He tried to peer into the gloom, but the wind buffeted his face with such force that he could barely keep his eyes open. His garments and wings flapped noisily and he shook his head.

"We will need to fall together to combat the wind. You will need to put your arms around my torso and leap with your wings open!" Faraii shouted. "Otherwise the winds will dash us upon the ground. It is either that or a much slower, more challenging descent clinging to the inside of the shaft upon my back!"

Adramalik pursed his lips and with a great effort opened his wings. He turned, took a few steps back, and then rushed at Faraii, his wings lifting and swooping them out into the void in one graceful motion. For a moment it seemed as if the wind would prevail and the pair hovered unsteadily above the abyss. But Adramalik laughed humorlessly and angled his wings downward and their combined weight and his flying expertise brought them into a controlled, braking dive.

In short moments, the Pit's entrance above receded into a small, near-round disk of luminous red sky. Smaller and smaller it shrank and soon they were plunged into near darkness as the walls of the chimney slid past. Faraii was heavier than his skinny frame had appeared and Adramalik, arms shaking, had to fight not to let go. He felt the air grow even chillier than that of the Frozen Wastes above, while below he began to see a faint blue luminosity as they dropped toward the floor of the chute.

The floor was perforated and the icy wind that tried to pull them into the large holes was even stronger closer to the source. It took all of the demon's strength and flying skill, fighting the pummeling wind, to place Faraii with some care upon the hard stone floor, away from the sucking holes. Without waiting the creature that had been Faraii bolted off and Adramalik, struggling to fold his wings, followed. They moved along a labyrinthine course of tunnels until, finally, they were away from the tugging of the winds. Panting, they both took some time to recover.

Adramalik moved to a nearby wall and reached out, touching the surface. The glowing emanated from tiny intricate patterns that covered the rock's surface. Up close it almost looked like writing.

"It glows. From what? An Art?" he said, a cloud of vapor puffing from his mouth.

"No. It is not my Lord Abaddon's doing. It's natural to this place. It is something that grows upon the rock."

"Really."

Faraii stretched his long neck and then nodded to be followed. He turned and cantered off, the rhythm of his bony feet against the foot-smoothed, flagged floor echoing far into the depths.

Adramalik sped to keep up, finding himself running at times, slipping and barely staying upright as the ice-rimed, polished paving stones afforded little traction. Time passed and the demon, having lost a sense of time passing, wondered how far they had traveled.

Their path opened into a huge cavern, surprisingly bright from the accumulated light of the glowing rocks. The pair stopped and Faraii turned to watch Adramalik take in the vista. A small outpost could easily have fit inside the space, an outpost with towers many times the height of a demon. The natural walls, curving seamlessly into the ceiling, were smoothed over and covered in vast mosaics, massive scenes filled with hundreds of dimly seen characters engaged in what appeared to be huge battles and strange rituals unfamiliar to Adramalik. At the distant center of the chamber he could just see a single huge figure depicted. It was, he imagined, a crude representation of Faraii's new god.

And, oddly, there were Salamandrines in the images. *What are those vermin doing* here? *What place* is *this?* Adramalik wondered.

Overhead, darting among the tiled-over stalactites, were formations of flying Abyssals, hissing and spitting and misting the air with their fine spittle. Their slick bodies were emblazoned with red spots that in the darkness appeared to separate and come together in flowing, hypnotizing patterns as the flocks made their careening, convoluted way through the air.

So distracted by the spectacle of winding murmurations of Abyssals was Adramalik that when his gaze finally lowered to the floor of the cave his eyes widened. Stretching across the floor were tumuli of darkly transparent husks beyond count, each shaped like a demon, each glistening and dripping from the falling saliva. The nearer ones, he could see, were split apart as if two great hands had twisted and cracked them open. Inside they were hollow and

empty of any skeletons or organs. Many were partially filled with
saliva.

"What are they?"

"I thought it might be clear to you," Faraii said. "Have you
never wondered what becomes of demons when they are sent
down here?"

"Rarely."

"This place is where their spirits go. This place is where they
are . . . changed. These spirit-shells are what they inhabit when
they are destroyed. And what is pulled free from them . . . my lord
transforms and makes new. What you see here is the currency of
Death in Hell. To be found and hoarded and then spent by my
lord."

"And all of these images. Including the Salamandrine filth?"
Adramalik indicated the walls.

Faraii looked sharply at Adramalik.

"Be *most* careful when you speak of them thusly. They are the
most beloved of my lord. And know, demon, the Men of Wrath
were good to me once. A very long time ago."

This fervor surprised Adramalik and he held his tongue and
simply bowed his head in deference.

Without another word, Faraii swept past the demon and continued down a narrow passage that hugged the cavern wall. Adramalik was not sure whether the creature had truly taken offense
at his words or had simply run out of things to impart, but his
sudden silence weighed heavily. Adramalik followed apprehensively.

*What kind of god is this that favors the miserable, dwindling Salaman-
drines over demons?*

12

THE WASTES

It was the worst firestorm either of them had ever witnessed. And while they were sheltered from its wrath, they were squarely in the heart of it. The air was incandescent and the ground seemed to melt from the shimmering heat waves. Peering out from deep within the rock cleft's hollow, Lilith and Ardat winced whenever a particularly ferocious blast roared past. The air was almost sucked from their shelter with some of the fiercer blasts. Incredibly, they had seen a Salamandrine in the distance, bundled from head to toe in protective Abyssal skins and bent against the fiery wind, trekking in no particular hurry. It was just another walk for him.

Embers surged and hissed partway into their cleft and Lilith put her arms around Ardat as much for her own comfort as that of her handmaiden. Ardat looked up and smiled tensely. And a look passed between them that had flitted on both their faces before, a look of longing that, now, was the unexpected stepchild of the storm.

Lilith drew Ardat's face close and looked deeply into her eyes. Embers danced there . . . were they reflections from the storm or motes of Ardat's yearning soul? Their lips came close, brushed, and she felt the heated breath tingle upon her face. In a moment they were plying kisses upon each other's faces, their lips brushing each other's cheeks, chins, and necks. They had waited millennia, circled their feelings without even knowing their depth. Ardat's loyalty, Lilith's devotion . . . two sides of the same coin.

The winds blew in small handfuls of embers, which fell and gathered on the cleft's rocky floor like glowing tesserae. The effect was almost magical. Lilith scooped up a thumb-sized ember and blew on it until it blossomed into white heat. With one hand she clawed open Ardat's traveling skins and then the robes beneath, layer by layer. Eyes meeting, Lilith slowly pushed her down upon the rock floor, the handmaiden's pale skin glistening in the half-light. Lilith's hands pulled away the skins, ran up and down the smooth, inviting curves of Ardat's thinly muscled torso, and reached behind to caress her firm buttocks.

Lilith took the ember between thumb and forefinger and put it against Ardat's neck and with a moan the younger demon arched her back. The ember traveled slowly, teasingly, upon the handmaiden's body and left a faint wisp of steam as it made its inevitable way downward. Lilith circled Ardat's nipples with it and smiled as she watched her handmaiden's breath come in short, excited bursts. And, she laughed as she playfully traced tingling glyphs upon her flat belly eliciting small high-pitched noises. But her hunger grew along with Ardat's gasps when her fingers slid farther down, parting her already-moist lips. Ardat's hips rose as the sizzling ember entered her and the trembling that followed only grew as Lilith's mouth descended hungrily between her legs, her sharp teeth pressing into the soft flesh. The spasms that followed did not subside until the handmaiden's cries rose about the howling wind, echoing in the confines of the small cave.

Ardat, eyes wide, shakily reached down and pulled her mistress up so that she could reach into Lilith's traveling skins and between her legs as she kissed her. Lilith closed her eyes, smiling, sighing, as the insistent, probing fingers caressed her, finding their goal. She found herself growing more oblivious to the shrieking wind, to the world around her, as those clever fingers eventually found their way inside her. For all her quiet demeanor, Ardat was bold and expert when it came, now, to pleasuring her mistress. For a moment her fingers withdrew, but only a moment, and when, after a gasp, they returned they held the ember. When she applied it, Lilith growled in satisfaction, a look upon her ivory face that her handmaiden had never before seen. And when she pushed it easily, deep inside Lilith, she felt her mistress' body tense and felt, too, the building release to come. Lilith, the White Mistress, champion of souls, consort to Lucifer, to the Fly, and to the Ascended Sargatanas, was no longer there. In her place was an ancient creature of purest lust. She snarled, snapping down with her mouth agape, sank her small, sharp teeth deep into Ardat's breast. The pain was undoubtedly profound, and at first Ardat clawed frantically at Lilith's bare back trying to dislodge her, but this only made the demon sink her teeth deeper and slide her hand between her handmaiden's legs once again. The pair twisted on the cave's floor, locked together, but as the moments wore on, the terrible pain subsided and Ardat found herself climaxing along with her mistress.

Time and thought seemed to stop. Winds seemed to dwindle. And the ember, now tossed aside, faded and blackened.

The pair slept the restless, dreamless near sleep of Hell. The storm passed and when they both stirred, smiling faintly, it was to find their arms around each other, the scratches still visible. They rose, put on and adjusted their traveling skins, strapped on their weapons and packs, and exited the cleft, saying nothing. A welcome threshold had been crossed.

Lilith spotted the distant soul caravan before her handmaiden. They were so far off, Lilith at first thought her eyes were playing tricks in the ever-shifting ash fields. But her eyes were every bit as keen as they had been all those millennia ago when she had targeted far-off humans in their swamps.

Lilith, squinting into the distance, saw something in the way the souls were moving across the landscape that aroused her curiosity. They seemed to be dragging things behind them. Ardat and she wordlessly nodded to each other as they took up the pursuit.

The winds from the firestorm had blanketed the ground in dark, now-cooled embers that made soft crunching sounds as Lilith and Ardat set out. After crossing a flat, gray plain crisscrossed by thin ribbons of lava, they picked up the souls' trail and found themselves following not only the many footprints but also six furrows that were clearly drag marks.

The pair picked up the pace but were careful to stay concealed as they drew nearer, keeping to the far sides of hillocks and the deeper, shadowed parts of gullies. Lilith's mood toward the souls had, if anything, hardened over the days since her last encounter. The sense that she had been following a lost cause for all those long millennia in Dis only served to make her more bitter.

They were something I needed to focus upon to deflect my own misery. I can see that now. Could I have survived without them? I wonder.

She frowned as she made her way toward the souls and Ardat, seeing that dark expression, knew to keep silent.

When they were a few hundred paces from the party, Lilith and Ardat finally saw the authors of the long drag marks. Six tied figures, females it would seem, were being dragged roughly by two to three souls each. The females were succubi by the look of them, their garb shredded and hanging in tatters. Watching them being pulled over the sharp terrain twisting in pain raised Lilith's anger to a point that was soon barely controllable.

She and Ardat edged closer until they were only a few paces from the muttering gang. Lilith silently slid Lukiftias from its sheath, stalked forward deliberately, and jerked her chin fiercely toward them. Ardat understood and quietly pulled out her own blade.

With a growl Lilith leaped from behind cover, followed swiftly by Ardat. The souls were so shocked that, as one, they shrieked and scattered, dropping the ropes by which they had been pulling the unfortunate succubi. Many, clearly new to the ways of war, dropped their weapons in their terror and surprise. Rather than pursue them—they had fled in every direction—the pair sheathed their weapons and set about freeing the demons.

"What are your names?" Lilith asked as she tried to work free the tightly knotted tendon ropes that crisscrossed their bodies.

"Mine is Araamah," the succubus said hoarsely as Lilith freed one arm. She jerked a thumb at the others. "Hers is Liimah. That one kicking one of the souls is Kaasah. Those three are Dimmah, Mashtaah, and Asaakah."

The knots were uncooperative and, with an annoyed groan, Lilith pulled a small Abyssal-tooth knife from her satchel. Its serrated edge made easy work of the tough ropes and Araamah was freed quickly. She stood unsteadily, pain creasing her delicate features, and rearranged her tattered garments.

"Go free them, Araamah. Take this. And kill the soul Kaasah is kicking," Lilith said, handing the succubus the black knife. "I want to make sure those souls aren't regrouping to come back."

Lilith moved up a small hill to Ardat's side, feigning scanning the horizon.

"What are we going to do with them?"

Lilith shrugged.

"We cannot leave them out here. They would wind up just as we found them. Or worse." Ardat was clearly sympathetic.

Lilith shook her head slightly. *This is just not what I had in mind. Finding Buer . . . getting back to Dis as quickly as possible . . . this is just going to slow us down.*

"You are right, Ardat," Lilith said with a sigh. "We can drop them at the next demon outpost. That is, if we find one that has not been overrun. Otherwise they are just going to have to keep up with us."

Lilith turned and headed back down the hillock. The succubi were kicking away their bonds as Araamah finished with Dimmah.

"Pick up whatever suits you," Lilith said, indicating the souls' lost weapons. The various pieces looked mostly like swords and pikes "liberated" from demons—good, solid weapons.

For a few moments the succubi tentatively picked through the swords and dirks and hatchets until eventually they were satisfied. Oddly, Lilith noted, whether it was by agreement or not they all seemed to select the same crooked blades—forged weapons, these were, meant for demon officers—which they hefted and twirled in mimicry of their former captors.

Ardat joined Lilith, smirking.

Lilith was not about to slow her pace just for some itinerant succubi even if they were cast about Hell's five points against their will. And to their credit—and Lilith's and Ardat's quiet approval— the younger demons kept up admirably. It was, Lilith reflected, almost as if the release from their imprisonment and servitude put added strength in their legs and enthusiasm in their breasts. They were, as it turned out, low-level succubi, pleasure givers to Dis'

decurion class and young, by Hell's standards—a millennium or
two for each of them. And none of them had been outside the confines of the Keep before.

Algol rose and set before the party found a sheltering cliff's
overhang. Winds were kicking up again.

Lilith and Ardat listened as they rested, half-interested, while
Liimah, the most forthcoming of the succubi, explained their escape.

"We were never even aware a war had been going on for so
long. The decurions never said anything. We were just sweet meat
to them." Liimah's three eyes flitted from Lilith to Ardat looking
for sympathy from the two demons and found none. They had
been through far worse at the hands of the Fly than the compara-
tively pampered existences of these creatures. And they had seen
too many atrocities since leaving Dis behind to consider the succubi anything but truly fortunate.

"When the Keep was forcibly emptied of its occupants just before they razed almost all of it, the victors came in to claim their
spoils. Us. They used us no better or worse than the decurions of
Dis. And, for our troubles, we learned little bits of information
about the war. Sargatanas' army would be unforgiving to anyone
from Dis, especially from the Keep. So, we fled."

Lilith felt a pang in her heart momentarily as *his* name was pro-
nounced. She saw Ardat shoot the succubi a look, but they could
not have known what their transgression was and they ignored her.
*It has been so long since I lost him and yet it is still so hard to hear his
name. Maybe that needs to end.*

"The mandate was tolerance in exchange for fealty."

Even as she said it, Lilith knew better. Knew that demons from
Dis beyond count, far from Put Satanachia's idealistic gaze, were

humiliated or destroyed and that very few of the Fly's hierarchy were found guiltless enough to be absorbed into the government of Adamantinarx. A mere handful. The corruption had been too deeply ingrained, the sadism too pervasive, to be so easily expunged. *So be it,* she thought. *They got what they deserved.*

"The mandate was . . . overlooked in most cases. We saw the mountains of rubble that had once been the demons of the court and government of Dis. The executions were unending. The air was thick with their dust. And we were sure we would be treated the same. We escaped by way of the underground arteries that come from beneath the Keep. Once that thing . . . Semjaza . . . was loosed it was easy to find our way into one and then to evade the armies up above."

Lilith maintained her studied demeanor of indifference. These succubi were little more than playthings, pampered pets of the entitled military. Why should their misadventures be of any interest to her or Ardat?

Liimah carried on despite Lilith's obvious aloofness.

"When we finally did make it away from Dis we headed out into the Wastes. We thought we would be safer away from the armies."

"You were wrong," Lilith said flatly.

"Yes, we were. We wandered for what seemed like forever. And then Araamah had an idea. She had heard about Adamantinarx and Sargatanas. Had heard what he did. And she got it into her head to go there."

Lilith sucked in her breath and turned away. She had heard this kind of thing so many times from other travelers.

"And *I* had the idea to find *you.*"

Lilith turned and looked intently at the succubus. A trace of a smile crossed her face. "So, you enlisted a gang of soul brigands to capture all of you and then had yourselves dragged to my feet? Good plan. It worked."

Liimah laughed, a not-unpleasant sound.

"That was not really the plan, Mistress. The plan was to find you and to appeal to you to let us follow you."

"Follow me? Where?"

"Not where . . . how. We all decided that Sargatanas' cause, his sacrifice, was . . . holy. We want to become your . . . disciples. Acolytes, if you will allow us."

Lilith looked at Ardat. She shook her head almost imperceptibly. *I'm suddenly someone to be followed? Simply because* he *and* I *were together?*

Ardat smiled wryly, clearly reading her thoughts.

She turned back to the tattered succubi who straightened under her gaze. Despite their effort to look hardy, they looked, instead, weak and pampered, more fit for the court seraglio than the fiery Wastes.

"So, you want to be my disciples." She paused, took a deep breath, nodded toward the piled weapons. "Pick up your weapons. You have a lot to learn."

13

THE WASTES

Boudica grew bolder and more zealous with each venture into the once-unknown Wastes. The demon-hunting patrols that K'ah led were well organized and exhilarating. He was a natural leader, one who planned as carefully for the destruction of his enemies as he did for the safety of his fellow warriors. And he was more than attentive when it came to her. In some ways she felt liked a well-trained pet or mascot kept at heel for the sport of it, yet in others she sensed that he actually cared about her. But she could not deny the importance her mentor placed on her being along during the raids. There seemed to be some kind of underlying motive to his thinking, some larger reason for his inclusiveness. It took fewer than a dozen raids before she was riding next to him, helping him with tactics and decisions. And she could not fail to notice that the raids were edging closer and closer to outlying cities.

Between raids, the Salamandrine taught her the ways of the sword she had earned. It was a weapon designed for stabbing and thrusting from a distance. Its long blade was thick and powerful and yet flexible enough to bypass other weapons and find its mark. Its purpose had evolved over millennia to destroy demons, to pen-etrate their heavy armor and deal a killing blow from a distance great enough to prevent them from striking first. She immediately understood its potential. K'ah trained her hard and once, during a rest period, she had asked him whether he found it odd to be training a soul and he had replied that it was but that another tribe had once trained a demon, eons ago. This extraordinary demon had fallen from the sky so far from his kind that he had asked to be adopted by the nearest tribe. That, K'ah said, had been the oddest thing he had ever heard of. The demon's name had been Faraii and his exploits had been sung for millennia. The name meant nothing to Boudica, but the tale was, she admitted, strange.

The demons, Boudica saw, were pulling back and sending out supply caravans less frequently, guarding them when they did venture forth with larger and larger forces of foot soldiers. Which was not especially worrisome to the Salamandrines. It simply meant that K'ah had to send out runners farther afield to get more raiders. This was not a problem. There was no shortage of young warriors eager to sharpen their newly crafted swords in the rough rubble of fallen demons.

Algol rose and fell six times more before K'ah's intentions became clear. On the sixth rising of the star he woke her, tapping her shoulder lightly with the tip of his black sword.

"Are you ready for something different?"

"I am ready for more rest. That's different, yes?"

"Rest is for the egglings. We are grown past it. Rise, B'udik'k'ah. The clans from afar are gathering . . . we have dark work ahead."

Boudica stumbled out of her stall, her weapons and outer garments gathered hastily and hanging in disarray, as she tried to get her bearings. She clambered clumsily up and out of the camp and saw a few hundred warriors encamped a small distance from where she stood. They were silently preparing for battle. That was something very different from the garrulous warriors in her Life.

As she stood watching them, willing the sleep from her eyes, K'ah approached, mounted and holding Andrasta's reins. Boudica adjusted her new robes. They fit perfectly thanks to the skill of the Salamandrine who had labored over them. She slung her long sword's baldric over her head, smiled unfathomably at K'ah—he still could not fully read her facial expressions—and climbed onto her saddle. All of her Salamandrine things, the beast's tack, her own personal items, all seemed familiar now and somehow right. And owning things again felt good.

A horn blew and, as one, the clans' warriors mounted. Boudica frowned and pointed at the lowering sky. A long swathe of black clouds, pregnant with shimmering fire, slid along the horizon. K'ah nodded.

"Tsak'ka rolled her weather bones and told me the clouds would rain fire . . . that they would favor us. They are gathering just as she predicted."

Boudica, who was still not exactly accustomed to the firestorms, simply frowned.

"Come, we have work to do."

"Dark work?" Boudica ventured.

"Indeed."

K'ah led the way at the head of nearly two hundred warriors. Mounted on various kinds of Abyssals—some, Boudica noted, heavily armored and powerful-looking—the large force soon stretched out in a long train as some creatures were not as fleet as others. This was, as she saw, advantageous, as the broken terrain would be nearly impassable had the war party stretched from side to side.

"We head for the demon garrison near the Sheets of Fire, B'udik'k'ah."

"You're talking about the border outpost, Char-zon? Near the Flaming Cut?"

"The same."

"That, K'ah, is a very ambitious target."

"I am a very ambitious man."

Boudica stared for some time at the back of Andrasta's head as they made their way through the ravines.

"From what I remember hearing, that garrison is lightly manned. But, like many key outposts, it was built over a summoning pit. By design. Most of the demons stationed there are decurions. Capable of conjuring countless legionaries."

"Yes. We know that."

"You will have to be quick about it. Quick enough to penetrate their walls before they can summon large numbers of legionaries from the conjuring pits."

"That is our intention."

The embers rained down gently, making the sparkling landscape indistinct. At first, there was little or no wind, but as the storm descended, the wind picked up and Boudica pulled her hood down, adjusting the heavy, full-face mask so that the eye slits were well placed. She cinched it tight with cords from behind. It had taken her longer than she had expected to get used to the tight, closed feeling inside that hood and mask and also to the strong musk of the Abyssal leather it was composed of. Now she quite liked the scent.

The war party had dismounted and spread out on a rocky shelf near the outpost, its flank pocked with craters and lined with gullies. It was, Boudica noted, a perfect spot for them to gather unseen.

K'ah was hunkered down next to her. Both were hidden in a wind-carved scoop in the rocks. Apart from the falling embers, the view of the distant outpost was clear. His mask was down, the markings upon its smooth, layered surface beautiful and terrifying at the same time. Behind the four slits his eyes glittered.

"Timing will be everything, B'udik'k'ah. We need to launch two attacks at exactly the same moment. We will attack the garrison at its gate and where they least expect it. From behind. The Rockcrawlers that we brought along . . . they will tear down the wall and move in to cover the lava pits. They are slow but impossible to resist. The Conjurers, those decurions, won't be able to summon enough soldiers before we have sealed off the pits."

Boudica considered all of this, eyeing the outpost through the slits in her mask.

"They are no fools, K'ah. These are not decurions-of-the-line. They are better than that. Smarter and faster. That's why they are out here in the middle of nowhere. And, worse than that, no matter how fast your attack is, they will send a glyph back to their patron city. For help."

"I'm counting on it. The war has weakened them. Perhaps we can weaken them even further."

"A dream. A dream of regaining what you will never have. Even with the war their numbers are growing as yours are dwindling."

"You will not help us?"

"You know I will. I've been on the losing side before. It just makes things that much more interesting."

K'ah made a noise that she knew to be equivalent to a laugh. She smiled inside her hood and turned, again, to the outpost.

Reaching into his satchel, K'ah brought out a fist-sized object composed of a dozen or more smaller globes—polyps plucked from artery trees tied together. This he threw out so all the Salamandrines could see where it landed. Immediately it sparked to life, the falling embers setting it alight and causing the globes to separate and burst into flames. Any demon seeing it would have thought it to be an exploding cinder. The Salamandrines knew better. The signal caused the Rockcrawlers to move slowly forward, their heavy, armored legs seemingly impervious to the lava channels they sank into as the creatures crossed through them. Their riders hunkered down so as not to be detected should the decurions chance to look out into the Wastes.

K'ah pulled three more grenades from his pouch, threw one, waited, and then tossed the remaining pair into the air. Rising from the shadows, the Salamandrines on foot began to run, hunched over, through the low gullies toward the front gate of the outpost. Clearly, they had practiced this maneuver.

Boudica watched the awkward Rockcrawlers muscle their way toward the outpost, their thick belly armor shielding them from the rocks they slid over. Were it not for the sizzling winds and the cover the ember clouds lent, she was sure the creatures and their riders would have been spotted. But K'ah was a canny tactician and had picked his time for the assault perfectly.

The heavy creatures descended into the wide ditch that surrounded the outpost and then slowly reemerged to stand on their many hind legs, freeing their massive clawed paws, waiting in the shadow of the wall. They did not have long to wait.

An outcry could be heard and suddenly Boudica saw five large conjuring glyphs rise above the buildings. When she looked back at the Rockcrawlers they were already pulling down the substantial wall, filling the ditches with huge chunks of rubble.

K'ah leaped out from the rocky hollow, raised his long sword, and roared to the other Salamandrines to follow. Boudica ran after him, sword in hand. His long strides soon took him farther ahead than she wanted and she soon found herself at the back of the ragged ranks of running warriors. Up ahead she saw K'ah leaping nimbly from one chunk of rubble to the next, crossing the ditch easily, and then clambering through the wall and into the garrison. It was only moments until, trying to keep up with the warriors, she was struggling to jump from one chunk of wall to the next. She slipped, caught herself, and carried on, grateful her mentor was not watching. She made a final leap onto the broken wall and into the chaos that was the outpost.

She took in the entire scene of carnage rapidly, her battle-trained mind picking out the safe spots, the areas of greatest conflict. She saw the rough soul-brick towers surrounding the flagstoned courtyard, the stables for soul-steeds, the simple soldiers' quarters, and finally the all-important summoning pits, centrally located in long, shallow depressions. The mandate to break down soul bricks did not seem to have reached this far-flung outpost.

As slow as they had seemed from afar, Boudica immediately saw that the Rockcrawlers had made remarkable time getting to the conjuring pits. Most had positioned themselves atop the bubbling lava pools, precluding any more summoned demons from emerging. There, beneath the large creatures, the legionaries would be held, quickly sizzling back into the element from which they were born for lack of the hardening exposure of the air.

Boudica pulled her long Abyssal sword and together with her smaller sword she weighed into the fray, slashing and stabbing at those heavy legionaries who had managed to emerge before the pits had been shut down. There were a few hundred of them and the Salamandrines were challenged by a force that held a slight edge in numbers.

The decurions, easily identified by the transverse-crested helms, were mounted on wheeling soul-steeds, controlling the waves of demons with cascades of command glyphs issuing from summoning staves as they clashed with K'ah's warriors. Despite being conjured only moments before, they were organized and disciplined, and a few Salamandrines fell under their blades. As she joined the fight, Boudica began to realize that the decurions were the key to victory. She set her eyes on the nearest decurion and fought her way toward him.

Created with an innate sense of duty, the decurion sent a large alarm glyph up into the sky, and she saw it flash away to its capital. Was it heading to Adamantinarx or another city? She could not tell.

As she approached it, the decurion's soul-steed eyed her dumbly, saliva hanging from its mouths, its enormous head, composed of dozens of souls' heads moving from side to side to avoid being cut. It pivoted on its massive legs with more agility than Boudica had thought possible for a creature so large. The decurion hardly noticed her, so intent was he on casting his fiery glyphs into the melee. And that proved his downfall. Boudica leaped upon a low wall and then squarely onto the broad back of his steed and, with a piercing scream, thrust out with her Abyssal blade. She felt the odd bite of the sword into something that was not quite flesh, not quite stone. His body burst into a gritty cloud of debris as his head flew into the air, the look of surprise on his disintegrating face plain to Boudica. Beneath her, the riderless soul-steed spun on its heavy feet as she jumped down, narrowly missing being trampled. For the briefest of moments she looked across the tumult of battle, through the flailing swords, the frenzied combatants, and caught K'ah's masked gaze. He nodded, clearly pleased.

Encouraged, Boudica suddenly realized that her relatively diminutive height was an advantage. She could stalk her way through the fighting toward the decurions unseen and, when the opportunity arose, leap from the rubble piles of the destroyed demons to dispatch them just as she had the first of the officers. She set about her self-appointed task with a terrible grin and an equally terrible resolve to make as many demons as possible pay for her miserable millennia of enslavement.

The second and third decurions fell as the first had, unsuspecting and without any opposition. The fourth decurion, however, saw her coming for him at the last moment and, glaring at her, skillfully wheeled his mount around to face her. Perhaps he had watched his brethren fall, suddenly and perplexingly, and surmised what had happened to them. Perhaps he was simply keener of sight and intuition. Boudica tried hurriedly to gain the top of a cairn of dead demons, stumbled, and regained herself only to see the decurion's summoning stave pointed directly at her, a fiery glyph curling outward to combat her. It shot from the stave's tip and twisted around her, its slitherings burning her through her skins.

She tumbled from the pile of rubble and fell heavily, writhing and clawing at the incandescent ribbons as they attempted to find a way inside her. She rolled upon the flagstones and just as the huge steed lifted a front leg to crush her she saw the decurion's head explode into powder, the blur of a sling bullet barely seen hurtling through the dark cloud. The steed reared and twisted, its foot missing her by inches, and then she felt rough, gloved hands snatch her up, lifting and carrying her through the dwindling battle, past the massive Rockcrawlers, to place her down next to a steaming summoning pit. Through the haze of pain she watched her Salamandrine rescuer pull up the ground-skin and tear away a chunk of the black matrix beneath. She looked up, dazed, knowing that had to be K'ah.

Of course he had seen what happened! He was watching me throughout the whole battle.

Like a lodestone, the tarry chunk drew off the ribbons of fire into its inky core, and, once Boudica was free, K'ah tossed the bubbling mass into the fiery pit, where it sizzled and vanished. She had no idea why it worked. She did not care—it had simply and completely stopped the pain. She sat upright, shuddering.

"Those were made to kill Salamandrines. You are very lucky, B'udik'k'ah."

K'ah extended his hand.

"My swords," she said, breathing hard and patting his forearm in thanks.

Another Salamandrine who had followed K'ah put them almost reverently in her hands.

"A true warrior," he said quietly. "A truer leader. We have all seen your quality here, B'udik'k'ah of the Blades. By T'Thunj, Lord of the Second World, we have seen the birth of a leader!"

Looking around her, she saw small clusters of warriors dispatching the last of the conjured demons. Some turned, briefly, to look at her. The winds abated and a muffled silence descended as the Salamandrines finished their grim task. A sooty cloud of coarse black powder settled slowly over the garrison, dusting the victors in their victims' remains.

K'ah dropped his mask to his chest. His pale face and short beak were slick with sweat and streaked with the grit, but his four eyes were bright, wide with the post-battle zeal that Boudica had so often seen in her own warriors so long ago. He turned to his lieutenants who stood around him, exhausted but eager for orders.

"Disperse the Rockcrawlers and the tribes who joined us. Tell them to take what they will from the outpost. We travel on our own now."

He looked at Boudica for approval and when she nodded the Salamandrines headed off. The sound of carved trumpets could be heard. K'ah studied her, put his hand on her shoulder.

"I could not have imagined a soul to be so ferocious."

"We are a ferocious lot, K'ah." Boudica grinned.

K'ah clicked his beak three times. Boudica knew he had caught the irony. She had told him many times why so many humans had found themselves in Hell, that they were a destructive race filled with jealousies and self-interest and intolerance. Perhaps, she thought, she should someday tell him about the good aspects of her race. Or not. The Salamandrine might never believe her given what he had witnessed of humans. And her.

"What now, K'ah?"

"Now we wait to see if our message was received."

Boudica nodded. She was certain it would be. She was not as certain the cities would mobilize a response. The war had shifted priorities beyond what K'ah could imagine.

"And," K'ah added, "you have one last ritual to perform. There are dead to be eaten."

Boudica closed her eyes. She would have to get past this last hurdle.

14

THE PIT

Ice crunched and sizzled beneath Adramalik's careful footfalls as he edged his way slowly along the cavern walls. The floor had fallen away and was concealed in the lower shadows far below. Faraii, incomprehensibly surefooted, managed the narrow strip of icy rock much better. *Perhaps, four feet are better here than two,* Adramalik thought. He would never have thought so, but the fact was that he was having trouble keeping up.

Adramalik frowned. He heard something in the cavern far ahead, a muffled cacophony of distant raspings and rendings and, perhaps, low speech blending into one steady susurration. It was disquieting and set the demon's nerves on edge. He clenched his teeth, trying to ignore it, but the deep sounds seemed to flow through his body.

The creature that was now Faraii halted and turned his head toward the demon. The crown-like flames darkened his face in flickering shadows and only his eyes glittered back at the demon.

"Do you see that tiled arch up ahead? Not the dark one—the big one lit from behind? You must pass through that one on your hands and knees. And continue on into the Presence in that manner."

More *degrading rituals! As if kneeling before Ai Apaec was not enough! The Court of the Fly was like a dream compared to these upstart gods and*

*their ridiculous self-aggrandizing formalities. I served the Prince of Hell
and now this? Will my fall never end?*

As the pair made their way toward the archway, Adramalik had
to admit to himself that he almost welcomed the notion of crawling given his constant slipping. Still, it rankled him.

When they reached the huge arch, he dropped to his hands and
knees, but it was an almost involuntary act as he saw laid out before him the vast tableau of Lord Abaddon and his attendant court.

The ancient cavern, eerily illuminated by the glowing growths
on the rocks, was easily as vast as the Prince's Rotunda had been,
a space that should have defied the physical supports it would need
to keep it from collapsing. As no supports were visible, the enormity of the amphitheater was staggering, but Adramalik had little
time to consider issues of fantastic architecture.

Recumbent in a lake of trembling quicksilver was Abaddon.
The god was gigantic, nearly the size of Semjaza the Watcher, and
he was unlike any thing or being that Adramalik had ever seen in
Hell. He had a head. That much was apparent, but even that was
not like any head he had encountered before. It was impossible to
tell which direction it was looking, which were its features, and
which were simply strange ornaments projecting from its round
skull. Surrounding it was a dark and wavering nimbus, a huge version of the Faraii creature's, that seemed to pull the light in from
all around it.

The rest of the god's partially submerged body was equally
puzzling. Angular limbs disappeared beneath the rippling liquid
metal to reappear in unexpected places, attaching themselves to
the torso in ways that Adramalik had trouble understanding. *Perhaps,* he concluded, *this is because it is hidden. Perhaps if it rose up. . . . ,*
but the thought of this enormous, unfathomable being standing

before him actually frightened him in a way nothing had ever done before. While the Fly had been a unique and undeniably disturbing figure he, at least, had attempted to be *something* recognizable while in the presence of his court.

As hard as it was to take his eyes from the abstraction that was Abaddon, the surroundings were nearly as bizarre. It was pure chaos. Flocks of Abyssals swooped and careered and rocketed through the air, screeching as they darted between the stalactites. Dotting the quicksilver lake were small islands of countless discarded spirit-shells, some of these floating rafts surmounted by chanting demonic Conjurers, the source of the low voices he had heard from far back in the caverns.

Adramalik watched them as some pounded on drums and intoned their throaty phrases while others used long wedges to pry open the dead armored demons that were constantly being pushed into the lake by equally malformed helpers. The naked Conjurers, each one twisted into a wildly unique, multi-limbed form, had clearly been imbued with some kind of Art Transfigurative. Strange glyphs flew as thickly as the incantations allowed and from each cracked and shriveled demon a new creature was pulled, covered in the black tar of its rebirth. Even as the Conjurers were casting away the remains of the demons—the so-called spirit-shells—the new creatures gaped their distended jaws wide, stretched unsteadily, and then leaped into the quicksilver pool to swim to shore. By the time they had managed to make land they had grown large and strong and were cleansed of their black slime. Another unnatural feat of transformation! A constant, chittering stream of them faded into the darkness to join their brethren somewhere in the icy bowels of the caves.

The Faraii creature was different. Perhaps he had been designed with the simple purpose of speaking to him. Or, more likely, he was a higher form, created to lead the masses of these transformed demons. He lacked the robust jaws that seemed so obviously designed to rend and tear.

Adramalik was convinced that Abaddon had gifted his Conjurers with some small portion of his own vast power, an Art well beyond anything the demon had ever heard spoken of. It did not seem to matter in what way a demon was destroyed on the battlefield. Drawn here by Abaddon they were all intact, all fodder for transfiguration. This being was something to not trifle with. He shook his head slowly, partly out of admiration, partly out of fearful respect, partly out of sheer incomprehension. After the Fall the demons' Arts had flourished and grown powerful. But deep inside he knew they could not compete with the primal power of resurrection itself.

Faraii stood back, watching the awestruck demon as he took in all of the sights. A smile, not unlike his old, grim smile, crossed his face.

"The only true god in Hell."

And Adramalik, on hands and knees, found himself unable to contradict the creature.

"We must make our way down to that ledge. And await your audience."

"*My* audience?"

"I told you. He was waiting for you. You did *not* think I brought you here to simply gaze upon his majesty, did you?"

Fear rose up in Adramalik's chest. Unaccustomed fear. *Why does this thing wait for me? What could I possibly do for him that he could not have done by any number of other means?*

Adramalik moved forward, down toward the ledge, perhaps more slowly than was physically necessary. Each crawling step brought him closer to the god, closer to his unthinkable questions being answered. And, as he descended, edging past moaning, incense-shrouded Conjurers in blind-eyed, gyrating trances and through low, crackling hummocks of stinking spirit-shells, the last shreds of his former confidence vanished entirely and he realized that he was . . . nothing.

He had, indeed, fallen further still since his fall.

The creature that had been Faraii moved easily through the chanting demon-things and the detritus, trotting ahead until, reaching the ledge, it turned and watched Adramalik approach.

The demon slipped on the ice and bits of shell and went down on an elbow. A multi-armed Conjurer reached down and helped him back up on all fours. And Adramalik marveled at how little kinship he felt for the creature, how he could hardly see the demon in it. He had no desire to thank it, to address it at all. Without a word, he simply continued creeping forward until he was at Faraii's cloven feet.

He spun slowly until he was facing Abaddon and sucked in his breath. Closer to the god his enormity was even greater. His musty scent somehow penetrated the foul stink of the Abyssal birthing ground, permeating the air, filling Adramalik's lungs. Age. Vast age. He sensed it even without the pungent odor.

The god sat up to regard the demon. Quicksilver slithered from him in long, wobbly worms that seamlessly blended into the lake. Abaddon's shadow-shrouded head bowed, but even with this orientation, Adramalik was just as challenged to discern any recognizable features.

There was no voice and yet the demon heard it. Over the flapping and screeching of the Abyssals, the chanting of the shamans, the crackling of the shells, over it all Adramalik heard Abaddon's brittle words.

"You are finally here, Adramalik. After all these millennia."

Adramalik nodded, speechless. How could this be? How could *he* be awaited by this being?

"This world, as you know it, this world is nearly at an end. Your kind have reigned here far too long and wrought changes upon the landscape that I find intolerable. I will see that dominion end. And, in its place, I will give back to my children their world as they knew it before you and your degraded race arrived."

Abaddon shifted slightly and the heavy ripples in the lake caused the small rafts and their occupants to bob briefly.

"You demons have claimed this world as your own, as if it were your right to colonize it. It was mine, mine and others' before you and so shall it be again. I am nearly ready to take it back. I need only a Summoning . . . a final sacrifice . . . to set about the changes. And, that, Adramalik, is why I waited so very long for you."

Another shift and the silver waves lapped thickly at the ledge.

Adramalik's mind raced. Were all his dark heroics, his darker schemes, his fealty to the Fly and loyalty to his brother Knights, was his entire existence in the Above and Hell, coming down to this? To becoming a simple, miserable sacrifice?

With all the hardships he had experienced descending into these vast caverns, he knew he could never escape. Even if he could manage to flee from this Faraii creature—and that seemed unlikely— he would surely be lost in the labyrinth of tunnels. And, worse yet, found.

He would have to argue for his life.

Nonetheless, Adramalik held his tongue. He needed to know more and remembered Faraii's warning about addressing Abaddon directly.

"Your instinct for self-preservation *is* remarkable, Adramalik. And unnecessary here." The god let that sink in. Nothing could be hidden from him. "A long time ago, demon, you craved a life of ease and plenty far away from Dis. You held high position in the spurious court of a false Prince who played at ruling Hell." Abaddon paused again and Adramalik could feel the hatred envelop him. The darkness that encircled the god's head roiled and agitated and the demon saw the briefest flickering of red lightning.

How could this thing have known my innermost yearnings? I shared them with no one.

"I knew your thoughts then, Adramalik, as I know them now because I am not a thing. I *am* Hell. I have been here since before the Salamandrines, living in this darkened realm, this second world beneath what you know. I watched you and your kind Fall. But I had no host to stop it. Now, with the constant slaughtering of one another that you demons seem to delight in, you have provided me with the materials for your own undoing. The more your kind wages war the larger my army becomes. Your own dead and destroyed are the very foundation of my Horde. My Abaddim."

A flock of the circling Abyssals landed on the god, covering what served as shoulders in red-glowing, folded wings. Abaddon took no notice.

"You are not to be sacrificed as you fear. To the contrary. I will give you what you have craved . . . that life of indulgence and comfort. . . . I will anoint you the new Prince of Hell. But it will come at a price. You will be alone to enjoy it. And you will have to bring me the creature that calls himself Ai Apaec. It is *his* demise that will bring me forth."

"And what of the world above?" Adramalik spoke out loud.

Faraii took a step toward him.

Abaddon lifted an appendage, staying the creature.

"It will change again to what it once was and my scions, my *brood* . . . my Abaddim . . . will flourish and repopulate it. That is my wish."

"Why me?"

"Because of your power and your cunning and your instinct for self-preservation. Even as that thing you called a Prince was fighting to save himself, you were gauging how to stay alive. I had to compel you to leave. That Watcher was too potent to be fought, too powerful and wild. He needed to be released, to turn the tide. To bring you here."

"*You* released him?"

"I broke the ground beneath the great fortress and his chains fell away."

Adramalik, awed, humbled, pressed his forehead to the frozen ground.

"I will do as you require."

The Faraii creature left him in a tunnel near the base of the Pit, just before the winds could be felt. No words passed between them, but a connection had been forged. After all, Adramalik reasoned, Faraii was no stranger, and while this bizarre version of him was both unexpected and horrific, it was certainly an improvement over the mindless Husk he once had known. Perhaps there was something of the old demon left in that misshapen, four-legged thing.

Alone, the demon made his way to the chimney's base. Wings spread and catching the terrific updraft, Adramalik rose into the frigid air with a mixture of relief, exhilaration, and purpose. The dark, ragged mouth of the Pit spat him forth, falling away beneath him as he tried to combat the wild winds above it. But, ultimately, his wings betrayed him and he plunged back to land heavily upon the ice. He read no portents in that small fall.

15

THE WASTES

Ardat and Lilith sat on a rocky promontory watching a small herd of Abyssals pulling up a crimson patch of arterial growths to get at the more tender vessels belowground. Each creature was adorned with floating antler-like growths that hovered above their heads and backs and a pattern of red-orange spots that glowed brilliantly in the semi-gloom. They were quite attractive, Lilith thought. She was sure that the vessel fields had not been present before the arrival of the Fallen—she remembered that distant past with clarity—and marveled that the Abyssals had adapted to carving away the layers of tissue that had come with the descent of the demons and souls. The corruption of the native land that had occurred since their ancient arrival had been thorough and completely invasive. She somehow felt guilty for that, as if her association with the demons made her equally culpable, but she knew better than that. It was *their* doing.

As the pair watched, the six acolytes silently, stealthily moved in behind the herd, positioning themselves behind rocks for the imminent ambush. Liimah, sharp as ever, was the leader and with crisp hand signals she directed the others to wait and be patient. The Abyssals were skittish and even the two distant Watchers could hear their periodic nervous croaks. It was as much a hunt for food as it was a proving ground. Lilith had watched them training with their newfound weapons and had actually been impressed. These Abyssals should be a small but instructive challenge. The creatures' many curling horns would give the succubi something to consider.

It was a simple thing. Liimah would startle the herd and in its pell-mell attempts to rush away it would fall into the waiting blades of the hidden succubi. Lilith had seen this ancient tactic work countless times in both of her existences before and after the Fall.

Liimah saw her fellow succubi settle into position and then turned back to watch the herd. A large, old Abyssal tore at the fleshy ground with his paw near her, oblivious to the threat, the fiery lights upon his scarred flanks etching his silhouette against the dark ground. Liimah kept her eye on him and when he had turned and ambled in the opposite direction she stood up suddenly and began to call out, her high-pitched ululating piercing the air.

The old Abyssal paused and bugled a warning to his herd-mates. Then, instead of racing away with the frightened herd, wheeled around and in a flash of blazing light came for Liimah. It took only a moment for the creature to cover the ground before he was upon the succubus. With a flick of his antlered head he lifted her into the air and tossed her high over his broad back.

Liimah landed squarely on the splayed antlers and Lilith winced. But luck was with the succubus. Undaunted, she twisted around, hacking furiously at the Abyssal's neck. Lilith counted seven blows and he was down on his knees, screaming, still fighting but spraying spattering fans of black blood. His end was quick.

Lilith shifted her gaze and saw the other succubi swiftly running after a pair of creatures that had separated from the herd. The Abyssals were driven into a steep crater from which they could not easily escape. The air was soon filled with the sounds of slaughter.

While each Abyssal had relatively little meat upon them the three creatures provided a grand meal for the party. The succubi were chattering, as they did, each describing some moment in the hunt with relish. Liimah, eyes glittering, occasionally rubbed her bruised ribs, mostly nodding along, her eyes more than occasionally darting to Lilith and Ardat for any signs of approval. She found none.

Lilith sat quietly, chewing a stringy bit of thigh-meat, looking at Zimiah shining clear and cool in the otherwise fire-streaked sky. It seemed an astral antagonist to Algol, a body that harried by its very existence the old red star in its journey across the dark sky. She asked herself the same question she had done a thousand times before: Was that his sign? And again, she found herself agreeing with the legend, that it seemed more than a coincidence that Zimiah had appeared immediately after he had Ascended. Just the sight of it brought back so many bittersweet memories.

She lowered her gaze, her eyes alighting upon the succubi, and nodded almost imperceptibly to herself.

It won't be hard to create a cult around him. All of the raw materials are there—his stoicism, his nobility, his enigmatic departure, and above all his aspirations. He has captured their imagination. This world has changed for the worse since his war. He could have never seen this coming. It is the right moment, the time for me to ask them to follow him—and me. To look to that star.

Lilith tossed the gnawed bone into a nearby pool of lava.

"Liimah, what is it you seek? From your life?"

Liimah blinked and stopped chewing, her expression suddenly serious. Ardat, who had been carving another chunk off the remaining Abyssal, turned and looked at her mistress. This question was not totally unexpected. They had been talking about this possibility off and on ever since they had left Adamantinarx.

"I want to survive here. I want to find a peaceful place for myself where I can . . . be myself. And not be used by anyone for their pleasure. Or anything else."

"That seems attainable. As long as you are far enough away from the souls. Peaceful coexistence does not seem like something they are about."

Liimah nodded.

"But what about your inner self? Is there nothing that you can imagine that might bring you more than just peace? A sense of . . . purpose, perhaps?"

Silence.

"It was the Ascended Sargatanas' wish that those worthy of redemption seek it."

"But I have done nothing that would warrant punishment. Save being born *here*. Why do I need redemption?"

Lilith cringed inwardly. She was right. The succubi, simple creatures that they were, had been used, had been a party to the evil that had been Dis, but had not overtly committed any punishable acts and certainly not any acts that might preclude them from redemption. If anything, they were to be pitied. Lilith did not like where she was going to have to take the conversation.

"Being created here, being a part of this place, is enough, Liimah," Lilith said plainly. "It is a dark stain upon your soul. But it need not be there for all eternity."

The other succubi gathered closer.

"There are still demons and, yes, now souls here whose designs are dark and whose souls are even darker. I would say, still the majority. They strive for chaos, for a Hell of ceaseless carnage. It is their way. It is why they are here. And, yet, it is their presence that gives us a way out, a way toward salvation."

Ardat sat down and offered up the chunks of Abyssal meat she had worked free.

"Sargatanas took up the sword in an effort to purge Hell. To start to cleanse and change it, and, in so doing, he showed that he was worthy of divine reconsideration. Against overwhelming odds, he succeeded. But his success was limited. He knew it could never be completed by him. He knew it was just the beginning."

"But we were never *of* his former world. Or of any of the fallen demons'. We cannot go *back* to someplace we have never before been!"

Lilith felt a pang in her chest. How many times had she said the same thing to him about herself? Would these naïve creatures have a better chance at the Above than she? And the answer made her bitterness rise up. For no matter what she did in Hell, the path was forever barred to her.

The same was probably true for them.

"It was his fervent belief that that path he opened would be open to all," Lilith said with all the earnestness she could muster. "Sargatanas told me that he envisioned a select group of demons . . . females all . . . a sisterhood that would be his missionaries here in Hell. He wanted his message spread."

Ardat's eyebrows arched fractionally as she heard this.

A feral smile brightened Liimah's face, her pointy teeth glistening.

"I would be a Sister of Sargatanas!"

She had named her own cult. There was more to this creature, Lilith saw, than a simple, mindless courtesan. She was a clever one.

Araamah, Dimmah, Kaasah, Mashtaah, and Asaakah, each one vehemently repeated the sentiment; each one bore the same wide-eyed, fervent expression. In a moment their lives had been given meaning. In a moment they had become acolytes. And in the same moment Lilith and Ardat had become something more. They were now priestesses in a cult dedicated to Sargatanas the Ascended.

It suited them both. They had suffered so much for simply existing. This would be a cult of retribution, a cult that expiated the sins of the souls and demons alike at the point of a sword. There were, Lilith reflected, so many who deserved that in Hell.

"There is a bend of the Acheron not too far from here. When our bellies are full we will make our way there."

They heard the river Acheron long before they smelled or saw it. Its distant, muffled cries reached for the party with thin, tentative fingers long before they could grasp their souls more firmly. Sheets of mist hung above the pale, viscous river, its thick curtains undulating like living things. As the party made their way toward it, the sting of the mist in concert with the mournful wailing brought a great sadness down upon them all. Lilith remembered that effect well. It was why most avoided the river, why, other than the once-great city of Adamantinarx, there were so few settlements along its banks. The sorrow it created was too deep. And only a leader steeped in his own sorrow for a lost world and life would choose it as a residence.

The succubi grew silent and all that could be heard was their soft footsteps on the moist tissue of the ground.

Lilith had thought long and hard about how to initiate the succubi. This would do well.

The riverbank dropped nearly vertically into the slowly flowing river below; the edge of the land looked etched and eaten away by the bitter waters. It had been a very long time since Lilith had seen the Acheron. The sad memory of her lord immersing himself in it was as vivid and shocking as when she had watched him. It had never left her and now, it would seem, it would take on a new meaning.

At the river's edge, with tears involuntarily streaming down her ivory face, Lilith stripped off her garments and embraced the Acheron.

Ardat, almost as willingly, did the same, watching her naked mistress wade farther into the river. The succubi, seemingly astonished, hesitated but then one by one unfastened and dropped their garments and tentatively walked into the sluggish currents until they were ankle-deep.

Lilith had to admit to herself that the sensation was very nearly unbearable. It was her heart that nearly burst from the torrent of sadness that filled it to overflow. Here was the collective misery, both immense and trivial, of every thinking species that had ever populated the world she had once inhabited. Here were the terrible losses, the victims of awful crimes, the casualties of wars beyond count, the neglected, the sick, the abandoned, the shamed, the regretful, the unloved—all of their tears joined and magnified.

They drowned her in their immeasurable sorrow.

She saw but did not see. Somewhere on the darkened fringe of her awareness she saw the others, now knee-deep, stopped and watching her. Eyes wide. Were they seeing her reaction? Was it their own?

Suddenly Ardat and the succubi and their initiation rite faded like dissipating smoke as a dolorous intoxication seeped into her mind.

She grew dizzy and faint and fell forward, the river enfolding her as she sank. The bitter waters entered and filled her, the voices in her head roaring. A deep blue began to suffuse her inner vision and she began to feel a strange sense of rushing forward while floating in place. She traveled like that, trapped in the thick water, for some time, the pain of the medium she barely moved in caressing her body with a thousand claws.

The blueness took some form. She saw a distant plateau hovering in cold space, indistinct in its full shape. From beneath the enormity of that timeless dream landscape she grew to understand that upon this plateau was a city—the tiny blue lights in the azure shadows glittered, casting a cool radiance from what she thought might be windows in countless small domiciles. But, too, tiny lights were flashing in her mind against the drone of voices and she could not be sure of anything she perceived.

Pain and Sorrow were her psychopomps casting Lilith upward, atop and over the plateau and into the blazing, frigid light, urging her forward, the odd, rounded ghosts of buildings passing beneath her by the thousands. A vast white mount, tiered by an Intent beyond her understanding, loomed ominously over the landscape, a shaft of purest light reaching from its peak into the blue Nothingness above. Incomprehensible. Cold.

The Above!

She saw ahead with greater clarity, jutting into the deep azure Void, a white tower, one among many, from which an elliptical balcony extended. Toward this tower she flew, her eyes unblinkingly fixed upon the balcony. And leaning on the parapet, she saw gazing into the emptiness a single lonely figure. Wings floating motionless, garbed in iridescent, nacreous armor, the language of his body was forlorn. He turned, his sad copper eyes meeting hers and widening, a look of surprise lighting his pale face. He began to smile and—

—hands grasped her roughly, clutching at her slick body, pulling her free of the viscous bosom of the Acheron. Lilith screamed. He had been right there! She knew he had seen her! And now these fools had ripped her from him!

She lay gasping for breath upon the river's shore, her eyes unblinking, staring up at the blue star. The succubi gathered around, attempting to get her to sit upright, but she batted them aside, the disappointment and sorrow making her blows harder than was necessary. As one they turned and slowly walked off, eventually sitting by the shore and casting furtive glances at her. Only Ardat had the sense to busy herself making cords from the Abyssals' tendons.

Lilith lay there for some time. The irony of the situation struck her. She had had confidence that the powers imbued in the waters of the Acheron would be transformative. She had been trying to create a bond between them all, to fashion the foundations of something much larger than these foolish creatures and their prattling admiration for Sargatanas, a demon with whom they had had no actual contact. Each was to have been a vessel to carry forth the spirit of his enlightenment. Instead, the river had chosen her to be the vessel. Perhaps that was fitting.

That star! It was the same cold azure of the Void above that tower. And Sargatanas. His demeanor had been disconsolate. Almost that of a prisoner. How much of that vision had been real? How much had been her wild imaginings? She gathered herself and sat up, head pounding, brow furrowed. Ardat came to her side to lend a hand as she got to her feet, but Lilith waved her away. The images lingered in her mind, not in small part due to the vapors of the river. They would haunt her every step as she made her way to Buer.

16

PYGON AZ

It was some time before Adramalik could speak again. His training—the Knights' special Art Protective—had staunched the pain of the vigorous clubbing by Ai Apaec's champion for quite some time. Until it had not.

Between blows, as if he were an outsider watching the torture, he had noticed odd things: the way the ornamental bones embedded in the headless giant's torso had rattled with each stroke, the dust clouds raised on the floor with each scuffling readjustment to better the blow, the cold sweat running in thin rivulets down his sides, the way the ropey tendons tightened on his improbably thick arms.

Perhaps the headless giant had known how long it would take to batter the demon's defenses away. Demospurcus' execution may have been informative. Maybe the giant had been instructed to keep beating him until he started to scream. Or stopped. Or maybe the mindless thing had simply been told to hit him until his huge arm grew weary. Without a head, he could not see the Glyphs of Protection that surrounded Adramalik's body, one by one, dissipate into ineffective embers.

No matter. The outcome was inevitable and the beating did stop. Adramalik's punishment for leaving Pygon Az without permission was complete. His voice long since gone from screaming, he had been deposited back into his domicile to curl up in a

corner and contemplate his immediate future. The Bearer of
the Knife, who had been present throughout the clubbing, turned
as he left the dark room.

"When Algol rises again . . . and it will do so shortly . . . you
will come and explain to your god why you were disobedient to
him. And perhaps he will spare your Knights. You had best be
persuasive. He is an angry god."

The pain in Adramalik's joints and ribs was like the gnawing of
some toothy Abyssal. He was convinced more than just his leg
bones and plates had been seriously damaged. He could no longer
open his right wing and hoped that it would mend on its own.
He was not optimistic. He regained himself enough to chant the
palliative spell from the Litany of the Arts Curative, but he made
disabling mistakes the first three times and grew furious with
himself as he limped miserably behind the Bearer. After he took
extra care with his enunciation, the spell finally took hold and
the demon stood a bit more erect, strode with a little more confidence. Not that he felt in any way in control. He had no idea
how the message he had been given to deliver would be received.
But he could guess.

Ai Apaec did not disappoint him in his wrath. As Adramalik
approached on all fours yet again he saw the Decapitator standing
squarely before his throne. In his huge hand he held Lucifex dangling by the head, his palm across his mouth and his fingers tight
around the Knight's skull. And with little effort, he squeezed the
writhing demon's head until it burst, brains flying and gore drib-
bling over his hand and down onto the dais. The ensuing ash cloud
settled slowly to the floor.

Adramalik dared to say nothing.

"I gave you asylum here, Adramalik. And you pissed on it. Why should I allow you and your companions to continue to thrive in my city?"

And so it began.

"My god," Adramalik whispered hoarsely, "it was out of my control. I was summoned by a force much greater than myself. An irresistible force. It pulled at me until I had to seek its origin."

The Decapitator crossed the blood channel in one quick stride and stood over the prostrate demon.

"What force?"

Adramalik swallowed hard.

"A god . . . a god native to this place, to Hell. He has many, many followers. And many names. For you, he chooses the name Abaddon."

"Abaddon," Ai Apaec rumbled, weighing the name upon his tongue.

The mounds of heads began murmuring the name as it had been spoken. The murmurs grew in intensity, filling the space with their echoes. Ai Apaec glared into the gloom and the vast chamber grew silent again.

"Yes, my god. And he wishes to hold council with you and your court. He has heard of your kingdom and your power and your wealth and wishes nothing more than to form an everlasting alliance with you and your subjects."

"Why? Why do I need *any* alliances when I am secure upon my throne here in Pygon Az?"

Again, Adramalik swallowed. "Because my god, if you do not ally yourself with him, you will find him to be an enemy worth fearing."

Ai Apaec roared in outrage.

Around him, the huge champion and the other headless body-guards rose to their feet.

"A *council*? To take the measure of me? To see if I am as powerful as he has heard? Adramalik, are you now his envoy, his creature that he can command to deliver his demands?"

"No, my god, I am nothing." And this Adramalik actually believed. "I am nothing more than a go-between, caught against my will between two gods. It brings me no joy to relate this message."

Ai Apaec paced and fumed, came very near kicking the demon who crouched before him.

"Can you send a message back to this Abaddon or must you return to him in person?"

"I can, my god. Your words will be heard just as you speak them." And that Adramalik now knew to be true, for he was sure that the God of the Second World was paying close attention to this exchange.

"Tell him, demon, that I would meet him halfway, at the Pit's edge. I will not descend into its bowels of his world and will not ask him to enter my city. This I will do at the setting of Algol."

"So soon?" the Bearer asked.

Ai Apaec turned on him and he flinched like some cornered Abyssal. "You cannot make the arrangements hastily?"

"Of course, my god . . . of course I can." But clearly, the Bearer was in doubt and knew what would befall him were he to fail.

Ai Apaec turned to Adramalik. "Send the message!"

"One thing, my god. Abaddon made a request that we bring my Knights along. He has never seen any demons other than myself and would like to set eyes upon them to enjoy the variety."

Ai Apaec looked down at the demon and Adramalik heard the deep-bellows intake of breath. Had his creativity gone too far? Had he, in an effort to free his Knights from Pygon Az, shown his hand? He waited for the blow, but it never came.

"Send the message, demon!"

Adramalik made a fine show of tracing fiery, complicated, and meaningless glyphs upon the floor, waving his hand and sending them speeding away, but he knew the message had already been received.

The winds slid through the black ice fields, whining and clawing at the hollowed formations of ice like a hungry beast. Overhead the sky was dark with heavy clouds lit red from above, churning and corkscrewing in constant movement; it all added to Adramalik's sense that everything was in motion. And out of his control.

The processional that wended its way through the black ice fields was slow and stately, befitting a god and lord of the realm. At the front were two dozen standard-bearers each holding aloft standards ornamented with short, flapping banners and ice-glazed heads arrayed in various patterns and surmounted by the Decapitator's personal symbol—the ubiquitous *tumi* blade. Adramalik's remaining Knights trudged alongside these standard-bearers, dazed by their own sudden release from incarceration, silently— perhaps resentfully—regarding Adramalik and undoubtedly wondering what game he was up to. Behind them rode the court officials, mounted on white-shelled, multi-legged Abyssals that seemed only half-tamed and barely appeared to be capable of staying in formation. The air was frequently rent by the snapping of the officials' whips and the hoarse whinnying of the protesting beasts.

Ai Apaec, dazzling in his gold-threaded Abyssal mantle and layers of golden finery, further encrusted in bone and gold jewelry, was carried in a massive gold sedan chair borne by twelve souls almost of a size to rival the redoubtable champion who strode arrogantly alongside. The Bearer of the Knife, less ostentatiously bedecked in dark robes festooned with silver plates and chains and crescents, walked stiffly on the ice with a staff made from a single stretched soul. His stride, Adramalik thought, was less arrogant than it had been, slowed perhaps by his tireless efforts to organize the elaborate expedition on such short notice. He was flanked by his underlings, each dressed in simple ceremonial garb but nonetheless exuding an air of studied, and to Adramalik's eyes ludicrous, self-importance.

Trailing far behind the important personages, winding through the wind-carved ice formations, stumbled a long line of souls, garbed not against the cold but for show in thin, gaudy robes pulled from Lucifuge's musty warehouses. None could have guessed that the souls normally never ventured outside of their dark, dank domiciles, let alone the wide ice world that lay outside the city's walled perimeter.

Adramalik, walking only a few paces from Ai Apaec, thought the procession not very dissimilar from those that had entered Dis from far and wide by the thousands over the eons. Like this one, most had had an air of cheap, forced regality, but this one was different in one way. Only he, his Knights, Ai Apaec, the Bearer, and twenty other officials had heads upon their shoulders. And this simple fact lent the entire march an air that made the demon shake his head in silent bemusement.

There were no encampments, no pauses to rest beast, demon, or soul, along the way to the Pit. The perilous trek through the mountains was endured silently and, notably, without complaint. When souls fell from icy ledges no one stopped to watch their twisting forms plummet, nor were those frequent losses even acknowledged. Ai Apaec sat upon his movable throne, a look dark and dangerous upon his scowling face. Adramalik felt his baleful eyes upon him, watching him intently as he sent glyphs forward, guiding the procession. The hatred was clear and it made the demon wary of his back.

Eventually, after a labored climb, the front of the column topped a low mountain and Adramalik saw the foothills of the carved mountains that he had been so careful flying over. This short mountain—a tall, craggy hill really—had the first of what would be many of the totems set upon it to warn travelers away from the region. Something about the discouraging spells it projected made Adramalik's stomach turn, and he understood the power that the totems held. But Ai Apaec seemed unaffected by them and with a clipped chop of his hand he waved the column on.

Adramalik watched as the fallen god grew more impatient and angrier with each mountain slowly negotiated. Ordering the column to halt for the first time, the god rose from his throne and stalked back among his subjects. Without any warning he moved among them, randomly grabbing them and tossing them off the mountain, rending others apart and crushing even more of them in a fit of displeasure. Adramalik watched as the god's rage ebbed, his anger sated by the violence. The demon had to admit that none of it was any worse than what he had witnessed at the hands of his former master, the Fly. His mood improved, Ai Apaec resumed his throne, and the column moved ahead again.

Finally, as Algol began its slow dip below the horizon and the gloom deepened, the ragged edge of the Pit was spied and the column picked up speed as it descended the last slope.

Adramalik peered into the growing shadows and saw a familiar shape. Once again, Abaddon's herald, Faraii, awaited them, his wiry form squatting a hundred paces from the yawning opening. He got to his feet as the party approached.

Ai Apaec raised a hand and the column halted. Whether it was the first whiff of foul air from the Pit or an overabundance of caution, the god determined that coming any closer was unnecessary. He rose from his throne and stepped down. The Bearer hurriedly moved aside, as the god made his way to Adramalik.

"I see no welcoming officials, no putative puissant god of the lower world upon his throne to greet me as an equal. Instead, I see . . . *that!*"

"Indeed, my god, I, too, am surprised at the lack of pomp and fanfare." Adramalik tried to sound earnest. In truth, he had had no idea what to expect. "This is as it was when I first came here. That creature and I have a passing knowledge of one another. Please allow me to confront him on this dreadful oversight and find out why you are not being shown the respect you are due."

"I will allow you to do as you ask, demon. But the Bearer of the Knife will be close by your side to witness your exchange."

"Of course, my god."

Adramalik broke ranks with the column and without turning to see if he was followed made his way past his puzzled Knights and on to the creature that was once Faraii.

As he drew closer, the creature extended a foreleg and bowed down almost gracefully, a gesture if not sincere, certainly disarming.

Adramalik heard the clinking of jewelry as the Bearer stopped a pace behind him.

"Adramalik, you are as good as your word," Faraii said, rising. "You have acted as go-between in a delicate situation. My god is pleased with you."

The Bearer snorted.

Adramalik said nothing but nodded appreciatively.

"And who is this?" Faraii indicated the Bearer with a short jerk of his head.

"He is called the Bearer of the Knife and is first among many in the exalted court of the Great God Ai Apaec."

"I see," Faraii said, his expressionless face taking the Bearer in. "And I see you brought your Knights along as I requested. Fewer than I recall."

"Yes, much has befallen us in our stay in Pygon Az. They were all too willing to make the journey and leave that city behind." Adramalik suppressed a grin as he heard the Bearer inhale sharply at that.

"It will be their last as Knights, Adramalik."

"What?"

"They are powerful. My god has decided in his profound wisdom and majesty to bestow captaincies upon them. They will be at the head of his glorious legions."

"*That* was never agreed upon, Faraii!"

"They are the final sacrifice, the final necessary offering to Lord Abaddon. *Your* offering and token of fealty. Be proud. It is an honor not lightly bestowed. *And* not able to be refused."

The Bearer snorted contemptuously.

"You see, Adramalik," he sneered, "the last shreds of your power and influence have finally fallen away."

The Faraii creature turned to the Bearer.

"As has yours," Faraii said, cocking his head as if listening to some distant sound. "It approaches."

The ground trembled.

"What does?" the Bearer asked.

"The end of this time."

A sound like the blaring of unthinkable numbers of horns issued from the bowels of the earth and the Pit, itself, glowed fiercely with a blinding, golden effulgence. The frozen ground around the

Pit bellied upward with a groan, causing the rocks underfoot to shudder violently and break apart. A sound like the bass rumble of thunder grew beneath them, growing in volume, and then the ground sagged downward.

Only the Faraii creature seemed unaffected by the massive tremor, standing on a patch of solid and immovable rock that floated serenely amidst the churning ground. Adramalik, flapping his broken wing furiously, clawed the air to stay upright. He turned and saw Ai Apaec, roaring, leaping from his overturned throne. His champion rushed forward, knocking the shocked retinue aside with his huge club, clearing a path for his god as they charged toward the Pit. The Knights, despite the chaos and disciplined as ever, saw the enraged god approaching and leaped aside while the headless champion bludgeoned anyone too slow or clumsy who blocked his god's progress. In an instant the standard-bearers at the column's head, steadfast and oblivious to the oncoming pair, were shattered and catapulted into the air.

Ai Apaec hurtled onward and, bellowing in rage, launched himself toward Adramalik and Faraii. Suddenly the Pit erupted, vomiting a steady stream skyward of dark Abaddim, their heads dark with flame and huge jaws agape, Abaddon's solitary black glyph hanging within the fire. They climbed over one another's backs in a frenzy to reach the open air, forming a huge mound of writhing bodies. Bony mandibles wide, screaming, they twisted in midair and descended upon the column. Ai Apaec's silent champion rose, a terrible mountain of flesh. His club hand flailed to and fro, smashing into the Abaddim and sending them flying, until it was grasped by three of the creatures and sheared off by their mandibles. The champion stumbled, black blood geysering from his wrist, caught and weighed down by numbers until he hit the ground with a tremendous thud. Adramalik saw him struggling even as his great body was torn apart.

Eight Abaddim caught Ai Apaec in their jaws and, before he could utter a word or incantation, scissored his giant body to pieces, the blood-spattering chunks of him tumbling around Adramalik. That creature that was Ai Apaec, himself, fell separately, heavily, and frantically tried to scuttle to cover, but he was snapped up by two Abaddim that tussled over him before bursting him in a spray of fluids.

Too late, the horrified Bearer grasped his chest and wrenched apart his rib cage, reached inside, and pulled a large, glyph-wreathed golden knife from within. He brandished it at the Faraii creature, which deftly sidestepped the Bearer's thrusts. Adramalik saw two arms suddenly appear that had been hidden from sight within the Faraii creature's torso. He reached out and, in an instant, the right hand elongated into a semblance of the black sword Adramalik so well remembered in Faraii's previous incarnation. This he used with familiar and blinding dexterity to rapier the Bearer through an eye, and before the spasming demon could fall to the ground two Abaddim swept him up and away toward the Pit. The Faraii creature turned, eyes alight, something like a ferocious grin on his features.

Adramalik crouched down into the settling rubble and cast his protective glyphs, but he was less than certain they could keep the creatures' mandibles away. And, yet, none came for him.

What have I unleashed? What have I done? He saw Faraii standing placidly, staring back at him as the Abaddim Horde streamed around and past. And he saw his Knights valiantly charging into the attacking whirlwind of dark, chitinous bodies only to be swiftly disarmed and lifted, struggling but unharmed, and spirited away and down into the lambent Pit. He shuddered involuntarily. He knew their fate to come and hoped, for his own sake, he would never encounter them again.

It was not long before the demons and souls of Pygon Az's court were no more. With snarls and roars, the Abaddim had consumed anything organic in their path, leaving behind the metal of ornaments and weapons and standards and a smudge of darkness in the air. Only Ai Apaec's smashed throne bore testimony to his former presence.

Adramalik watched the waves upon waves of Abaddim pouring forth from the Pit and saw how their powerful armored jaws begin to immediately tear at the frozen ground. The hard, icy flesh covering was no match for their mandibles and the incandescent saliva that spewed from their mouths and melted the very ground they moved over. Nothing would stop Abaddon's spawn. As the Horde moved away, consuming all the flesh in their path, they left behind a dark, heavy cloud over the landscape hanging low in the frigid air like a noxious cloak thrown over the world.

Abaddon's cloak. And, after the Abaddim had done their work, Adramalik thought, when finally the hot winds of change blew and the old god removed that cloak and Hell was once again revealed it would be a very different place.

Adramalik realized that he was trembling. He tried to put that down to the raw and frenzied energy he had been surrounded by as the Pit had disgorged its denizens. But deep within himself, he knew better.

17

THE WASTES

Mave and Cammi tumbled in the grass, laughing and throwing clods of earth at each other and laughing even harder. They were irrepressible red-headed balls of energy when they were like this and Boudica, her heart smiling, did nothing to interfere. Times were stressful and this was a wonderful respite from the worries of the events that seemed bent on fracturing her people's way of life. She sat on the moist sward, letting her restless mind wander over recent events. The invaders cared little for the deeply rooted customs of her tribe, let alone for their gods. Theirs was a world of things built of stone and taxes and military might. It was all becoming intolerable. And it was all coming to a head. Something was going to snap; Something was going to smear the sky with smoke and ash and the land with blood. She felt it coming—

She burst out laughing when her daughters catapulted themselves at her, knocking her over. They smelled like wet grass and clean sweat and sun-drenched hair—a wonderful scent. They tussled and laughed and—

The trembling ground woke her with a start, as it did the dozens of Salamandrines who rested beside her. It was moments before it subsided, before the hanging Abyssal-oil lamps stopped swinging and the wide-eyed young started breathing again.

Boudica rose hurriedly like the warriors around her and climbed out of the encampment to survey the land. Nothing. She peered far out into the murky distance and saw no mighty Abyssal herds that might have shaken the grounds and no advancing army from

Adamantinarx or Dis to threaten them. Only the briefest flickering of lightning flashing on one horizon and a high-altitude firestorm glowing in the clouds in the far distance caught her attention.

That as it was, it would be prudent, she thought, to break camp, and K'ah agreed. This they did with their usual quiet efficiency and it was a very short time before the Salamandrines were on the march.

K'ah pointed out the promontory long before Boudica's soul's eyes would have spotted it. Clouds nearly obscured the curving jut of rock that rose above the surrounding plain.

"There is a settlement there . . . more a single huge keep . . . called Dolcha Branapa in the tongue of the demons. It is supposedly a place of learning and records, or so I have heard. Souls can be found there as well as demons. They keep their histories there, copying them and sending those copies out to the cities. We've destroyed so many of their caravans going in and out of there."

"Why didn't you destroy the keep a long time ago?"

"It seemed inconsequential. Why would we care about the demons' history here?" he said. "But now, now with the demons still reeling from their war, we would erase the very memory of their existence from our lands."

Boudica's mind swirled around the word "records." Could this be where the Books of Gamigin lay, secreted far from the cities? She had to stay calm, to somehow persuade K'ah not to destroy everything he and his warriors found within those walls.

"And what are your plans regarding the place now?"

"My plan is to destroy everyone within its walls."

"But might it be useful for us to study what we find?"

"Study what?" K'ah turned his head jerkily to look at her.

"Our enemy. To understand him fully is to have the advantage over him. There could well be information there about the legions, their strengths. And weaknesses. We could force them to find this information for us." It was the best she could come up with.

The Salamandrine, his four eyes unblinking, regarded her and made a small whistling sound through his beak. K'ah agreed but not enthusiastically.

"You have taught us much about being more cautious, B'udik'k'ah. This is wise." And he added wryly, "We will be measured in our slaughter and destruction. And consult you before we break anything."

Boudica grinned. It was as close to humor as K'ah could come. She tried not to get her hopes up, tried not to fantasize that the answers to her daughters' whereabouts would be found within the walls of that keep. But it was impossible not to be hopeful. And that thought—hope finding its way into Hell—made the corner of her mouth go up.

The keep grew larger as they cautiously approached. There was no need to be quiet—the winds had picked up and howled, taking with them cinders from afar. Boudica was used to the steady, sometimes forceful patter of cinders against her back. It reminded her of something from her Life, but she could not quite remember what.

When the Salamandrine war party was a few hundred paces from the building Boudica and K'ah crawled up an escarpment that overlooked the keep. From that vantage point it was clear that there was not going to be any real fighting. Looking down into the settlement, Boudica could see that it was completely undefended, devoid of legionaries or even legionary-conjuring decurions just as K'ah had said. Boudica could easily see souls and demons carrying manuscripts, walking upon the keep's walls, oblivious to the threat that hunkered down yards away in the rocks outside the walls.

Boudica took in the place ever more astonished that it was still entirely intact from lack of attacks or the erosion of time. Surrounded by a thick wall, the buildings within, hewn from the living stone of Hell, descended into the heart of the promontory in a corkscrewing spiral. She imagined the oldest texts deep down at the base of that spiral—it was only logical that the scholars would have some chronological system for their archives—but she had no evidence that was the case. That would be remedied presently. Apparently, the scholars who lived within its stone walls took excellent care, repairing any damage caused by wind, firestorms, or the buildup of ash and cinders. The place was immaculate. And the archiorganic buildings—a disturbing anachronism after the post-war freeing of souls—were of an older type not unlike the more ancient buildings of Adamantinarx that she had reworked in her former days on the work-gangs. Again, she imagined that the soul bricks were still in place not out of demonic stubbornness or contrariness but by dint of the remoteness of this outpost.

The pair scuttled back down to the waiting warriors and K'ah gave Boudica a crisp nod. The Salamandrine's deference to her was now fully accepted within the ranks of the warriors. The strange soul whose fierce hatred of their eternal foe, proved by the mountain of demon rubble and remains she had left behind, was their war-band leader and they followed her without hesitation. She gave the silent signal for swords to be drawn. A hundred Salamandrine hands were filled and without another order the war party began to filter down through the rocks toward the walls of Dolcha Branapa.

Grapple-hooks were tossed and the Salamandrines easily scaled the wall, dropping onto the wall's wide upper platform. Any unfortunate enough to be caught there were quickly killed whether they were demon scholars or soul assistants. And then began a methodical descent, filled with blood and the cries of the unarmed scholars. Boudica was not entirely at peace with this. Two factors seemed at play. She knew that no one here was directly responsible for any of the calamitous events that had preordained hers and all the other souls' fates in Hell. And yet she saw them as the functionaries in a much larger scheme. In fact, she rationalized, the notion that they were so unaware of the massive changes that had occurred in Hell made her feel a cold resentment, which easily turned to indifference for their fate. Why had the word not gone out to every one of the five corners of Hell that souls should be freed? Or had these far-distant outposts chosen to turn a blind eye to the mandate? At one point, resting from the slaughter, she glanced at the wall she was leaning upon and her eyes met a solitary green eye staring back at her. The fear in it was real. She felt a welling up, a combination of anger and deep sadness that surprised her and redoubled her resolve to purge the place of its demons. Bureaucrats or not, this keep was a symbol of the oppressive regime that had tormented her for millennia.

She caught up to K'ah, who was leading the warriors ever deeper into the funnel of ancient buildings. As they descended the long steps that led deeper into the sanctuary Boudica saw some of the Salamandrines split off and head into the curved buildings.

"I need to search these rooms, K'ah. You know what I'm seeking."

"Your daughters. The Books, am I right?"

"Yes, the Books. There is to be no torching of the buildings until I agree it's time."

"I have already given that order, B'udik'k'ah. I've told them that disobedience will result in banishment."

"Perfect." She knew what banishment meant to a Salamandrine.

Boudica spotted an entrance that seemed promising. Surmounting an archway and carved beautifully from native stone were what she took to be scrolls. She was completely unsure of what the Books of Gamigin looked like or what books of any kind looked like. For the thousandth time she regretted not asking Eligor. She had asked K'ah, but he was equally ignorant. Were they the rolled scrolls or the things she had seen scholars carrying— flattened leaves caught between covering boards? Were those books? What exactly would demons have written upon? All of these thoughts made her task all the more difficult. She was searching for something that she could not even describe.

She entered the gloomy antechamber and saw cases that held objects in rows. From her lowly position as a brick she had seen demons writing or tabulating things on scrolls, using objects like the ones on the shelves. They were writing implements. Next to them were wells that contained dark red liquid. Blood? Perhaps.

She went farther inside, the screams of the scholars diminishing, and saw row after row of seats at small desks and beyond that, disappearing into what was essentially a beautifully wrought cave, were larger shelves holding scrolls beyond count. She stopped and sighed, her mouth slightly agape. This was just one of the dozens of buildings that lined the funnel of Dolcha Branapa.

The black candles were still lit on the small desks and she took one and wandered back into the silent stacks. A small tear quivered on her lower lid. It was an impossible task. And she had been a fool to think that she could find them amidst the souls who had gathered for millennia in Hell.

She threw the candle down and then remembered her admonishment to K'ah. No torching. But oh, did she yearn to rid Hell of its history.

Back out on the wide spiral stairs she caught up to K'ah. Bodies of souls and demons alike littered the featureless rock steps, some still clutching their scrolls.

"Did you find anything?" he asked with genuine concern.

"Frustration and anger."

"The warriors are feeling the same. They are eyeing the candles with intent."

"I'm not sure there is much point to searching here anymore, K'ah. I feel drained."

"Shall we set the place ablaze, then?" His eagerness was unmistakable.

"Not yet. I want to descend to the very bottom of the well."

"So be it."

The pair negotiated the ever-tightening spiral steps until the buildings gave way to a smooth cylinder at the base of the funnel. The floor of the circular space was thirty paces across and completely without decoration. It was flagstoned in natural rock.

Boudica looked around the drum-shaped space and then back up at the sky. She felt a heaviness born of despair. All these many risings and settings of Algol, all of the raiding parties crisscrossing the Wastes without even a trace of information as to the Books' whereabouts. And this, the most promising of locations yet—another deadening disappointment.

She stamped her foot, angry with herself for her failure. Almost immediately she and the Salamandrine heard a faint whispering. The round space, barren of doors and windows, gave no clue as to the source of the sound. They separated, putting their ears to the cold stone of the wall.

"Could it be coming from above?" she asked K'ah.

"You know how thorough our warriors are. They heard nothing like this."

"It sounds like a crowd."

But after a few moments of fruitless searching the whisperings died away.

K'ah shook his head slowly. Boudica frowned and stamped her foot again and, as before, the whisperings began anew.

Still frowning, she bent down and rapped on a flagstone with her sword hilt.

"It sounds hollow. There is something or someone beneath us. In a room, perhaps. Hiding."

K'ah whistled and a dozen Salamandrines appeared overhead. They ran down and surrounded Boudica, looking inquisitively, where she pointed at the ground.

"The floor. Pull up one of the stones."

The Salamandrines set to work, jamming their grapple-hooks into the spaces between the flagstones to pry up one of the heavy stones. Boudica dropped to a knee and peered into the darkness below. As she did, the whispers grew in intensity.

"I can't understand a thing they are saying! And, I can't see a thing. Dr'a'ak, get some candles from above. Let's see what we are getting into before we release them."

The young warrior nodded and raced away, climbing the steps four at a time in her haste to accommodate her leader. Boudica and K'ah exchanged looks. They both looked down at the floor.

"More scholars for us to skewer, I'd wager."

K'ah clacked his tongue softly in affirmation.

Dr'a'ak reappeared, bounding down the steps with an armload of thick, still-lit candles.

Boudica took a candle and held it down toward the opening.

"It looks as if the floor is not too far down! *You* might even be able to touch it, K'ah."

K'ah moved into position and reached down.

The whispers were loud now, loud enough to be understood were it not for the confused number of whisperers.

"I can feel something, but I can't actually grab on to it."

Boudica took a deep breath. "Pull up the floor!"

The Salamandrines set to work, and with the fifth flagstone yanked up Boudica's eyes widened. Arranged in the recess were at least a hundred large bound volumes set side by side so that their spines were facing up. Though she could not read it, she easily recognized the demonic script. She could see that the Books of Gamigin—for surely these were the treasured Books—had been well hidden and had she not woken them no one would have been the wiser. It was a stroke of fantastic luck!

"The face that you are making with your lips? What does it mean?" K'ah asked, genuinely concerned.

"It means that I am pleased."

She reached down and pulled a huge, oversized volume from the collection. As she opened it and ran her fingers down the names inscribed on the first soul-vellum page a hundred different voices rang out, each one coaxed forth when her fingertip brushed the ink. Again, she smiled. These were her people. And, while she did not love them and knew full well why they were memorialized in the Books, she felt a kinship to all of them. So odd, she thought, and unexpected. For an odd moment, she realized her own name was in one of the Books and wondered what it would say if she touched it.

"Did you leave anyone alive up there?"

"Perhaps."

"We . . . I . . . need someone to help me read these."

K'ah looked up and, without asking, the warriors headed back up the steps.

"And, K'ah, I am sorry, but there will be no burnings. We need to remain here for a bit."

The Salamandrine clacked his tongue.

They had arrived at Dolcha Branapa when Algol was low on the horizon. Now it was climbing into the fiery sky once again and the Salamandrines were uncomfortably ensconced in their stony encampment. Their surroundings could not have been further from their accustomed outdoor camps. As one, they found the confinement and odors of the demons and souls to be unappealing, and rumor had it that they were restlessly contemplating leaving the sanctuary and camping up on the walls or, better yet, the open plain. But K'ah kept them patient and they had gotten used to the routine into which Boudica fell. She would retire alone to one of the lower buildings and sleep deeply—something they could not entirely understand, as parts of their brains were always awake—and then upon rising she would call the five surviving demons to her side and they would descend to the Books.

With the promise that none of them would be harmed, the demons sullenly set about going page by page through the many Books. It was exhausting work and Boudica drove them to stay with it for far longer than they were comfortable. For her part she sat, sword across her lap, watching and waiting. But after many sessions even she grew bored. Eventually, she asked K'ah to watch them and then climbed the long steps and ventured onto the surrounding wall. It became a habit, her way of distracting herself from the anxiety of the search. Whether it was on K'ah's orders or simply their own common sense, the Salamandrines knew to leave her to herself.

Time dragged on. And perused volumes were put aside as new ones were taken up.

When Algol was directly overhead she once again left the demons to their murmuring Books and ascended to the open air. She stepped out onto the wall's platform and was shocked to find eight female demons staring at her. Their weapons were drawn and the light in their eyes was anything but friendly.

Boudica thought to call for the Salamandrines below, but even their fearsome speed would not be enough to save her. Instead, she chose to look the apparent leader squarely in the eyes. She was a fierce-looking pure-white demon with bird feet, clad in white skins and carrying an enormous sword. She exuded an unmistakable air of lethality.

"What are you doing here alone, soul? Dressed and armed as a Salamandrine?" the white demon demanded. Her eyes were piercing red and unblinking and she towered nearly twice her own height. Boudica, remembering well her trembling confrontation with another demon so long ago, fought to conceal her fear.

Those feet! Her hand unconsciously reached for the necklace she wore. She could feel its comforting shape under her skins.

"I am *not* alone. Below is a war party of Salamandrines who can be by my side before you could climb the wall to escape."

"There is no need for that, soul. We are simply passing through. And we have no grievance with the Men of Wrath."

Boudica nodded. The white demon's tone was neutral.

"The same cannot be said for them."

"Not all demons feel that the Salamandrines are inferior, to be destroyed for sport. Some actually believe this place is theirs."

"My Salamandrines are less equivocal."

"Yours?"

"In spirit only. They are no one's pawns. I lead them where they would go without me. And you, what are you doing out here?"

The white demon glanced from side to side at her compatriots.

"We are ridding Hell of its . . . undesirables."

Boudica almost laughed.

"Souls, in particular," the white demon added dryly.

"Not all souls are undesirables. Some would simply like to be left alone."

"And those we leave in peace. But after we get what we came here for. I seek someone and the demons here know where she is."

Boudica considered this. These female demons did not seem a threat. Despite her bold statement, they could have easily dispatched her. What was the harm in letting them wander the empty buildings?

"I, too, came here looking for people . . . my two daughters." She hesitated. K'ah would not be happy sharing this space with demons, no matter how benign they seemed. "I will have to discuss this with them," she said, nodding down toward the Salamandrines.

"Of course. We do not seek anything but information."

"That will not impress them. They were eager to rid *this* place of *its* undesirables. Also, I have enlisted the demons that we allowed to live. You will have to search the scrolls for yourselves."

The white demon's eyes remained unblinking.

"Tell them we will stay out of your way."

It took much convincing on Boudica's part to dissuade the restless Salamandrines from breaking up the monotony with the shed blood of the female demons. But she managed it and K'ah respected her wishes enough to threaten his own harsh punishments if any warrior was disobedient.

Despite her near certainty of the white demon's identity, Boudica was not sure why she was so easily swayed to grant permission to the demons. What difference was it to her if they found the information they sought or not? Perhaps her own frustration, her own seemingly endless search, was what made her more agreeable. And, perhaps, too, it was the undeniable charisma of the white demon that had worked upon her. She raised an eyebrow at that thought.

As they continued to wait while the demon scholars turned ancient page after page, she and the Salamandrines saw little of the eight demons. If she did pass them on her frequent climb to the wall, Boudica only saw fleeting glimpses of the female demons methodically moving from one gloomy chamber to another, searching for the elusive scroll that they sought. Seeing their determination, she wished, deep inside, that she could enlist their aid in her own quest but knew that was a fantasy.

Time passed slowly. Algol began to sink toward the horizon when, as the soul peered out into the Wastes, the demon and her succubi joined her on the roof. A faint smile played upon the white demon's lips and Boudica, envious, knew what that meant.

"We are finished here."

"You are. I am not."

"There was a time I might have offered to help you . . . a time when I felt pity for souls. That time has passed. I have seen too much of the changes wrought in souls since the war and it sickens me. Despite that, there is one that I have to help. He suffers because of me."

Again, Boudica was surprised. What kind of demon was this?

"What is your name?"

"Lilith."

She tried to conceal her admiration and thought to reveal the necklace but decided against it. It might convey the wrong idea. She worshipped no being. Not anymore. But, still, the power of this female demon's message had gotten her through many trials.

"Boudica."

"Well, Boudica, I wish you good fortune in your search."

Boudica nodded. Memories of what she had heard about this demon came flooding back. Lilith! The First Consort to Beelzebub. The White Mistress! The legend standing before her! She shook her head. The war had, indeed, changed everything.

The band of demons turned and walked to the wall where their grapple still held firm. Boudica watched as, one by one and without a look back at her, they grasped the rope, swung over the wall, and disappeared. Lilith turned and regarded Boudica. She bowed her horned head, clambered over the parapet, and dropped out of sight.

As their pale forms vanished into the gloomy landscape Boudica knew one thing. Lilith was not someone she could soon forget.

18

THE WASTES

The familiar sat looking at its mistress, its head rotated quizzically so that its hollow eye sockets were one atop another, and Lilith smirked wryly. It seemed none the worse for wear, having been stuffed into her satchel. Her carving tools had made soft indentations into its wrinkled skin and wings and she spent a few moments smoothing the thin, pale flesh.

The Dolcha Branapa demons' record keeping had been, predictably, meticulous. It seemed, Lilith thought, that when demons were tasked with bureaucratic efficiency they could be nearly flawless in their attention to detail. She fondly remembered the wonderfully organized Library in Adamantinarx and its fastidious and fussy lord of detail, the head Librarian, Eintsaras. For millennia she had frequented the Library to learn more about the Fall, the souls and their role in the Fall, and demons whom she met up with in Sargatanas' capital. Eintsaras had been a brilliant guide through his dusty kingdom. Now he was gone. Like her lord, he had perished in the last days of the Rebellion. And while the loss was nowhere near as significant, it was great.

That female soul, Boudica, had caught her attention. She was clearly an exceptional being, driven and fierce, and self-possessed. She reminded her in many ways of Hannibal before his fall. She wondered if the demons of Dolcha Branapa would find her daughters. It had been easy to corner one of them, when Boudica was not watching, and ask him the nature of her quest. The demon had been all too eager to talk to her, hoping, she was sure, that she could free him from the forced labor of winnowing through the thousands upon thousands of pages of the Books. That was not to be. Lilith truly did not care about this former functionary in the Fly's bureaucracy. When that became clear, he had grown less communicative and Lilith had had to resort to other, more persuasive means. And so, eventually, he had told her what he knew and she had walked away leaving him angry, sputtering. What the Salamadrines did to him once they were done with him, she thought without remorse, was their business.

She wrinkled her brow, thinking hard about Boudica's quest and her devotion to her daughters. This imperative was something she had seen before her fall, something she had witnessed in nearly every mother she had riven of daughter or son. It was a fierce thing, a thing as powerful as her own drive had been for revenge. She had not fathomed it then and only now, finding it in Hell, did she truly grasp what it meant. She had taken away those mothers' hearts and left them gutted and hollow. And she had shattered women by the thousands. It shamed her. She closed her eyes and tried to imagine the grief, the heartache, she had created. Now, here in Hell, it had all come back to haunt her. Justification for her presence in this place. Boudica's love, almost animal powerful, transcended time and place and not even the horrors of Hell could erase it. That was something to respect, to be in awe of.

She understood the power of devotion. It touched her. She had felt a surge of love and meaningfulness with Sargatanas and had treasured every moment with him. Now, when her guard was down and she remembered, his loss still sent a pang stabbing into her heart. She could only imagine the pull of the maternal yearning to be there for one's daughters that drove Boudica relentlessly across the infernal Wasteland.

Lilith sighed heavily. She had lost touch with those things that had once made her the champion of Hell's souls. Certainly guilt had been a factor, but human resilience and the better human emotions had been attractive to her. This soul on her virtually hopeless quest reminded her of those qualities. How she could move forward in this new world of chaos and conflicted feelings she could not say. Lilith guessed she would simply take the souls as they came and try hard not to judge them all by their vilest representatives.

And, in time, perhaps she could become their advocate and champion again. But not yet.

She stroked the familiar's round head and spread its triangular wings remembering how it had flown all the way from Dis to Adamantinarx to tell that city's lord of her plight. It must have been a hard flight—its white skin was ember pitted and scorched from the journey. This task had no such urgency and she was confident the familiar would have no trouble keeping a discrete eye on the extraordinary soul during her journey.

Lilith picked up a small chisel from her kit and poked her finger. She let a trickle of black blood dribble down into her palm and then dipped her nail into it and, with it, wrote a glyph upon the maquette's body.

"Go, Ukuku, go and follow her. Watch her. And show me her progress."

She was, for some reason, yet obscure to her, unwilling to reveal what she had learned at Dolcha Branapa. Was she so bitter toward the souls that even this act of kindness was beyond her? Perhaps. While she could feel pity and respect and even admiration for the soul, she could not reach out to help her. Not yet. She would have the soul watched and find the right time to tell her what she knew of her daughters. For now, she had other, more pressing issues at hand.

Again, she dipped into the blood and drew the glyph onto the little winged thing. It leaped into the air, circling briefly on rapidly flapping wings. Lilith saw it find its target—back toward Dolcha Branapa—and she watched its pale form grow tiny and disappear into the distance.

Lilith put her tools away, rose, and roused Ardat and the slumbering succubi. Wrapped in sleepy embraces around their weapons, they were barely recognizable since she had first encountered them. Armed and armored and clad now in white Abyssal hides, they looked potent and even a little dangerous despite the yawning and stretching.

She smiled faintly. Her Sisters of Sargatanas. What could she make of them?

A newfound sense of urgency permeated her every move now. The library of Dolcha Branapa had provided her with the last bit of arcane guidance necessary to find Buer. The old spellcaster had certainly found the most out-of-the-way spot to dwell, well past the last settlements and in the shadow of the foreboding Watchtowers that bounded in the known world of Hell. It was still a long way off and it was impossible for her, for the thousandth time, not to wonder how the thing that was Hannibal fared.

Even as that thought crossed her mind she discerned roughly two dozen spots, growing larger with every moment, approaching in the flame-washed sky.

"Weapons out!" She pulled her huge sword from its sheath and stood pointing it skyward. She was pleased to see her companions moving swiftly, forming a circle as they took in the aerial nature of the enemies that were nearly upon them. They looked to Lilith, wide eyed, for further orders but were shocked when she suddenly dropped her guard and smiled.

"Lord Eligor!" she hailed as the red demon dropped from the sky. He knelt, folding his wings and bowing his head.

"My lady! I am pleased to find you well."

Lilith looked at the demon's face and saw a darkness there she had never seen before. Something was very wrong.

"I am well. As are my companions. I see you did not travel alone. A Guard Flight? Is Adamantinarx at war?"

"Not just yet, my lady. But the city . . . what is left of it . . . is in great peril. Lord Satanachia had Agaliarept—"

"Agaliarept?" Lilith's lip curled, remembering Beelzebub's unfathomable Conjurer. "*That* nightmare?"

"Yes, Satanachia thought it best to spare the thing. It has its uses. Such as locating you in this forsaken land. As I was saying, Satanachia is throwing every possible measure into defensive walls and battlements."

Lilith knit her brows. "Who is threatening the city? Surely no demon lords are left with the power to cause Adamantinarx any great harm."

"No. You are quite right. It is not a who, exactly. Something has been unleashed, something that imperils every living thing in Hell. We first heard about this from panicked traders who fled into the city babbling about legions of 'Eaters.' At first, Satanachia did not put much stock in the stories. Much is not right about Hell and much is cause for endless dark speculation and consternation. You know this. But this is different. Too many traders and travelers were coming in with the same tale. Flying scouts were sent out to the four corners of Hell and returned with reports of a massing of creatures, a vast army of . . . things unlike any demon, Salamandrine or Abyssal. Of creatures that split and split again and multiplied as they consumed everything before them. And they told of something else leading them. A true Abomination. Eventually, whispers from the Salamandrines came to our ears. *Abaddon.* And that is what *we* have whispered about since we learned of it. *They* say it is the coming forth, foretold in their legends, the Coming of Dark-fire. They have a sacred legend cycle that speaks of it . . . How Dark-fire Spirit Returns the Lands. It is an apocalyptic tale meant to give them hope, meant to end with them returned to their rightful place as lords of their land." He paused. "Tellingly, it originated when we Fell."

Lilith was silent.

"And that is not all. There is a demon with the creatures. We do not know who, but he is powerful. And feared."

Eligor let his words sink in.

"We need you back in Adamantinarx, my lady. We need every possible warrior to combat this threat." Eligor paused. "And we need the souls to take up arms."

"The souls. Again, we have to rely upon them. Except now there is no Hannibal. No leader to bring them together."

"That would be you."

Lilith frowned. "Perhaps. My opinion of the souls has changed since the fall of Dis. How long before the city is besieged?"

"Perhaps six risings of Algol. No more."

"I am bound to find Buer. You know that."

"I do. And I know, too, that Hannibal does not improve with each setting of Algol. My Guard, in what used to be Dis, brings me tales of madness. That as it may be, Adamantinarx needs you more. And that is why I am here with a full Flight. I had no idea how many of you there would be. They will carry you and your party to Buer to speed your journey along. Once you have what you seek we will carry you back to Adamantinarx. We cannot waste any time, my lady. Do you know of Buer's whereabouts?"

"I think I do. Buer is in the Margins among the Eastern Watchtowers. Supposedly in a straight line toward setting Algol. I hope."

"Then we have no time to waste, my lady."

Lilith nodded and turned to Ardat. "Tell them to bring only their weapons. We need to leave everything else behind for the sake of speed and lightness. We leave straightaway."

As they watched the Sisters pile their belongings Lilith turned back to Eligor. He had grown in so many ways since Sargatanas' Ascension. A Demon Major now, Elevated for his heroic service to Sargatanas by his new Lord Satanachia, he carried himself with more authority. And more gravity.

"I came across a rather unusual soul recently, Eligor. Very impressive. Commanding even. She was with a rough band of Salamandrines. Remarkably, she seemed to be their leader."

Eligor cocked his head.

"Really."

"Yes, she was searching for her daughters. She and her warrior-band had overpowered the sanctuary at Dolcha Branapa with hopes of finding out their whereabouts. It was . . . touching. The deep yearning she felt for them . . . What?"

The demon was staring at her, mouth slightly agape.

"Did she carry a straight sword? A sword both beautiful and made for a soul?"

"Yes, that and one made for Salamandrines. You know this soul?"

Eligor smiled. "Oh yes, *that* one I know. Let me tell you about her."

Eligor's steady wingbeats lulled Lilith into a state of calm she had rarely ever felt in Hell. He cradled her in his arms gently, protectively, and she peered below at the infernal landscape as it slid beneath them. And, strangely, she found beauty in it.

The dark terrain was alternately cracked and folded into intricate and unexpected patterns, some of which seemed to echo the very glyphs the demons created. Over many hours the twisted ground gave way to vast plains ribboned with incandescent snakes of lava that stretched as far as the eye could see, and farther on steam rose in places suffusing the ground in a gentle, lambent orange lending the inferno a dreamlike delicacy belying its true and fierce nature.

They flew through the tattered veil of clouds, over a seemingly endless charred landscape.

Remarkably, for the Margins were notorious for their winds, the air was warm and calm and Lilith found herself drifting, her lids heavy, her limbs loose. She fell asleep to the rhythmic whooshing of Eligor's long wings. And, not for the first time, she dreamt of Sargatanas in his tower, the coldness of the scene, the look in his cupric eyes tugging at her heart.

It was Eligor's soft voice that wakened her. "My lady, the Eastern Watchtowers."

"How long have we been aloft?"

"Long enough, given these winds."

Yawning, she peered into the dense, sulfurous air and saw the immense silhouettes of the fabled Watchtowers. She had known of their existence, of the fact that all five of the far-flung Margins owned their own towers to guard against whatever might lie beyond. Few in the cities had ever laid eyes upon them, so distant were they from Hell's populated centers, and descriptions of them were unreliable. She knew, too, that they marked the edge of the known world. Beyond lay only the darkness into which no demon had ever ventured. Or so Lilith had heard. All of the tales had seemed like nonsense to her. How could there really be an "edge of the world"? And yet, at this distant point, so far from Adamantinarx and Dis, it didn't seem so unrealistic.

She looked down and saw sharp-edged lines of lava converging at and disappearing under the towers' bases. Why? Did the archiorganic buildings need the lava to sustain themselves? Who had fashioned these runnels? Unknown demons eons ago? She shook her head to clear it. What did it matter?

The towers stretched in both directions, fading away into the sulfurous miasma.

"So many of them, my lady. Do we know which one is Buer's?"

"It will be the only one guarded by Beasts. Or so the scrolls said. Find the Beasts and you will find Buer."

"Beasts. I thought they had been hunted away."

"Not out here, apparently."

Eligor took them closer to the towers. They were huge piles of barely designed architecture and huge organs crackling from within with a force that made the air surrounding them vibrate and shimmer. As they drew nearer, Lilith's skin tingled faintly, a sensation that at first annoyed her but eventually grew endurable.

The base of each stack was composed of countless rough organic cubes sparsely perforated by what looked like windows and doorways and tailored for flying demons. None appeared at the point where the base met the ground for fear, Lilith suspected, of unwanted intruders.

As her eye wandered upward, she saw that the cubes diminished and gave way to huge, flat slabs of flesh that formed vague cones, each surmounted by two giant tooth-lined jaws. And set within each of these was a monstrous glassy and lidless eye. As these were facing inward, toward Hell's center, Lilith imagined that another eye, equally expressionless, must be facing outward toward the unknown on each of the towers. She was vindicated in this when Eligor took the Flight through the colossal structures and she caught a glimpse of their far sides.

"Are they Abyssals, Eligor?"

"Yes. From what I have read in the earliest texts, they were found in this vertical position, their bodies mostly buried. These creatures are a colony that surrounds Hell. There is nothing like them within its confines. They seem immortal. The ancient architects . . . Mulciber and his lot . . . simply built around them, encrusting them with their buildings. They thought to establish a vast settlement here. Imagine that." He paused. "It did not work out well."

"So odd," she mused. "Wait . . . there! Did you see that?"

Instead of answering, Eligor stooped and dove, and Lilith could not help but smile as the wind whistled over his wings. *The sheer power he has at his command!*

The Flight was right behind them, diving in concert with their leader.

She focused ahead and saw a great, dark leg as it disappeared behind a Watchtower, dust kicked up by it, obscuring its path.

Eligor banked steeply around the tower and came suddenly face to face with the Beast as it turned, mouth agape, to confront him.

It was the largest Abyssal Lilith had ever seen. Black, horned, and glowing with searing lines of fire, it reared up on its hind legs and swiped at Eligor, missing only because the demon rose up and over the creature with practiced, fluid confidence. Never missing a wingbeat, he arced back toward the Beast to make sure his Flight had not been knocked from the sky.

"I guess we found Buer," Lilith said wryly.

Eligor grinned.

The Beast twisted and again clawed at empty air. The demons

were too seasoned from countless battles to be so easily overcome. Or so Lilith thought.

In a snarling fury, the Abyssal spun and crashed into the nearest tower, sending a cascade of debris into the air. A shower of bricks collided with the demon carrying Ardat and the pair were sent hurtling into the tower's side. As Eligor came around, Lilith, stricken, saw them lying motionless on a shattered terrace. Ardat's side was crushed and bleeding.

A piercing whistle filled the air and a wave of glyphs poured from one of the darkened cells on the same side of the tower that Ardat and the demon lay. Lilith watched the glyphs circle the Abyssal and weave around its body. The Beast's reaction was immediate. No longer enraged, it slunk off and lay down some distance from them. Another creature, only slightly smaller, joined it and began grooming it. Both kept their dark faces turned toward them as the whistling died away.

Moments later, a wiry figure emerged from within the tower and descended the rubble to the broken terrace. It knelt down to inspect Ardat and her crushed side. Eligor open his wings and coasted down, landing a short distance from the three figures.

Lilith leaped from Eligor's arms and ran toward Ardat. Glyphs cast by the wiry old demon were already touching the handmaiden. As Lilith knelt by Ardat the demon rose and hurried to the fallen flyer, but it was clear from his crushed face that there was one death from the encounter with the Beast. Eligor looked down, his face grim. He did not acknowledge the other demons as they landed with their succubi.

Tears trembled on Lilith's face as she kissed Ardat's lips. She stood shakily and regarded the demon.

"Buer, I presume? You are . . . female."

"Yes. To the first question. For now, to the second."

"Will she live?"

"Yes, but she may never be as she was. My glyphs can only do so much to mend her. Much inside of her is badly damaged. And much of it seemed to have been damaged before." The voice was as thin as the demon who wielded it.

"She has been through some terrible changes." This was not the time to explain Beelzebub's wrath.

"She will walk and talk as she did, but pain will be her constant companion for some time," Buer said gravely.

"For how long?"

"I cannot say. I am not boasting, but truly no other demon could do more for her."

Lilith's heart sank. Had she come all this way for Hannibal's salvation only to have her trust in this legendary demon's abilities immediately shaken? And, worse still, Ardat, poor Ardat, was awfully wounded.

Buer reached out and put a gnarled hand reassuringly on Lilith's shoulder. Lilith wondered if she could read her thoughts.

"You did not come all this way for naught."

Lilith closed her eyes for a moment, calming herself. Anger was just below the surface.

"Was that you . . . the whistle? The glyphs?"

Buer nodded. "My . . . guardians . . . they get overzealous in their protectiveness. I *am* sorry." She turned to the demon flyers. "Pick them up carefully and follow us."

The wizened demon turned and led the party into the tower. Eligor glared angrily at the distant Beasts and helped lift his fallen comrade. Lilith, fighting back her rage at the unpredictability of Hell, was the last to follow.

19

THE PLAINS OF DIS

It was all that he could have hoped for and more. Carnage, complete, and chaos, without end. Hell was falling to bloody shreds before his very eyes and he was there at the forefront of its destruction.

And his rewards were just as he had hoped for, as well.

I am, he thought, *perhaps the most fortunate demon in all of Hell. To have survived the downfall of the Fly and the madness of the Decapitator and, now, to be allied to Abaddon . . . it seems I truly can survive anything Hell has to offer.*

Not for a moment did Adramalik consider again the steep price he had paid for this latest alliance, nor did he allow any thoughts about his decision to sully his unbridled elation. While he had felt, at times, some camaraderie with them, his Knights had always been a fractious and dangerous lot and he had always had to look behind him to make sure his authority was complete and plots were not forming. In many ways he regarded his newfound freedom from them as a boon.

Now, before Adramalik lay a Hell ripe for the picking. And, better still, Abaddon's promises to him were being kept. Since the Abaddim had begun their devastating march across the landscape his place at the head of the Horde and at Abaddon's side had been assured.

Adramalik considered all of this for the hundredth time as the ragged front line of Abaddim approached the plains where Dis had once stood. This Horde was unlike anything any demon lord had ever created. Demons had been destroyed since the Fall many, many millennia past and Abaddon had been collecting them, biding his time, for all those long eons. They had not just surged up from the dreaded and stinking frozen Pit but also from hellmouths throughout the inferno. Faraii told him that his Knights had valiantly led the Abaddim from those many points of egress, leading the Horde on a path to eventually converge upon Adamantinarx, the final capital of Hell. Abaddon knew well that to break the demons it must remove Put Satanachia from his seat of power.

Mounted on a huge Abyssal that Abaddon had created just for him, he urged the great beast forward, fascinated by the Abyssal's many floating limbs, shifting fins, armored plates, and spines. Abaddon had been at his most creative conjuring this creature and, Adramalik knew, it spoke to his trust for his demon general that such a magnificent thing could have been fashioned just for him.

He surveyed the glass-smooth plain and shook his head slowly. There was nothing there. Only a handful of massive chunks of Keep, floating on conjured lightning, their crackling audible even from this distance. Where once had stood a city he had known as well as anyone could have done, a city whose twisted alleys and imperial avenues were as familiar as the wrinkles and veins and callouses on his hands, there was only a dark landscape riven by channels of lava. That, and the imposing tower of Moloch, its shattered shards floating high into the surging cloud banks. Put Satanachia's enormous personal glyphs guarded it, rotating slowly around its base. Of the Keep there was no sign. *It is incredible,* he thought, *that a demon-made mountain, the Keep, could have been be so thoroughly razed. As if a giant sword had simply scraped it into the lava.* He was sure Satanachia's sorcery had aided in its demolition. There was no other way. *And yet why had he left that tower? Moloch was, thankfully, no more. Perhaps as a marker of the battle that had been won? Or was it a reminder of his now-supreme power?*

Without the massive Keep and its mantles of flesh obscuring the base of the tower, he thought it looked more than ever like one of Moloch's awful Hooks. Even with as much time as had gone by his breath caught for a moment as he remembered those weapons.

He and the Horde drew nearer to the site of the destroyed city and he saw thousands of workers still slaving away at what little remained of Dis. Even the shallow grooves of the many thousands of foundations were to be erased. *Such hatred for the place! And such hubris that Hell would suddenly be transformed into a better place by the Heretic's vain gesture. Ascension, indeed! Pathetic mewling wishes of the weak-minded. He was a disgrace!*

But as the thought formed itself, Adramalik's eyes wandered up to the improbably blue star that hung over Dis' grave. And his eyes narrowed.

The demon swore and reassured himself by reveling in the vast army of Abaddim that surged around him. They were unstoppable. They had so rapidly carved away the surface of Hell that it had shocked him. Their advance had left behind a virtually unrecognizable Hell, smooth and black and covered in a pall of darkness. The waste of the Abaddim's voracious consumption of the mantle of flesh—Abaddon's cloak—hung low over the ground behind them. And somewhere in that seething, lightning-shot cloud, Abaddon himself followed, watching everything unfold just as he had, for so long, envisioned.

There was no denying Abaddon and his magic. It was not the refined magic, the various schools of Arts that Adramalik and other demons wielded that had their origins in the magic of the Above, but something strange and equally potent. A primal magic of creation that tapped into the spirit of things. The Lord of the Second World could re-form the ground they walked upon, level mountains, divert lava flows, but he could not singlehandedly rid Hell of its unwanted inhabitants. Why was this? Adramalik wondered. Could Abaddon only destroy through the act of creation, by adapting and re-creating the dead to do his killing for him? A god with paradoxical limitations? And while he had known his deepest thoughts, why had he not been able to see into the Heretic's mind? Or had he, and had he simply thought what he found there advanced his own plans? These were among the many ineffable questions about Abaddon for which he might never find answers.

As he looked about him, Adramalik shook his head at a not-unexpected result of Abaddon's rise. Intermingled with the Abaddim were war-bands of Salamandrines. While the very sight of them in their sooty Abyssal-hide garb turned his stomach and the memory of the countless successful hunts resulting in them piled high was easy to conjure, he grudgingly acknowledged their usefulness in scouting out the terrain ahead of the Horde. But oh, how he loathed them. They eyed him with the same revulsion and ferocity that he bestowed upon them. The ancient hatred went both ways. And he recognized that were it not for his elevated status among the Abaddim, they would surely have separated his head from his neck long ago.

The Salamandrines were allies now, uplifted, as he was, by their risen god. No matter his open hostility, Adramalik would not allow them to diminish his ecstasy in watching Hell be dismantled, one shred of flesh after another. Beelzebub had not appreciated his talents, Ai Apaec had treated him as a fool, and Abaddon—this bizarre god from below—had finally given him his due.

Adramalik raised his hand, cast a luminous command glyph into the sky, and spurred his mount. The creature bellowed in response and glided forward, its floating ebony spines fanning outward majestically. The demon, surrounded by jostling and chittering Abaddim, covered the ground rapidly and soon the first of the workers, demons and souls alike, were screaming, impaled on blood-slicked mandibles.

Adramalik carved away a few thousand of the Abaddim and maneuvered them toward the remaining fleeing workers, forcing them into a wide peninsula of rubble surrounded by what remained recognizable of Lucifer's Belt. Thousands of demons and souls suddenly found themselves with no avenue of escape and, satisfied, Adramalik halted the Horde. They might not understand the pleasure inherent in watching the workers' panic turn to the absolute certainty of destruction, but he certainly did. Again and again he wondered what the Abaddim remembered of their demonic lives. Perhaps somewhere deep in their chitinous skulls a shred of the demonic remained. It mattered not at all.

He moved his mount forward slowly. He wanted to see the workers' faces, their expressions, their eyes. And, best of all, hear their pleas. He was not disappointed. The chorus of entreaties was almost deafening. A thousand desperate voices, a thousand outstretched hands begging for clemency. It was all so satisfying . . . and arousing.

Adramalik slowly raised a hand, a gesture to calm them, to silence their fears, almost as if he were considering bestowing his mercy upon the herded workers. He smiled beneficently. And then dropped his hand sharply.

The Horde burst forward, past him, and he never once took his eyes from the slaughter that followed. The sheer press of the bodies and the frenzy of the Abaddim caused the workers at the back to spill into the lava and Adramalik, seeing this and enjoying it even more than the usual carnage, urged the Horde to push and butt the workers rather than carve into them. Whether they were whole or cut to pieces, the workers were toppled slowly into the bubbling lava. There, to the demon's profound pleasure, they would spend their eternities in incandescent agony.

"Come to me, Adramalik," intoned the voice of his new god in his skull, breaking his concentration on the delicious mayhem before him. Reluctantly, he turned his steed and headed back toward the lightning-riddled cloud. Thunder rolled from the sky and Adramalik grinned at the easy fear that must have induced in the superstitious Salamandrines.

He rode for some time through the Horde, noting how they did not pay him any attention, only moving aside as if he were a boulder rolling in their path. Somehow, Abaddon had conditioned them to obey him and never challenge him, and that made him feel prideful.

When he finally saw the looming form of Abaddon, now free of his quicksilver lake, he nodded, silently marveling, not for the first time, at the sheer size and strangeness of the being. He saw a throng of fifty or more high-ranking Salamandrines surrounding their god. The nomad chieftains, wearing their strange featureless masks and carrying carved staves, watched him approach through slitted eyeholes and he had to admit that they were intimidating. Covered from head to toe in Abyssal-hide robes, decked out in bone ornaments, and armed with their characteristic long swords, they appeared barbaric and ferocious. After watching them in battle, he had come to respect them despite his hatred. And, more important, he knew that with one dark word Abaddon could have him set upon by them and he would not last long. He knew he could never show them his true revulsion or, worse, any sign of weakness, and so he rode head up, eyes directly upon them and hand lightly on his sword hilt. That said, a defensive glyph was always on his lips should he need it.

Abaddon was robed in heavy, ornately worked deep-red hides covered in what Adramalik imagined were sacred patterns picked out in fine, black bone work that were unique to the Men of Wrath. He could only imagine how long it must have taken for their females to create such huge robes, and the effect, despite the truly bizarre aspect of the god, was one of genuine, regal holiness. Less holy were the hundreds of small winged Abyssals that had accompanied him, perched, wings folded, on his back, shoulders, and head, chirruping, shifting, squabbling, and defecating. The once-lavish robes were streaked with their dung. Of them Abaddon seemed to take no note.

"Prince Adramalik," the voice said. The demon looked up at the darkness that shrouded Abaddon's head. Red flashes of lightning hinted at what lay within the shadows.

"These Exalted Chieftains and Shamans are agitated. They wish me to focus solely on the cities. They say that is fitting punishment for millennia of genocide. Further, they say the Abaddim are corrupting their land. What say you?"

Adramalik did not hesitate. "The cities must fall, my god. As for the land—"

Abaddon uttered a phrase to the throng of Salamandrines and they turned and glared at the demon. One of them raised his staff and shouted at Adramalik and soon the remaining chieftains were chanting angrily.

"They do not like you, my demon prince."

"That is unfortunate."

"They see in you everything they have despised about demons for millennia."

Adramalik sucked in his breath. The Salamandrines certainly had their reasons. He needed to tread carefully.

"My people have wronged them."

The web of lightning intensified around the god's head, as did the chanting.

"And I am using your dead to right that wrong, Prince. There will be many more demons joining the Horde before I am finished. This does not trouble you?"

"No. They are of no concern to me. Only my enemies remain." He had learned to answer quickly, before any negative thoughts could color his words.

"And to that point, Prince, your former Knights will be joining us in the push toward the next city . . . the one called . . . Adamantinarx."

It was impossible for Adramalik not to react.

"But, my god, they will remember—"

"They will and they do. But they obey me."

"Am I to lead them?"

"They have their orders. And yours will be to stay away from them. If you value your existence."

Adramalik's mind raced.

"As you will it, my god."

Adamantinarx! That much, at least, gave the demon great pleasure. To utterly demolish the Heretic's own city, to make his successor, the upstart Put Satanachia, kneel before he wiped him and his "enlightened" capital from existence. Now that would be the culmination of everything he had dreamt of since before the fall of the Prince Regent!

The dark clouds flickered briefly. Abaddon spoke to the Men of Wrath. As the god spoke, the gathered Exalted Chieftains knelt and began to carve away at the ground, reaching deep down until they yanked free chunks of the blackness from below.

Adramalik had seen this practice many times along the way during the march of the Abaddim. It was some kind of offering to Abaddon, a rite that the chieftains believed symbolized the rebirth of the land. Or some such nonsense.

The Salamandrines briefly lifted their masks, licked the black substance, and immediately spat upon the ground. It was clear to Adramalik that something was wrong. The Salamandrines were growing more agitated by the moment. Each of them, their faces again hidden in their elaborate masks, was turning to look upon their god. Each of them was carrying a heavily ornamented staff and the bolder ones had the temerity to be shaking them at the recumbent god.

"They say it does not *taste* right. They say they are offended! *OFFENDED BY WHAT I HAVE DONE TO THEIR LAND!*"

Abaddon's rage was barely contained and the demon involuntarily cowered, not wanting to misspeak and bring disaster down upon himself.

Adramalik feigned cluelessness.

"Idiot of a demon. The *ground*!" Abaddon roared, reading his thoughts, and even the Salamandrines in their arrogance flinched. "*They* say it tastes . . . of *your* kind! Their 'sacred ground tastes of the vomit of demonkind' is exactly how they put it. They say it is because the Abaddim are of *your* kind . . . originally demons! *They* hoped it was not the case everywhere, but it is! They say they cannot live on land so befouled! The land that I am cleansing for *them*!"

Remembering Faraii's warning, Adramalik caught his foul

thoughts about the Salamandrines before they fully formed. "But their camps . . . they chop them deep into the black ground they call sacred."

"They have a purification rite for that. They sprinkle it with Abyssal blood before they settle on it. They say, now, there is not enough Abyssal blood in all of Hell to purify what has been corrupted."

Adramalik's jaw clenched. *These things, these miserable creatures, are confronting their god? Outrageous!* And yet would he not do exactly the same thing in their place? *Am I feeling respect for them?*

"Respect? You feel *respect* for them, Adramalik? Perhaps you should follow them back into your so-called Wastes where they are threatening to retreat? And see what they would do to you."

With a vast effort the demon cleared his mind and shook his head slowly as he looked up at the bizarre, enraged figure of Abaddon.

T'Zock, the World Eater, looked down upon his disillusioned children, his Salamandrines. Instead of cringing, they stood, almost defiant, in the face of their god. Words did not need to be uttered.

"Go . . . go, then, and find your way back to the lands that you find so acceptable. There will be little enough of them left to live upon when I am through!"

The Salamandrines turned their backs on Abaddon and started to filter away, their anger clear in their contemptuous gestures toward their god and especially Adramalik. The demon tried to conceal his pleasure at their departure, but the god before him would have none of it.

"This gives you joy?" the god roared. And winds began to rip through the air. *"My children turning their backs on me! When all I am doing is freeing their land?"*

Stunned, Adramalik reflexively fell to his knees and pressed his forehead to the ground. The black substance beneath him filled his nostrils with a rank, foul odor.

"No, my great god. Forgive me. For too long have I wrong-fully despised them. Do as you will with me."

The blackness around Abaddon pulsed as the lightning within him crackled incessantly, angrily.

"We will march at the next rise of the star you call Algol. De-spite my children's abandonment, I *will* destroy that last bastion of demonkind. Your kind. Go back to your tents, wallow in your pleasures, and wait, Prince. Once the Arch Abaddim . . . your Knights . . . arrive we will venture forth."

Adramalik rose slowly, unsteadily, the winds howling around him. His Knights were coming. And he could barely keep his fear in check. He did not remember reaching for the saddle on his mount.

The demon turned his steed and left the divine presence, pass-ing aggressively through the Salamandrine chieftains. True to form, they pushed back as he pressed forward. He could already see the Men of Wrath withdrawing from the field. He sucked in his breath in one long and deep intake, spurring on his Abyssal as if in an effort to distance himself not just from the god but also from the dark revelation he had just imparted.

His betrayal of his Knights had weighed upon his mind since the moment it had happened. Not because of some misbegotten morality. No, this was purely about his survival. Soon, while fight-ing the demons of Adamantinarx, he would also have to look over his shoulder on the battlefield as if his former demons-in-arms were the enemy itself. *Every move I have made has had dark conse-quences.*

His tents were lavish, befitting the Prince of Hell he had

become and the future ruler of whatever demons and souls Abaddon permitted to live in Hell. Due payment for leading the Abaddim and if he alone of the demons survived, then so be it. When this was all over, Abaddon would look after him.

He dismounted, scowling, and, with a glyph shot into the ground angrily staked his steed outside his entrance tent. He pulled aside his tent flaps, entered sending a half-dozen glyphs speeding into the tents to shed some pallid light on their interior. With the Salamandrines leaving, how would he transport these fine things? Would Abaddon fashion new creatures for him to carry the tents and their contents along? Unsure, he sighed and looked around, pleased with his possessions. Campaign furniture made for him by resentful Salamandrines, simple but light and sturdy, filled the tents, as did the random spoils he had looted from towns and outposts that had fallen to the inexorable advance of the Horde. In one corner a table stood, laden with a huge, bloody Abyssal joint he had begun to eat and surrounded by small dishes of exotic organ fruit plucked from various artery trees along the way. Scattered about were small, precious things he had collected: carved skulls, ornamental braziers, chests of fine stones, goblets, hides from exotic Abyssals, and weapons. Many, many weapons. He had become something of a discriminating collector, choosing different and strange arms to use as the Abaddim moved across Hell. It was interesting to him how many different ways he could dispatch souls, for example. One moment crushing blows were something to investigate, another broad full-arm slices. In his days under the Prince, the favored weapons had been fiery swords—metal at their core but flame enhanced by powerful glyphs—and eventually those had become the sole weapons the Fly would allow his Knights of the Priory. Those feared swords became associated only with them and, now, Adramalik saw just how limiting they were and so he collected as many different kinds of weapons as he could. He relished every first moment with each of them, testing them and gauging their efficiency and discarding the inferior ones with complete indifference. It was how he kept himself from growing bored.

Most recently he had begun to favor two massive axes, stripped from some petty godling he had encountered during the long march. He had enjoyed wresting them from him and using them on the hapless demigod. A fine memory.

He threw his satchel and weapons down at the foot of his pallet when a sharp sound made him twist around and peer into the shadowed corner of his sleeping tent.

She or it—Adramalik still did not quite know how to quantify the creature—emerged from the shadows, draped in one of the long, glow-spotted Abyssal hides.

She was dark as pumice and covered in her own spots, tiny and red and concentrated around her breasts and pubic area, and she flashed them like a lure when he looked upon her. Abaddon had done well in her creation. He had tapped into every fantasy that Adramalik had, both known to him and not, and constructed the ultimate sexual plaything. An Abyssal seductress far more potent than any succubus, she could engulf him with orifices unimaginable, enfold him in limbs unthinkable, and wrap around and into his mind with tendrils both creative and intoxicating. When he lay with her, Adramalik lost any sense of where he was, who he had been, and what had meaning. Abaddon had, indeed, done well.

He looked at her and could not deny his appetites. He wrenched the hides off her and picked her up by her thin neck. Her green eyes opened wide in mock alarm and she made a cooing sound in her throat. That only inflamed him more and, with a growl, he picked up the fiery Abyssal stalk he used as a crop and threw her down on his sleeping pallet. When her hide was welted and tender he watched her part herself for him. The scent of her wafted up and a part of him collapsed inward, thrillingly resigned to the spell of her body. He buried himself deeply in her and felt her change around him.

Claws came out, both hers and his, and for a while they drew black blood. They lapped at it, smeared it upon each other, and drew more. She moved her ribs apart and yet another set of limbs pulled free to caress him, to stab at him. He was lost. All thoughts of angered Salamandrines, vengeful Knight-Abaddim, Adamantinarx, even her creator, Abaddon himself, vanished in the fog of lust.

He came with a roar in a blinding flare of fire that set the thin hides on his pallet ablaze. And the two lay there amidst the flames for some time, panting and dripping, entangled in a mass of her claws and pincers and spread body plates. She gradually recomposed herself into something like what he had seen when he entered and sat up. Silently, she picked up the smoldering hides and draped herself in them. Adramalik, the fire still burning upon him, turned his head to look at her through the flames. Her head was now shrouded in the same shimmering dark veil that surrounded Abaddon's head. A not-so-subtle reminder of the god to whom he now owed his very existence.

20

THE WASTES

"We are being watched, B'udik'k'ah," K'ah said, pointing into the sky with his sword.

Boudica followed his finger and saw a tiny white speck floating against the shredded clots of low clouds, hard to see in the scurrying shoals of embers.

"Who . . . ?"

"Not who . . . what. It is some kind of flying *thing*. Not natural."

Boudica squinted, but the pale dot was too far away for her to discern any detail. Why were they being followed? And who would care about their whereabouts? Was it Eligor's doing? She sighed. It was just another enigma added to her already-frustrating existence.

Dolcha Branapa had proved to be an exercise in futility. Despite her and the Salamandrines' extreme cajoling, the demon there had been utterly unable to find her daughters in the vast Books of Gamagin. Had they missed their names? Or could it be that they were *not* in Hell? She considered this over and over and it brought her some small joy. To imagine her beloved children not witness to the things she had seen was her greatest dream. But the uncertainty of it made her uneasy.

It had taken far longer than she had expected to go page by page through the massive tomes. She sat listening, sometimes from a distance, sometimes near at hand, and she thought she would always, maddeningly, remember the unending sibilance of the souls within them who had been given voice. Ultimately, she had simply reconciled herself to the seeming futility of the exercise and turned away from the demons, tears streaming from her eyes. She had left the demons squatting amidst the Books, looks of misery, defiance, and anger written upon their faces. The Salamandrines, for their part, had not been as emotional. Coldly, they had set upon the last demons of the sanctuary and, instead of quickly dispatching them each with a merciful sword thrust in final bursts of ash and rubble, chopped them slowly into small bits with their bone skinning-daggers. But, according to Boudica's instructions, they had done this away from the Books so as not to sully them with the demons' blood. She had asked K'ah to have the Books replaced beneath the floor for anyone else who might come searching for them. Strangely, they had respected her wishes without a word of contest. Perhaps they felt some sympathy for the souls beyond number who had fallen victim to their common enemy, the demons. And no amount of explanation from Boudica that the overwhelming majority of souls were in Hell for a reason could shake them of that notion. She was, it would seem, simply too good an exemplar of her kind.

They left Dolcha Branapa a hollowed bone of a structure, rising in the middle of the plains. Not a demon was left alive. And its secret was safe.

Boudica stared morosely at the wrinkled, bobbing head of An-drasta as the party left the sanctuary. Her demeanor was anything but a secret to K'ah. He had become quite good at analyzing her moods through her alien body language. And he had learned, too, when to leave her to herself. Instead, he set his warriors back on a path to their semi-permanent camp.

In no great hurry, the war-band of roughly forty warriors moved steadily ahead and, instead of retracing their steps, deviated from the shorter route. K'ah was curious about the reaction the

cities might have to their raid on Char-zon, but sensing her dis-
interest in fighting and, therefore, wanting no skirmishes, they
took a more oblique route that led them past many soul encampments. It seemed to Boudica that he was almost offering her a way
back to her people, but she had little interest in anything to do
with them. Which, she thought, was probably reassuring to him.

The towns, if they could even be called that, were meager things,
scattered across the landscape. Most were comprised of a few somewhat sturdy buildings made of Abyssal bones and thick, chopped
slices of the fleshy ground cover surrounded by a few dozen elaborate lean-tos and weird tents. She knew that the skills the disparate
peoples brought from their Lives to Hell would be employed in
creating dwellings, but the mixture of designs was visually dishar-
monious and arresting. As they passed these dismal settlements,
ragged souls would come out of their dark hovels to either stare,
sullen faced and eyes narrowed, or brandish primitive weapons at
them threateningly. Souls knew all too well not to take on Salamandrines in force and the threats seemed perfunctory at best.
Boudica watched them hurriedly head back into their homes as
soon as it was clear there was not going to be a confrontation.

Despite her having been in Hell for eons, the sight of souls—
her kind—still made her uneasy. No two were alike. And far too
few of them looked as she did, more or less human. Even with the
once-ubiquitous punitive black spheres now gone, most were, in
a word, horrific. Monsters in any other context. Had one of them
burst out of the woods near her old tribal village, they would have
been killed without hesitation. Such was the work of the demons
upon her kin. And such was the nature of humanity that they had
earned their place in Hell.

Boudica shook her head. How could she go on without any
resolution to her daughters' fate? She could spend her inexhaustible

life in Hell traversing its five points and yet still never find them. And then, to further confound her, there was the notion that they were not even in Hell. She closed her eyes as the wave of sadness and depression and confusion washed through her. She started to drift into sleep, lulled by the padding of Andrasta and the monotony of the landscape.

Cries woke her. She opened her eyes and blearily scanned the flat horizon. She recognized the minimal landmarks as just outside the immediate region of the settlement. In a moment saw what the Salamandrines had reacted to. A low pall hung over the plains in the direction they were heading. With a nod from her, K'ah sent some of the warriors speeding ahead to reconnoiter the camp and its surroundings.

They did not return. Instead, as Boudica and Ka'h and the rest of the warriors made their way to them she saw the land around them change dramatically.

The foul and oppressive flesh layers that blanketed Hell—brought down upon the land when the Fallen had arrived—were gone and only the black, yielding substrate remained. The warriors began to dismount with looks of astonishment on their beaked faces. Openly elated, a cry went up.

"Our god has Risen! Our god has Risen. The Second World is upon us!"

This was taken up by all of the Salamandrines and even K'ah seemed excited and genuinely pleased.

One by one the feared Men of Wrath knelt to press their beaks reverently against the newly revealed and near-sacred ground.

Boudica and K'ah dismounted and fell to their knees. She felt the warmth and soft texture of the blackness beneath her fingers and saw how dully the surface reflected the ruddy light. K'ah sat transfixed for a few moments before leaning forward.

"It is the prophecy made real," he said quietly to himself.

But before Boudica could press her face against the surface she recoiled as a cry of outrage rang through the air and, one by one, the Salamandrines rose with revulsion visible in their movements. Something was terribly wrong.

"It is corrupted!" someone shouted. "Our land has been fouled!"

K'ah stopped in mid-bow, just as he was about to press his beak to the ground. Instead of standing, he slowly lowered himself down and kept his beak just above the black surface. His tongue came out and tentatively rasped the ground and he then closed his mouth. He raised his head a bit. Boudica watched him hold this position for a few moments and then he straightened and rose.

"The Burning Land . . . *our* land *is* being corrupted. Something is very wrong."

"But the God of the Second World would never . . ."

K'ah did not answer but, without a word, ran to his mount. Boudica only hesitated long enough to see the other Salamandrines following his lead, racing to their own Abyssals. Once they were all in their saddles K'ah spurred his mount and set off at a fast gallop.

They rode for a very long time, negotiating so many similar dark hills and valleys that Boudica soon wondered if they were going in circles. Only when they approached a singular rock formation did she know they were nearing K'ah's settlement.

The large pit was still there, its edges torn and disfigured, but the destruction within it was significant. The once neatly arranged partitions were shattered, some lying outside the periphery of the encampment, apparently dragged by some kind of stampede. Sleeping skins, Abyssal-hide curtains, small possessions, were all scattered about as if they had been trampled, picked up, and flung without any restraint. Only the black idol, the image of the Lord of the Second World, remained upright and untouched as it had been. Boudica saw the tribe hard at work trying to reconstruct the clawed embankment of backfill that the Salamandrines had carefully put in place. Strangely, though the chaos of destruction was profound, none of the females or young or elderly seemed injured apart from minor cuts and bruises. All this K'ah took in as well. Spotting the chief, M'ak, he pivoted his mount and headed toward the old Salamandrine.

"What has happened here?"

"Prophecy has happened here. Abaddon's Horde has risen from Below along with our Lord and 'cleansed' the Land."

K'ah looked stunned.

"How can that be?"

M'ak looked down. Boudica's sympathies rose for the old Salamandrine.

"It can be because it is, K'ah. Prophecies are only perfect when they are explained by the willingly fooled. The prophecy only predicted a new world . . . a Second World . . . would be brought into being. It said nothing about its hardships upon us. T'Thunj is of this world. The demons are not and, therefore, the Horde is not. I am told by some of the tribe that saw them that the Abaddim are 'demons in disguise.' Perhaps that is why this has come about."

K'ah flinched, the equivalent of rolling his eyes.

"What, then, is the *point* of our worshipping a god for eons that does nothing to help its worshippers? That, in fact, hurts its worshippers?"

It was as if M'ak had not heard the question, and he seemed even older and frailer than he had when Boudica had last seen him. His eyes were fixed upon the horizon.

"The Abyssals have fled. Our time here is over. We must move away. To lands that are not 'cleansed.' Since the fall of the demons we have changed as a people. Adapted. We will continue as we have in the past."

K'ah sat down heavily on a pile of hides. Boudica could all too easily imagine what was flooding his mind. She and her people had had to deal with the same kinds of concerns. They had chosen to stay. To fight. And to ultimately be eradicated.

"B'udik'kah," K'ah said without looking at her. "I cannot disagree with the decision of my chief. Nor do I think he is entirely wrong. You heard him. We are going to move away from these, our ancestral grounds. Probably to the Margins. We could use your leadership out there."

A hot wind was whipping up. The charred smell of it was not pleasant. Boudica looked down at her feet and saw a small bone object—a carved child's toggle fastener—begin to roll across the black ground. She bent to pick it up, clasped it tightly, and put it in her pocket.

"A memento?"

"Yes, K'ah. I cannot go with you. I think you know that."

K'ah went down on his knees, arms outstretched. This was a rare thing, she knew. Any sign of affection was viewed with suspicion, seen as weakness. But their relationship had been unique from the start. He enfolded her in his arms, the fierce Salamandrine and the fierce soul, both finding something they had only touched on for all this time.

"Where will you go?"

She had not thought too deeply about her next move. Would it make sense to simply roam the Wastes in search of her daughters? To travel from one misbegotten or dangerous soul village to another in a vain effort to describe them to the souls she encountered? In a moment she made up her mind.

"Adamantinarx."

K'ah looked surprised. "Probably best to not mention anything about Char-zon when you get there."

Boudica grinned. Affection *and* sarcasm. K'ah was a changed Man of Wrath, indeed.

Head bowed, M'ak had heard all of this and slowly reached for a pendant hanging around his neck, pulling it with shaky hands over his hooded head.

"Take this, B'udik'k'ah Two-swords. Remember us and what we were about. Tell them in the demons' capital that we simply want to be left alone. To hunt and live until we are no more." He paused and his four old eyes glittered fiercely. "And tell them, too, that if they follow us into the Margins we will shred them."

Without examining it Boudica nodded and put the necklace around her neck. She watched M'ak-aka-tua turn and walk slowly, solemnly away.

K'ah gently took Boudica's arm and peeled up the Abyssal skin until the spiral tattoo was visible. There were many more than just the first one she had earned.

"Remember, you are always a part of us. And you can always seek us out and know there is a place for you. Take your mount and ride swiftly."

Boudica felt a welling up.

"I will never forget you, K'ah-aka-tuk. And, never is a very long time in the Burning Lands."

K'ah bowed his head. As if they had heard her, the other Salamandrines bowed their heads, and Boudica had to bite her lip to keep tears from flowing.

She cinched her swords and satchels and turned away from him and, as she walked toward Andrasta, she heard him quietly say, "Keep your swords sharp, little one."

Boudica's fingers idly worked over the Finder's bone and metal surface as she stared into the distance. Fiery dust devils skirled across the low hills nearby and she found she could not take her eyes from them. Their unpredictable courses mirrored her own. Did she really want to go back to Adamantinarx? What would she find there? That demon, Eligor, might try to be helpful, but she was sure he had other things to attend to. And it had been he who sent her off on her quest in the first place. Yet the new capital seemed the only place remaining that bore any semblance to civilization in Hell since the war had upset the long-standing order of things.

She was not in any hurry and the pace she set included the occasional feeding detour, affording Andrasta frequent opportunities to inhale the tiny airborne creatures that swarmed around the fumaroles. This, in itself, was fascinating to watch under normal circumstances, but Boudica's distraction was all-consuming and she barely paid the spectacle any attention. At least the creature was content.

For a while she avoided soul villages. Her interest in other souls was marginal, and, from what she had seen of their ferocity and total lack of conscience, they were well to be given wide berth. And, so, when any hint of humanity and its settlements became evident she veered far off course to remain unseen.

All of this care at avoidance had worked well until she stumbled directly upon a hidden settlement that had been tucked away in a dark cavern, a pocket in the black substrate. As she passed, the souls within came streaming forth and, instead of meeting her with naked belligerence, blades bared and threats thrown, they beckoned her to stop and tell them what she knew. She sighed and dismounted and cautiously approached the small band, noticing that most of them were far less grotesque than souls she had been familiar with. This was a comfort to Boudica, who found herself opening up to them without even knowing why.

"Where did you come from?" "Why are you wearing Salamandrine garb?" "How long have you been alone?" "Why *are* you alone?" "What kind of device is *that* and how did you get it?" "How are you riding that Abyssal?" All these questions and many more she answered patiently, and soon she was asking them questions of her own.

She discovered that when the Horde had passed through, the souls had hidden well beneath the surface flesh and had, thus, escaped any detection. Their descriptions of the sounds and sights of their passing were chilling. The horror at what the souls had seen was still preying upon them. And, despite what they told her of the ravaging Horde, they bravely wanted to fight. This was something to which Boudica gave great thought.

She lingered with these souls. She listened to their tales and heard their fears and her sympathy began to grow. To her amazement, she found something welling up within her, something comforting in being with them. Was it their simple humanity? Or, perhaps, their unbridled adulation of her? That made her a little uneasy. Was she ready to lead again? All of these mixed feelings were a surprise to her, particularly since she found herself desperately missing K'ah and his people. Had she not been driven by the urge to find her daughters she might well have followed K'ah into the Margins for good.

When at last she decided it was time to move on, the souls to a one clamored to go with her. They were eager to leave the foul-smelling protective ground pocket they had hidden in, but when Boudica saw them leaving their weapons behind she sighed deeply and shook her head. A new course was offering itself to her.

"Take your weapons. You are going to need them."

21

THE MARGINS

Buer led them deep inside the Watchtower and it was almost immediately obvious that they were traveling inside an ancient living creature, albeit one that the demon had somehow manipulated. To her surprise, Lilith thought the smell inside the massive Abyssal was pleasant and it reminded her of burning candle wax. As they traveled the lengthy corridors, Buer gestured to and lit glyph lamps that gave a warm glow to the smooth walls carved into the Abyssal's flesh.

They wended their circuitous way into the Watchtower, past blind arteries and over protruding knobs of flesh. Buer kept a running monologue going, which Lilith at first thought was annoying and then embraced. It took her mind off Ardat.

"When I first Fell here," Buer said, her voice creaky, "I lived in a small overhang at the foot of this tower. I hunted and kept to the shadows, endlessly afraid of the Beasts. I was not sure my protective glyphs could hold against them. I tried out many glyphs against them as well . . . maybe some of them worked. Then, in time, I prevailed and when they began to take my offerings of food I realized the Beasts were not a threat and I could take care of myself here. Fortunately, I did not long for companionship. . . . I was never really alone." Lilith glanced at Eligor at that but held her tongue. The party slid their way down a short, moist sloping tunnel. Buer's voice trailed off for a few moments. ". . . I grew bolder and began to climb and explore and I found my way into the creature. It took a very long time for me to carve my way into its belly and I was always afraid I might injure something vital when I dug deeper inside. But I was lucky and the great beast was hospitable. I was little more than a tiny pest to it, I think. Centuries passed and I finally arrived at a space I was happy with. . . ."

The demons and Lilith entered a vast, humid chamber that appeared to have no ceiling. Instead, the walls leaped upward into a titanic, roughly triangular open vault, the apex of which was shrouded in darkness. The walls of the room were clearly organic and the suggestion of ribs and arteries was evident. That they were deep within the creature's chest was clear and she was sure that she felt the suggestion of the inhalation and exhalation of hot air. But, to Lilith, by far the most amazing aspect of the already-amazing interior was the innumerable glyphs that rose on every side and ascended into farthest regions of the vault. There were thousands of them receding into tiny pinpricks of lights. It was, in Lilith's mind, magical.

The party picked their way across the wide floor, through head-high stacks of manuscripts, Abyssal bones and claws and beaks, minerals, bits of demon armor, rolled hides, a variety of transparent polyps from arterial trees and pots. Hundreds, if not thousands, of ceramic pots of every shape and size and color. Most contained small amounts of pulverized elements, some recognizable to Lilith, most not. A mound of valuable demons' phalerae lay spread in careless disarray across the middle of the room.

"How did you get all of this out here? So far from any city or trade route? Did your companion bring it?"

Buer did not stop to answer but continued on to a low pallet spread over with the softened hides of Abyssals. She pointed to it.

"All of this was brought to me over time. As payment. For services rendered. By me."

Ardat was laid gently out on a pallet with six floating glyphs shedding a dull glow upon her broken body. Buer removed the handmaiden's traveling skin and the thinner skins beneath them and Lilith could easily see the crushed ribs and the side of her face. Her heart sank.

Buer closed her eyes and, under her breath, chanted a short invocation. The sound of it was odd to Lilith's ears.

A being began to coalesce from azure pinpoints of light. The pinpoints merged to form the strange, luminous glyphs Lilith had seen before in Sargatanas' Shrine. They quickly filled into the outline of a figure in the gloomy chamber. In a few moments the androgynous being stood, wavering in the realm between dream and fire.

Lilith saw its face, formed of hundreds of tiny glyphs, turn to regard its creator. Its smile was unmistakable. And beautiful. Crowning it all, circling its head was a glorious corona of sigils pulsing with prismatic light.

"Fetch me these, would you?" Buer asked, her tone kindly, as she traced three arcane glyphs in the air before her. The glyph spirit moved immediately to one of the walls. Four large, glowing wings sprouted from its back and it floated upward.

"What *is* that?" Lilith's eyes followed the being's ascent upward. Buer's companion was extraordinary.

Buer hesitated as she attempted to put Ardat in a comfortable position. "A Legate. My personal Legate." The demon smiled faintly. "A memento, if you will."

"Of what?"

"More like 'of where.'"

Lilith looked at Eligor. His expression was such as to imply that he knew the answer to the question on Lilith's tongue. She looked at the strange figure of Buer. The small demon was wearing a wing-flanged bone cap, a belt of organ containers and many tiny amulets that clicked and clacked as she moved. Her forearms were actually elongated fingers terminating in even more fingers. These she used to tug and pull the soft bedclothes around Ardat, creating a nest for the wounded handmaiden. A small tail protruded from beneath Buer's robes, twitching with her every movement. Lilith had rarely seen a more unusual demon. But for some reason she liked Buer.

"It was my constant companion in the Above. My rank and station in the Above required it. Somehow, I managed to keep it through my Fall. As far as I know there are no others like it here in Hell."

Lilith could not help but be impressed. Here was a creature of pure Light that, if not fully tangible, was unchanged from its form in the Above. And it was glorious.

"I know why you are here, Lilith. Why you made this journey. And why Eligor is here, as well."

Lilith tried to not show her surprise.

"Then I need not bore you with a long-winded entreaty."

"No. I have what you will need. But it will cost you. Not just in your repayment to me."

"Repayment?" Lilith began to reconsider her newfound affections.

"Yes. As I said, how do you think I got all of this?" She grinned a toothy grin and spread her hands indicating the pots, the manuscripts, and the furnishings.

"Whatever the cost, Buer. Much hangs on Hannibal's recovery."

Buer turned and looked intently into Lilith's red-irised eyes, her own age-filmed eyes narrowed.

"Indeed. And even more hangs on other choices that you will have to make."

Lilith did not respond.

Ardat groaned and Lilith's breath caught, the sound stabbing into her heart, sharp and deep. She clenched her jaw and reached for her, but Buer gently pushed her hand aside.

"Time for me to get to work." The Legate floated down by her side and offered the demon the glyphs. Eligor nodded to his demons and the succubi to retreat into the dark corners of the chamber and, once in the shadows, they crouched, attentive and concerned. Lilith sat herself down on a pile of dusty tomes and watched as the glyphs broke apart and stretched into arcane webs, hovering above the handmaiden's injuries. Like fine lines of fire the patterns shifted, dipped and fused, intersected and diverged, symbols flickering into existence and disappearing just as unpredictably.

Buer stood back supervising the spells, uttering guiding words under her breath, and waved her gnarled hand. A few pots of mineral elements sparked and sizzled and smoked, sending wreathing tendrils of vapor into the air. The acrid odor filled Lilith's nostrils and she saw glyphs form within the smoke, curling one into another and forming elaborate equations only to blow away into the darkness, leaving behind the strange smells. It was all very hypnotic and soon Lilith found herself looking inward as she sat, motionless, entranced.

She simply could not get away from the sadness of loss. That and love, that most impossible of Hell's emotions. Everyone whom she had grown close to had left her. Lucifer, Sargatanas, and now Ardat? The old familiar numbness was threatening to take her again and she was not sure how she would handle it. Not this time. Her bond with Ardat was complicated. Not like the infatuation she had had with Lucifer or the deep soul sharing she had experienced with Sargatanas. Ardat's love was the love of a near equal, of someone who had shared so much with her from the very beginnings in Hell. And, to be entirely honest to herself, Ardat's suffering at the Fly's hand had imposed a heavy burden of guilt that had stayed with her, since the handmaiden's punishment had been undeniably her fault. She had only been able to push that guilt aside when they had finally consummated their love for one another and she had told her about it. Ardat had held no grudge and that had only made Lilith love her all the more.

A complex network of luminous dotted lines soon covered Ardat, the myriad, multi-layered intersections concentrated on her caved-in side and face. As she watched Buer conjuring she saw the demon's face changing, bone plates hidden rising and sliding across her countenance, puzzle-like pieces locking and unlocking, tiny teeth emerging and melting back into bone, until the small demon was no longer recognizable. Lilith knew what this meant, saw the strain the conjuring was putting Buer under.

Suddenly the curving lines, the tiny glyphs, the ancient symbols and patterns ceased to shift, locking in place inches above the handmaiden's skin.

Ardat began to tremble, but the curative web work never moved and Lilith saw the slowly mending bones shifting under her bruised skin. The muffled grinding of bone was unmistakable and unsettling as ribs began to re-form.

Buer stepped back, never taking her eyes from her charge, moving slowly toward a worn bone bench. She sat heavily, exhausted, and drew her feet up. The Legate dissipated away in a cloud of blue sparks.

"Just as difficult as I thought it would be," she muttered to no one but herself. "Nothing to do but wait."

She pulled her robes around herself and closed her three eyes and, as she grew still, her face began to resume its former aspect.

Lilith rose and approached Ardat, followed quickly by Eligor.

"Do *not* touch her! Or all will be undone!" Buer was staring wide eyed at her.

The shrieked command hung in the air. And, somehow, the Legate was suddenly, urgently, in front of Lilith, who stopped in her tracks. She started and Eligor put a hand softly on her shoulder.

"It was not your fault, my lady."

She looked up at him and shook her head. She turned and walked toward the bench, the cool light of the Legate's presence fading away again behind her.

She sat down quietly on the bench a few feet from Buer, who was already asleep. Nerves, exhaustion, and doubts filled Lilith's mind and she closed her eyes, taking shallow breaths perfumed by the wisps of whatever Buer had used in her ritual. Soon she was fast asleep, her paleness almost luminous in the gloom of the chamber.

A familiar cough woke her.

Ardat was sitting upright, her arms shakily propping herself up, her expression one of bewilderment.

Lilith hurried to her and knelt by her side, putting her hands delicately on Ardat's knees. The web of lines was gone from her battered torso and Lilith could plainly see, through the purple and red, the ribs had fully healed. She peered up at Ardat's face and, apart from the bruises, all seemed as it once had been. And yet there was something different in the handmaiden's eyes. A torpor, a distance, perhaps, Lilith thought. Or was it pain?

"Where am I?" Ardat's voice was weak, brittle, and dry.

"In Buer's chambers. Deep within a Watchtower."

Ardat looked around trying to focus on her surroundings, slowly peering up.

"Am I all right? I hurt. A lot."

"You have been healed. You were terribly wounded, my love."

Ardat looked back down and into Lilith's face. A tear streak glistened on her cheek.

"I do not feel right."

Buer joined them and said softly, "I did what I could."

She scuffed off and returned with a heavy obsidian goblet of thick red liquid flecked with gold, which she offered to Ardat. "Drink this."

"What is it?" Ardat's quiet and even tone bordered on angry.

"Certain Abyssals . . . tiny ones . . . eat the polyps on the artery trees. They expel this liquid. It is medicinal for demons," Buer said as she made for the center of the chamber. "And I have added a few things."

Ardat sniffed it, pursed her lips, and then drank down the entire potion in hungry gulps.

Lilith smiled when she saw Ardat's eyes grow more attentive. She stood, squeezed Ardat's shoulder for reassurance, and followed Buer some paces away to the pile of phalerae.

Buer began nudging the disks around with her foot. "Your handmaiden will never be alone," she said quietly. "Pain will always be her companion."

Lilith's face fell. "But this ritual . . . ?"

"As I said. It was the best I could do. She would have succumbed had I not been here."

Lilith looked down at the hundreds of charred phalerae at her feet. The squashed and distorted demons' faces on them, their teeth bared, their mouths set in grimacing smiles, seemed to be mocking her in her misery. She felt the bitterness welling up in her. But she had to be strong. She had to be clear eyed.

"When will she be able to travel?"

"She can travel now. But she cannot fight. That would be too much for her."

"Good. I need . . ." Lilith hesitated. Buer had already done so much for her that asking for any more help seemed greedy.

"I know what you need." Again, she summoned the Legate and gave it a brief instruction. But this time, instead of floating upward, it waved its hand, and slowly, almost serenely, the disks began to float up around them until the pair were surrounded in a cloud of them. The Legate briefly scanned the demonic trophies and plucked an especially large deep-red disk from the center of the cloud. This it handed to Buer almost ceremoniously.

The demon held up the phalera with thumb and index finger. "This."

Lilith reached for the disk, paused, and then took it from Buer, her hand dipping as she took hold. It was incredibly heavy for something so thin. She studied it and noticed that when shadows played upon its surface pits and wrinkles tiny faraway stars of light could be discerned. And when it was shaken slightly she could hear a distant deep sound, she thought, almost like war drums. *Am I imagining this?*

"Remarkable, eh? That is the *only* Disk of Transmutation I have ever come across, Lilith. My Legate identified it as such. It is the oldest phalera in my collection."

"Whose was it?"

"I do not know. But, to be sure, a powerful, forgotten god. Slain, undoubtedly, by a more powerful and forgotten god. Or demon. Something like this does not get passed along as time goes on. It is held on to. To be either used or secreted. You will find this interesting. It was found well beneath the Fly's Keep in a chamber intentionally flooded with lava. The Prince was clearly afraid of its power."

Lilith swallowed hard. She had not known the Fly to be afraid of anything or anyone.

Buer held her clawed hand out. And Lilith, confused, handed the disk back. The demon handed it to the Legate, who bowed, flared, and vanished, taking the disk with it.

"I am giving this to you, Lilith. And my Legate is going to bear it for you and help you when you need to use it. I will teach you how to summon the Legate when you require both it and the disk."

"You are sending your only companion away?"

"Yes." She frowned slightly. Buer shifted on her feet, uncertainty clear in her manner. "This is how you summon my . . . the Legate." And she whispered a phrase into Lilith's ear. Lilith mouthed it soundlessly until she felt she had mastered its inflection.

"I do not do this lightly," Buer said. "The need is great."

Lilith was shocked. Hannibal's plight was her guilt to bear. Why was it so important to Buer?

"And I do not do this without the expectation of repayment," Buer continued. "This is the disk of a fallen god. I expect payment in kind. A disk of equal value for a disk. I do not care how long it takes you to bring it to me."

"And the Legate . . . ?"

"Will return to me or not. I do not control it. No one can. I merely brought it here. Time will tell."

"There is more goodness in you than Hell deserves. You have our thanks."

Buer did not respond but bowed her head and withdrew, making her way slowly through the shadows and the dusty piles of specimens and crockery. A sudden sadness seemed to weigh her steps down. For the first time since she had met her, Lilith sensed the demon's age and sensed, also, the profound loneliness she knew was now going to be Buer's new companion.

Lilith made her way to Eligor, nodding to Ardat as she passed. The handmaiden seemed more herself, a trace of a smile upon her lips.

Eligor stood when she approached.

"Are we ready? Do you have what you need?"

"Yes to both questions, my friend." Lilith swung her satchel open and deposited the glass phials she had been carrying on a table. She caught Eligor looking on. "How was I to have known what form the cure for Hannibal would take?"

"Good point. And you will be lighter this way," he said with a slight grin that faded quickly. "We have no time to waste. We must take wing and be off to Adamantinarx."

Lilith nodded and Eligor's demons rose silently while the succubi, smirking to one another self-consciously, touched their forehead in salute and stood with a clatter of weapons, hands placed smartly on their sword hilts. *A salute? What next?* She shook her head imperceptibly.

They began to file out of the chamber and Lilith took Ardat's hand, helping her to her feet and guiding her to the tunnel exit. She walked stiffly and Lilith could not help but see the pain on her face. Ardat stopped and turned and peered back into Buer's chamber.

"Did Buer give you what you sought, Lilith?"

"Yes, and much more."

"I wish I could thank her."

"You can when we come back, Ardat. Someday."

The look on Ardat's face, a mixture of pain and puzzlement, was nearly undecipherable and Lilith wondered if Ardat would prefer to let it all fade into memory. She let the question go and the pair entered the tunnel behind the waiting succubi.

Eligor and his demons were waiting outside the Watchtower, readying themselves, flaring their flight glyphs for the journey back to the capital. With a nod from their leader the demons swept Lilith, Ardat, and the succubi up, ascending into the hot air and leaving Watchtowers, Beasts, and Buer in the smudge of ash below. The Margins quickly fell away to the horizon and the demons' wingbeats grew more tranquil as they took advantage of the fierce infernal thermals.

This time, fending off the usual drowsiness that would overtake her, Lilith intoned a few short words and cast her mind into her faraway familiar. The fog of distance parted and it was as if she were looking through her own very keen eyes.

Ukuku was silently hovering high above the gray-brown terrain and Lilith could quite clearly see the many figures streaming across the bleak landscape below. It appeared that an army was gathering. An army of souls.

Lilith sent Ukuku lower, guiding it toward the front ranks of the army as it marched across the steaming land. And there in the vanguard was Boudica, swords out and mounted on a Salamandrine war Abyssal, urging the armed host forward. It was impossible for Lilith to not realize that the army was heading toward Adamantinarx.

22

THE WASTES

It had not taken much—simply her single-handed defeat of three of the souls' key warlords—to bring the souls together. K'ah's training and her own innate prowess had made the outcome of the short matches a foregone conclusion and, in each case, she had left the warlord's body to writhe in pieces for eternity, kicked into a hastily dug hole. The resounding cheers for her as she left the makeshift arenas, bloody and defiant, only strengthened her new-found resolve. She had been reluctant to fight, but once she had committed to it her spirit had risen and her anger and bitterness had guided her hands. She barely remembered how she had dispatched each of them—the fights had been remarkably short—but she did remember how satisfied she had felt when she had raised her swords overhead in victory.

Not long after those battles the souls began to gather by the hundreds. Word spread that they once again had a leader and some even likened her charisma to that of Hannibal, the beloved Soul General, himself.

What had been difficult for Boudica was the transition back to leading her own kind. When she was being totally honest with herself, she admitted that here in Hell her attitude toward souls was dismissive at best. And, at worst, she could barely tolerate their proximity. That was different from her past, from her Life. She had loved her people and fought alongside them with pride.

Perhaps it was because in her Life she had seen the good that people had to offer. Perhaps her mistrust of her own kind, begun in the building pits of Adamantinarx with the likes of La and Div, had grown while she had spent time with the Salamandrines. While they felt sympathy with the souls, they had not in any way wanted to form an alliance with them. Whatever the cause, she simply did not trust her fellow humans. In Hell it was nearly impossible to see what might otherwise have been good motives as anything but opportunism at best. And, so, Boudica was careful to not make any serious alliances or friendships with the souls she now led. Instead, she adopted a cold and distant authority that belied the seething anger she now harbored inside, since she had realized that it might be millennia before she could ascertain anything more about her daughters. The frustration at having to ally herself with a rabble of souls in an effort to gain status with the demons to continue her search was almost maddening. *So be it,* she thought. *My Hell is my self.*

She was returning to Adamantinarx for better or worse. And the thought of it seemed almost absurd. For centuries she had toiled in its pits, abused and degraded and without hope. It took no effort for her to remember the sting of the whip upon her back. But she had been freed and the city was no longer what it once had been. And, from what she had heard, it would take every soul and every demon from the neighboring wards to defend it.

The march to the capital took Boudica and her growing army through what she was told had formerly been rough terrain. Now it was leveled, black and smooth. The rumors whispered about the vast Horde that had done this were true. And they were not too far behind it. It would be her job to keep her army from making contact with the enemy before they reached the capital. Scouts were sent out, some of whom did not return. But those who did were silent for some time before their reports were coaxed from them. Most described an ever-moving, cacophonous sea of dark creatures that stretched into the shadows cast by the clouds of debris that hung over the advancing tide. And some claimed to have caught sight of something else, a huge Being limned in red lightning, moving slowly at the rear of the maelstrom. Boudica could make no sense of any of it except that it was a threat to everything that thrived, for better or worse, in Hell. And that, in turn, meant a threat to her daughters if they had been cast into this horrendous world. The uncertainty gnawed at her.

Hell is my self.

Eligor shifted his hold on Lilith. While he and the other flyers had skimmed along the high, hot thermals with little or no effort they had been aloft for a very long time and, as lithe as Lilith was, she weighed more than the usual complement of weapons. Still, Eligor seemed more than content to carry her, shifting her weight rarely, never uttering a word of complaint.

Despite her dark mood about Ardat and the imminent threat to Adamantinarx, Lilith could not help but look upon him with fondness. Eligor was a stalwart companion to her, a demon of good nature and loyalty. She knew well how fierce he was in combat and that only made her admire him all the more for his kindness. She was glad he had been Elevated. With such a sterling character, how could he have ever Fallen? The answer lay upon Lucifer's lips. Truly Eligor should have stayed away from the war in the Above, but it was because of that same loyalty that he had followed his lord, Sargatanas, as he, in turn, had followed Lucifer on his ill-fated journey. Though she had never asked, she was sure he wished he could have followed Valefar and Sargatanas back to the Above.

"Where are we?"

"Getting close. We passed the Flaming Cut a short time ago."

"And the Horde that marches on Adamantinarx?"

"No sight of them. Yet."

Lilith looked across at the other flyers. Their huge wings made slight adjustments on the hot winds, the flames from their heads trailing behind them. She could see the succubi enfolded in the arms of the demons and she could also see Ardat cradled protectively by the farthest demon, Eligor's most trusted First Lance.

Suddenly a bright spot appeared before them, growing against the dark sky. In moments it was recognizable as a packet of fiery orange glyphs, a message sent out on the winds.

Eligor craned his neck as it whizzed by, its trail sizzling in the ether.

"That was from Adamantinarx. An entreaty from Put Satanachia, himself, for any and all demons to gather in the capital. To bring arms."

"That does not sound good."

"No."

"What will happen if Adamantinarx falls?"

Eligor looked down at her.

"It will be the end of us here."

Lilith's mind raced for any answers, anything that could help the threatened city.

"What if I could heal Hannibal . . . bring him to the city?"

"He is deeply corrupted, my lady. This I know from reports and you know from visiting him. It would take time for him to become himself again, yes? And even if he regained himself swiftly, he could never muster enough souls in time."

Lilith knew he was right.

"It is up to us, Lilith. The irony of demons saving Hell has not been lost on me. The inmates saving their prison so they can remain incarcerated."

Eligor fired off his own glyphs.

"The Proconsul should know we are inbound."

Lilith was silent. Should she mention Boudica?

"That soul . . . Boudica. The one you were so impressed by. She is raising an army."

This time it was Eligor's turn to be silent. He remembered well that soul's anger.

"She hates us, Lilith. And with good reason. She may well join in against us."

Lilith remembered her encounter at the keep of Dolcha Branapa, trying to recall every detail of the soul's behavior to see if what Eligor suggested was plausible, and, ultimately, she had to agree it was.

She looked into the distance and there, between some ragged clouds and far below, was a wide, light strip, bending fluidly across the dark landscape. The river Acheron!

Eligor soared on a straight and level course and, after some time, when the tiny, distant fires of the city were visible, he pulled up, beating his wings to maintain altitude.

"We can glide in or be a little more . . . energetic."

Again, Lilith smiled at the demon.

"I like the sound of 'energetic.'"

With that, Eligor gathered himself and, holding more tightly on to his companion, angled down toward the city. Folding his wings, he stooped into a combat dive. Lilith glanced hurriedly behind and saw the other demons following their wing leader. She chuckled wondering how the succubi were reacting.

Eligor gathered speed and the air whistled around them as they plummeted toward the city. Breaking through the clouds, they dropped at a furious speed. Lilith saw demons beyond count on the wing, some in formations, many hurrying about their tasks. She saw Eligor aim for the Central Mount and its huge palace complex, saw the countless new buildings lit by torches, saw tiny workers and legionaries on the streets, and saw, too, the city's surrounding wall illuminated by a glowing tracery that outlined Adamantinarx in fire. All of this rushed toward her at an almost harrowing speed until, suddenly, Eligor snapped open his wings and braked just above the palace dome.

The flight alit on the wide plaza that lay before the palace gate and Lilith stepped down onto the flagstones delicately and slightly dizzily. Still, her face belied her exhilaration.

"Thank you, Eligor. For that and for everything."

Eligor bowed in answer. "My lady."

"Where to?"

"I think Proconsul Lord Satanachia will be eager to see you after all this time."

Lilith nodded and took a very deep breath and a moment to look around her. Adamantinarx was thriving, once again. She could easily see, even from this high vantage, the various torchlit arteries below bustling with activity. The rebuilding of the capital was in full swing. Spires leaped skyward again, warehouses crouched along the Acheron, municipal buildings, forges, stables, armories, as well as a hundred other types of buildings all lined up and down the resurrected avenues and side streets. The quarrying of vast quantities of natural stone had seemingly not impeded progress on the city's rebuilding and Lilith liked its new look.

Gone was the smell of blood on the air. Gone, too, were the endless cries of souls. Only the whine of the wind, of an impending cinder storm, perhaps, could be heard.

One thing did stand out to her. The forges were belching out copious amounts of smoke. Clearly, the city was preparing.

The plaza was newly flagged with finely dressed travertine marble that felt warm beneath her bare feet, not at all like the former clammy blocks. And surrounding the octagonal space were new, heroic statues of various demons bearing arms—heroes of the Rebellion, she guessed. She turned to follow Eligor, admiring the palace's new appearance. It still looked like Sargatanas' world, but, by dint of the fact that no souls were used in its construction, it had, to her, a more inviting look.

The demons and succubi gathered around Ardat, and Lilith thought her handmaiden looked, if anything, weaker than when they had taken flight. But Ardat insisted on walking alongside her lady and Lilith measured her steps, trying to make her slower pace seem less obvious.

Eligor led them through the huge, impressive front gate, built of granite and arched overhead as it was with magnificent carved demons, their outstretched wings interlocking, and behind the first pair, forming the ceiling of a long corridor, floated a hundred more like them. This was a new feature to the palace, replacing the old vaulted ceiling originally composed of soul bricks. Lilith took in the fine masonry and craftsmanship and then, as her eyes dropped to the end of the corridor, her heart skipped a beat and her mouth parted in astonishment. Standing in the glow of a great skylight at the corridor's end was her Lord Sargatanas staring upward, hands clasped in prayer.

Has he come back to me?

Slowly, disbelieving and incredulous, she approached the figure, her heart pounding. She almost spoke out, waiting for him to open his arms and embrace her, but then the realization took hold of her, her chest aching from the bitterness. He did not lower his gaze, did not greet her, did not smile or speak. Sargatanas was no closer now than he had been before she walked into the palace.

Carved from a single block of the purest white nephrite, the Demon Major's features, his armor, robes, and sword, and very stance, were reproduced to utter perfection. Lilith saw in the curved and angled bones of his face the nobility, the sincerity, and . . . was she imagining it? . . . in his eyes the pain and longing that had always lain just beneath the surface. It truly was a sublime and transcendent work of art.

And nothing more.

"We found the most amazing sculptor among the souls. He based this upon the older statues, court drawings, and our descriptions," a voice said behind her. "He truly captured him, yes?"

Lilith turned and saw Put Satanachia in all his splendid regalia, his smile fading a bit as he looked into her eyes.

"And we had something else to go by," he said, looking to Eligor, who, reaching into his satchel, produced a small statue— the piece she had carved and given to him long ago.

"A lovely work of art, Lilith," Satanachia said.

Lilith could not find words. She simply returned Satanachia's gaze. The burden of rule had not diminished him. He was just as charismatic, just as regal, as he had been when she left. His opalescent armor was as she remembered it, the five-pointed starbust of flame motionless in the still air. Around his neck hung a heavy livery collar made of gold and jet, the only indication of his governorship of Hell.

"I thought it best not to put him on a pedestal. He would not have wanted that. Not in here, anyway. There are many more statues of him out there . . . many more dramatic ones. Here I wanted him to be . . . accessible. To seem . . . like he was still one of us."

"You succeeded, my lord. I was, indeed, . . . fooled." The sadness in her voice was unmistakable. Ardat came close and put her arm around her.

"I am sorry, Lilith." Satanachia's voice lowered. "I should have realized how you would feel."

Lilith swallowed, biting back her feelings.

"It *is* wonderful, my lord," she said quietly. "Perfect."

Satanachia smiled faintly and looked at Eligor. Clearly, he was aware of the emotions that the statue stirred in Lilith. And equally aware that the subject needed changing. He started to walk toward the arcades and Eligor, Lilith, and Ardat followed.

The succubi, seeing their opportunity, gathered around the statue and, as one, dropped to their knees. It was a tableau of reverence. As Lilith slowly walked away she could hear them praying. What they were saying, what they had made up for their devotions, was lost to the echoes of footsteps in the corridor.

Eligor cocked his head and shot a look at his First Lance, who nodded in understanding. The Wing would look after them while he and Lilith attended the Lord of Adamantinarx.

Satanachia's small retinue of aids and courtiers appeared, filtering silently out from the shadows of an adjacent chamber where they had been waiting.

"We have much planning to do," the Proconsul said. "The host is making its way here rapidly and without rest and we are in the process of fortifying the city. We have one, at the most two rises of Algol before they are upon us. I have had Architect General Halphas draw up plans and these I would like to review with you both. And," he added gravely and portentously, "with Lord Agaliarept's aid, I now know what and *who* we are facing."

"Agaliarept."

"Yes, that . . . thing . . . has been most cooperative since we liberated him from Dis."

Lilith could barely hold back her curiosity but Ardat's listlessness was concerning her. Satanachia sensed this.

"I have had your chambers prepared. Rest and gather yourselves and we can reconvene with my cabinet. But do not rest for too long, Lilith."

Eligor knocked softly on the door of Lilith's chambers.

"Enter." Lilith said softly.

He pushed the door open and saw that only one of the small braziers was alight, casting a dim glow in the room.

Ardat was lying, motionless, upon a pile of soft sleeping skins. Lilith, sitting next to her on the floor, held her hand lightly. She patted it, placing it upon the skins, and rose.

"We should join the Proconsul, my lady. Time grows short and he needs our counsel."

She nodded.

"You have not rested?"

"I am not the one who needs to recover, Eligor."

Eligor did not press her. Instead, it became apparent to her that they were heading through the arcades toward Satanachia's Audience Chamber. The way was all too familiar to Lilith and she was not surprised that Sargatanas' world had been adopted nearly completely by the new regent.

"While you were in your chambers I visited the Shrine. The Proconsul has allowed it to become a place of pilgrimage for those of us who want to remember the Above."

"Sargatanas would approve."

But would he? That place had been so secret, so private. It is hard for me to imagine his reaction to crowds moving through that place. And, yet, he wanted them all to strive to regain the Above.

She sighed. Nothing was easy anymore. All of the causes and beliefs she had held for millennia were being challenged. Her distance from him was almost as great as the distance she felt from the souls she had sought so desperately to help.

The pair entered the Audience Chamber and walked in silence the long way to the flat-topped pyramid that dominated the space. Above hung Put Satanachia's huge multi-colored sigil, its interior crowded with the sigils of those demons he now counted as allies. Many had shifted their alliances from Sargatanas to the new regent of the city. Some of them she recognized and a few, the more aggressive or contentious, surprised her. Dropping her eyes back to the platform atop the pyramid, she could see a large gathering of demons milling about, some apparently female, and that surprised her.

The many stairs to the pyramid's summit proved to be a bit more challenging than she had hoped—she was more tired than she cared to admit to Eligor. When they topped the pyramid she stopped in her tracks. The females she had seen from a distance turned to look at her and her stomach rolled.

"First Consort, it has been—"

"'Proconsul Minor Lilith,' 'Co-Regent of Hell,' 'Consort to the Ascended One,' 'Bearer of the White Sword,' 'Bearer of the One Heart.' Any of those will do, *Naamah*."

She had never been one for titles, but Lilith found herself suddenly, stonily, set on them when it came to the former consort of Beelzebub.

Naamah's eye's widened, nostrils flared ever so slightly, as she gathered her elaborate robes and knelt.

"Forgive me, Proconsul Minor."

Agrat, Eisheth, Lamatsu emerged from the small throng and gathered around Naamah. Eyes lowered, expressions blank, they knelt.

Lilith took a deep, slow breath. As it happened, she had barely given them a second thought when she had heard of the last battle in Dis. She had thought them destroyed in the conflagration in the Keep, and that would have been fine with her. To have the Fly's consorts back in her life, to have these venomous succubi in proximity, was something with which she was going to have to contend.

Satanachia stepped forward, solicitously extended his hand, and took Naamah's, bringing her to her feet. She looked adoringly at him, smiling demurely. But Lilith knew better. There was not a faint or affectionate bone in her body. For millennia Naamah had worked tirelessly against her using dark innuendo, acid lies, and poisoned gossip as her tools to influence Beelzebub. Ultimately, she had not succeeded—Beelzebub had relentlessly favored that which he could never fully have—and Lilith had remained First Consort. The irony was that not a moment had gone by in all those eternities in Dis when Lilith had not wished the Prince had listened to the Second Consort and had her banished or destroyed.

Times were different now. Hell was different now. She recognized and accepted her elevated place in it and recognized, too, these creatures for what they were—dangerous plotters to be watched more carefully than ever before. Somehow, they had managed to worm their way into the usually canny Satanachia's good graces, and Lilith did not rule out the Art Deceptive. Naamah was more than schooled in that Art and it seemed quite possible that, in concert with the other three cunning consorts, she had deflected the Proconsul's wariness.

But how can I tell if Satanachia's feelings for Naamah are real? How can I protect him from them? And myself?

Lilith looked at them coldly. It was as if Time had rolled backward. But this time, Lilith vowed, things would be different.

Naamah smiled ingratiatingly back at her and Lilith wanted to tear her lips from her face.

Satanachia regarded Lilith. She was sure he had heard the grit in her voice, seen the hardening of her features. And, powerful as he was, he did not want to get between her and her old rivals.

Instead, he gathered his robes and sat heavily down upon one of the two nephrite thrones that he had had installed atop the pyramid. He indicated to Lilith that she should occupy the other. For a brief instant she wondered to what storeroom or chamber Sargatanas' white throne had been removed, and that thought made her heart sink.

She looked at her co-regent, superficially confident and potent, and thought she saw a shadow of exhaustion and concern that darkened his features.

"We have much to discuss. Very soon the city will be besieged, and we are not close to being fully prepared. While demons and even souls have been streaming into Adamantinarx by the hundreds every rise of Algol, they have not filled out our standing armies' ranks as much as we would like. Added to that, the cursed Salamandrines have been depleting our troops out in the field and calling them back has proved less rewarding than we had hoped . . . some outposts are simply not responding. It would seem we must rely on the two resources we have at hand. Our limited troops stationed within Adamantinarx and Architect General Halphas' ability to fortify the city."

"And what of the souls?" Lilith asked.

"There are many thousands of them returned here, but they are, truthfully, no match for the host that approaches."

Lilith nodded. The souls' physical strength was, unfortunately, not matched by their deviousness. Under the command of Hannibal they had been an effective second line of defense and skirmishers and had evened out the field of battle by sheer numbers, but to use them as frontline troops was unthinkable. Add to that the fact that the souls' most brutal individuals were, as she'd seen, ruling their small fiefdoms in the Wastes and had no interest in helping demons and what one was left within Adamantinarx were the weaker souls. Not much to work with.

Halphas stepped forward, map-scrolls tucked under his long arms. Little had changed with the tall and wiry Demon Major. His ornate bone-encrusted robes were, if anything, more elaborate since she had seen him last. Once easy to smile, Halphas looked dour, even grim. And tired.

"Proconsuls, long have I been working to solve the problems we face. I have scoured every text in our library on the sieges of cities since Hell was founded so long ago. And that includes parchments appropriated from Dis after its fall. I have some answers, maybe even some solutions."

Satanachia leaned forward on his throne. Lilith could hear the deep breath he took.

"I have two possible means by which we may not only hinder the advancing host but defeat them, as well. Both are reliant upon the natural resources of Hell itself. But both are difficult and dangerous to achieve. First, I have asked Lord Agaliarept if there is any way we can create significant conjuring pits within the actual confines of the city and the Conjurer is working ceaselessly to find an answer to that problem."

"That is something no lord has ever managed to accomplish. The conjuring magic is too destructive to be attempted amidst buildings. And there are no lava fields in proximity," Satanachia said with a tone of resignation. He looked disappointed, as if his own answer had closed the subject.

"My lord, that is only partially true. Lava runs very deep within the rocks beneath the city. In warrens and vast chambers it flows. Waiting."

"Too deep to be mined?"

"We have almost reached it as we speak! Because of the imminent threat, I took the liberty of beginning to seek it and drill down for it as soon as Agaliarept broached the subject. Two thousand souls and demons are hard at it as we speak. And I am using the backfill to shore up our walls."

"Brilliant, Halphas! Well done!"

Even Lilith was smiling. And of course the consorts were clapping their hands in a disagreeable display of newfound solidarity.

"Further, Proconsuls," Halphas went on, his tail stiff with pride, "I am having deep channels cut beneath the walls and into our streets to divert the mighty Acheron so that it may be controlled and flow within the city and serve as additional barriers. I suspect its dolorous waters may have the same effect upon the host as they do on everyone who comes in contact with them. All this in preparation for a wall breach."

"But would those same waters not also affect our own troops?" Lilith asked.

"Yes. Lords Agaliarept and Charnyx . . . she is a Sixth Tier Master of the Arts Curative . . . are working on an incantation to counter it, my lady."

"Will it be ready in time?"

"I cannot say for sure. It is beyond complicated, particularly when you consider that it needs to be effective for souls as well as demons." He looked dubious. "Some part of it may be."

Satanachia gave a great sigh.

"Finally, and most urgently, we must take down the five bridges that cross the Acheron."

Satanachia and Lilith looked at each other. Both knew just how hard it had been to reconstruct those bridges from natural stone once they had been dismantled. In fact, they had asked the souls who had comprised them to lend a hand. Not one agreed. None-theless, the reasoning to demolish them was sound.

"Unfortunately, that does make sense," Satanachia said grimly. "Do begin their demolition as soon as possible."

"Yes, my liege. May Sargatanas' spirit be with you."

"Thank you, Lord Halphas. All of this seems promising. Urging you to make haste with all the preparations would seem pointless. I can see you are doing what you can."

"And for that we are grateful, my lord," Lilith added.

Halphas bowed and moved back into the line of attending demons.

Naamah put her hand on Satanachia's shoulder. "Would it not be wise to send out flying cohorts to scour the Wastes for allies and provide protection for returning demons?" She turned to Lilith. "And souls?"

Eligor looked sharply at Lilith, who said nothing.

Satanachia pursed his lips as if in thought.

"No, First Consort, I think not. Eligor's flying troops are the backbone of our army right now. Our strength lies in our ability to attack from the air. We cannot weaken that line of defense or, if we are fortunate, offense."

Lilith watched Namaah's reaction closely, saw her nod as if in complete agreement. And, yet, why would she have made such a dangerous suggestion? Satanachia's points were so obvious a young demon could have outlined them. *Am I being too suspicious of her? Has she changed? Or is she simply a fool?*

"Lord Eligor," she said, "tell us of your troop strength."

"Yes, my lady, my lieutenants tell me we can lift three full legions of flyers . . . that's fifteen thousand demons. This includes new arrivals as well as my old guard. Flyers have been coming in steadily from many of the outlying wards. Word has gotten around."

"As the Proconsul said, they are the backbone of Adamantin-arx's defense, Lord Eligor. Is there any way of finding more without jeopardizing our position here?"

This last she said with her eyes firmly on Naamah.

"I have sent glyphs far and wide, my lady. We can only hope, in these final moments before the assault, that more find their way here. I will not risk my officers or this city."

"Fair enough."

"One small note, Proconsuls," Eligor said. "Our forges have not cooled down since we became aware of the threat. They have been working tirelessly to create new weapons for this battle . . . long-handled scythes. We have tested them and they are very effective against large numbers of enemies. Not all of our flyers will be equipped with them . . . there simply is not enough time to put one in everyone's hands . . . but there will be enough to make a difference."

Lilith saw Satanachia's face brighten somewhat. *Nothing like new weapons to perk up a demon,* she thought wryly.

"And a difference we will need, Lord Eligor. I mentioned to all of you that we now know whom we are facing. The few spies who have returned have painted a clear picture and there is no doubt in my mind. We face an enemy of legend. An enemy that no one ever thought was actually real. The Men of Wrath whispered about a god from below that would come and save them in their time of gravest need. They gave him many colorful names. I will not sully this Audience Chamber with their utterances. I will call this god by the name we gave him when we became aware of those myths. His name is Abaddon and he and his vast army of Abaddim exists solely to wipe us from the fiery fields of Hell."

23

Satanachia's delvings into the origins of the primal god known to the demons as Abaddon came at the price of much Salamandrine blood. Small parties were sent into the Wastes to ambush them— few returned; fewer still returned with captives. But those who did, laden with one or maybe two tied-up Salamandrines, were richly rewarded. The prisoners were summarily dragged into the pits of Adamantinarx, never to be seen again. So much for the tolerance of all after the War of Ascension—the Men of Wrath garnered no such sympathies. Lilith attended additional sessions after the Proconsul's revelation, and while they were difficult to witness—while not particularly a friend to Salamandrines she was not an enemy either—she reluctantly recognized the value in saving her city.

This is Hell. This is what we do in Hell. There are no morals here. No repercussions for our deeds. We set our own rules. This is Hell.

She thought this over and over as her ears filled with the bubbling screams of torn and broken Salamandrines and almost grew to believe it.

What they pieced together of the weaknesses of the army of Abaddon was gleaned mostly from meager snippets of myth and even more meager facts. And from those there was little to derive in terms of tactics and less still in terms of comfort. It seemed to

Lilith the fate of the city rested precariously upon the sharp blades of its defenders.

Lilith shared none of this with Ardat. She sat by her side as the handmaiden slept and left only for her most basic needs and when she was called upon by Satanachia. She was not eager to walk the halls of the palace knowing she would eventually have to engage the consorts in conversation. Or worse. Given the proper circumstances she would not be hesitant, now that she was co-regent, in dispatching one or all of them and taking her chances with Satanachia's good will.

She knew, too, the time was drawing close when she would have to pick her sword up. If she was being completely honest with herself, a deep and enervating melancholia was threatening to overcome her. And, now more than ever before, she wished her lord and love Sargatanas sat upon his throne.

Eligor's summoning glyph melted through the chamber's door and whisked into the darkened room, sizzling faintly as it drew close. Lilith, eyes half-closed, flinched awake.

She stood, sighed, and bent to kiss Ardat's forehead. She was cool upon her lips and that was encouraging.

Lilith followed the glyph until she emerged from the palace. As she passed under the great threshold Liimah, Araamah, Dimmah, Mashtaah, and Asaakah emerged from beside the doorway's flanking columns and formed up around her. They were joined by ten more Sisters of Sargatanas. All were swathed in white bone-spined, armored cassocks with long sleeves, and flowing white coifs framed their ash-dark faces. Each carried a newly forged crooked white blade, which they did nothing to hide as they walked protectively beside her.

Lilith nodded crisply to Liimah and said nothing, taking in the full meaning of the Sisters' presence. She found this new guard comforting, especially given the consorts' proximity. Things were very different, indeed.

She found Eligor standing in the broad plaza. He was fully armored, ready for war. He had formed a beautiful panoply of crimson armor and in his hand was the graceful *ialpor-napta* that Sargatanas had given him. She had not seen it in person. The blue flames of this weapon of the Above, nearly as light as air itself, were rippling with energy. It had been Valefar's weapon and just the fleeting memory of that lost demon made Lilith frown for a moment. His nobility had been second only to Sargatanas'; his lightheartedness was much missed.

She jerked a thumb at the Sisters.

"Your doing?" Lilith asked, indicating the Sisters with a tilt of her head.

"I might have had something to do with guiding them along a certain path." He looked wry. "I think I know how you feel about your old friends from Dis."

Lilith smiled. "Was I that obvious?"

"Only to me."

Eligor turned to face the Acheron. The tall red demon pointed wordlessly toward the river and beyond. Out over the entire horizon a long black cloud hung, blotting out the sharp edges of the distant mountains' peaks. Red lightning flashed within it.

"It will not be long now, my lady. Abaddon approaches."

"Are we ready for him?"

"The gates are sealed; the summoning pits are ablaze; the Acheron's channels have been dug; the forges are finally cooling. We are as ready as we ever will be, my lady."

"Then let Abaddon come. Let that *god*, that *thing*, throw his army at our walls. Let the great river, let the streets of Adamantinarx, fill with the bodies of his minions. We will resist to our last demon and soul. And maybe, just maybe, we will prevail."

The city rose in the distance, its spires and domes veiled by the pallid haze that hung over the accursed Acheron. It was a prize he had coveted since the Heretic had fomented his revolution, and already Adramalik could feel his blood rushing in anticipation of the slaughter to come.

He was experiencing a euphoria he had never imagined before. With the Salamandrines gone and with his elevated role in the eyes of the Abaddim and despite Abaddon's anger, he wanted for nothing. He had all the carnal pleasures he could demand, all the spoils the ravaging Horde had left behind, and all of the exotic meats to fill his belly. Only the sweet, imagined taste of total revenge upon his fellow demons was missing. And there just over the horizon was the wellspring of that anticipated draught.

He had shucked the trappings of civilization and rode naked upon his terrible steed. Gone were his cloak, armor, and satchels. This simplicity of purpose pleased him. He now felt himself a thing of pure primal rage.

The Abaddim squatted around him, awaiting the order to advance. Their acrid scent filled his nostrils and their incessant chitterings filled his ears, and as irritating as he found both sensations, he wished he had had an army as powerful as this when he was confronting Sargatanas. In many ways he had—these were, after all, demons transformed. *But oh, what that transformation had wrought. I actually feel proud leading them on the field.* But, even as a smile creased his face as that thought formed, he remembered the four Knights whom he had betrayed and the smile vanished as quickly as it had appeared. Beleneth, Rahab, Vulryx, and Chammon.

Once allies, now powerful enemies. Eventually he would have to deal with them. Perhaps, one by one, on the field of battle, perhaps by less obvious means. He still knew things they had never dreamt.

From behind him, a massive signal of black lightning seared through the sky and, as one, the Abaddim rose. The bolt hung in the air unnaturally and suddenly broke apart into a million black motes that descended upon the Abaddim below. Each mote found an upturned forehead and ignited a dark flame atop the creature's skull.

It begins!

Adramalik tugged excitedly on the reins of his Abyssal, which pivoted uneasily with pent-up energy. It bellowed and the ground shook.

The Abaddim surged forward. And Adramalik roared at the sky.

Lilith's breath caught in her throat. The dark line of the distant Abaddim suddenly grew even darker with the black fires of Abaddon. She watched as they moved like an oozing wave of tar dipping into the creases in the terrain and cresting the low hills. She watched as the blanket of creatures grew in size until it spanned the entire horizon. And she saw five tiny, fiery sigils, equidistantly spaced, and knew those marked the generals' positions. Rumor suggested that at least one of them was a demon. *Who is it? What demon would make such an alliance?*

"Araamah, fetch my sword."

The Sister turned on a heel and departed.

Eligor sent a massive command glyph skyward. It passed through the low clouds and then split apart into a dozen different glyphs, which, in turn, descended into disparate wards of the city.

"My lady, I must be off."

She took his hand and looked up, into his eyes. "Fly high and strike true, my dear friend."

The demon's eyes were fixed on the horizon.

"I will do my best. Fortune now rests on our guile. Stay safe." He turned to look at her. "*He* would be so proud of you, Lilith."

He took a moment gathering himself, then spread his wings and rose into the air. Lilith watched him ascend on slow, powerful wingbeats and then purposefully dart away. She swallowed hard, knowing that she might never see him alive again.

Lilith's gaze returned to the dark tide of Abaddim as it drew closer to the Acheron. The distance was great and it seemed to take forever and she found herself agitated. *Odd how impatient I am to get on with the fight. Our world may be at an end and I'm eager to bring it to a close?*

She watched the oncoming Horde in fascination for some time and then shifted her gaze down to the swarming city below. Legions of highly trained *malpirgim,* eager to wield their flaming javelins, were rushing down the Rule and the other wide avenues to mount the seven great gates and the walls. Overhead, Wings composed of hundreds of demons of Eligor's Flying Guard, new scythes brandished, climbed and dove, their fine training and discipline evident in their tight formations. She saw them all eventually settle into their ready positions, great cube-like formations of hovering demons forming a partial half dome over the city's waterfront. She could even hear the formations closest to the palace spiritedly reciting their war chants.

Souls tasked with domicile-to-domicile fighting were carrying weapons of every description, lining the streets and clambering up onto the lower rooftops.

A glyph bearing Halphas' signature blazed from the palace, separated, and headed down toward the river. There Lilith could just

see it rise and then drop quickly into the flagstones at the foot of
the wall. Moments later, activated by unseen sluices, the mighty
Acheron, diverted by Halphas, began to flood beneath the wall
and into the geometric channels cut into city streets. Soon a vast
network of pale waters was etched into the dark streets adjacent
to the walls far below. The pale pattern, which to Lilith's eyes
looked to form ancient and arcane symbols, did not reach too far
into the city, but Lilith could see how it might impede the invaders. But for how long? And it would undoubtedly affect the defenders, as well.

Footsteps behind her made Lilith turn and she saw Araamah
and Put Satanachia approaching. Araamah held out the oversized
sword and Lilith slung its baldric over her head and cinched it in
place. She immediately felt a surge of confidence and power. Was
Sargatanas' spirit lurking somewhere in that blade? As frivolous as
it was, she smiled inwardly at the thought.

"Finally! I thought they were going to sit out there forever,"
Satanachia said, grinning. Gone was the troubling shadow that she
had seen darkening his demeanor since she had returned to Adamantinarx. In its place was the demon's old confidence and
bravado. And she was grateful for it.

The Proconsul looked every bit the commander of Adamantinarx's legions. He had invoked his Panoply of Spines—armor
that flared spikes aggressively and protectively when in combat—
and while the armor was dormant before battle on the palace plaza,
Lilith still found its cloud-gray and nacreous surface captivating.
He carried a light lance with a blade at each end, each of which
glittered with tiny coruscating glyphs. He could not help but
notice her staring at it.

"Would you prefer this weapon to the one you carry, Lilith?"
Satanachia smirked. He already knew the answer.

"I think not. Too light for me. I need something with some heft to it. Some real killing power behind it." *As if Lukiftias weighed much,* she thought.

Satanachia grinned, studied the oncoming Horde.

"Where shall we begin?"

"I and my Sisters will be heading down to the Seventh Gate. It fronts the river fully. May I suggest you remain up here? We cannot have both Proconsuls in the field at the same time. And the palace needs to remain in our hands. If I grow weary I will return and you can take my place."

"You had better grow weary! I cannot have rumors circulating that I was not willing to lend a sword arm to this."

"Fair enough," she said lightly.

Lilith nodded to him and then turned to the waiting Sisters. Each was already saluting her, bent swords vertical against their noses.

Lilith drew her sword, saluted Satanachia, and headed to the long stairs that led to the Rule and, taking them three at a time, was down amidst the troops in no time. While not chaotic, the tumult caused by milling souls and legionaries was serious, and the Sisters formed a moving wedge around Lilith to better clear the way toward the looming gate.

It was impossible for Adramalik to not keep looking toward the other generals' floating sigils as he closed on the Acheron. Perhaps it was the early effect of the mist that affected his thinking, permeating him with a sense of sad foreboding. Or maybe it simply was his own paranoia. Either way, the prospect of his former Knights converging upon him sapped some of the exhilaration from the moment and he found himself swearing, even as he looked with relish upon the distant city.

The Acheron was, in his opinion, the biggest challenge the Abaddim would face. A noxious barrier, to be sure. The pervasive sobbing he heard coming from the river underscored his unease. He was confident that, once on dry land, his forces would annihilate any opposition, but this cursed river was a very real obstacle. Had its threat taken the form of rushing sulfuric liquid like the Styx, its danger would have been obvious. Not any more easily negotiated but obvious. The Acheron, in contrast, was slow flowing, languorous. Deceptive. Its danger was hidden and insidious—the danger of complete and profound and immobilizing mournfulness.

Adramalik had speculated as to whether something already dead and yet resurrected would feel anything at all. He now had his answer.

As the Abaddim drew near the river's edge they dipped their front legs and mandibles into its pallid eddies and, immediately, Adramalik saw the effect. It was like a creeping malaise. They stopped, looked skyward, some dropping to their knees while others climbed atop them in an effort to move forward. And there, in that struggle, repeated all the way along the river's edge, in their misery, was the answer to fording the river.

Ignoring their plight, Adramalik urged them forward, first with glyph commands and then with a ceaseless conjured cascade of burning darts, a method he had perfected to motivate unwilling demons in countless battles fought for the Fly. With his eye ever on the huge gate on the opposite shore, he goaded the Abaddim to a frenzy until they were climbing frantically atop one another in an effort to evade the harrying darts.

It took a long time. And the conjuring was exhausting. The number of Abaddim expended was incalculable. As they tried to cross they sank and, pushed down by the weight of their scrambling fellows, drowned. When enough had perished beneath the waters and their bodies had accumulated, a small distance had been gained. And so it went all the way across the wide river of sorrow. Adramalik estimated that perhaps a million of the creatures had drowned to provide the others a bridge. It was no matter—there were plenty of Abaddim to spare. He saw the other generals slowly emulate his strategy and wondered what incentive they had employed. None of his Knights had the Art to accomplish what he had done. Nonetheless, eventually six ragged and squirming bridges finally reached across the Acheron. With the completion of the bridges, the river ceased to flow.

Dammed as the Acheron now was, the crossing became easier, and Adramalik guided his steed onto the bridge. Despite the damming, the river's lingering vapor filled his lungs and he felt the oppressive weight of remorse and sadness for the truly countless number of sins he had committed descend upon him. The shredded thing that was once a conscience ached inside him, but he knew it was an artificially induced pain. Intellectually and coldly, the demon recognized that he had enjoyed every brutal transgression.

Adramalik ground his teeth and fought the Acheron's effects as he forged forward toward the gate. His Abyssal seemed immune and they crossed the uneven bridge easily. With the Abaddim finally landing on the outer perimeter of Adamantinarx, the siege of the hated capital could begin in earnest.

24

The chittering of the Abaddim on the opposite side of the gate was so loud that many of the demons and souls were pushing ragged plugs of hide into their earholes as they looked at one another with apprehension writ large upon their faces. Lilith had never heard such a din. And she had never before seen demon legionaries show any fear.

Overhead, the flying demons were waiting, hovering in place with steady wingbeats, scythes in hand, awaiting orders to dive. Lilith suspected they were going to let the forces build up before swooping down upon them. But even as she watched them she also saw the dark pall that floated along with the Abaddim begin to obscure her view. How would that affect Eligor's troops?

She and the Sisters mounted the many corkscrewing stairs to the top of the massive Seventh Gate and finally, atop its wide platform, she looked down toward the wharves and warehouses and saw them being utterly destroyed and overrun. The unabated wave kept coming and she saw the Abaddim close up for the first time. The sight took her breath away. They looked more like Abyssals than anything else, but the most disturbing aspect of their appearance was the parody of a demon's face that each bore—a face distended by immense mandibles. She found them revolting and she also found herself eager to destroy them. As she looked down at their efforts to climb the high tower she knew she would not have long to wait.

The Abaddim were, as one, single-mindedly clambering upon one another to gain the top of the wall. What they faced were thousands upon thousands of lightly armored demon *malpirgim* lining the length of the wall hurling fiery javelins down into their midst. As quickly as a javelin left their hands the defenders conjured another. But as many Abaddim as were destroyed, more filled the gaps and inexorably the mass of the gathering creatures rose to nearly the level of the wall's platform.

Lilith, red eyes fixed on the enemy, slowly pulled her sword overhead from its scabbard. The Sisters around her tensed. When the first dark Abaddim reached over the parapet it was met with three blades that cleft it apart. As its limbs and mandibles fell asunder on the platform's floor two more of the creatures surmounted the tower and then five more.

Lilith firmly grasped her sword with both hands and began the business of hacking away at the onrushing Abaddim. With perfect footwork and fluid strokes and avoiding their formidable mandibles she waded in, sending a head flying, cleaving a creature from head to shoulders, chopping clear through the torso of another. Sargatanas' drills with the very sword she now wielded were serving her well.

With quick over-the-shoulder glances, Lilith saw the Sisters weaving and darting expertly, dismembering Abaddim with abandon. Two of them were even smiling! How had Eligor gotten them to this level of proficiency so quickly? She really had to ask him, now that he was a Demon Major, exactly what his abilities were. *If* they survived.

The flood of Abaddim cresting the parapet did not let up. As she hacked at them she saw, down by the river's edge, the nearest of the Abaddon's generals' sigil. Whoever he was, he had finally joined the fight. Elements of his sigil looked familiar, but she could not, in the frenzy of battle, place them. He drew nearer by the moment, but it would still be some time before she might be able to confront him.

The mound of dead and dying Abaddim grew beneath the feet of Lilith, and the Sisters, making the defenders' footing slippery and difficult. The fiery missiles of the *malpirgim* found their marks less frequently, for the writhing of the dying creatures and the instability of the carcasses underfoot made taking aim all the more difficult. Suddenly the battle seemed to be turning against the gate's defenders despite Lilith's best efforts, and it seemed the gate might be overrun.

The Abaddim slowly gained access to more and more of the wall and she watched the *malpirgim* begin to fall to their powerful pincers. It was not long before Lilith and the Sisters, fighting valiantly, were alone atop the gate.

Suddenly Lilith heard a great chorus of battle cries and without fully understanding what she was witnessing felt the rushing of air around her. A stream of red-winged bodies flashed past and the chaos of the moment became profound. Hundreds of flying demons, scythes in hand, fell upon the Abaddim around the gate, slashing and hacking, carving them up, tossing their cleft bodies from the walls and platform in the hundreds upon their fellows below. No troops could have easily withstood the hammerblow of their assault. The Abaddim were flung into the air, beaten down and back toward the shore.

The Sisters laughed as they dropped their guard and took in the whirlwind of carnage. Lilith, too, was elated. Dripping from horns to claws with black Abaddim gore, she was relieved that the demons had chosen that moment to fall upon the enemy. Smiling, she wiped her face with her sleeve.

Her relief was short-lived. The unknown general had gained much ground and was in position to rally his Abaddim by sending a terrible fountain of conjured arrows skyward. While the invocation only lasted moments, it was a murderous display of power that accounted for many fallen flyers. The flyers veered up and away and the cacophony from the Abaddim grew in its enthusiasm. The dark tide turned once again toward the city.

Lilith looked out toward the river and saw it pooling behind the bridges of drowned Abaddim. She pursed her lips, thinking about that, and then ran to the opposite side of the gate's parapet. She glanced down to where the channels cut for the river were meant to be and to her shock she could not see them. She suddenly realized that, by damming the river, the Abaddim had inadvertently removed that impediment to their progress. And improved their chances of taking the city.

He was fairly certain who he had seen, albeit briefly and from some distance, atop the beleaguered gate. The white skins and the flashing white sword were enough. *It is the Fly's whore. His First Consort, the bitch, Lilith! What good fortune!*

Even as he reached the foot of the gate, Adramalik began fashioning plans for what he would do with and to her. Nothing would be off-limits. Without the Fly looking possessively over his shoulder, he could take his time with her as he had always, secretly, desired. And he could be as creative with her as his fertile imagination allowed. Once the city was taken and properly dealt with, the palace would be his—so Abaddon had promised—and it would truly become a place worthy of his darkest ambitions. Lilith would be his plaything there, forced to await his pleasures. Abaddon would create a court for him and provide him with whatever his whims dictated. And all would be as he had, so long ago in his chambers in the Priory at Dis, envisioned.

In the meantime, he had a city to take. Adamantinarx would not fall without furious opposition. As easily as he had batted aside the flying demons, he knew he could not make that invocation too many times. Even a Demon Major had his limits. This was a siege of brute strength, not Art, and he was confident that, even with great losses, the numbers were on his side. And he could not discount Abaddon. He had no real idea what marvels of mayhem the god was capable of.

Adramalik urged the Abaddim on. He had them gather and press against the gate's massive doors in such huge numbers that the pressure became almost too much for the structure to bear. Only the great seal behind the gate, conjured no doubt by Satanachia or, perhaps, Halphas, held it in place.

Adramalik bowed his head and closed his eyes. He insinuated a Version Tenebrous of his own seal beneath the heavy doors and began to work away at the gate's last remaining protection, occluding its light-scribed elements bit by bit. It was a skill he had learned from his colleague Lord Nergar, the former secret-police chief of Dis, for whom entering any space was a necessary Art. No door could have held its secrets for long if Nergar had need to enter. Adramalik had never been quite as good as his tutor at this ability—truly no demon had been his equal—but the former Chancellor's abilities were far from poor. He set to work eating away at the seal, reducing it by degrees.

He could hear the hundreds of Abaddim growing frantic, clawing at the doors. Adramalik, picturing his progress in his

mind's eye, saw the seal slowly being occluded. He was methodical, calculating, leaving no light speck of any symbol untouched.
Nergar would have been smiling his toothy grin. Finally, the seal
vanished completely. A great groan went up from the gate, rising
above the din of battle, as the hinges were challenged and then,
with a crack like a terrific bolt of lightning, the doors collapsed
inward.

The Abaddim streamed through the shattered gate, the creatures climbing atop one another in their eagerness to enter the city
precincts. Adramalik felt pride swell up within his chest. This was
his doing, almost as much as Abaddon's. He glanced back out over
the tortured river basin and into the darkness beyond. And almost
as he formed his prideful thought he saw red lightning spidering
out from where he knew the god to be. That, alone, was enough
to dampen his exhilaration. He had to tread so carefully with
Abaddon.

He turned to look back at the besieged city. He looked up and
saw that most of the flying demons were again hovering in formation. Waiting. There were small gaps indicating their losses.
There will be a lot more of those before much longer.

His eyes darted to the parapet and he grew angry. A formation
of demons was stooping, wings tucked tightly on a direct course
toward the gate's platform. They never slowed and, arms extended,
scooped up Lilith and her fellow fighters and banked steeply up and
away. It all happened so quickly that Adramalik barely had time
to swear, let alone fashion an invocation to stop it. Instead, well
after the fact, he hit his steed with the flat of his ax so hard that
the beast roared in pain and lurched forward trampling a dozen
Abaddim underfoot. He vowed he would get her soon enough.
Adramalik's mood improved almost immediately as he quickly
found himself passing beneath the Seventh Gate of Adamantinarx,

the city he had always hated most in Hell. A finer moment he could not remember.

Despite her halfhearted protestations, the demon who bore Lilith carried her back toward the palace plaza. She peered down into the city and saw just how far the Abaddim had penetrated. The streets and alleys and avenues clogged with fighting demons and Abaddim thinned out the farther up the Central Mount she was borne.

The Sisters were dropped there just before Lilith alit, and even though she was disappointed, she thanked the flying demon who had lifted her away from the battle. She was met by the Proconsul and his guard.

"Who ordered me removed from the gate?"

"I did."

Lilith frowned. There was nothing to be done about it now. And no point in recriminations. She looked out into the distance and saw no end to the Abaddim.

"The walls are overrun. Their numbers are too great. And their general is no novice."

"Who is it?"

"No idea. His sigil was not normal. It had elements I did not recognize woven into it making it hard to read. And much of it was darkened."

"Who holds such a grievance against us that he would ally himself with that god-thing?"

Lilith did not venture any guesses.

"What now?"

"Now we fight fire with fire, Lilith. I will command Agali-arept and the other Conjurers and decurions to redouble their efforts at the pits to summon as many legionaries as we can to stem the tide."

"And Eligor's troops . . . ?"

". . . are our last defense. We can use a third of them to harry the enemy, but we dare not use more. I am pulling the remaining two-thirds back, overhead . . . up here. For a final defense."

Lilith looked down.

"I am not staying up here, Satanachia."

"I know."

She looked at him. His armor was thickening. And he was firing up his lance. In a moment it was ablaze with sharp glyphs that skimmed across its surface.

"You really did not think I was going to stay up here and let you do all the fighting, did you, Lilith?"

She smiled at him and then at her Sisters.

"Well, then. Why, in the name of the Ascended Ones, are we just standing here?"

With that, once again, Lilith headed to the great stairs, followed closely by Put Satanachia and the Sisters.

Already, she could see the effect the conjuring pits were having on troop strength. The streets were nearly impassable and the avenues were little better. Cohorts of still-steaming demons seemed to be moving in every direction. Everywhere command glyphs were flying and troops were hastening to their positions. Lilith knew that the apparent chaos was, in fact, better organized than it appeared. But she also knew that movement and fighting within a city was one of the things generals dreaded most.

As she considered that, a glyph arrowed in to the Proconsul and Satanachia absorbed its meaning. Lilith was grateful she had been away and was not bearing the brunt of all the command decisions as was her co-regent. As they tried to make their way through the crowded avenue the Proconsul sent a large glyph back and shared what he had learned.

"My field commander, Lord Belmathagor, tells me that our troops are holding ground in most of the city. Just. The Seventh Gate was the focal point of the heaviest attack. As you know, we failed there, and he is sending three full legions to attempt to staunch the flow of the enemy that continues to enter there. Thankfully, as we hoped, the pits are doing their job. Legionaries are pouring out at an unprecedented rate. We barely have enough centurions to lead them."

And then he said almost as an afterthought, "Also, Belmathagor tells me neither Halphas nor Agaliarept nor the decurions know how long the pits will be useful before they are spent."

That thought lingered in Lilith's mind.

Up ahead she could hear fighting, and eager to push the thought of empty lava pits aside and join the fray, she elbowed her way through the marching demons.

She did not have long to wait. Down at the foot of the Rule the Abaddim were making steady gains and a somber and disturbing cloud of destroyed demons' ash hung low over the avenue. Anger flooded through her and she redoubled her pace down the avenue.

They hit the Abaddim like a firestorm. Satanachia, swinging his lance with two hands to and fro, set to clearing a wide swathe before him. Lilith's nostrils filled with the stench of burned Abaddim. She and the Sisters widened the swathe even more. For some time they fought the many dozens of Abaddim that crossed their paths and yet it seemed to make no difference. It was, as the demons sometimes quipped, "like trying to blow out a lava field." The odds were simply too great.

Satanachia's spines flared and he bent to his slaughter with even more vigor, leaping into the thickest of the Abaddim and roaring with fury. The flames above his head grew until they covered his entire torso and burned to cinders anyone who came too close. He became a thing of fire and destruction. And even this was not enough.

Lilith, pausing and breathing hard, saw the hollow expressions on the Sisters' faces. As fierce and adept as they had become, this was proving to be too much.

Three glyphs suddenly converged upon Satanachia, and Lilith watched him drop back. The Sisters covered him, blades swinging, as he faced Lilith.

"Reports are coming in from Flying Guard captains. They think they can see the rear guard of Abaddon's army. It is not infinite. We knew that. They also think they can see Abaddon himself in the darkness."

"Is Abaddon moving forward?"

"So it would seem."

Lilith sidestepped a thrust from the mandibles of an Abaddim and severed his head. She reached down and picked it up.

"This looks like a demon."

"It is. Or was. We are fighting our own dead."

"How do you know?"

"Because Eligor just told me that he recognized one of their captains. The Knight-Brigadier named Melphagor he slew back in Dis."

"A Knight. From Dis. And a captain, no less." Lilith grew thoughtful. Who *were* the generals who actually led this host? Something was eating away at her, but she could not put her finger on it.

"We must keep going." Satanachia looked grave. "It hardly matters who these things were in another life. It only matters what they are about now."

"Agreed."

They, once again, leaped into the fray and did not stop swinging their weapons until Algol had sunk below the horizon. When the gloom finally set in, she and Satanachia looked at each other in silent affirmation. They were weary and had done what they could for now and must let others fight on. The Abaddim had thinned out around the gate, pushing buildings new and old down in an effort to evade the fury of Lilith, the Sisters, and Satanachia. Their flanking attempts did not succeed.

"I am going to send in the contingent of flying legions, so we may rest for a bit," Satanachia said, panting. "With any luck they will keep the Abaddim busy for a while. And I am needed in the Fifth Ward, Lilith. You can handle this, right?"

Lilith nodded, exhausted. She was unscathed, but two of her Sisters were bleeding from minor wounds. She saw Satanachia form a large purple command glyph and saw him launch it into the sky. She did not even look back as she and the others withdrew. But she could hear the deep rushing of wings from above, the shouted battle cries and the scythe-inflicted carnage that was ensuing as she made her way back up the Rule. The Sisters needed their wounds attended to and Satanachia did what he could with glyph work as they filed away. While the palace beckoned she resisted the urge to withdraw completely and return there.

Instead, she found a broken corner of a building and crouched, chin resting on her sword, watching the darkness grow and the red flickering of lightning on the horizon.

25

The ranks of her army had swelled into the hundreds of thousands. She looked behind and it covered the rough terrain far into the gloom. Souls. Her people. Her followers.

She had been a queen in her Life and was a queen again in Hell. She had become a living legend. A soul who could hold her own against demons. A soul who had been accepted by the fierce Men of Wrath. A soul who, even though she was consigned to Hell, thought in large terms. As they had marched, she had brought them together in a common cause. What she had offered was not the petty internecine squabblings of greedy warlords and their fiefdoms but, instead, the dignity of nationhood. Nationhood in Hell. She told them the time was right, that after what they had endured for millennia they deserved the respect of the demons. And they loved her for it.

And from where had this idea sprung? She fingered the white necklace, the precious carving of the White Mistress, she wore and knew the answer.

In moments of quiet reflection, surrounded by her growing army, she knew, deep down, that the only way she might get the demons to respect *her,* to take her seriously and answer her greater question about her daughters, was at the head of a great host. Every leader had his or her reasons for leading, This was hers and she was not going to let anyone stand in her way. Doubters and malcontents were left behind. Violent opposition was met with more violence. This was no pacifist army.

But the notion of statehood for souls? More often than she cared to admit, she heard herself discussing the eternal future of the souls and could not really believe much of her own lofty rhetoric. Was she seriously thinking souls could break entirely away from their dependency on demons and truly be left alone to build their own future? It was a grand idea, an idea to fire the imaginations of souls, an idea that she felt she could present to the demons who had set her free. They had even said she was special, that their lord, Sargatanas, had considered her important. Why not go back to Adamantinarx and make a case for independence instead of codependence? And with an army of this size behind her how could they refuse?

They had had to march more quickly than the Abaddim so as to stay undetected and had veered well past them, losing sight of the enemy. Boudica remembered that the Acheron bowed around the back of the city, and there, where the river was somewhat narrower, and at great risk, they would have to suffer the river's punishment to gain entry without the Abaddim seeing them. With all the souls in her host, that was a risk. But it had its advantages, as well. In an army this large she felt certain someone would figure out a way to ford it. She had still not made any close alliances with any of the souls and so she would have to rely on word of mouth to find that individual. As much as she wanted to see her people treated fairly, she, herself, still had many reservations about them.

They marched the final leg to Adamantinarx without stopping to rest. In a show of solidarity, Boudica gave up Andrasta so that she could march on foot alongside her fellow souls.

It was not easy to send the Abyssal on its way. She had grown truly fond of it and its strange ways. But, with a lump in her throat, she removed its tack and consulted her Finder and pointed the creature as best she could in the direction of K'ah's last camp, swatting it hard on the rump. It never looked back as it trotted off, its biolights eventually fading into the gloom, and Boudica thought that was just as well.

When she saw the city she actually felt a dark pang of nostalgia. She had been away a very long time and yet that place had been her home for far more time. It had not been a good home and she shook her head, silently wondering if going back was the most foolish decision she had ever made. She took a deep breath and moved on.

They crested a ridge and Boudica frowned. The river should have been sliding through the landscape before her, pale and luminous and dangerous. Instead, she saw only darkness where it used to flow. As she drew closer to the banks she saw that it was gone. Or, more probably, elsewhere. Had some unknown force diverted the mighty river? It was not her concern. The way was clear!

She turned to look at the far side of the city and saw dense, ashy clouds lying low, obscuring the taller spires and statues. In the distance, command glyphs were silently tearing through the artificial darkness and occasionally red lightning flickered. The Abaddim were already there and laying siege!

A few keen-eyed souls closest to her pointed into the turbulent air high above the closest gate. A sentry had spotted them and, hovering for just a moment more, suddenly took wing, bolting away.

Boudica grew uneasy. She signaled that the army should begin to cross the dried riverbed in haste and make their way to the gate. Best to make a bold statement. Trumpets fashioned from Abyssal horn blared and the army surged across the wide riverbed. No need for stealth now, she thought.

Despite the lack of flowing water, the Acheron's effect began to eat away at her. It must have still been in the air or rising from the mud of the riverbed. She found tears streaming down her face. Uppermost were the sad memories of her daughters, their sweet childhoods, their trials, their rapes. Sobbing, she recalled the death of her father, the countless deaths of her ancient tribespeople. It all washed through her. And, she could see, the others all around her were just as affected. Perhaps she and her army would fill the riverbed again with their tears.

The army began its slow way across the wide and muddy riverbed. It passed a few abandoned transport barges deeply mired in the ooze, their triangular sails flapping, their cargos of natural stone from far away still secured on deck. The ships only highlighted the melancholic mood of the place.

Boudica insisted on crossing first, in the vanguard of her army, and, all the while negotiating the uneven footing, kept her tear-filled eyes toward the sky. She was convinced that the demons would confront her from the air. She was only partially right.

Just before she had made it to the opposite shore, she saw a flight of demons approaching. One bore a brilliant blue-flame sword unlike anything she had ever seen in Hell. It shone almost like that blue star they called Zimiah. They were only six in number and so Boudica ordered weapons to be lowered. These were emissaries.

The demons alit and as they moved toward her a look of recognition crossed Boudica's face.

"My scout described you to me. There is only one soul who could lead an army like this."

"Eligor?"

"Yes. I do not have much time to spend on pleasantries, Boudica. As you can see, we are under attack; the city is under siege. Are you here to aid us?"

"No. We are here to demand our freedom and see what terms we can work out so that our two peoples can live alongside one another. That is all."

"That is a lot and nothing at all. Your people already live harmoniously with us. Many in our city. Here."

"As second-class citizens. We have no leaders equal to yours governing us. We *want* more."

Eligor looked back at the city. His hand tightened on his sword hilt.

"'Here' will not exist for much longer if you will not help. And then where will your petition for freedom get you? I daresay you will not get what you want from that god-thing."

Boudica audibly sucked in air as she stiffened.

"Everything comes at a cost, Boudica. Especially freedom." He raised his sword. "We demons tried our bid for freedom eons ago in the Above and look where it landed us."

Boudica looked toward the city. He was right. But this was not the souls' war. Or was it?

She took a deep breath and turned to the souls around her.

"It seems that our freedom from the demons is to be bought with some of our lives!" she shouted. "We are being told that unless we fight that host out there, alongside demons, there is little or no chance for our own nation, let alone our eternal existence. We came here to negotiate and now we are being *asked* to fight. For them. *With* them."

She let that all sink in. And she waited for her words to spread.

"I leave it to you all. But *I* think we have little choice. What say *you*?"

She looked toward Eligor, who met her eyes clearly and without guile. She sensed the urgency in him and felt, despite the fact that he was a demon, a sense of indebtedness to him. He had raised her from oblivion and she could not forget that. And he seemed a demon of character, even nobility.

Whether the souls were answering their innate, base selves and the urge to shed blood or they recognized, politically, that the situation called for them to join the battle for Adamantinarx, their response came in a huge wave of shaking weapons and cries of, *"Fight!"*

She looked out at the sea of souls, saw their answer, and turned to the waiting demons.

Eligor was smiling fiercely.

"Thank you, Boudica." He absorbed a series of incoming glyphs. "You have become more than Sargatanas could have ever imagined. Or hoped for."

Boudica did not know how to respond to that. She bowed her head slightly. After all, that demon lord had consigned her to becoming a brick, even as he had ordered her freedom.

Eligor's wings opened and the other demons behind him rose into the air.

"Where shall I send my troops?" Boudica's steady voice belied her apprehensions.

"The Seventh Gate . . . do you remember where that is? The fighting is still heaviest there. Other wards are nearly equally at peril, but the Proconsuls both feel that if we break the siege there we may have a chance."

"I do remember. The Proconsuls?"

"Put Satanachia and Lilith."

She unconsciously put her hand to her necklace. Eligor could not have missed it.

"Know this. I will keep watch over you and your souls, Boudica. I will not let them perish needlessly."

She raised the sword he had presented to her long ago in salute.

And he was off. She watched him fade into the clouds and then turned to her army.

Raising her swords, she cried, *"Follow me!"*

He sensed Abaddon moving up from the rear of his army. He would soon be in the thick of things. And then the Heretic's city would fall. The fighting had been far more difficult than Adramalik had imagined. The counterattack by the city's Flying Guard had been a real mauling, but eventually his Abaddim had prevailed and the ground lay thick with the winged enemy. And perhaps, too, it was the addition of the souls. While they were destroyed easily, they were much quicker than he had remembered and they harried his Abaddim from within buildings, a cowardly tactic that he disapproved of. It had forced him to waste valuable troops on the demolition of many of the smaller buildings hugging the wall and beyond.

But now he was making steady gains and the fact that they were nearly halfway up most of the main avenues of the city—halfway to that accursed Central Mount and its gleaming palace—was something he could point to Abaddon as real and promising. The battle for Adamantinarx was far from over. The real resistance would come when the Demons Minor had been destroyed and whatever Demons Major were left to defend their palace came into their own. Experience had taught him to never underestimate cornered Demons Major.

Adramalik dismounted, glyph-staking his steed inside a partially demolished building. He pulled his two axes from his saddle and stalked confidently onto the ruin of the avenue called the Rule.

The twisted and cleft bodies of souls lay amidst the ashes and broken remnants of demons and he trampled both underfoot without a second glance. When he felt something alive beneath his horny clawed foot he pressed all the harder until it gave way with a crack or a scream.

Any fleeing or resisting demon or soul whom he encountered alive he cut down without even trying. They were exhausted and he was not. And he was, he had to admit to himself with a snarl, an indomitable force of destruction. He would see this city broken and bleeding and forever his vassal.

He followed the Rule up its gentle slope, passing collapsed and smashed shops, massive toppled statues, and piles of Abaddim cadavers. The ground had not been given up easily. And he had no idea what Abaddon would make of the losses. As long as he survived, he did not care. So far, he thought, he had acquitted himself well.

A dozen demons leaped from behind a pile of rubble. One, a Demon Minor, flashed a glyph at him and it stung momentarily, angering him. He piled into the demon with both axes flying and made a point of chopping away each limb before delivering the fatal blow as the demon lay on the pavement. The others attacked him en masse and were dispatched with a single blow each. *This is almost too easy!*

He did not even bother to scoop up the vanquished demon's disk. What possible use did he have for it?

As he turned back to ascend the avenue, a strange sight met his eyes. Seven females, clad in white, weapons extended, faced him. One he knew immediately.

"You!" she spat, her red eyes wide and flashing.

This was almost too good to be true. Adramalik felt himself getting aroused by the very sight of her. It would be nothing at all to destroy her bodyguard, for certainly that was what these other demons were. Then he could take her, perhaps have her right on the avenue before Abaddon appeared. His chest swelled in anticipation.

"Yes, it *is* me, whore to the Fly. From your million yesterdays and your million tomorrows. You have no idea what I will do with you for eons to come."

"He is mine." She squared off with him, the huge white sword held out. That sword, he thought, looked familiar.

She waited, her hands moving the blade almost like a lure, the tension in her stance obvious. He towered over her, naked, dripping with souls' black blood, fire wreathing throughout him, embers ablaze on his face. And yet she seemed not in the least intimidated by him.

He spun suddenly, powerfully, both axes outstretched, and, for a moment only, he thought he could take her by simply smashing her into unconsciousness with the sides of his axes. It was a good move, a move he had practiced many times. A move that did not work.

She was very quick. Perhaps, he thought in a flash, those feet were what enhanced her agility. He felt her blade slice lightly into his side, deeper than he had been hit ever before. He leaped back, grimacing, sparks flying from his nostrils.

He said nothing, did not even feel the wound to see how deep it really was. Instead, he spat on the ground at her feet, a look of utter contempt on his face.

He watched her white hands change her grip slightly and she dropped the point of the blade, providing an open target of her chest if he chose to go for it. But he did not go for the obvious blow. He dropped his axes nearly to his sides, an echo of her movement. His own invitation. He circled her slowly, like a predator and she pivoted deftly with each of his steps.

He took her in, licking his lips as he studied her face, her eyes, her lips, the horns on her head, the full breasts beneath her ivory skins. She was panting, slick with sweat and Abaddim blood. A crooked smile split his face.

Lilith raised her blade, dropped it again and then lashed out toward his head with a blindingly fast move. The smile had worked. *Too easy!* He dodged that slice, feinted to one side, crouched, and hurled himself toward her with a great arcing of both blades. He swept her feet out from under her with the flat of his blades and she twisted in midair trying to regain her balance. She fell hard but did not lose her grip on the white sword. With one hand she held the blade out to parry any blows that might follow.

Adramalik saw the white-clad female warriors crouching, their eyes darting, blades at the ready. What were they? Succubi? One of them looked familiar, almost like one of the playthings his Knights had shared. It did not matter. They would be destroyed soon enough. He expected an attack from them the moment Lilith was out of the fight, whereupon he would easily take them on and litter the ground around her with the ashes of her companions. It would be an enjoyable way to complement his capture of Lilith.

He closed on her, one ax held up, one leveled at the former Consort. He smashed the upraised sword away. She rolled, but his ax hit her solidly on the side of her head. She spasmed and lay still.

And just as he had predicted the succubi lunged toward him. He dodged two of them, but the others were quicker and their blades found their mark on his legs and arms. One jumped onto his back, clawing her way up and putting an arm around his throat.

Adramalik roared, dropped an ax, and tried to get the arm locked around his neck free. It was surprisingly powerful. He felt a blade begin to painfully saw away at his armored throat, quickly working its way between the plates and finding his windpipe. Shocked, he thought to summon up a Glyph of Protection, but the world around him was growing dim and the words could not easily come to his lips. He felt things in his throat snap, cut clean through. The pain was sublime and he watched in astonishment as a geyser of black blood spouted from his mouth. He dropped his other ax, reached up to pry the arm away, and immediately felt three blades stab deeply into his belly, carving downward until, revoltingly, he felt his bowels bursting outward, his genitals hacked away.

Is this how I die? At the hands of filthy succubi?

He swore.

And then nothing.

26

ADAMANTINARX-UPON-THE-ACHERON

Boudica saw the huge demon fall in a dark, dense cloud of ash as she rounded a corner. Her army had encountered only sporadic fighting as it had negotiated the streets and plazas and avenues of the city's flank. Only when they had approached the ward containing the Seventh Gate had the fighting begun in earnest.

Eyes wide, she took in the tableau of the Sisters standing, blood dripping from their crooked blades, turning to kneel around the demon she had met on the parapets of Dolcha Branapa—Lilith. She gave orders to the souls to form a fighting perimeter and ran to join the Sisters, pushing her way next to them. They looked at her only briefly, saw her anguish, while one of the succubi held Lilith's face in her hands, looking for any sign of life.

Lilith's eyelids fluttered and the reaction was immediate.

"Back to the palace!" the succubi shouted.

Boudica ordered a hundred heavily armed souls to surround the Sisters as four of them carefully lifted Lilith and began to move up the avenue. But then something caught her eye. It gleamed dully in the pile of ash that had been the great demon lord. A disk! She reached down and hurriedly swept it up and followed the departing Sisters.

One of the Sisters looked at her, the tension written upon her face.

"I am Araamah. Who are *you*?" the succubus demanded.

"Boudica, leader of the souls."

Araamah's eyes alit on the pendant of Lilith.

"Come, if you want."

Boudica was torn. She could remain at the head of her army or accompany Lilith back to the palace. In a moment that she knew swirled with import, she elected the latter, delegating command to one of her captains. Lilith had been her Light through all of her long millennia as a slave. She could not abandon her now no matter what the souls might think.

She turned and followed the Sisters up the Rule, stepping over the dead and dying, through windblown hummocks of ash and rubble. It was slow going and the confusion of the soul army flooding down to fill in the gap left by the retreating Sisters did not make it any easier. Up above, surmounting the Central Mount, she could see the palace. She had never been there. It would have been unthinkable. As a slave, she had glimpsed it vaguely, a very long time ago, through the fire and ash, and wondered what it looked like, what treasures lay within, and who resided within its forbidden confines. Now events were leading her there and she almost felt as if she were dreaming. None of this felt real.

They continued laboriously up the inclined avenue as demon flyers screamed overhead, their heads fiery, their scythes bloody. She took a moment and glanced back from where they had come. Something was happening down there. The darkness had gathered and something huge was making its way into the city, knocking down a section of wall and then buildings. It frightened her more than anything she had ever seen in Hell. Shaking, she turned away and busied herself climbing and lending a supportive hand to the Sisters when she could.

They finally arrived at the great, marble staircase that led directly to the Palace Plaza. Here the going was easier. There were

no bodies or piles of rubble to work around and the simple repetitive rhythm of the stairs made carrying Lilith predictable and
a bit easier. The din of the battle diminished somewhat and she
heard the Sisters whispering among themselves. Were those
prayers?

Another female demon, one who looked very similar to Lilith,
waited at the top of the stairs, a look of terrible pain written upon
her face. She rushed to Lilith's side as the Sisters lay her down on
some hastily provided skins.

Boudica saw Lilith's eyes open.

"Where am I?"

"The Palace Plaza, Lilith," Ardat said quietly.

A terrible look crossed her features, one of both concern and
pain.

"Adramalik?" she said, spitting out the name.

"Destroyed," Araamah said. She smiled, showing her tiny
pointed teeth. "We finished what you began."

A faint smile crossed Lilith's face that lingered until she saw Ardat, holding her side.

"Why are you out here? You need rest. And to be safe."

"Something made me come out. I guess I could not stand being
shut in like that." She looked out over the dying city. "It . . . the
city . . . it is falling."

Lilith propped herself up. She looked at two of the Sisters, silently asking to be lifted to her feet. They knew better than to
refuse.

She stood and Boudica saw her take in the full measure of what
was happening to Adamantinarx. It was a spectacle of destruction.
Great billows of smoke rose from every quarter; flames licked the
sky. Command glyphs soared and flying demons banked and attacked. Battle cries rose from the streets. And then she looked

toward the great darkness that approached. The darkness Boudica had so feared.

She turned and faced them. Her eyes turned to Boudica.

"You. You came to help us. Why?"

Boudica nodded and looked down. The necklace made the words easier.

"Because once you believed in us."

Lilith walked slowly to her and folded her arms around her.

"I do still, Boudica. It has not always been easy."

Lilith drew away and shook her head.

"The city is falling. Somewhere out there Satanachia is fighting for it, along with Eligor and the rest. And I feel powerless to stop it from happening. The need is great to . . ."

Boudica saw a strange look come over Lilith's features.

"The . . . need . . . is great."

Lilith turned again to the vista of the burning city and turned back again.

She began to whisper a phrase and immediately a pinpoint of azure light glowed before her, growing in intensity, separating until myriad pinpoints had formed tiny glyphs, which in turn coalesced into a winged being of Light the like of which Boudica could have never imagined.

"Legate," Lilith said almost breathlessly.

The being's corona flared, the sigils within it pulsing.

"Legate, do you have the disk?"

The Legate slowly nodded once. It produced the disk as if from thin air. It floated out in front of it, red and gleaming.

A huge thunderclap rent the air and all gathered turned as one and stared out at the abomination that was Abaddon, fully revealed and wreathed in red lightning. The ground shook and buildings near the god toppled.

Boudica looked up and saw Eligor drop down and hurry over. He looked haggard and harried and bore more than a few minor wounds. One eye was missing. He carried a severed Abaddim head, which he angrily tossed aside.

"The city cannot endure this for much longer, my lady. Can anything be done?"

Instead of answering, Lilith addressed the apparition.

"Legate, the . . . need is great."

The being nodded again. It regarded Lilith for a moment and then spoke in a voice that resonated like chimes.

"The need *is* great. And so shall be the sacrifices. A being of True Light must be created."

"How? From what?"

"From those you love."

Lilith's eyes hardened. "But why?"

"The sacrifice must be real."

Lilith frowned.

"But my lady. Hannibal!"

"Hannibal be damned. He will have to find his own way to redemption! Or destruction."

She looked at the Legate, the fierceness apparent in her eyes.

"Who?"

"A demon. A soul. And myself."

That last caught Lilith by surprise.

Boudica's mind raced. *A soul.*

Eligor immediately knelt, head lowered. "I can think of no better way to serve my city. And you, my lady."

But before Lilith could speak, Ardat, wincing, pushed her way forward and put a hand upon his shoulder.

"No, Eligor, it will be me."

He looked up and was about to object when Lilith silenced him.

"Ardat, my love, why? *Why?* You are healing—"

"Our journey together is at an end. It should have ended back by the towers. I was not meant to live, Lilith. Buer gave me the gift of eternal pain. Maybe it was to fulfill this . . . to be part of this. The pain is beyond anything the Fly ever did to me. Every movement is torture. I feel as if I am dying by inches." Tears were streaking her cheeks. "I cannot let you watch this happen to me. I will not."

Another thunderclap blasted through the city.

Lilith shook her head, swallowed hard, and said nothing. She took Ardat's face in her hands and kissed her until the tears were streaming down both their cheeks.

Boudica watched this and suddenly everything became clear. With the prospect of enduring in Hell forever without her daughters by her side she, too, had felt that her life had grown meaningless. With every rise and fall of Algol, she had felt more and more hollow. The souls' cause had been a noble one and, with any luck, another leader would rise to take up the staff, but it would not be her.

"I will do it," she heard herself saying. "I want to be part of this. I *must* be part of this."

Lilith and the Sisters looked at her. And Eligor rose and approached her.

"Boudica . . ."

"Please, Eligor."

The demon took her hand. "I will do everything I can for your people. This I pledge to you."

She did not answer but, instead, removed the necklace M'ak had given to her.

"Try to make peace with them, too. Find K'ah-aka-tuk. Tell him of the end of my story."

A flight of demons flew low overhead. Boudica saw them approaching Abaddon and saw, too, a web of red lightning reach out and incinerate them.

"Time is running out, Lilith. This must be done now."

Lilith nodded.

"There is something you need to know, Boudica. Something I had hoped I would be able to tell you if our paths ever crossed again." She paused. "They were never here."

Boudica felt as if someone had struck her.

"How do you know?"

"I asked them at Dolcha Branapa. They did not find their names because they had never been written in the Books. My way of asking was more persuasive than yours."

"If they are not here . . ."

"They are where you will be," the Legate said. "After this."

Boudica nearly collapsed. Eligor caught her and held her steady.

Ardat moved to her side and helped her to stand. Eligor let go and stepped back.

The Legate floated in front of them and said gently, "It is time. If we wait any longer it will all be for naught."

The soul who had been Boudica and Bo-ad and B'udik'k'ah and then Boudica again nodded shakily. She had not experienced joy in all the millennia of her existence in Hell. Nothing but sadness and yearning, bitterness and exhaustion.

She felt joy now.

She watched the winged Legate approach, holding out the red disk before her. It was saying something in a strange tongue as it pressed the disk against her. And she felt no pain, no remorse, no reluctance. Only the joy at the prospect of seeing her beloved Cammi and Mave once again.

The Legate looked into her eyes and said, "That which was will cease to be. That which ceased to be will begin anew."

Vaguely, she heard Eligor say, "May Sargatanas' spirit be with you."

And then only Light.

Lilith shielded her eyes as Boudica's burst of light entered the floating disk and then watched the Legate glide in front of Ardat.

Her love was smiling. The pain in her eyes was still there and yet there was something else. Relief. She was looking not at the Legate but at Lilith and mouthed, *I love you.*

Lilith reached out, but it was too late. The Legate pressed the disk against the handmaiden's chest and she vanished.

Lilith's breath came in short, shallow bursts. The world, her world, was changing too quickly. She barely noticed Eligor's arms around her, supporting her.

The Legate turned to face them.

"What name do you go by?" Eligor asked.

"I am become Mahniel."

The red demon bowed his head.

The Legate that would become Mahniel flared its corona, and within it sigils began to move, to interlock and change. Blue-white flames bled from its eyes.

"Vonpho zirdo!"

The bells of its voice made the ground tremble. The air sweetened.

She watched it push the disk into its luminous chest. The myriad glyphs began to stir, forming curls within curls, each one identical to the next, each one an expanding symmetry unto itself. Chaos and order working against and with each other. The Legate was growing, changing. It turned to begin its descent of the great stairs, down toward the god it would soon confront.

The sky had darkened considerably and Adamantinarx had the appearance of a city already destroyed. It was nearly impossible to see more than halfway down the Rule and the Seventh Gate, at its far end, was invisible due to the roiling clouds of ash. The demons were paying dearly for their city.

The terrible creature that once was the Legate and Boudica and Ardat stalked down to the avenue. It was now larger than the largest statue of Sargatanas the demons of Adamantinarx had erected. A ferocious thing of blue fire, its many-horned head was set upon a long and sinuous neck upon which a mane of flames guttered. It bore six wide wings and four sweeping arms and in its many-fingered hands were four flaming swords.

As Mahniel strode down the length of the Rule, it swung its long swords and cut down the panicking Abaddim by the hundreds. Long gouts of fire were left where clusters of the enemy had tried to flee.

Lilith watched its progress with a mixture of awe and horror. There truly was no other way to view this creature born of pure wrath.

Mahniel worked its way down the avenue and as it drew close to Abaddon red lightning began to lick at it. It seemed not to notice but, instead, moved from a plodding to a ground-shaking trot. With all of its swords raised it rose into the air and swooped down, charging Abaddon, and a deafening crack of thunder rolled through the sky.

Four swords tore through the dark deity, converging on his center, and then, reversing, tore their way back out.

A blinding blue light bathed the lower ward and, when it faded, only Mahniel remained, majestic in its wrathful potency. Lilith gasped. It had been so fast, so decisive. So overwhelmingly powerful. She saw the black flames of the Abaddim gathered in the streets below gutter out and then the life leave them. She saw the dark clouds that had lowered over the city begin to dissipate. And there, up in the sky, was the blue star, shining more brilliantly than it had ever shone.

Mahniel's light began to fade and even as it was growing fainter it raised it swords toward Lilith. It was gone in a moment, the sound of bells echoing in the air.

Silence fell over the city. A breeze began to blow.

Lilith turned to look at the Sisters and then Eligor.

"Take me down there, Eligor. Please."

The demon put out a hand and gathered her up. They flew in silence. Neither knew what to say. Neither said anything.

A crater lay where Abaddon had been. Lilith pointed to its center and Eligor descended, landing lightly.

The ground was hot and glass smooth, smoking from a thousand azure embers. She walked gingerly, until she found what she was looking for.

She knelt and, brows knit, picked up the hot black disk that had been Abaddon. She was frightened of it as she turned it in her hands. It seemed too weighty and smelled foul. But she kept hold of it as she walked up and out of the crater.

As she emerged, she saw Eligor looking up. She followed his eyes and stared at the sky. The star seemed to be moving. But then she realized that it had split and the brighter half was moving toward them.

In a moment the blue radiance had grown much larger and suddenly the ground shook and a single huge peal as from an unthinkably large bell rang out. Lilith took a deep breath and a lush, heady perfume filled her nostrils, a scent the like of which she had never encountered or even imagined.

The blue radiance glowed even brighter and then took the shape of a winged being carrying a standard. It settled before them and raised a hand in greeting.

"A Herald, Lilith!" Eligor whispered.

The being stepped forward, its breastplate gleaming blue, purple, and green, its gorgeously hued wings trembling.

"I bring a message from the Above," the Herald said in a voice full of strange and rich harmonics. "He returns."

The Herald bowed ceremoniously, spread its wings, and in a few short moments was gone.

27

The acrid smell of cinders and fire had penetrated the Audience Chamber. A miasma of fine ash particles suffused the air of the vast space and Lilith realized she could barely see the chamber's far, curved wall. When her eyes traveled up to the oculus she could only see smoke, torn by the winds, skimming across the sky.

Algol had risen and fallen four times since Abaddon had been destroyed and the city was still burning.

Lilith sat upon her throne atop the pyramid and saw her Sisters climbing the last few steps. Satanachia had gathered as many of the city's higher demons as could be spared from their pressing duties for the investiture.

In all of the urgency of the moment, as Boudica had been embraced by the Legate no one had noticed the disk of Adramalik fall to the pavement. Only after the destruction of Abaddon did Lilith see it and stoop to recover it. It was not long before the Sisters recounted how the demon had been overcome. And it was clear to Lilith what the fate of the disk should be.

She could not have been prouder of her Sisters. Fierce and loyal, they would serve her well. And, even as she formed that thought, she saw Naamah, Lamatsu, Agrat, and Eisheth gather around Satanachia's throne as he gathered his robes and sat. Naamah and Lamatsu put their hands upon his shoulders, and Lilith saw them both gently caress him. It chilled her.

Only Satanachia could perform the Elevation. Lilith saw the disk in his lap as the Sisters gained the platform and approached. As one they knelt, with Araamah at the front, and stayed motionless upon their knees, coifed heads bowed.

Put Satanachia rose and stepped before Araamah.

"With this disk, Araamah of the Sisters of Sargatanas, I Elevate you to the status of Demon Minor. Yours will be some of this former demon's powers. Be strong when you discover them; be careful when you choose them; be wise when you use them. Rise, now, Araamah, that you may receive this token."

Araamah rose to her feet and, as she had been instructed, she parted her white robes to expose her dark gray breastbone.

Satanachia held the disk forth and pressed it against her chest and Lilith could hear its high-pitched sizzling as it embedded itself into her. It glowed red for a moment and then faded. She did not flinch.

A small sigil appeared over her breast, simple yet beautiful.

Lilith could not help but smile.

Lilith gazed out at a city in ruins, at a river dammed, at a world changed. She sat, knees up and bird feet tucked, on a marble bench on the Palace Plaza overlooking the smoldering city below. She turned to Eligor, seated nearby on a step.

"So, are you going to tell us how you lost your eye, or not?"

Eligor scowled. He was fingering the Boudica's Salamandrine pendant hanging around his neck.

Satanachia, seated opposite Lilith on a bench, put down the scrolls he was reading. He looked pointedly at the red demon, a light smile playing upon his lips.

"It is not exactly something I am happy about, Lilith."

Lilith simply looked at him and tapped one of her clawed toes impatiently.

"Fine. I met up with an old friend. From my days before the Rebellion. Perhaps you remember him . . . the Baron Faraii. Only this was not exactly the Baron. He had been changed by Abaddon into one of the Abaddim. Only a special form. He had arms. And he had something like his old sword . . . the black one made from Abyssal horn . . . which he could conjure from his hand. We recognized each other across an avenue and we fought. For what seemed like an eternity. Me flying in tight circles, he turning so quickly it was amazing. He had lost nothing of his abilities. In fact, his four legs made him even more dangerous, more agile, more unpredictable. My sword barely touched him. He knew well enough not to let my sword touch his sword . . . the flames would have destroyed it. So he weaved and dodged and touched me with it until one blow took my eye. It was a performance of unthinkable skill. I was quite overmatched. Until he made a mistake and my sword took him."

"What did you do with his head?"

"Oh, that. In a box. Somewhere."

Lilith looked at him, not a little disbelieving. A loud sound—a building collapsing—made her turn back to the city below.

"What is left for us here, Eligor? Just look at it."

Eligor stretched, his wings shaking.

"It looks like Hell to me."

Lilith snorted, despite herself. She felt numb, disengaged. The loss of Ardat was almost too much to bear. She found herself welling up at the strangest moments.

"We should open the palace up to survivors. Most of the city is uninhabitable. Rebuilding is going to take forever."

"We have nothing but time, Lilith," Satanachia offered. "First, we will need to set the river straight again. Break down those disgusting bridges and rebuild ours and cleanse the riverbed with fire. None of that will be easy. Perhaps we can ask the souls to help. Once they appoint a leader to sit alongside us, that is."

Eligor nodded.

"We can ask." Lilith smiled gently. She closed her eyes, remembering. "She *was* remarkable. Boudica, I mean."

"Yes. Sargatanas must have known just how remarkable. Must have seen something deep within her when he first encountered her. It was his Art, after all . . . to see things hidden."

"It was," Lilith said. "He certainly found things hidden within me."

Another pang of sorrow stabbed her in her aching heart. She had lost too many loves.

She looked up at Zimiah. The gate. And wondered for the thousandth time who was returning.

EPILOGUE

THE MARGINS

A lone figure made his way across a lava river, picking his way over the sharp rocks. He was swathed in dark traveling skins that bore the faded emblem of Pygon Az. He used to respond to the name Lucifuge Rofocale. But now, when he was approached by far-flung travelers, he gave up no name. And when he asked, in a voice that buzzed oddly, of any word of the sighting of a giant Watcher named Semjaza, he was very careful to keep his hood lowered so as to not allow anyone to see that his head was formed of an angry mass of flies.